MULATTO

The Texas Pan American Series

MULATTO

Aluísio Azevedo

Translated by Murray Graeme MacNicoll

Edited by Daphne Patai

Introduction by Daphne Patai
and Murray Graeme MacNicoll

UNIVERSITY OF TEXAS PRESS AUSTIN

Printed in the United States of America

First University of Texas Press edition, 1993

Published by arrangement with Associated University Presses, Inc.

♾ The paper used in this publication meets the minimum requirements of American National Standard for Information Sciences—Permanence of Paper for Printed Library Materials, ANSI Z39.48-1984.

Library of Congress Cataloging-in-Publication Data

Azevedo, Aluísio, 1857–1913.
[Mulato. English]
Mulatto / Aluísio Azevedo ; translated by Murray Graeme MacNicoll ; edited by Daphne Patai ; introduction by Daphne Patai and Murray Graeme MacNicoll.
p. cm.
Originally published: Rutherford [N.J.] : Fairleigh Dickinson Univ. Press, 1990.
Includes bibliographical references.
ISBN 0-292-70438-0
1. São Luís do Maranhão (Brazil)—Fiction. I. Patai, Daphne, 1943– . II. Title.
PQ9697.A93M813 1993
869.3—dc20 92-43072

Contents

Introduction

Daphne Patai and Murray Graeme MacNicoll

Aluísio Azevedo's *Mulatto* is a young man's novel, full of passion, venom, and caricature. Written at a time in Brazil's history when many young men were, as historian Thomas Skidmore has stated, "caught up in the converging tide of abolitionism, anticlericalism, and republicanism"[1] its themes are the corruption of the church, the evils of slavery and racism, the malice, savagery, and political ignorance of provincial life—but also love and desire, the search for one's past, the consequences of a personal and cultural amnesia, the struggle between individual and society. Its characters are individuals and types, one-dimensional sadists such as Dona Quitéria, haughty bigots such as Maria Bárbara, idealized domesticated blacks such as Mônica, admirable but simple types such as Raimundo, the very model of a young positivist hero. The novel also contains carefully delineated figures such as the cunning Luís Dias, the bore Freitas, the villainous Canon Diogo, and the sensual, defiant, and practical Ana Rosa. Even when character seems to veer into caricature, however, Azevedo is remarkable in his attention to details, especially details of a powerfully physical kind, indexes to moral and spiritual traits, as befits a writer usually credited with introducing the naturalist novel into Brazil.[2] Thus *Mulatto* is filled with compelling descriptions of nails, teeth, ears, skin tone, body size, as well as posture, dress, gestures, glances, tones of voice. The novel is also the intricate portrait of the city of São Luís, capital of the northern province of Maranhão, of its rhythms and hues, its work and play, its hierarchical divisions—male and female, white and black, parent and child, priest and penitent, owner and worker—and the pathways by which chal-

---

Parts of the introduction were first published in Murray Graeme MacNicoll's "*O Mulato* and Maranhão: The Socio-Historical Context," *Luso-Brazilian Review* 12, no. 2 (Winter 1975): 234–40, and are used here by permission of the *Luso-Brazilian Review.*

lenges to these hierarchies arise and the ways people deal with them.

Mulatto is the work of a man with an artist's eye, and indeed Azevedo's first artistic aspirations were in painting, not literature, and he had a special aptitude for caricature. Translated into the written word, *Mulatto* reveals Azevedo's ability to capture verbally the beauty of his native Maranhão and the colors, tastes, and smells of hatred, fear, and suffering, of dining tables, festivals, and salons, and of the grotesque features of moral turpitude.

Azevedo (1857–1913) was in his early twenties when he wrote the novel, and was once again living in Maranhão. Born out of wedlock to Portuguese parents (his father, the Portuguese vice consul in Maranhão, recognized Aluísio as his legitimate child when the boy was six; his mother had separated from her husband after an unhappy marriage), Aluísio, at the age of nineteen, went to Rio de Janeiro to study painting. There, through the influence of his older brother Artur, who was also to become an important Brazilian writer, Aluísio was drawn into journalism as a cartoonist and illustrator. After two years in Rio de Janeiro, he returned to Maranhão when his father died. Still with the intent of becoming a painter, he began to write under a pseudonym in an illustrated humor review called *A Flecha* (The arrow), published in São Luís. Azevedo's plan to study painting in Rome was thwarted by his failure to obtain the necessary financial assistance from Maranhão's Provincial Assembly, which refused his request owing to the clearly anticlerical position the young man had assumed in his writings, particularly in the anticlerical publication *O Pensador* (The thinker), whose subtitle was: "An organ in the interests of modern society."[3] In 1879 Azevedo published his first novel, a melodramatic romance entitled *Uma Lágrima de Mulher* (A woman's tears). Then, under the influence of Zola and Eça de Queirós,[4] Azevedo produced his second novel, *O Mulato,* a fictional transposition of the polemical stance already adopted in his journalistic activities. The first announcement of the work indicated that the novel's anticlericalism more than its attack on racial bigotry was expected to attract readers. A few months before the book's publication, it was described in the 10 January 1881 issue of *O Pensador* as a work "in which the author proposes to confront religious abuses occurring in this city."[5]

Upon its publication, *Mulatto* was greeted with critical acclaim in Rio de Janeiro, but aroused such scandal and resentment in Maranhão that Azevedo, using the proceeds of his novel, returned to Rio de Janeiro later that year. Determined to live by his work as a professional writer—an unlikely way to make a living at that time—he cultivated a variety of genres, producing dramas, short fiction, and chronicles, as well as novels. Almost all of Azevedo's novels after his return to Rio de Janeiro were first published as *folhetins,* newspaper serials that then attracted a broad reading public. In this way, and under pressure of deadlines, Azevedo composed several more romantic novels, seldom read today, as well as three further naturalist works, of which *O Cortiço* (1890; published in English as *A Brazilian Tenement*),[6] is generally regarded as his best work. Finally, at the age of thirty-eight, having been unable to make a living with his writing and disenchanted with his career, he abandoned literature and became a diplomat, occupying posts in Japan and Argentina, among other countries. When he died in 1913, he had not published any literary work for eighteen years.[7]

Apart from *Mulatto*'s status as a pioneering book—one of the first and certainly the most famous of Brazil's early naturalist novels—and the novel's importance as an indictment of racial prejudice in provincial Brazilian society in the years preceding 1888, when slavery was abolished, what stands out in this work is the author's biting animus against the decadent society of Maranhão, the "Athens of Brazil," as it was known in its heyday earlier in the century. In Azevedo's pen the term drips with sarcasm and emendations, as when the "beauties" of this Athens are depicted in a perpetual state of incompletion and disrepair (p. 92), or when Raimundo bursts out: "This narrow-minded little land of petty intrigues and overblown jealousies!" (p. 227).

The novel describes in considerable detail the extremely closed social life that was played out in São Luís's private homes, as well as the material setting in which these personal dramas occurred. Lavishly furnished dwellings in town contrast painfully with primitive rural housing. Heavy furniture, massive dressers of holywood and huge hand-carved oratories fill the more prosperous residences, whereas in the interior of the province, as the novel shows, "freed" blacks live in run-down shacks or steal onto the properties where they used to work, for a night's sleep.

In this society, white women's rights did not greatly exceed those of slaves. Indeed, to consolidate fortunes or partnerships, a veritable traffic in white wives existed among the various commercial families. As an adolescent, Azevedo had worked as a clerk in a Portuguese-owned warehouse, an experience that undoubtedly accounts for his familiarity with the inner workings of a wholesale firm. The typical Portuguese-owned firm in the novel resembles a feudal organization. The head clerk, Luís Dias, rules his underlings like a despot and is expected to become a son-in-law, partner, and eventual successor. From the viewpoint of this organization of both family and commercial life, Raimundo is a mere interloper, and the eventual extermination of this threat is necessary and inevitable if the traditional norms and patterns are to be upheld.

Many of the local Portuguese feared the lack of discipline of their own Brazilian-born sons, and *Mulatto* portrays the continuing prominence of Portuguese immigrants in the commercial life of Maranhão. In this context, Azevedo does not miss the opportunity to echo the vogue for "scientific" explanations of Brazil's backward condition in comparison to northern Europe. The ideas of such European writers as the English historian Henry Thomas Buckle and the Frenchman Arthur de Gobineau promoted belief in climatic and racial determinism, with the climate and races of northern Europe conspicuously placed at the acme of the Social Darwinist pinnacle then thought to explain the rise and fall of civilizations.[8] Immigrant Portuguese boys, such as the novel's lonely and frightened ten-year-old Manuelzinho, were brought to Maranhão in the belief that they would be better able to withstand the rigors of life in Brazil than the native Brazilians and would contribute to a more desirable racial balance.

Interestingly, Azevedo reflects the climatic determinism of his time but not the thesis of "mongrelization" (which was to become far more powerful as eugenic ideas developed in the late nineteenth century),[9] by which, through miscegenation, the enslaved race was envisioned as wreaking its revenge on its masters. Thus he depicts even the Portuguese quickly succumbing to the supposedly degenerative climate and mores of Maranhão. Gustavo de Vila-Rica, one of Manuel Pescada's employees, is initially described as a youth of sixteen, "with his superb Portuguese coloring, which the climate of Maranhão had not yet managed to destroy" (p. 51). In the novel's closing pages, however, Azevedo cannot resist a parting shot on this theme, and Vila-Rica, after nearly a decade in Maranhão, is seen to have "completely lost his lovely European coloring; his face was now mottled with syphilitic scars" (p. 294).

Mulatto does not provide a single-mindedly negative vision of Maranhão. Rather, through Raimundo's fresh eye, the reader is exposed to the province's natural beauty as Azevedo engages in detailed and at times loving descriptions of the landscape (see, for example, pp. 130–31). These descriptions, by way of contrast, focus the reader's attention on the true objects of Azevedo's scorn: the people of Maranhão and especially the clergy. For, as the Brazilian critic Josué Montello observes, the novel must be seen in the context of the bitter struggle against the clergy of Maranhão, in which Azevedo participated.[10] In the novel's possibly most fascinating caricature, Canon Diogo is shown to be totally without a conscience, guilty of every possible sin, venial and mortal, an adulterer and liar, ready to achieve his ends by suggesting Ana Rosa have an abortion, and not flinching at the murder of father and son. The church, under his leadership, is nothing more than a stage set, the occasion for well-off local families to display jewels and clothes, presided over by the carefully costumed Canon Diogo, whom Azevedo, in a stinging characterization, calls "the great actor." Diogo's power, however, depends on the confidence of his parishioners, whom he manipulates with exquisite skill, capitalizing especially on the susceptibility of the women who worship their favorite priests more than the symbols of Catholicism.

Azevedo's combative prose nonetheless repeatedly gives way to the artist's realistic brush as it depicts the broad sweep of ordinary life.[11] Because *Mulatto* is specifically a representation of Maranhão as a physical, social, and cultural space (it would be a gross misreading of the work to see it merely as a symbolic space occupying Azevedo's literary imagination), some historical information about Maranhão, and the roots of the conservatism Azevedo so abhorred, is indispensable.

Unlike most of Brazil's provinces, which, after gaining independence from Portugal in 1822, aspired to a Brazilian identity, the Maranhão of the 1870s depicted in Azevedo's novel is a province still clinging firmly to its Portuguese traditions and maintaining close commercial and cultural ties with the mother country. Following Brazil's independence, an atmosphere of mutual political antipathy quickly emerged in Maranhão between those still loyal to Lisbon and those who considered themselves Brazilians. The provincial lower classes were, for the most part, Brazilianized. But the elite, and especially the merchant class, struggled tenaciously during the nineteenth century to maintain Maranhão's Lusitanian traditions—and this rear guard action, in particular, is satirized by Azevedo throughout his novel. In fact, the older residents of Maranhão were considered to be so Lusitanian that when Brazil became independent, the Lisbon government took the extraordinary step of offering Maranhão the great honor of remaining a transatlantic province of Portugal.[12] Maranhão indeed hesitated until 1823 before adhering to Brazil's independent status. In the novel, such attitudes are exemplified several generations later by the Portuguese immigrant Manuel Pescada and his family's pride and sense of superiority over "Brazilians," and by the haughty and bigoted

Maria Bárbara, Manuel's mother-in-law. It is Maria Bárbara who most often refers to Raimundo as a *cabra*—literally meaning "goat," a term used to refer to mulattoes, which we have translated as "nigger" to retain its distinctly pejorative connotations.[13] Blaming everything on the changes going on in independent Brazil, Maria Bárbara foresees the onset of a republic as the culmination of a long sequence of disasters. Such attitudes have their roots in the special relationship that formerly existed between Maranhão and Portugal.

At the end of the sixteenth century, eleven Hereditary Captaincies existed in Brazil, and the capital was Salvador, in Bahia. But in 1621, as a result of the greater ease of maritime communication directly between Lisbon and the northern Brazilian port of São Luís, the State of Maranhão, with its capital in São Luís, was created as an administrative entity separate from the State of Brazil. The new State of Maranhão, consisting of Maranhão, Pará, Amazonas, and parts of Ceará and Piauí, had a separate government administered directly from Lisbon.[14] Nevertheless, colonial Maranhão suffered the crown's neglect and remained economically undeveloped and backward. Geographically isolated and semiautonomous, Maranhão stood at the periphery of colonial Brazil.

Because of its relatively infertile soil, which was in sharp contrast to the rich black *massapê* earth (suitable for sugar cultivation), of Pernambuco and Bahia, Maranhão was unable to produce a marketable agricultural product. Instead, Indian hunting, accomplished either independently or through government-sponsored expeditions known as *entradas,* became an important enterprise. Amerindian captives provided a source of labor for small-scale farming and gathering activities.[15] Although invoking the wrath of Padre Antônio Vieira (1608–97), an important Jesuit orator and writer who spent most of his life in Brazil and not only defended the interests of the colonists against the greed of the Portuguese but also took on a virtual campaign against the enslavement of the Indians,[16] the pursuit and enslavement of Indians familiarized Maranhão's colonists with their hinterland, its forests, and its tropical products. Consequently, during most of the colonial era, Maranhão languished in a cycle of primitive hunting and gathering.

The industrial revolution in Great Britain and the subsequent demand for cotton awakened Maranhão from its lethargic past, and it finally received Lisbon's attention. A royal cotton monopoly, the "Companhia Geral do Comércio do Grão-Pará e Maranhão," was created by the Marquês de Pombal. Lasting from 1755 to 1778, the company financed African slaves, credit, equipment, and plantations for the province.[17] Opposed and criticized, both in Brazil and in Portugal, by many groups whose activities it threatened, including by the Jesuits who had organized the economy of Pará and Maranhão, and with whom Pombal was in a bitter struggle,[18] the company nonetheless contributed to Maranhão's economic growth. So extensively did the province, especially the Caxias area in the interior, prosper during this period, that Pombal sent his brother to govern the territory and oversee the company.

When Brazilian ports were opened in 1808, following the 1807 Napoleonic invasion of Portugal and the subsequent transfer of the Portuguese court to Rio de Janeiro, British merchants established themselves in São Luís to control the cotton trade, and French interests arrived to operate the traffic in luxury items.[19] In the final decades of the eighteenth century. Maranhão was the only province of colonial Brazil that was not in a serious economic depression. During the first decade of the nineteenth century, 150 vessels visited the port of São Luís yearly, and one million pounds sterling in cotton was exported.[20]

Before the demand for cotton, the number of African slaves brought to Maranhão had been negligible. In 1760, however, ever-increasing numbers of slaves began to arrive. Between 1756 and 1778, the Companhia Geral do Grão-Pará e Maranhão shipped more than 28,000 slaves to the captaincies of Maranhão and Pará (out of an estimated 2,000,000 slaves thought to have reached Brazil in the eighteenth century).[21] In the early 1800s an average of 3,500 slaves entered Maranhão annually.[22] Between 1812 and 1820, more than 36,000 slaves are recorded as having entered São Luís do Maranhão.[23] An 1819 estimate listed 133,000 slaves and 60,000 free whites in the province.[24]

Unlike Pernambuco and Bahia with their much older sugar economies, however, Maranhão had not experienced two centuries of contact with African slavery. The black person who reached Maranhão was introduced as a foreign element into a previously established society. Despite reported cruelty on the part of the provincial masters, compared to other parts of Brazil few slave revolts occurred in Maranhão. Of these, the most important was the antiplanter uprising known as the "Balaiada" (1838–41), which attracted slave participants.[25]

Maranhão's economic prosperity was, as it turned out, short-lived. During the 1820s and 1830s, Britain began to obtain the bulk of its cotton from the more efficient southern United States. Because of instability in the world cotton market, a substitute product, sugar, was planted in several interior zones of Maranhão, and by

1860 the province had 410 sugar mills.[26] Maranhão's sugar was inferior in quality to that grown in Pernambuco, but no matter how the market in the interior of the province fluctuated, São Luís, the capital and only port and by then a highly organized trading center, always prospered as its merchants did a steady and brisk business with the hinterland.[27]

Azevedo's attempt to root *Mulatto* firmly in Maranhão's past is evident in the way he works into the novel's opening chapter historical events such as the Revolution of August 1831, led by José Cândido de Morais e Silva, known as "Farol," which ousted the pro-Portuguese provincial president. Closely following the account of Farol that had been published eight years earlier in Lisbon, Azevedo depicts him as a fiery-eyed revolutionary, clever orator, and journalist who unsuccessfully sought to destroy Portuguese influence in Maranhão during the first decade following Brazilian independence.[28] An intriguing link is implied between political and personal events in the frustrated passion Ana Rosa's mother had experienced for this romantic figure, which becomes the fulcrum of her daughter's own bid for freedom later in the novel.

A further demonstration of Azevedo's serious (and not merely satirical) interest in Maranhão's culture occurs in the lengthy description of the Remédios festival (chapter 4). Here Azevedo shows his indebtedness to the writings of an earlier *maranhense* (native of Maranhão), João Francisco Lisboa, a noteworthy literary figure of the midnineteenth century. The bore Freitas's description of the Remédios festival owes much to Lisboa's long and detailed 1851 article on this most popular of São Luís's festivals.[29]

With the abolition of slavery in 1888, Maranhão's economy, essentially agrarian and dependent on slave labor, collapsed. Seventy percent of the sugar mills were closed, and 30 percent of the cotton ranches were abandoned.[30] Although these events take us beyond the time frame of Azevedo's novel, it is important to note those earlier laws affecting slavery that play a part in *Mulatto.*

In 1830, a treaty with Britain went into effect that made the slave trade in Brazil illegal. In practice, however, there occurred merely a lull in the trade.[31] Only in September 1850, with the passage of the Queirós Law, following two decades of weak and inconsistent efforts to suppress the traffic in slaves, was the slave trade finally abolished. Great Britain thereafter forced Brazil to respect its own laws, and the slave traffic from abroad effectively came to an end. Given Brazil's continuing shortage of labor, however, the Atlantic trade was replaced by an interprovincial slave trade in which slaves were purchased in poorer regions of Brazil and sold to richer ones.[32] This internal commerce is alluded to in *Mulatto* through the character of Mônica, Ana Rosa's faithful *mãe preta* (black mammy), a recently manumitted slave who had suckled and loved Ana Rosa because her own children had been taken from her and sold in the South of Brazil (p. 102). Reference to the internal slave trade is also made in the scene at the port, as Canon Diogo and Manuel Pescada await Raimundo, when a little mulatto girl is described as crying over the separation from her older sister, who has been sold to Rio de Janeiro (p. 231). Thus Azevedo interweaves with his main plot sympathetic depictions of the emotional plight of slaves, as well as more sensationalistic descriptions of the indignities and barbarous punishments they suffer. In addition to these details of slave life, Azevedo, in his depiction of São Luís's responses to the atypical Raimundo, crystallizes some key ideological features of the transition from slavery to freedom in Brazil.

As in all other slave regimes, so in Brazil the child of a slave mother was born a slave, even if, as in Raimundo's case, the father was a free man. If, however, the father acknowledged the child as his, the child became free when the father died.[33] Raimundo's father had done more than merely recognize the child, and the infant had been freed on his baptism and officially adopted by his father. Raised as a free man, his father's heir, Raimundo had been educated abroad and protected form the knowledge of the "disgrace" of his birth to a slave woman.

Of all the piecemeal efforts to manumit certain categories of slaves before the final abolition of slavery in 1888, the most important was the Rio Branco Law, passed in September 1871. This piece of legislation, known as the Law of the Free Womb, effectively assured the eventual disappearance of slavery in Brazil, for it declared free the children born to slave women after that date. But, like other manumissions, which were often susceptible to revocation, so the Rio Branco law hedged this freedom in conditions designed to ease and delay the passage to a nonslave society: these children were to remain with their mothers until the age of eight, after which the mother's owner could either take a financial indemnification from the government or use the minor's labor until the age of twenty-one.[34] Even this law, however, was unacceptable to some slaveholders who saw their entire way of life at risk, and Azevedo depicts the complicity of the clergy in backdating slave infants' birthdates so that their masters might evade the new law.

Despite the evidence of these precise historical details, many critics have faulted Azevedo's novel for its unsustained attack on slavery as an institution. It is indeed accurate to see the novel's drama as set in motion primarily by the conflict between a corrupt cleric whose every move is designed to protect and promote his own power, and two star-crossed lovers. As Wilson Martins notes, two lines, until then running parallel to each other, converge to produce Azevedo's novel: naturalism and abolitionism.[35] At times, these two lines lead to separate emphases as the novel works out its main themes.

As befitting a positivist hero, Raimundo is a thoroughly enlightened character, and Azevedo repeatedly contrasts his ideas with those of the narrow-minded gentry of Maranhão, who still dwell mentally in an earlier era. Only Raimundo is well educated, atheistic, an experienced traveler, liberal, open-minded, and appalled at the treatment of blacks. Only he is depicted as having an interest in science. Through this single character, Azevedo pursues several important naturalist themes. First among these is abolitionism itself, which can, in fact, be subsumed under naturalism's characteristic nineteenth-century political philosophy: liberalism.

A second theme that appears in Brazil's naturalist novels of this period is anticlericalism, which is found in only one other of Azevedo's eleven novels, *A Mortalha de Alzira* (Alzira's shroud, 1893). Even though this theme appears to be central in *Mulatto,* it is somewhat weakened by its embodiment in one truly villainous character. For Azevedo's target is known to have been a particular contemporary priest of Maranhão, who Azevedo believed exercised a pernicious influence on the province. Whereas Eça de Queirós, in *O Crime do Padre Amaro* (1875), proposed that the corruption of society as a whole resulted in a generalized clerical decadence, Azevedo, by contrast, suggests that one priest, Canon Diogo, single-handedly corrupts his office and his parishioners, who are part of a relatively innocent, if ignorant and pretentious, society.

Ridicule of the bourgeoisie is a third naturalist theme prominent in *Mulatto.* Manuel Pescada, the successful and prosperous merchant, emerges as a mercenary incapable of sentiment even toward his daughter. The upwardly mobile head clerk, Luís Dias, appears as a lout molded by a tedious commercial regimen. Many of the other characters in the novel are ridiculed for their crass ignorance, superstitious beliefs, provincialism, and bigotry, unsuccessfully concealed by their condescending and superior airs.

Antimonarchist sentiment, also characteristic of novels of this period, is found in *Mulatto.* In the early 1870s, when the novel takes place, many Brazilians favored a Republic, as does Raimundo, reasoning that it would correct the political and social problems neglected by the Brazilian emperors. Maranhão, however, was staunchly pro-Empire and looked on the Emperor Dom Pedro II not so much as the ruler of Brazil but as a link with Portugal.

Finally, naturalist novels, in their exposure of the seamy sides of life, frequently favored the underdog, as is apparent in *Mulatto*'s antislavery attitude, thus bringing the two currents—naturalism and abolitionism—full circle. Azevedo persistently exposes and attacks the cruelty of the slave owners. The presence of the bigoted and shrewish grandmother, Maria Bárbara, a symbol of intransigent racial hatred and prejudice, is one of Azevedo's contributions to the Brazilian abolition campaign. Many of the novel's details relate not only to racial attitudes, but to slavery as an institution and to the society it animates. Even stereotyped characters such as Mônica, the very model of a faithful, maternal black mammy, can be seen as an indictment of the fear and dependency provoked by slavery, for not only was manumission itself conditional but freed slaves found few options available to them, especially in the agrarian north, and many of them continued in their former occupations. A pointed contrast is also drawn in the novel between Mônica, Ana Rosa's substitute mother, integrated into Manuel Pescada's family, a captive to her love of the child she raised, and Raimundo's own mother, a crazed black woman, also manumitted, an outcast with nowhere to go, a former slave-concubine without a master. She is the reject, the black woman who has no social role in a society that reduces the options of black women, in particular, to lives tied in one way or another to the white masters and their households.

But it is above all through Azevedo's depiction of Raimundo, the mulatto, that the novel's representation of black oppression must be gauged. For Raimundo progresses from an arrogant and privileged young man, whose European education endows him with a (wholly traditional) feeling of superiority to those around him, to an embittered, thwarted individual who discovers that he is defined, ultimately, by the stigma of his birth. Although he is repelled by the aptly named Maria Bárbara's barbarous treatment of her slaves (p. 112), Raimundo, in his ignorance, initially dismisses slaves as of no relevance to his own life. Only after he learns his mother's identity does he engage in a genuine antislavery speech (pp. 226–27). In many of the earlier scenes, he simply feels superior to the bigotry and malice he sees around him, whereas once the mystery of his birth vanishes, his bitterness and disillusionment threaten to permanently mar his hitherto unblemished character. Raimundo discovers that the word "mulatto," like a parasitic idea" he cannot free himself of (p. 204)—note the biological language so cultivated by writers of naturalist fiction, and which

Azevedo amply uses throughout the novel—has altered his existence.

Raimundo's lack of knowledge of his personal history is both a psychological and an existential failing. It is also the occasion of one of the novel's subtle parallels, for just as Raimundo does not know "who he is," so Maranhão's society does not know what it is. The key difference is that Maranhão's white society most desires to avoid knowledge, to continue to live in the shadow of a largely mythic past, whereas Raimundo's passion is to cast off the myths and uncover his real history. His efforts to recollect the past lead to some pre-Proustian moments of reminiscence and observation regarding the functioning of memory, as well as to an early fictional use of stream of consciousness.

Azevedo's narrative perspective in one important respect approximates Raimundo's: an estranged eye, able to see what this benighted society willfully ignores. Blind to his past, Raimundo nonetheless sees clearly the nature of the society that surrounds him. They, knowing his past, live in illusion. Raimundo cannot know "who he is"—but the rest of the city, and the reader, knows that he "is" the son of a slave woman, and that he himself was born a slave. This knowledge is the feature that defines him most significantly in the eyes of his society. In depicting Raimundo, ironically, as a creature of privilege, Azevedo is separating class from race as components of the prevailing social hierarchy. Raimundo is an anomaly, hence the unease he causes in those around him: he belongs to the "right" class by virtue of his appearance, education, and, most important of all, his wealth. But he belongs to the "wrong" race by virtue of his mother, and, like her, he experiences the taint of race and class: black and born a slave.

The novel limns the story of Oedipus—another man who did not know who his mother was, whose search for his origins led to his destruction—with the significant difference that the good Raimundo engages in no violence, not even against Canon Diogo, who easily outsmarts him and deprives the reader of what would be a most gratifying revenge scene. In pointed contrast to one another, the innocent and blind Raimundo is tormented by his lack of knowledge, whereas the evil Canon Diogo, who knows and sees everything, always has an easy conscience and sleeps well. Here the novel projects lack of knowledge of oneself and one's history as leading to helplessness and passivity. Even Raimundo's sexual transgressions, as the novel makes abundantly clear, are provoked by Ana Rosa's daring insistence, predicated on her belief that her father will care more about the gender hierarchy that requires her to be redeemed by a proper marriage (and cousin marriages were common) than about the race hierarchy that makes Raimundo an unacceptable son-in-law. The fact that she is wrong in her evaluation of the relative importance of these hierarchies is one of the novel's fascinating touches. For Azevedo's denouement argues for a hierarchy within the hierarchy—with the prejudice against blacks and slaves (the two being intimately intertwined) appearing as deeper than the female virginity complex characterizing the sexual double standard of Manuel Pescada's class.

From another viewpoint, the two systems of domination—whites over blacks and men over women—articulated in the novel are ironically affirmed at the book's end. Ana Rosa is returned to her place as a woman, a dutiful daughter turned dutiful wife, at the same time that the danger to the family represented by Raimundo's tainted blood is thwarted. Several reversals are thus set right: the proud mulatto dies, and the rebellious young white woman is restored obediently to the bosom of white male authority. Her challenge to her society, made explicit when she defends her pride and virtue at the cost of her virginity and thus (so she thinks) assures her marriage to Raimundo, comes to an end with his death and her miscarriage.

Motivated by passion and her discovery of her maternal destiny, Ana Rosa had disregarded the lessons of her society and the racial hierarchy in which she was brought up. Despite the naturalistic flourishes, she is a true romantic heroine in that she had believed love conquers all, a belief the novel bloodily explodes. Unlike a romantic heroine, however, Ana Rosa survives and gets on with her life and its biological imperative, whereas Raimundo is sacrificed to the prejudice and pride of Manuel Pescada and—not to be forgotten—to the machinations of Canon Diogo. Azevedo is not lacking in subtlety, however, and perhaps the reader is meant to detect the parallel between Mônica, the "free" black mammy who has a stereotypical doglike fidelity to her charge (see p. 248), and our last glimpse of the "free" white woman Ana Rosa, once again integrated into her society, apparently having learned to love her oppression. To be sure, more than a hint is given here of a latent attack on the bourgeois family and its pretensions, an attack also apparent in one of Azevedo's later novels, *Casa de Pensão* (Boardinghouse), first published, as a serial, in 1883.

In some respects, however, Azevedo, not surprisingly, seems to have absorbed elements of the dominant racial and sexual ideology of his time. This ideology emerges, for example, in his unquestioning use of conventional color metaphors to indicate moral qualities, as when the narrative refers to "the whiteness" of Raimundo's unblemished character (p. 205), an image that needs to be distinguished from Canon Diogo's perfectly consistent reference to Raimundo's "black soul" (p. 259); or when Raimundo's despondency is described as "an immense black cloud in his spirit" (p. 205). It is evident as well in the novel's depiction of women such as Ana Rosa's mother, who had fallen in love with the hero "Farol"; these women discover—so we are told—their unavoidable fate in loving a "superior" man. Moreover, both Raimundo and Canon Diogo express the belief that it is a woman's nature to slavishly obey the father of her child—a view that disregards contradictory elements such as Ana Rosa's strategic and carefully reasoned seduction of Raimundo, part of her vigorous defense of her "happiness."

Azevedo, however, can be, and indeed has been, criticized for making Raimundo a totally unlikely "mulatto"—right down to his blue eyes.[36] But this conventional representation of an unjustly maligned hero has to be understood within the context of Azevedo's critique of race prejudice, which he portrays as resting on cultural, rather than biological, categories. This sense of what we would today call the social construction of race first emerges early in the novel when Canon Diogo rejects Manuel's suggestion that Raimundo should have become a priest. Outraged that many dark-skinned priests already exist, Diogo acknowledges the political, and not biological, imperative at work in the oppression of blacks. Protesting Raimundo's privileged status, he comments: "it seems pure spite for a black boy to be born with such opportunities as this one was. . . . One can recognize an intelligent man right away! But they ought to be jackasses! Jackasses! Good for nothing but serving us! Damn them all!" (p. 48). The implication that biology cannot be relied on to keep blacks ever inferior to whites is reiterated when Maria Bárbara, enraged, expresses the classic opinion that "they no longer know their place" (p. 220). Brazil at the time had a significant population of free blacks, and, as many of the novel's details also indicate, individual black- and brown-skinned men did succeed in attaining positions of power and influence, thus challenging further the linkage between social and biologic definitions of "race."

The clearest expression of the social construction of the black occurs when Raimundo, having discovered "who he is," connects his personal past to Brazil's history and considers the effect on his life of the label "mulatto":

> That simple word revealed all he had desired to know until then, and at the same time denied him everything; that cursed word swept away his

> doubts and cleared up his past, but also robbed him of any hope for happiness and wrenched from him his homeland and future family. That word told him brutally: "Here, you wretch, in this miserable land where you were born, you shall only love a Negress of your own sort! Your mother, remember it well, was a slave! And so were you!"
>
> "But," retorted an inner voice, which he could scarcely hear within the storm of his despair, "nature did not create captives. You should not bear the least blame for what others have done. And yet you are punished and damned by the brothers of those very men who introduced slavery into Brazil!" (p. 205)

Contemplating the gulf that separates his birth from his education, Raimundo, whose "taint" is not even visible, begins to understand some of the words and categories in which he is enmeshed. He identifies what is happening to him as a maneuver to "blame the victim." As a man in a liminal category, neither black nor white, through whose presence Azevedo explodes the myth of Brazil as a racial paradise in which miscegenation was widely accepted, Raimundo is uniquely situated to demonstrate the strength of choosing a "white black" as protagonist.

Such a choice had already been made some years earlier by another Brazilian writer. In 1875 Bernardo Guimarães published *A Escrava Isaura* (The slave Isaura), a romantic abolitionist tale about the daughter of a mulatto slave and a Portuguese man. Isaura has ivory-colored skin, speaks French, and plays the piano. Her trials and tribulations are largely the result of the lascivious desires of the white men who have power over her, but her savior, the novel's romantic hero, is also a white man. This ambiguous novel, which was immensely popular in its time, is, like Azevedo's work, routinely criticized for focusing its antislavery argument on an atypical heroine. Although *Isaura,* unlike Azevedo's novel, is in many respects a standard romantic work, it raises similar problems about the significance of choosing white blacks as protagonists of ostensibly antislavery and antiracist fiction. On behalf of such novels, it can be and usually is said that in their time they allowed the white reader to identify and hence sympathize with the protagonist's plight, thus breaking through a conditioned acceptance of the institution of slavery and the practice of discrimination as things that happen to "others," to people essentially unlike "oneself." Although this position is true as far as it goes, such a line of argument misses some of the deconstructive potentialities of the white-black character.

In his study of race relations in the United States and Brazil, Carl Degler affirms that observable physical differences can easily translate into intellectual and moral distinctions.[37] Such a view implies a biological basis for racial and sexual domination. It cannot, however, explain the absence of domination when other perceptible physical differences exist—for example, in hair or eye color, body height or weight—nor can it help us understand why it is one particular group—whites rather than blacks, men rather than women—that dominates over and discriminates against the other. The white-black character in fiction, it can be argued, elevates the entire discussion to the level of social rather than biological constructs, for the absence of the characteristic "taint," as these novels show, does not automatically alter status or life options. Instead, by their very presence, which points to the arbitrariness of the dominant society's rationale for exclusion, such characters call attention to the real motive behind the attribution of inferiority to others: the protection of privilege, both material and psychological.

Brazil has a history of denying the existence of racial prejudice, embracing instead the category (more apparently innocuous, perhaps, because wholly respectable within capitalism) of "class" prejudice as an explanation for the oppression of blacks. Indeed, racial categories in Brazil are a highly ambiguous matter, worked out in detailed codings of hair color and texture, shape of nose and mouth, and skin tones.[38] This complex coding, which suggests extraordinary acuity regarding racial distinctions, rather than lack of awareness of them, seems to deflect attention from the social construction of racial meanings.

In Raimundo's case, what is apparently objectionable is the social fact that his mother was a slave, and that he was born a black slave (these are the phrases that are repeated again and again). Raimundo, in the passage cited earlier, objects precisely to the social stigma he suffers because of this "fact." He objects, in other words, to his society's penchant for historical amnesia. Given such amnesia, when the enslaved or inferiorized person is visibly black, it is more difficult to sort out the social from the biological characterization, for indeed "black" and "slave" were largely coterminous for more than three centuries of Brazil's history. The special identity of the two categories is further indicated in Portuguese by the use, in both cases, of the verb *ser,* expressing "to be" in an essential and permanent sense, as in: to be human, to be male, to be female, to be black, to be a slave. This grammatical norm finds its complement in the verb *estar,* meaning "to be" in a contingent or temporary sense, as in: to be busy, to be sick, to be hungry, to be sad. "To be black" or "to be a slave," then, is to have imputed to one an essential and inherent quality. Not the historical act of enslavement, but the identity of "being a slave" is affirmed by such language.

Might not the function of the white-black character, suffering the stigma of race, be precisely to call into question the entire system of coding, encompassing both praxis and ideology, that sustains domination? Even the hapless Isaura, who is a slave, raises, by the mere fact of her white appearance and accomplishments, the issue of society's definitions of her identity.

Such novels can be attacked for appearing to imply that no critique need be made of the plight of, for example, slaves who look like proper slaves—dark skinned, not French speaking, piano playing, not educated as is Raimundo. But this perception is by no means a necessary implication of such works. At least as strong a case—and certainly a more interesting one—can be made for the alternative reading: these works pointedly expose the artificial categorization on which racial oppression depends, in which social and politically functional designations of race are passed off as having an inevitable "natural," because ostensibly biological, base.

The white-black protagonist, then, can be viewed as a device for protesting against the "self-evident" quality of racial labels and the social categories ensuing from them in a slaveholding society. He or she lays bare these labels as cultural categories lacking invariable biological referents. Furthermore, such characters make the important point, which found little theoretical articulation until our own day, that the meanings of biological categories are socially created, and that these creations serve to sustain inequality (whether of race or gender) and justify the domination on which inequality must rest.[39]

From this point of view, white blacks, objects of derision and hatred to whites and also, as Azevedo acerbically notes, to other mulattoes who have internalized their own oppression, are a special threat to the dominant society because they call attention to the arbitrariness of the society's rationale for exploitation and discrimination. They force a perception of the difference between "seeming" and "being," between what a human being "is," and the roles he or she is made to enact. In its promotion of such an analysis, as well as in its unforgettable portrait of Maranhão in the 1870s, Aluísio Azevedo's *Mulatto* continues to be a work demanding our attention, claiming our respect.

Notes

A note on orthography: No attempt at regularization has been made in the following notes. The orthography of the original Portuguese has been followed in all cases.

1. Thomas Skidmore, *Black into White: Race and Nationality in Brazilian*

Thought (New York: Oxford University Press, 1974), 9. For a survey of Brazil in the years during which Azevedo was coming to maturity and writing his most important books, see Emília Viotti da Costa, "Brazil: The Age of Reform, 1870–1889," in *The Cambridge History of Latin America,* vol. 5, ed. Leslie Bethell (Cambridge: Cambridge University Press, 1986), 725–77.

2. The novel's status as *the* first naturalist work in Brazil is the subject of much debate. The eminent critic Lúcia Miguel Pereira, for one, reserves that label for Inglês de Sousa's 1877 novel *O Coronel Sangrado,* which she considers to be far more in the spirit of naturalism than *O Mulato:* "in the spirit, but not in the technique," as she says. "Writing in the years before Zola and Eça de Queirós became popular in Brazil, Inglês de Sousa lacks the tics and mannerisms that soon thereafter would tightly link almost all the novels published in Brazil in the last two decades of the 19th century. . . ." See her *Prosa de Ficção (De 1870 a 1920),* vol. 12 of *História da Literatura Brasileira,* ed. Álvaro Lins (Rio de Janeiro: José Olympio, 1950), 155. Wilson Martins, *História da Inteligência Brasileira,* vol. 4: 1877–1896 (São Paulo: Cultrix, 1979), 51, criticizes literary histories that see realism as suddenly arising in Brazil with *O Mulato* in 1881, or even with Inglês de Sousa's *O Cacaulista* in 1876, for realist novels existed long before these, and some even had a clear sense of a realist "school." Conversely, Martins notes, romantic stereotypes extend long beyond 1876 and 1881. This is apparent, too, in Azevedo's own subsequent novels. For an English-language study of naturalism in Brazil, see Dorothy Scott Loos, *The Naturalistic Novel of Brazil* (New York: Hispanic Institute, 1963).

3. Josué Montello, *Aluísio Azevedo e a Polêmica d' "O Mulato"* (Rio de Janeiro: Livraria José Olympio/INL, 1975), 8–9.

4. For a discussion of Azevedo's introduction to positivism, see ibid., 39–42 and 48–51.

5. Ibid., 21–22. Montello's argument is that the novel is a *roman à thèse,* the thesis being principally anticlericalism rather than racial bigotry.

6. Aluízio Avezedo, *A Brazilian Tenement,* trans. Harry W. Brown (New York: R. M. McBride, 1926).

7. Herberto Sales, *Para Conhecer Melhor Aluísio Azevedo* (Rio de Janeiro: Block Editores, 1973), 12–14. See also Raimundo de Menezes, *Aluízio Azevedo: Uma Vida de Romance* (São Paulo: Martins, 1958).

8. Skidmore, *Black into White,* 27–32.

9. See Skidmore for a detailed exposition of Brazilian racial ideology toward the turn of the century and thereafter.

10. Montello, *Azevedo,* 3. Martins, *Inteligência Brasileira,* 7–9, points out that the anticlericalists of the late 1870s were not irresponsible revolutionary radicals attempting to destroy institutions; rather, they defended a whole complex of liberal ideas—democracy versus monarchy, compulsory and secular education, coeducation, and so forth—and even counted among their adherents several conversative figures and groups.

11. Montello, *Azevedo,* 55. For other accounts of life in Maranhão at the time, see Giorgio Marotti, *Black Characters in the Brazilian Novel,* trans. Maria O. Marotti and Harry Lawton (Los Angeles: UCLA Center for Afro-American Studies, 1987), 51–72.

12. Carlos Studart Filho, *O Antigo Estado do Maranhão e Suas Capitanias Feudais* (Fortaleza: Imprensa Universitária do Ceará, 1960), 343–44.

13. Mary C. Karasch, *Slave Life in Rio de Janeiro, 1808–1850* (Princeton: Princeton University Press, 1987), 6, notes that, unlike some other racial terms

used in Rio de Janeiro during the period she studies, the word *cabra* had no positive connotations. The label *mulatto,* to be sure, is itself a racial insult; it means a young mule, hence an animal of mixed parentage, presumably sterile.

14. Helio Viana, *História do Brasil,* (São Paulo: Melhoramentos, 1961), 1: 121–30.

15. Celso Furtado, *The Economic Growth of Brazil* (Berkeley and Los Angeles: University of California Press, 1963), 74.

16. *Dicionário de História do Brasil*, 4th ed. (São Paulo: Melhoramentos, 1973), 554.

17. Caio Prado Júnior, *The Colonial Background of Modern Brazil* (Berkeley and Los Angeles, University of California Press, 1969), 172–73.

18. Furtado, *Economic Growth,* 96–97.

19. Mário Martins Meireles, *História do Maranhão* (Rio de Janeiro: D.A.S.P. Serviço de Documentação, 1960), 213.

20. Prado Júnior, *Modern Brazil,* 173, and Furtado, *Economic Growth,* 98.

21. Robert Edgar Conrad, *World of Sorrow: The African Slave Trade to Brazil* (Baton Rouge: Louisiana State University Press, 1986), 31. See ibid., 30–34, for a discussion of different estimates of the number of slaves brought to Brazil.

22. Prado Júnior, *Modern Brazil,* 459, n. 53.

23. Conrad, *World of Sorrow,* 33.

24. Octávio da Costa Eduardo, *The Negro in Northern Brazil: A Study in Acculturation* (1948; reprint, Seattle: University of Washington Press, 1966), 13.

25. See Adolfo Serra, *A Balaiada,* 2d ed. (Rio de Janeiro: Bedeschi, 1946).

26. Meireles, *Maranhão,* 286.

27. Ibid., 287.

28. See Antônio Henriques Leal, *Pantheon Maranhense* (Lisboa: Imprensa Nacional, 1873), 221–32.

29. João Francisco Lisboa, "A Festa de N. S. dos Remédios," in *Obras de João Francisco Lisboa,* (Lisboa: Typografia Mattos Moreira & Pinheiro, 1901), 2:515–31.

30. Meireles, *Maranhão,* 288.

31. Conrad, *World of Sorrow,* 194.

32. Ibid., 195. See also Leslie Bethell, *The Abolition of the Brazilian Slave Trade* (Cambridge: Cambridge University Press, 1970), 364– 387.

33. Katia M. de Queirós Mattoso, *To Be a Slave in Brazil: 1550–1888,* trans. Arthur Goldhammer (New Brunswick, N.J.: Rutgers University Press, 1986), 155.

34. Ibid., 155–60 ff.

35. Martins, *Inteligência Brasileira,* 101.

36. Ibid., 102, for example, notes that Raimundo is a typical Brazilian "moreno," a physical type well within the dominant patterns acceptable at the time, and points out that Raimundo looks so little like a mulatto that, in chapter 5, someone seeing him on the street comments: "I've heard he's a mulatto" (p. 110). Martins further argues that racial and color prejudice play no significant role in the development of the plot and action. As for Raimundo's blue eyes, Azevedo wrote before the laws of genetics had been understood.

37. Carl N. Degler, *Neither Black nor White* (New York: Macmillan, 1971), 207–8. In this work Degler suggests that the mulatto occupies a special place in Brazilian society, neither black nor white. This situation created a "mulatto escape hatch," by which mulattoes, but not blacks, could rise in the social and economic hierarchy (109). Rejecting such a view, Nelson do Valle Silva, "Updating the Cost of Not Being White in Brazil," in *Race Class and Power in Brazil,* ed. Pierre-Michel Fontaine (Los Angeles: UCLA Center for Afro-American Studies, 1985), 42–55, concludes, based on statistical analyses of racial income differentials in

recent decades, that "to consider Blacks and mulattoes as composing a homogeneous 'nonwhite' racial group does no violence to reality" (42).

38. The "myth of racial democracy," or the "prejudice of having no prejudice," are terms used by Florestan Fernandes, *The Negro in Brazilian Society,* trans. Jacqueline D. Skiles et al. (New York: Columbia University Press, 1969). Skidmore, *Black into White,* 26, notes that the famous abolitionist Joaquim Nabuco subscribed to the popular view that Brazil should be "improving" itself eugenically; at the same time, his classic work *O Abolicionismo* (1883) expresses the idealized view of race relations in Brazil: "[S]lavery, to our good fortune, never embittered the slave's spirit toward the master, at least collectively, nor did it create between the races that mutual hate which naturally exists between oppressors and oppressed." On racial terminology, see Marvin Harris, "Referential Ambiguity in the Calculus of Brazilian Racial Identity," *Southwestern Journal of Anthropology* 26, no. 19 (Spring 1970): 1–14. Harris gathered 492 different racial categorizations in five different states. For further references on this subject, see D. Patai, *Brazilian Women Speak: Contemporary Life Stories* (New Brunswick, N.J.: Rutgers University Press, 1988), 10–15 and notes.

39. This line of analysis draws on a lecture by Etienne Balibar at the University of Massachusetts at Amherst, on September 27, 1988. Balibar spoke on the subject of "Racism and Nationalism," tracing the changing signification of the term "race" and demonstrating the politically motivated attribution of a biological meaning to the term.

A Note about the Translation

This translation was originally done by Murray Graeme MacNicoll, working from an unspecified edition. Daphne Patai, before editing the translation, verified it against the Editora Ática seventh edition (São Paulo: Editora Ática, 1987), which itself is based on *O Mulato,* 3d ed. (Rio de Janeiro: B. L. Garnier, 1889). Explanatory notes were composed by Murray Graeme MacNicoll.

MULATTO

1

On a sultry and oppressive day, the decadent city of São Luís Maranhão lay sprawled in the tropical heat. It was nearly impossible to go about on the streets: the cobblestones were scalding hot; the window glass and street lamps flashed in the sun like mammoth diamonds; outer walls were shining like polished silver; the breezeless air made silent statues of the trees; water wagons moved noisily on the streets, shaking the buildings; and water sellers, with shirt sleeves and pantlegs rolled up, invaded the houses without knocking in order to dispense it to jugs and bathtubs. In certain zones no living soul could be found; everyone was huddled indoors, dozing; only a few Negro servants were out shopping for the evening meal or selling their meager wares.

The Praça da Alegria emitted a funereal air. From a dilapidated house with one door and window, the squeak of rusty hammock hooks could be heard and the shrill, consumptive voice of a woman singing in falsetto "sweet Caroline was beautiful"; from the other side of the square, an old Negro woman, bent by a heavy wooden tray that was dirty, tallowy, soaked with blood and covered by a cloud of flies, cried out in a drawling and melancholy voice: "Liver, kidneys, and hearts!" She was a vendor of entrails. Here and there naked children pursued their paper kites, squealing as they ran, their skinny legs bowed from being carried on their mothers' hips. Their heads were reddened by the sun, and their skin was scorched except for those bloated little bellies that looked jaundiced. One or two whites, having been driven from home by necessity, were crossing the street, cooking in their own sweat even though their ample umbrellas protected them from the sun. The dogs, stretched out twitching on the sidewalks, moaned like humans, and bit angrily at mosquitoes. In the distance, near St. Pantaleon Church, the cry of "Venetian rice! Mangoes! Green coconuts!" was faintly audible. The empty stands on the corners were thick with the acrid smell of cheap soap and fermenting brandy. One stall owner, flopped over his counter, was sleeping off his drowsy lassitude and absently caressing his monstrous bare foot. From Santo Antônio Beach the monotonous sound of a horn announced the return of the fishermen, drawing the fish women eagerly to the scene; most of these were hefty black women, balancing trays on their heads and swinging their vibrant flanks and opulent breasts in cumbersome rhythm.

Praia Grande and Rua da Estrela, however, contrasted sharply with the rest of the city because at precisely that hour they were bustling with the urgencies of commerce. Panting men, their faces flushed by the heat, mingled everywhere; black porters and clerks running errands jostled one another; those wearing gray canvas jackets had sweat-stained backs and armpits. In the open light slave buyers were examining the Negroes and their little ones who were about to be sold; they inspected their teeth, feet, and groins; they asked endless questions; they tapped some on the shoulders and thighs with their hat brims, testing the muscle tone as if buying a horse. At the Commercial House, or under the almond trees, or in the entrances of the supply houses among high stacks of crates filled with Portuguese onions and potatoes, hummed private discussions of the exchange rate, the price of cotton, the sugar tax, and the tariff on national products; amply padded rural colonels confidently concluded dealings, made transactions, losing, winning, trying to outwit one another, with the cleverness innate to shrewd businessmen, using their own slang, exchanging off-color jokes, but with a general spirit of camaraderie. Auctioneers loudly intoned the price of their merchandise, with an exaggerated opening of their vowels. "Ooo-uun" thousand, they said, instead of "one" thousand. Curious onlookers and prospective buyers alike clustered around the doors of the auction halls. A sultry and heavy drone of voices blanketed the entire market place.

The auctioneer winked his eyes meaningfully; excited, with the gavel always in one fist, his countenance serious, he would raise his arm to display a jug of crude brandy, or squat comically to poke at the baskets of flour and corn with a sharp-pointed rod. And when the time came to part with his goods, he would shout out and repeat the price many times, finally bringing down the gavel with a powerful thud and dragging out his voice in a high-pitched finale.

The presposterous bellies of the rich merchants could be seen gliding around the square; bald and red heads were seen, and beads of sweat dripped from beneath costly hats; defensive smiles, unmoustachioed mouths swollen by the heat, agile and sweaty little legs encased in canvas trousers from Hamburg. Incessant motion, though much of it feigned, pervaded the teeming scene; from the idle rich who had gone there to pass the day, to clerks who sought to kill time, and even to the jobless vagrants: each according to his own talents pretended important business.

The veranda of Manuel Pescada's two-story house—it was a large veranda with an open ceiling so that the shingles and rafters supporting the roof tiles could be seen—had a more or less picturesque appearance with its expansive view of the Bacanga River and its lattice work painted a Paris green. The structure opened onto a long and narrow backyard where, for want of sunlight, two sad pitanga trees withered and a peacock paced solemnly back and forth.

Inside, the walls were lined with blue Portuguese tiles, except for the part around the top where wallpaper, once glorious with hunting scenes, was whitish gray and partially paintless, leaving spots that resembled trousers threadbare at the knees. Off to one side, an old well-polished mahogany china cupboard looked haughtily down on the dining room table, its shining glass doors displaying the latest style of silver and porcelain; forgotten in a corner lay a Wilson sewing machine sleeping in its varnished pine box—it had been one of the first to arrive in Maranhão; between the doors hung four works of Julien, lithographs representing the seasons; near the cupboard a grandfather clock, its plate-sized pendulum swinging monotonously, sadly droned out the chimes. Two o'clock. Two o'clock in the afternoon.

The lunch dishes, however, were still on the table. A white bottle containing the last few sips of a Lisbon wine sparkled in the reflected light entering from the backyard. A thrush chirped in a small cage hanging between the windows on the far side.

Lassitude hung over the place. A breeze from the Bacanga River was freshening the veranda, giving it a lukewarm, agreeable feeling. The quietness of a weekend, a weary longing to close one's eyes and stretch one's legs, permeated the scene. On the other side of the river, the silent vegetation of the Anjo da Guarda estate invited good snoozing on the grass under the mango trees; the thicket seemed to open its arms wide and summon all to the calm tepidity of its shade.

"Well then, Ana Rosa, what's your answer?" asked Manuel, stretching out even more in the chair at the end of the table, opposite his daughter. "You know quite well that I won't go against your wishes. . . . I desire this marriage, yes, I do. . . . But, in the first place, I need to know if it is what you want. . . . Come now . . . Speak up!"

Ana Rosa did not respond but continued as she was, quite absorbed in rolling her pink-colored fingertips over the crumbs of bread she had found on the tablecloth.

Manuel Pedro da Silva, better known as Manuel Pescada, was fifty years old and Portuguese; he was strong and ruddy, obviously a hard worker. They said he had a knack for commerce and was a friend of Brazil. He liked to read during his leisure hours, and respectfully subscribed to the better newspapers of the province and even to some from Lisbon. When he was young, someone had crammed various passages of Luís de Camões[1] into his head, and he was not completely unaware of the names of other poets. He fanatically praised the Marquês de Pombal,[2] about whom he knew many anecdotes, and he had a membership in the Portuguese Cultural Center,[3] from which he benefited less than his daughter, who was crazy about novels.

Manuel Pedro had been married to a lady from Alcântara[4] named Mariana. She was very virtuous and, like the majority of the people of Maranhão, meticulously religious; when she died, she bequeathed six slaves to Nossa Senhora do Carmo Church.

Those years after she died were sad, not only for the widower but for the daughter, too—the poor thing left without a mother just when she most needed maternal guidance. They had been living on Caminho Grande in a modest single-story house where the mother's illness had sent them in search of a more benign air; Manuel, however, who was by then a merchant and owned his own store on the Praia Grande, immediately took his little daughter to the two-story house on Rua da Estrela, where on the ground floor he had been prospering for ten years through his business in the wholesale of fabrics.

In order to avoid being alone with his daughter, who was fast becoming a young lady, he asked his mother-in-law, Dona Maria Bárbara, to leave her small farm and come to live with him and her granddaughter. The child needed the kind of guiding hand that a man could never provide. And, if he should hire a governess—my Lord!—what would people say? In Maranhão they gossiped about everything! It would be ideal if Dona Maria Bárbara were to decide to leave the countryside and move in with them on Rua da Estrela! She would have nothing to regret, either. It would be just like being in her own home—a good room, plenty of food, and freedom to come and go!

The old lady accepted and went to live in her son-in-law's house, dragging along her fifty and then-some years, a battalion of black children she was rearing, and odds and ends from the time of her now-departed husband. In a short while, however, the good merchant was repenting the step he had taken. Dona Maria Bárbara—despite her highly pious manner, despite never leaving her room without her hair well arranged, without the clusters of black silk with which she extravagantly framed her furrowed and gaunt face; despite her great fervor for the church and the masses she babbled every day—Dona Maria Bárbara, despite all that, was a failure as a housekeeper.

She was a hag! A viper! She would strike the slaves through habit and her taste for it; she couldn't speak without shouting; and when she started to scold—heaven forbid!—she disturbed the entire neighborhood! Unbearable!

Maria Bárbara was like all the older Maranhão ladies brought up in the country. She frequently discussed her grandparents, almost all of them Portuguese; she was very proud, full of racial bigotry. She referred to Negroes as "filth" and called mulattoes "niggers." She had always been like that and, as a devout woman, she had no match: in Alcântara there had been a Santa Bárbara chapel where she required her slaves to pray in unison each night, with their arms spread, sometimes in manacles. Amid great sighs she recalled her husband, João Hipólito, an elegant, blue-eyed, blond-haired Portuguese.[5] This João Hipólito was a naturalized Brazilian who became an official of the secretariat of the provincial government. He was a colonel when he passed away.

Maria Bárbara dedicated an unlimited and exclusive enthusiasm to the Portuguese as a people, and in every respect preferred them to Brazilians. When Manuel Pedro, who was then getting his start in business in the capital, asked for her daughter's hand, she had remarked: "Well! At least I can be sure he is white!"

But Pescada never understood his wife, nor did he have her love. It was only virtue, or perhaps simply motherhood, that kept Mariana faithful; she lived solely for her daughter. It so happened that when the unfortunate Mariana was fifteen years old, in the irresponsible rapture of first love she had chosen the man to whom her soul would forever belong. This man still lives in the history of Maranhão; he was the political activist José Cândido de Morais e Silva,[6] popularly known as "Farol." She did everything possible to marry him, but all her efforts were in vain. Not only did such an idea encounter inflexible opposition from her own family, but political persecution inflicted a short lifespan on the phenomenal Farol.

Nevertheless, her destiny had become linked to the fate of this unfortunate young man of Maranhão. Who could have guessed that poor Mariana, born and raised in the backlands of northern Brazil, would sense like any daughter of the great cities the magic influence that superior men exercise over the feminine spirit? She loved him, without knowing why. She had felt the dominating force of his gaze, the revolutionary impulses of his Brazilian character, the patriotic heroism of his individuality—so superior to the environment that surrounded him. She had preserved within her heart the passionate phrases, vibrating with indignation, in which he fulminated against the exploiters of his precious country and the enemies of national integrity; and all this, though she could not explain it, drew Mariana to the dashing and fearless hero with the full ardor of a young woman's first love.

When, on the Rua dos Remédios, which at that time was still on the outskirts of São Luís, the ill-fated Farol, scarcely more than twenty-five years old, succumbed to the yoke of his own talent and political honor—an outlawed fugitive racked with misery, hated by some as an assassin and adored by others as a god—the poor young woman became possessed by an overwhelming melancholy, grew weak and became sick and ugly, until, ever sadder, she quietly joined her beloved one in death a few years later.

Ana Rosa had never known Farol; her mother, however, had secretly taught her to cherish the memory of the talented revolutionary whose fighting name still awakened among the Portuguese of Maranhão the bitter memory of the mutiny that had occurred on August 7, 1831.[7] "My child," the unhappy Mariana said to her on the eve of her death, "don't ever let them marry you off unless you truly love the man destined to be your husband. Don't marry in haste! Always remember that marriage must be the consequence of two irresistible inclinations. We should marry because we love, and not love because we marry. If you do what I say, you will be happy." She concluded by asking Ana Rosa to promise that she would refuse a husband forced on her against her will and that she would defy everyone and everything to avoid such a calamity, especially if she already fancied another. And for the latter—yes, whoever he might be—she should commit the greatest sacrifice, should risk her own life, for these qualities exemplified the true virtue of a lady's heart.

And Mariana gave no other advice to her daughter. Ana Rosa was still a child and did not understand what her mother had just said, nor did she soon try to understand. But Mariana's death and her advice were so firmly linked together that they haunted Ana Rosa, and she constantly pondered her dying mother's words.

Manuel Pedro, though a good fellow, was one of those men to whom the subtleties of sentiment were completely foreign. He might have been an excellent husband for another woman, but not for Mariana, whose romantic sensitivity did more to annoy him than to woo him. Despite his innate goodness, being a widower had little more effect than to create a certain displeasure within him, for he missed the presence of a companion to whom he had grown accustomed. Nevertheless, he had no thoughts of remarriage, convinced that his daughter's affection would more than suffice to soften the tedium of his job and that the prompt aid of his mother-in-law would guarantee the decency of his house and the balance of his domestic accounts.

So Ana Rosa grew up amid the insufficient devotion of her father and the raucous temperament of her grandmother. But somehow she conquered the Sotero dos Reis grammar book, did a small amount of reading, learned the rudiments of French, and played sentimental folk songs on the guitar and piano. She was far from stupid. She had a perfect intuition for virtue and a charming manner, and at times she lamented her limited education. She did intricate needle work—in fact, she could embroider better than most—and had a contralto voice that served her well. So well that, when she was a little thing, she sometimes played the part of the Veronica Angel in the Lenten processions. The canons of the diocese extolled the resonance of her voice and rewarded her with almonds in cardboard tubes decorated with crude and characteristic designs done in Gum Arabic and drugstore dye. On those occasions she felt radiant. With cheeks abloom, artificial curls atop her head, and wearing an abbreviated hoop skirt, she took on the air of a ballet dancer. Proud of her silver and gold braids and quivering silken angel wings, she paraded triumphantly in the midst of the group of religious orders, holding on to one end of a handkerchief while her father held the other. Ana Rosa was fulfilling vows made by her mother and grandmother on days when members of the family had been seriously ill.

And she grew into a well-shaped girl. She had her mother's dark eyes and chestnut hair, but her posture and teeth were sturdy and strong like her father's. As she began to mature, romantic whims and poetic fantasies commandeered her imagination. She revelled in moonlight strolls and serenades and the modest library of poets and novelists that she had arranged in the room adjoining hers. A ceramic Paul and Virginia dominated the top of her bookshelf, and hidden behind a mirror was the portrait of Farol that she had inherited from her mother.

Lamartine's *Graziella* was her favorite tale. It made her cry, and each night before she fell asleep she would instinctively imitate the innocent smile that Graziella offered to her lover. Mariana's daughter undertook good deeds for the poor, adored baby birds and could not bear to see a butterfly killed. She was only slightly superstitious: she never left her slippers upside down under her hammock, and she trimmed her hair only during the fourth crescent of the moon. "It's not that I believe in those things," she would say to justify herself, "but I do them because other people do." For some years, a colored lithograph of Nossa Senhora dos Remédios hung above her dresser, and she prayed to her each night before going to sleep. Nothing was as familiar and pleasant to her as a stroll through the Cutim suburb of the city, and, when she heard that there was to be a streetcar line out to it, she shivered with goose flesh.

Her fifteenth birthday steadily brought her new and strange changes; she saw, she felt, that a significant transformation was taking place within her soul and body. Groundless terrors often assailed her; sometimes she felt disheartened with no cause. Finally, one morning, she awoke with a troubled heart, and as she sat up in her hammock lost in thought, she was startled to notice the sudden roundness of her arms and legs; she saw that throughout her body curved lines had replaced straight ones and her shape was in every respect that of a woman.

She was at first struck with delight, but the feeling soon gave way to despondency; for now she felt very much alone; her father's and grandmother's love was no longer enough. She wanted a more exclusive affection, something more her own.

She remembered her past flirtations and laughed a little. How childish, she thought.

When she was twelve she had liked a boy at the Lycée. Although they had spoken only three or four times in her father's office, they thought they were truly in love; then, the student went off to school in Rio de Janeiro and was forgotten. Next was a naval officer. How handsome he looked in his uniform! How charming and elegant! How well he dressed! Ana Rosa even started to embroider him a pair of slippers, but before she finished the first one, the fellow was off on his patrol boat, *The Bahian*. After that it was a store clerk. A good fellow—very careful about his clothing and his fingernails. She could still hear him as he so methodically chose the words with which to request of her "the high honor of dancing the next set."

So long ago! Long ago!

She didn't want to think any more of such foolishness. Childish things! Childish things! Now she must have a husband! Her own, the genuine article, legally! The master of her house, the owner of her body, whom she could love openly like a paramour and obey secretly like a slave. She needed to give herself, to devote herself to him. It was essential that she put her newly found confidence into action and have a household of her own and bring up many children.

Along with this daydreaming came hot chills and palpitating

excitement. The ideal man of her imagination was strong, courageous, superbly clever, and capable of killing himself for her. And in her restless dreams she sketched out the form that was vague but enchanting, leaping over cliffs to be at her side merely to court the good fortune of her smile, with a poignant hope of marriage. In her dreams she pictured her wedding day: a resplendent feast and, next to her, within reach of her lips, a handsome and impassioned young man—the epitome of strength, charm and kindness—who would writhe at her feet burning with impatience and devour her with his blazing look.

Next she saw herself as mistress of her household. Preoccupied with her children, she imagined her happiness, very dependent within the prison of her nest and the tender domination of her husband. And she dreamed of fair-haired, adorable little children, babbling cute and touching nonsense and calling her "mama."

Oh! How wonderful it would be! And to think there actually were women who refused to marry!

No! She could not conceive of celibacy, especially in a woman. A man could fend for himself. He would be sad and alone, but at least he was a man, he could find other diversions. But a poor woman? What better future for her than marriage? What more rightful pleasure than motherhood? What more joyous companionship than that of her children? Those bewitching little imps! Aside from which, she had always liked children. Often she would ask her friends to send their children to keep her company, and while romping through the house with them, she allowed no one else to care for them. She claimed the exclusive right to fix their meals and wash, dress, and cuddle them. She was forever making them little shirts and pants, bonnets and woolen house slippers, and everything with such loving patience, exactly as she had played with her dolls when she was small. Whenever one of her girl friends married, Ana Rosa begged for a carnation from the bridal bouquet or one of the buds from the orange-blossom wreath; whichever she received was devotedly affixed to her breast with one of the bride's pins. And then she would stand gazing down at it, a distant look in her eyes, until finally her lips would part in a long, very long, sigh, not unlike the traveler who, after only half his homeward trip, already feels tired.

Wherever could her sweetheart be? That handsome fellow, so impassioned and eager. Why didn't he appear? Of all the men Ana Rosa knew in the province, certainly none of them could be he! But in the meantime she kept loving.

Whom?

She could not name him, but she was in love. Yes! Whoever he might be, she loved him, she could feel every fiber of her body vibrate when she thought of her "special someone," intimate and unknown though he be, that "special someone" whose absence was making her melancholy and filling her life with tears.

Months passed—and nothing! After three more years of this, Ana Rosa began to look thin. She slept less and lost her color. At the table she scarcely touched her food.

"Oh, my dear child, something's troubling you," her father said to her one day, by now disturbed by his daughter's sickly state. "You're not yourself at all. What is it, Anica?"

"It's nothing, father."

She felt frightened, as if she had fallen short of his expectations. "Fatigue, nerves. Nothing to worry about."

But she was crying.

"Look! Oh, there we go now, crying! Nothing, eh? I think we need to call the doctor."

"Call the doctor? Now, Father, that isn't necessary!"

She coughed. Why couldn't they leave her in peace? Why couldn't they stop pestering her with questions?

And she coughed even more, choking.

"You see? You're ill! You go about coughing, coughing, coughing, and your only reply is that it's not worth bothering about. Not necessary to call the doctor! No, young lady, we're not going to play with sickness!"

The doctor prescribed ocean baths at Ponta-d'Areia Beach.

The three months Ana Rosa spent there passed delightfully. The coastal breeze, the chilling swims, the extended walks along the beach—all restored her appetite and enriched her blood. She grew stronger and even gained a few pounds.

At Ponta-d'Areia she made a new acquaintance, Dona Eufrasinha, the widow of an officer of the Fifth Infantry, a battalion whose members had perished during the Paraguayan War.[8] She revelled in romance and spoke amorously of her husband, embellishing his brief history: "Ten days following our marriage, he went off to the battlefield where, daringly courageous, he was cut down by an artillery shell. He died soon after, with the name of his beloved spouse on his bloodied lips."

And with a sign indicative of unsatified desire, the widow sorrowfully confided that in this life she had known only ten days and nights of pleasure.

Ana Rosa's heart went out to her friend as she listened in good faith to her tales. With her candid and excitable temperament, she could easily identify with the singular story of that marriage—so tragic yet so charming. More than once she found herself crying over the death of the unfortunate young infantry officer.

Dona Eufrasinha instructed her new friend in many things of which she had hardly dreamed; she taught her certain mysteries of married life; one could say that she gave her lessons in love. She spoke much about "men" and told Ana Rosa how an experienced woman should deal with them. She listed the whims and weak points of both husbands and sweethearts, told her which types were most preferable, and the significance of limpid eyes, thick lips, and a long nose.

Ana Rosa giggled. "I never took her foolishness seriously," she told herself.

But without realizing it, she was using the widow's instructions to piece together her own ideal man. She made him more human and less spiritual, more real, more capable of being discovered. He was assuming a personality of his own as though, at first barely outlined in her dreams, he had been given his final touches by a painter. And after seeing him complete, all trimmed and perfected, she loved him even more, much more, as much as she would have loved him if, in fact, he had been a reality.

From that time onward, he was her ideal, complete and perfected, the basis of her resolutions concerning marriage; he was the gauge she would use to rate all those who would court her. If the young aspirant did not have the nose, the look and the gestures, in short, the overall appearance to match the figure in her dream, he had no hope of gaining the favor of Manuel Pedro's daughter.

Eufrasinha moved to the city. Ana Rosa was already there, and they continued their visits.

And those visits, which became quite frequent and intimate, served as a mutual consolation for the persistent celibacy of the one and the precocious widowhood of the other.

At that time, a young Portuguese by the name of Luís Dias was employed in Manuel's store—a businesslike, thrifty, discreet, hard-working fellow with distinctive handwriting. He was highly respected in the city's commercial circles for his enviable share of business acumen; no one could say a word against such an excellent young man.

Strangely enough, though, people almost always referred to him as "the poor fellow," which, of course, was entirely uncalled for since, thanks be to God, he had everything—lodging, a daily fare, clothes properly washed and starched, and, on top of that, an income from his job. But, despite all those prosperous circumstances, he evoked pity. His problem lay in his confounded air of piety and supplication, his resignation and humility. The hearts of all who looked on him ached for that poor, submissive, passive creature, that beast of burden. Certainly, no man could raise a fist to him, lest he feel like a miserable coward.

But, in the meantime, they kept praising him: "And just to think what's hidden behind that air of modesty. You've got a first-rate employee there, Manuel!"

More than a few merchants had made him good offers, trying to lure him away; but Dias, always staring humbly at his feet, remained firm in his devotion. And so consistently did he reject the unending stream of offers that the entire business community was convinced of his future marriage to his employer's daughter. They all praised Manuel Pedro's choice and predicted that the couple would have a rich and happy life.

"It's all been planned," they said with knowing glances.

Manuel Pedro had in fact seen in this wretched, hard-working soul—passive as a wagon ox and thrifty as a usurer—the man most apt to please his daughter. He wanted Luís Dias as his son-in-law and partner; he confided to his colleagues that the young clerk spent barely a fourth of his annual salary for personal expenses.

"He's already got a fat nest egg," Manuel reflected. "The woman who marries him is getting a good deal! The fellow will make something of himself, he has a great future!"

And, little by little, he became accustomed to considering the fellow already a member of the family and giving him family privileges. The only thing lacking was his daughter's consent. . . . But wouldn't you know it! She couldn't bear to look at him! In fact, she despised him. She couldn't stand that closely cropped hair, the goatee without a moustache, the yellowed teeth, or his shameful tight-fistedness and puppetlike comportment.

"A miser," decided Ana Rosa, turning up her nose.

Her father had once touched on the subject of marriage.

"With Dias?" she asked in astonishment.

"Of course."

"Father, now, now," and she broke into giggles.

Manuel hadn't felt like pressing the matter further but that night he spoke of it privately to her godfather, his compadre and old friend Canon Diogo, who was practically a member of the family.

"Optima saepe despecta," was his reaction. "The girl needs time, my dear Manuel. Let nature take its course. I'm sure she'll come around."

In the meantime, Dias remained unperturbed; he waited silently, calmly, never staring anyone in the face and, as always, humble and resigned.

2

Thus it was that Manuel Pedro, on the veranda of his home, asked his daughter for a definite reply regarding her marriage. Three months had already passed since her stay at Ponta-d'Areia.

Ana Rosa sat silently in her chair, staring at the tablecloth as if it would bring forth some kind of solution. The thrush sang in its cage.

"Now, my dear, aren't you going to give us even a little hope?"

"Perhaps," and she got up from the table.

"Fine. That's how I like to see you."

The merchant passed his arm around her waist, intending to discuss the matter further, but he was interrupted by footsteps from the hall.

"May I enter?" said the canon, already standing in the veranda doorway.

"Come in, compadre."

The canon, smiling amiably and discreetly, entered slowly.

He was a handsome old fellow, at least sixty, but still strong and well preserved. He had lively eyes, a taut build, and was anointed with a sanctimonious kindliness. He wore carefully polished shoes and ordered special stockings and collars from Europe. Whenever he laughed he would flash his beautiful white teeth, each one containing a gold filling. His movements were well defined, and his white hands and snowy hair rounded out his elegance.

Canon Diogo acted as confidant and adviser to the good but dull Manuel, who never risked a step without first consulting his close friend. He had graduated from the University of Coimbra, the wonders of which he constantly related. Well-off financially, he never passed up the chance to slip off periodically to Lisbon "to relieve my shoulders of the weight of the years," he laughingly explained.

As soon as he entered, he extended, for Ana Rosa's kiss, his large, embossed amethyst ring made to order in Porto. And patting her on the cheek with his slender hand, scented with English soap, he said:

"Well then, my goddaughter, how is our little one?"

"I'm fine, thank you," she smiled. "How is my dear godfather?"

"The same as always. Is there anything new with Dona Bárbara?" She had gone out.

"Didn't you notice how peaceful the house is?" Manuel interrupted. "She went to mass and naturally is lunching somewhere with a friend. God keep her away! But tell us what miracle has brought you to our house at this hour?"

"A matter I want to talk to you about, somewhat private."

Ana Rosa immediately made as if to leave.

"Stay here," her father said. "We'll go to my office."

And the two compadres, conversing softly, walked to the little room in the front of the house.

The room was very small, with two windows overlooking the Rua da Estrela. The floor was carpeted, the wall papered, and the ceiling made of rosewood strips painted in white. There was a tall writing desk with an inclined bench, a cast-iron safe, a stack of account books, a simple printing press, a duplicating machine on the other side, and a dust-filled drinking glass that had a long-handled, flat paint brush resting on its rim, a wicker chair, a big box full of useless papers, and a gaslight jet and two cuspidors.

And also on the wall, above the desk, hung an annual calendar and a weekly calendar, the pockets of both filled with receipts and bills.

This was what Manuel Pedro pompously called his "office," where he prepared his commercial correspondence. There, whenever he devoted himself body and soul to those things in life that interested him—in brief, his speculations and business dealings—people could be dying just outside, and the good man was not likely to notice. He truly loved his work and would have been a saintly little creature if only he did not have the mania of speculating on everything, which at times cast a shadow on even his best intentions.

As they entered the room, he quietly closed the door while his friend settled comfortably into the chair with a sigh of relief, raising his lustrous and well-tailored cassock halfway up his shin. Manuel had taken a yellow-papered cigarette from its pack and eagerly lit it. The canon waited with news suspended on his lips; his mouth half open, he leaned forward with his hands resting on his knees, his head held high—staring through his crystal eyeglasses, his brows upraised.

"Do you know who is about to arrive here?" he finally asked, when he saw that Manuel was comfortably settled on his bench.

"Who?"

"Raimundo!" and the canon took a pinch of snuff.

"Raimundo who?"

"Mundico! José's son, man! Your nephew, the child your brother had by Domingas."

"Oh, yes, yes, I see, but what about it?"

"He's going to be here in a few days. Look at this."

The priest removed some papers from his pocket and pulled out from among them a letter which he handed to the merchant.

"It's from Peixoto, the fellow from Lisbon."

"What do you mean Lisbon?"

"Look, the Peixoto from Lisbon who's been in Rio de Janeiro for the past three years."

"Ah, yes, that's right, come to think of it, the boy must be in Rio de Janeiro by now. Oh, now I see, the steamer from the South just arrived bringing this."

"Correct, now read it!"

Manuel mounted his glasses on his nose and read the following to himself:

Rio de Janeiro

Esteemed Friend and Canon Diogo de Mello:

We trust that this missive finds Your Excellency enjoying perfect health. We are writing to inform Your Excellency that Dr. Raimundo José, whom you and Sr. Manuel Pedro da Silva placed in our charge when we were still established in Lisbon, will depart by coastal steamer from here for São Luís on the fifteenth of this month. Although we should have done it earlier, we feel we should inform you that we did our best to keep your ward employed within our firm. But unable to do that, we decided to send him at once to Coimbra to study theology. This attempt was also unsuccessful for after finishing his preparatory course your ward chose the field of law, in which he graduated with honors and high marks.

It heartens us to point out to Your Holiness that Dr. Raimundo was always esteemed by both his professors and fellow students and that he made a fine reputation in Portugal, as well as later in Germany and Switzerland and, most recently, in Rio, where, according to what he has said, he intends to undertake a very important business venture.

However, before settling for good here, Dr. Raimundo wishes to transact the sale of some land and other property that he holds in your province, and with that purpose will shortly arrive.

At this time we are also writing to Mr. Manuel Pedro da Silva, to whom we once again submit our accounts of the expenses we have incurred on behalf of his nephew.

The letter ended with the usual closing.

Having finished reading, Manuel called Benedito, one of his black errand boys, and had him go to the firm to inquire if the mail had come in from the South. The boy returned after a short while to say "Nothing yet, sir, but Mr. Dias has gone to the post office to check."

"So he's doing quite well, eh?" Pescada exclaimed. "The fellow is off and running and wants to liquidate his holdings here and settle in Rio. Looks like we're not good enough for him."

"Now, now, now," breathed the canon rapidly. "Let's not even speak about that. Rio de Janeiro is Brazil! He'd be a stupid ass to stay here."

"If he would . . ."

"I'll go even further. . . . Nor was it necessary for him to come here, because," he continued, lowering his voice, "everyone here is quite aware of his origins. They all know who his mother is."

"I don't say that he shouldn't come, because, after all, one is free to go where one wants or to send someone else. But if he's to come, let him settle his business and quickly go on his way!"

"Well said."

"And besides, just what the devil is there for him to do around here? Strutting through the streets and spending the little money he has? But, I guess he does have some things to settle—he's got that string of houses over in São Pantaleão. He must have a whole fistful of stock certificates. He's got his investment here in the firm where, to tell the truth, he's one of the silent partners, and he's got the ranches out near Rosário—that is, *the* ranch, because one of them is in ruins."

"That's the one nobody wants," the canon observed, and his far-away stare let on that he was caught up in a sad reminiscence.

"People say it's haunted," Manuel continued. "However, it's just that I've never been able to get the place going again. But remember, that's first-rate sugarcane land."

The canon remained absorbed in his recollection of the old, dilapidated ranch.

"Now," Manuel added, "the best thing would have been for him to have become a priest."

The canon came to life again.

"A priest?!"

"That's what José, his father, wanted."

"What nonsense!" retorted Diogo, getting brusquely out of the chair. "There are already too many dark-skinned priests in these parts!"

"But, compadre, look here, it's not that. . . ."

"What do you mean, my good man? Imagine—becoming priests!

Imagine! And you can see what's happening. Why soon there'll be prelates blacker than our cooking women! You think that's proper? The government," and he inflated his tone, "the government should take some serious action in regard to this problem! It should ban nonwhites from certain occupations."

"But, compadre . . ."

"I say put them in their place!"

And the canon grew heated with indignation.

"And then," he shouted, "it seems pure spite for a black boy to be born with such opportunities as this one was. . . ."

And he held the letter out, whacking it: "One can recognize an intelligent man right away! But they ought to be jackasses! Jackasses! Good for nothing but serving us! Damn them all!"

"But, compadre, this once you're wrong!"

"What do you mean, my good man? Don't be a fool! Would you like to see your daughter taking confession from, or married by, a Negro? Would you, Manuel Pedro, like to see your Missy Anica kissing the hand of Domingas's son? If you should have grandchildren, would you want them to catch spankings from a teacher blacker than my cassock? Really, my dear fellow, you seem so dense at times!"

Manuel, defeated, lowered his head.

"Now, now, now," the priest sputtered, like the last drops of a sudden downpour. And he paced vigorously back and forth in the room, shifting from hand to hand his fine imported Indian silk handkerchief. "Now, now, don't be this way, compadre! Stultorum honor inglorius!"

Just then there was a knock at the door. It was Dias with the mail from Rio.

"Let's have it."

The letter to Manuel said no more than the first one.

"Well, then, compadre, what do you think?" he said, handing the letter over to the canon after reading it.

"What the devil am I to think? The matter has gone beyond our control. Let things run their natural course. Didn't you once say you wished to negotiate over the Cancela Ranch? Now's the best chance—you can deal with the owner in person. Even the houses on São Pantaleão Street would be a wise investment for you. Look, if he sells them on account, I'll perhaps take one of them."

"But what I mean is, should I receive him as my nephew?"

"Bastard nephew, of course! What have you got to do with the blunders of your brother José? My goodness, fellow!"

"But, compadre, don't you think that will make me look bad?"

"Why bad, my good man? None of that has anything to do with you."

"Well, I suppose that's true. Oh, and another thing: should I put him up here in the house?"

"Yes, in a sense it should be handled like that. Everyone knows about the favors you owe your deceased brother José, and they just might start muttering if you failed to take in his son. But, on the other hand, my friend, I just don't know what to tell you!"

And after a pause during which Manuel remained silent, the canon said: "Look, compadre, this business of having young men in the house, it's devilish!"

"You mean . . ."

"Omnem aditum malis prejudica!"

Manuel, without understanding, added: "But I'm constantly putting up my customers from the interior."

"But that's quite different!"

"And my clerks? Don't they live here with me?"

"Certainly," said the canon, visibly impatient. "But the poor clerks are an innocuous bunch, and we have no idea what kind of fellow this doctor from Coimbra has turned into. My friend, this blackbird comes by way of Paris—he's probably a real dandy."

"Possibly not."

"Yes, but more likely he is!"

And the canon puffed up his double chin in a certain practiced manner.

"At any rate," ventured Manuel, "it'll only be for a short time. Perhaps less than a month." And, toning down his voice discreetly, and somewhat fearfully: "Furthermore, it wouldn't be wise to displease the young fellow. For sure, I'll be having to do business with him, and, just between the two of us, it would be a courtesy I've been owing, because after all you do know that . . ."

"Ah!" interrupted the canon, assuming a new pose. "That's another melody! That's where you ought to have begun!"

"Yes," replied Manuel, with a little more courage. "You know very well I'm not in the least obliged to worry about poor Mr. Mundico, and even though . . ."

"Pshaw!" exclaimed the canon, cutting short the conversation and saying: "Put the man up, then!"

And he left the room, at once donning his sluggish and studied air of piety.

When they reached the veranda, Ana Rosa, already in her strolling outfit, was awaiting them, leaning over the windowsill and lavishing a gaze both listless and full of uncertainty at the Bacanga River.

"Well, have you decided yet, my flighty little one?" her father asked.

And he gazed at his daughter with a small smile of pride. She was really quite attractive in her gay white piqué dress, smelling of jasmin from the wardrobe. Her Italian straw hat framed her fresh and well-formed oval face, and her thick, silky brown hair, parted evenly at the top of her head, reappeared at her neck unassumingly curled.

"You said you weren't going."

"Do go and get changed, Father." And she sat down.

"I'm going! I'm going!"

Manuel tapped the canon on the shoulder:

"Don't I fill you with envy, compadre? Just look how elegant the little one is, don't you think so?"

"Ne insultes miseris!"

"What's this?" the merchant interrupted, looking at the porch clock. "Four-thirty! And I still have to go out today to arrange a sugar shipment!"

And he went off to his room shouting for Benedito to bring him some warm water to wash his face.

The canon sat down facing Ana Rosa.

"Well then, where are you off to today, my precious goddaughter?"

"To Freitas's house. Don't you remember? It's Lindoca's birthday today."

"Excellent! Then there'll be roast turkey!"

"Papa is going to stay for supper. Why don't you go too, Godfather?"

"Perhaps I'll make an appearance this evening. There'll surely be a dance."

"Yes, but I think that Freitas is counting on a surprise visit from the music society," said Ana Rosa, busily straightening out the folds of her dress with the tip of her parasol.

At that moment, from downstairs, came the slamming of the warehouse doors, noisily being closed and locked, followed by the heavy sound of numerous footsteps on the staircase. The clerks were coming up to eat supper.

The first to reach the veranda was Bento Cordeiro, a Portuguese, some thirty years old and ugly, with reddish hair, and a moustache and beard forming a goatee. He liked to brag about his extensive experience behind the counter; they called him a sharp one. No one could match him when it came to dispatching orders from the interior. Cordeiro could easily handle even the smartest hillbilly.

Of the firm's employees he had been there the longest, but he had never managed to acquire a share in the firm. He remained an outsider, and as a result he had a deep hatred of his boss, a hatred that the rascal masked with an ever-present smile of good will. But his greatest defect, what truly set him off in the eyes of the young business "foxes" and explained to the commercial community his failure to acquire a share in the firm where he had labored for so long, was undoubtedly his weakness for wine. On Sundays he would go on a spree and become completely unbearable.

Bento silently crossed the veranda, greeting the canon and Ana Rosa with affected humility, and then continued off to the quarters at the top of the house where all the firm's clerks lived.

The second to appear was Gustavo de Vila-Rica, a pleasant and handsome youth of sixteen, with his superb Portuguese coloring, which the climate of Maranhão had not yet managed to destroy. Always in good spirits, he prided himself on his unflagging appetite and on never having fallen sick in Brazil. Within the firm, however, he had become famous for his extravagance, for the stylish cashmere suits he had made to order so as to go out for Sunday strolls and attend dances in private residences, and for the expensive cigars he smoked. His greatest defect was his membership in the Portuguese Cultural Center—which caused the good commercial people to remark that he was "a real scoundrel, an idler, always looking for something to read."

Bento Cordeiro on occasion yelled furiously at him. "What the hell! Hasn't the boss already made it clear to you that he doesn't like his clerks always reading newspapers? If you want to be learned, go off to Coimbra, you ass!"

Gustavo was constantly subjected to these and other affable remarks, but what could he do? He had to earn his living. Bento was the head clerk. So Gustavo resigned himself without a sputter and on certain occasions even seemed satisfied, thanks to his good disposition.

As he passed through the veranda he was less brusque in greeting the boss's daughter. He even came to a halt, smiling and bowing his head as he said: "My lady."

The canon chuckled.

"What a dandy," he thought to himself.

Next, a mere child of ten years, his hands hidden in the oversized sleeves of a double-breasted coat, the collar of which rose up to the nape of his neck, hurriedly crossed the porch. His hair was close cropped and his shoes terribly out of proportion. His blue denim pants were rolled up at the cuff. His frightened eyes, skittish gestures, and a certain rapid movement, hiding his head down between his shoulders, indicated that he was in the habit of receiving blows on the neck.

In every way this one was younger than the others: in age, service within the firm, and residence in Brazil. He had arrived some six months ago from his village near Porto. His name was Manuelzinho, and his eyes were always red from crying at night in longing for his mother and his native land.

As the firm's youngest employee, he swept the warehouse, cleaned the scales, and polished the brass weights. The others all picked on him mercilessly; he had no one to complain to. They amused themselves at his expense and sneered with disgust at his ears filled with dark wax.

His forehead was disfigured by a large scar caused by a crashing fall he had suffered on the first night when they had given him a hammock in which to sleep. The poor little expatriate, not knowing how to deal with such a contraption, foolishly tried to get in feet first, and bang—he fell right onto the top of a roommate's pine foot locker. From that day on, those in the firm gave him the nickname of "Floor diver." They called him other names, too, such as "Thing," "Rascal," and "Coward." They tagged him with every name they could, except his real one.

He crossed the porch like a frightened bird, almost on the run. The canon called out to him:

"Hey, little fellow, get over here!"

Manuelzinho turned, confused, and scratched the back of his neck, quite upset, without raising his eyes.

Ana Rosa's expression was one of pity.

"Just what is going on?" asked the canon. "You act like an animal out of the wilds. Address us properly, boy! Raise your head."

And, with his slender white hand he took hold of the boy's chin, lifting up the head that Manuelzinho persisted in lowering.

"This one is still shaggy!" he added. He then asked him all kinds of questions: if he wanted to become rich; whether he hadn't already dreamed of a benefice; if he'd seen the monkeybird; whether he'd found the money tree. The boy, with a distressed smile, mumbled inarticulate answers.

"What's your name?"

He did not answer.

"You aren't even going to reply? Certainly you must be Manuel!"

The little Portuguese nodded his head affirmatively and puckered his mouth to contain the giggle that was seeking an escape valve.

"So you only answer with your head? Don't you know how to speak, you little scamp?"

And, turning to Ana Rosa:

"This one is wily, Goddaughter! Look at those dirty ears! If your soul is in the same state as your body, you might as well hand it over to the devil right now. Have you been to confession here yet, scalawag?"

Manuelzinho, unable to hold back his lips, opened his mouth and, with the force of a kettle, let out the laugh he had restrained with such effort.

"Look, he's spitting on me. Hey there, scamp!" shouted the canon. "All right, then. Get away, get away!"

He pushed him away and wiped his cassock with a handkerchief.

Ana Rosa then ran her fingers around the boy's head and pulled him to her. She turned up his coat sleeves and inspected his fingernails. They were long and dirty.

"Ah," she scolded, "you're not so young that all this can be excused."

And removing a tiny scissors from her handbag, she began, much to the surprise of the little clerk and even the canon, to clean the child's fingernails, saying softly to her godfather:

"I can't imagine how mothers can part with children of this age. Poor little ones! They must suffer terribly."

Her voice was already heavy with the cares of maternal love.

The canon stood up and went to lean on the ledge of the veranda, while Ana Rosa, continuing to cut the child's nails, quietly asked him if he wasn't nostalgic for his native country, and if he didn't cry when he thought of his mother.

Manuelzinho was astonished. This was the first time in Brazil that someone had addressed him with such tenderness. He raised his head and looked at Ana Rosa. He, whose gaze was always downward, sought without wavering the young girl's eyes and looked into them, full of confidence and feeling a sudden respect for her, a kind of unexpected adoration. It seemed extraordinary to the poor boy scorned by everyone that this Brazilian lady, so clean, well dressed, smelling so sweet, and with such soft hands, should be there cutting and cleaning his nails.

At first this was a horrible sacrifice for him, an unbearable torture. He longed to put that uncomfortable scene behind him; he wanted to flee from that difficult position. He took short breaths, not daring to move his head, looking off to the sides out of the corner of his eyes, as if searching for a way out, a hiding place, or any pretext that would extract him from the spot.

He was uncomfortable with all that fuss, without a doubt! He didn't dare breathe openly, fearful that the young lady might notice his breath. Such was his restrained immobility that his joints already ached; not even a single finger fidgeted. After the initial minute of sacrifice, beads of sweat began to trickle from his head down to the collar of his coat, and the little creature had genuine shivers. But when Ana Rosa spoke to him about his native Portugal and his mother with that discerning tenderness that only a mother knows, tears burst from his eyes and silently streamed down his face.

No wonder, for it was the first time that anyone in Brazil had spoken to him of those things!

The canon witnessed all this, quietly, tapping his tinged and cigar-stained nails on his gold snuffbox and smiling his old gentleman's smile. And while Ana Rosa, her head lowered in deep concentration, hovered over the unfortunate little fellow, provoking his tears but holding back her own—God alone knows how—Dias passed catlike through the veranda without being noticed, his heart filled with rage on seeing the boss's daughter fussing over the boy.

Such kindness irritated him. No one had ever cut his nails! It vexed him to see "Missy" Ana Rosa occupied with such a scamp. Squandering herself on the little pest! Now just why did she have to do that! Dolling up that no-good! For sure she wanted him as a go-between, probably already counting on him to deliver her outrageous letters and bring her back flowers and messages from the local dandies! Ah, but he, Dias, was there to upset their trickeries!

Dias, who rounded out Manuel Pescada's staff, was as closed as an egg, but a spoiled egg whose shell scarcely indicated the rottenness within. However, even with his bilious facial coloring, his lack of cleanliness, and the patient restraint of his exaggerated economizing, one could decipher in him a fixed idea, a goal toward which he advanced like an acrobat, not glancing to either side, absorbed as if he were balanced on a tightrope. He disdained no means that would further his goal. Without question, he would follow any trail as long as it appeared shorter; anything was suitable, anything was good, provided it might carry him more rapidly to his desired end. Whether he had to pass through mud or over hot embers, he was determined to attain his goal—to become rich!

As to his person, it was repugnant; he was scrawny and emaciated, somewhat short and stooped, thin-bearded, narrow-browed, and had deep-set eyes. His constant use of braided slippers had given him enlarged and flattened feet. When he walked he flung them out sideways like the movements of a duck swimming. He detested cigars, outings, and gatherings on which it might be necessary to expend some money. When he stood near, one could immediately smell the sour odor of dirty clothing.

Ana Rosa couldn't conceive of how a woman of any status could tolerate such a pig. "After all," she would conclude, chatting with her friends when she wanted to give these women a precise idea of what Dias was like—"there are men who lack the courage even to buy a toothbrush!" Her friends would reply with an "ick!" But in general he was regarded as a well-intentioned youth with exemplary manners.

Only on Saturday evenings did he leave his boss's establishment, and then it was to go to a fish fry at the home of a fat mulatto woman who lived with her two daughters at the end of the Rua das Crioulas. He always went alone. "No need of revelry."

"I have no friends," he would constantly repeat, "I have only a few acquaintances."

On those outings he at times took along a bottle of Port wine or a tin of marmalade, and these he called his "extravagances." The mulatto woman regarded him with much admiration and confided in him. She entrusted her "gold trinkets" and other savings to his keeping. With this one exception, no one knew of his having any other individual friendships. One fine morning, however, the "exemplary young man" had shown up indisposed for work and had asked the boss to allow him to remain in his room that day. Manuel, anxiously concerned about his valuable employee, sent for the doctor.

"Well, then, what does the fellow have?"

"It's more a hangover than anything else," the physician answered, wrinkling his nose. But he did prescribe lukewarm baths. "Baths. Baths are all he really needs!"

And, when he saw his patient the second time, he could not restrain himself and said:

"Look here, my boy, personal cleanliness is also a part of the treatment!"

And he ended up demonstrating that a bath was as much a necessity for the body as proper eating, especially in a climate like theirs in which a man is always perspiring.

That night Manuel went to his clerk's room. He addressed him with paternal kindliness, grieved over his condition with amicable words, and let fly a protest in the form of a sermon against the climate and customs of Brazil.

"A land where one must exercise great care. Dangerous, very dangerous!" he said. "Our lives here hang by a thread."

Enthusiastically, he then spoke of Portugal, recalling the savory and filling Portuguese meals: "The kettles of rice, pig's ears with white beans, the soup made of bread, the thick broths, and the famous codfish from the Algarve!"

"Ah, the fish!" Dias sighed, longing for Portugal. "What a delicacy!"

"And our homemade figs, baked chestnuts, and the young wine?"

Dias's mouth watered as he listened.

"Ah! Portugal!"

The boss also spoke to him about Lisbon's comforts, its air, fruit, and, finally, its many amusements. He ended by relating stories about sicknesses, cases identical to Dias's; he laughingly went back to his boyhood, and, already standing up, about to leave, gave Dias an affectionate tap on the shoulder:

"Look, fellow, what you ought to do is get married." And he swore to him that he was well suited for marriage: "Dias, with your temperament and those manners, you would certainly make a good husband. Get yourself married, and you're bound to see what a difference it makes!"

"Look," he concluded, "I'll say the same thing as the doctor: baths and more baths, just so they're in church, you understand me?"

And laughing at his own joke and full of well-meaning smiles, he tiptoed out of the room cautiously so that the other clerks, whom he did not honor with similar visits, would not hear his footsteps.

When Ana Rosa finished clipping Manuelzinho's nails, she advised him to get some schooling. She promised to arrange to have her father enroll him in an evening primary class and told him to bathe every morning under the well pump.

"You do that, and I'll be on your side," she concluded, sending him away with a light pat on the head.

The boy, visibly moved, withdrew to the upper floor, but Dias, standing at the head of the stairs, awaited him, furious.

"And just what were you doing, you worthless rag?"

"Nothing," answered the child, trembling. "The young lady called me over."

Dias, giving him a cuff, pointed out that such a rascal shouldn't be chatting on the porch, neglecting his duties.

"And if," he added, becoming even angrier, "I see you again wailing at Dona Anica's side, you'll have me to face, you scoundrel! Everything will eventually reach the boss's ears!"

Manuelzinho moved rapidly on, convinced that he had committed a tremendous misdeed. At heart, however, he was pleased at the idea of no longer being so forsaken and he sensed the rebirth, in his dark and gloomy exile, of a joyous desire to continue living.

The gathering at Freitas's house was lively. There was guitar music, singing, much dancing. They even played some melodies from Bahia.

But, near midnight, Ana Rosa, after a waltz, suffered a nervous attack. This was now the third, and with no warning!

Fortunately, the doctor who was hurriedly called assured them that it was nothing to worry about. "Diversions and a healthy diet," he prescribed, and, on taking leave of Manuel, he whispered, smiling:

"If you want to make your daughter healthy, get her married."

"But what's wrong with her, Doctor?"

"What's wrong with her! She's twenty years old! It's nest-making time for her. But while she's waiting to marry she should be out taking walks. Cold baths, exercise, good diet, and diversions! Catch on?"

In his ignorance Manuel imagined that his daughter secretly nourished some unreciprocated love. He shrugged his shoulders. That was something he could do nothing about. And, in compliance with the doctor's orders, he inaugurated lengthy strolls in the crisp early mornings with the patient.

A few days later Canon Diogo, contrary to all his usual habits, sought out Manuel at seven in the morning.

Hurriedly, like a person bearing great news, he appeared at the store, and scarcely had he approached the merchant than he was telling him in a mysterious tone:

"Do you know what? It looks like a ship is arriving, and it's the *Cruzeiro*."

Manuel at once pushed away what he was working on, went up to the veranda, gave instructions for the guest's reception, and was soon down on the street with his friend.

As they were leaving the house the São Marcos Fortress shot off its cannon to announce the arrival of the coastal steamer. The two men caught a small boat and went on board.

3

A short while later, amid the questioning glances of the curious, a handsome young man crossed the Praça do Comercio accompanied by Canon Diogo and Manuel.

The event was immediately commented on. The Portuguese with their huge bellies appeared at the doors of their dry goods stores. The street vendors peered out over the rims of their tortoiseshell glasses. The stooped Negro porters halted "just to have a look at the new guy." A stout fellow, in shirtsleeves like almost everyone else, hastened to the street:

"Hey, you there, who's this new guy?" he loudly asked of a ruffian passing by just then.

"Some relative or contact of Manuel Pescada's. He's in from the South."

"Say, you over there, do you know who's that young fellow with Pescada?"

"I don't know, man, but he sure is a good-looker!"

Manuel introduced his nephew to several groups. There were courteous smiles and slapping handshakes.

"He's the son of Pescada's brother," they said afterward. "We know all about his life! His name is Raimundo. He was off studying."

"Has he come to settle here?" inquired José Bruxo.

"No, I think he's come to set up a business."

Others avowed that Raimundo was a shareholding partner in Manuel's firm. They discussed his clothing, his gait, his coloring, and hair. Luisinho the Silver-Tongued declared that the man had style.

Meanwhile the three men continued up the Rua da Estrela.

Upon reaching the house, where a room was already awaiting Dr. Raimundo José da Silva, the canon and Manuel outdid themselves with courtesy toward the young man.

"Benedito, bring some beer! Or do you prefer cognac, Doctor? Hey, black boy, prepare some guaraná![1] Doctor, come over here, it's much cooler. Don't stand on ceremony! Come out onto the porch. Think of this as your own home!"

Raimundo complained about the heat.

"It's horrible," he said, wiping his face with a handkerchief. "I've never perspired so much."

"Well, then, it's better you retire to your room and make yourself comfortable. You can change clothes and cool off. Your baggage should be along any second. Come now, Doctor, please enter and see if it's to your liking."

The three went into the room intended for the guest.

"You have here," noted Manuel, "windows facing the street as well as the backyard. Make yourself at home. If you need anything at all, just call Benedito. Let's have no formalities!"

Raimundo thanked him gratefully.

"I had a bed prepared specially for you," the merchant added, "since naturally you aren't accustomed to hammocks. However, if you wish. . . ."

"No, thank you, no. Everything is fine the way it is. All I want now is to just lie down. My head is still spinning."

"Well then, relax, relax, so you'll have a better appetite for lunch. Until then."

And Manuel, followed by his compadre, withdrew, brimming with courtesy and affable smiles.

Raimundo was twenty-six years old and would have been a typical Brazilian had it not been for his large blue eyes, which resembled those of his father. His hair was very black, shiny, and curly, his complexion dark and mulatto-like, but delicate. His white teeth sparkled under his black moustache. Tall and elegant in build, he had a strong neck, a straight nose, and a broad forehead. The most singular aspect of his appearance was his eyes: large, long-lashed, and filled with blue shadows. His eyelashes were thick and black, and his eyelids a hue of moist and vaporous violet. His eyebrows, well delineated on his face, as if with India ink, made the freshness of his complexion stand out so that instead of the shadow of a beard, his skin called to mind the soft and transparent tones of a watercolor done on rice paper.

He was quite measured in his gestures, which were orderly and lacking in pretentiousness; he spoke clearly, in a soft voice, without being affected; he dressed seriously and in good taste, and loved the arts, sciences, literature, and, somewhat less, politics.

During his entire life, always far from his native land, amid all kinds of peoples and full of different impressions, he had constantly been preoccupied with his studies and never succeeded in arriving at a logical and satisfactory explanation of his origins. He did not know with certainty under what circumstances he had come into the world. Nor did he know whom to thank for the comfortable life and wealth that he possessed. He did, however, remember having left Brazil as a small child and he could vow that he had never lacked for necessities and even had superfluities. In Lisbon he had had carte blanche.

But who was this person who had been entrusted to look after him from afar? His guardian, certainly, or the equivalent, or perhaps his own uncle, for, as far as a father was concerned, Raimundo knew that he no longer had one when he departed for Lisbon. Not that he had ever known him, or that he had heard on anyone's lips the sweet word "son," but he had learned it from his agent in Lisbon, and also by piecing together some vague childhood reminiscences.

His mother, however—who might she be? Perhaps some lady who was dishonored and afraid to reveal her shame! Was she a good person? Was she virtuous?

Raimundo grew absorbed in conjectures and, despite his detachment from the past, felt something attracting him irresistibly toward his homeland. Who knew if he might not discover there the answer to his enigma? He, who had always lived orphaned from legitimate and lasting affections, how happy he would then be! . . . Ah, if only he could discover who his mother was, he would forgive her everything, everything!

The portion of tenderness belonging to her still dwelled intact in the son's heart. He needed to surrender it to someone. He needed to unveil the circumstances that had brought about his birth.

But after all, Raimundo reflected in a natural flurry of past impressions, what in the devil did he have to do with all that if, until then, quite unaware of those facts, he had lived a respectable and happy life? Surely this was not the reason that he had returned to Maranhão! Therefore, he had only to settle his business, sell his holdings, and then take to the road! Rio de Janeiro beckoned him. On arriving there he would set up his office, he would work, and, with the woman he would marry and his future children at his side, he would have no need ever to remember the past.

Yes, and what better life could he desire? He had concluded his studies, traveled extensively, was in good health, and possessed valuable properties. He had only to proceed and leave behind the so-called past. "The past, the past! Farewell to it all!"

And having reached this conclusion, he felt happy, independent, sheltered from life's miseries, and full of confidence in the future. And why should he not have a successful career? No one could have better intentions than he. He was neither lazy nor subject to base instincts: he aspired to marriage, to stability, and wanted, in the quiet of his own home, to concentrate on serious work, to capitalize on his studies, on what he had learned in Germany, France, Switzerland, and the United States. He had only to return to Maranhão and liquidate his holdings. Well, then, here he was: ready to expedite matters and be on his way once more.

It was with these notions that he arrived in the city of São Luís. And now, refreshed by the freedom of his own room, after a tepid bath, his body still somewhat weary from the trip, and a cigar between his fingers, he felt perfectly happy, satisfied with his good fortune, and at ease with his conscience.

"Ah," he yawned, closing his eyes. "Just liquidate everything and I can get away."

And, with another yawn, he let his cigar drop to the floor and he fell calmly asleep.

Nevertheless, Raimundo's history, the history of which he was unaware, was familiar to everyone who had known his relatives in Maranhão.

He was born on a slave plantation near the small village of Rosário, quite a few years after his father, José Pedro da Silva, who had taken refuge there, had fled from the neighboring state of Pará during the anti-Portuguese rebellion of 1831.[2]

José da Silva had grown rich smuggling slaves from Africa, and had always been somewhat harassed and disliked by the people of Pará, until one fine day his own slaves rose in rebellion against him and would have killed him had not one of the young slave girls, Domingas by name, warned him in time. He succeeded in escaping unscathed to Maranhão, but not without having to abandon his holdings and running the risk of again falling into disfavor, for Maranhão, a neighbor and commercial tributary of Pará, was itself undergoing an uprising led by Farol against the Portuguese and naturalized Brazilians. He had, however, managed to put by a store of gold, which in those days flowed abundantly throughout Brazil and which the Paraguayan War would later transform into both military decorations and smoke.

They took flight, the master and his young slave, on foot over poor trails, cutting across the backlands. At that early time the coastal steamship company did not yet exist, and maritime travel depended on sluggish boats, some with both sails and oars, and at times pulled by heavy ropes through the narrow bayous. Exhausted, they ended up at Rosário. The smuggler set himself up as best he could with his one remaining slave and, later, at a place called São Brás, he purchased a small ranch where he grew coffee, cotton, tobacco, and rice.

After a series of miscarriages Domingas gave birth to José da Silva's son. The local parish priest was summoned, and, during the baptismal ceremony, the child and mother were solemnly presented with their certificates of freedom.

Raimundo was that child.

In the meantime the disorder in the city of São Luís was quelled. José prospered rapidly at Rosário, showering care on his mistress and his son. He established ties with his neighbors, made friends and, after a short time, married Dona Quitéria Inocência de Freitas Santiago, a rich Brazilian widow who was very religious and scrupulous in regard to blood lines and social status. To her, a slave was not a person and not being white in itself constituted a crime.

She was a beast! At her own hands, or through her orders, numerous slaves succumbed to the whip, the stocks, hunger, thirst, and the red-hot iron. Yet she never ceased being devout and full of superstition. On the plantation there was a chapel where, night after night, the slaves, their hands swollen from the ferules or their backs torn by whips, intoned prayers to the most holy Virgin, patroness of the unfortunate.

To one side of the chapel was a cemetery full of Dona Quitéria's victims.

She had married José da Silva for two simple reasons: because she needed a man—and in those parts there were not many to choose from—and because they had told her that Portuguese blood was as pure as the first rains of the season.

She had never had children. One day she noticed that her husband, under the guise of being his godfather, had singled out Domingas's son for special care. She then and there declared that not for one second longer would she allow that little urchin onto the property.

"You nigger lover!" she shouted at her husband, contorted with rage. "If you think I'd permit you to bring up in my home those children you begot from the Negresses! That's the last straw! And don't try to get rid of me! I'm the one who'll do the getting rid of—that black boy!—and it will be over there, at the side of the chapel!"

José, who knew perfectly well the extremes of which she was capable, flew off to the village to take the measures necessary for the child's safety. But, on returning to the ranch, horrible cries drew him to the slave quarters. Heartsick, he entered, and saw the following:

Stretched out on the ground with her feet in the stocks, head shaved and hands tied behind her, lay Domingas, completely naked and with her genital parts burned by a hot iron. Off to one side her little three-year-old son screamed like one possessed, as he attempted to embrace her. Each time he approached his mother, two slaves, on Quitéria's orders, would flick the whip away from Domingas's back and direct it against the child. The shrew, hideous and drunk with rage, stood there laughing, hurling obscenities and howling with spasms of rage. Domingas, half dead, lay groaning and writhing in pain on the ground. The incoherence in her speech and her uncoordinated gestures already denoted symptoms of insanity.

Raimundo's father, in an initial outburst of indignation, assailed his wife so furiously that he made her fall. He immediately ordered Domingas to be picked up and taken into the main house and given all possible care.

Quitéria, on the advice of the local parish priest, a young man named Diogo, the same priest who had baptized Raimundo, fled that evening to the ranch of her mother, Dona Úrsula Santiago, which was half a league away.

The priest, who often frequented the Santiago home, was said to be their kin. So it was in the role of confessor, relative, and friend that he accompanied Quitéria.

In the meantime José da Silva arrived in São Luís with his son. He sought out his younger brother, Manuel Pedro, and entrusted the little boy to his care. There the boy would remain, under his uncle's eye, until he grew old enough to enroll in a school in Lisbon.

With that accomplished, José returned to his rural property. Now he could expect to live more calmly. He assumed that his wife would remain at her mother's house. Knowing that they did not expect him that evening, on arriving there and seeing light coming from his wife's room he dismounted some distance away, to avoid meeting her, tied his horse and silently entered the ranch.

The dogs recognized him from his scent and scarcely growled. But at the moment he was passing outside Quitéria's room he heard from within the whispering of two voices. Impelled by curiosity, he moved nearer and placed his ear against the door. He immediately distinguished his wife's voice.

Who the devil could she be conversing with at that hour? He held his impulses in check and waited with straining ear. There was no doubt! The other voice was a man's!

Waiting no longer, he put his shoulder to the door and hurled headlong into the room. In a rage, he threw himself at his wife, who fainted on the spot.

Father Diogo—the other voice had been his—had no time to flee and fell trembling at José's feet. When the husband dropped the limp adulteress to attack the priest, he realized that he had strangled her. He stood there perplexed and numb.

An uneasy moment lingered. The panting of the two men could be heard. The situation was growing more tense, but the priest, recovering his sangfroid, got up, straightened his clothing, and, pointing to his lover's body, said firmly:

"You killed her! You're a criminal!"

"You dog, what about you? Are you less a criminal than I, by chance?"

"Before the law, certainly! But you'll never be able to prove my supposed guilt, and, if you tried to, the shame of the dead would fall onto you, while I, in addition to the crime of bodily injury against my sacred person, am the witness to the murder of my unfortunate and innocent parishioner. It's a crime I can easily document with the corpus delecti right here!"

And he pointed out the marks of José's hands on the corpse's throat.

José grew terrified and lowered his head.

"Well, then," said the priest finally, smiling and slapping the Portuguese on the shoulder, "one can arrange anything in this world, with God's divine aid. It's only death that has no remedy. If you so desire, the deceased will be buried with religious and civil formalities."

And, giving his voice a tone of authority: "In exchange for my silence about your crime, I demand in return only yours about my blame. Do you accept?"

José left the room, blind with rage, shame, and remorse.

"What a wretched soul!" he exclaimed. "My God, what a devil he is!"

The priest fulfilled his promise: Quitéria was buried at the São Brás chapel near her black victims. And everyone in the area, even her relatives, attributed her death to an evil spirit that had entered her body.

The priest confirmed those rumors and tranquilly continued tending his flock and being considered by all a very saintly man of great theological probity. His devout parishioners persisted in bringing to him over great distances the best suckling pigs, hens, and wild turkeys from their farms.

In a short time things returned to normal: José entrusted his ranch to Domingas and three older slaves whom he then freed, and, accompanied by the rest of his slaves, went off to the city of São

Luís, with the intention of liquidating his holdings and returning home to Portugal with his son.

Raimundo's mother was finally able to repose. Legends about São Brás grew and little by little it gained renown as an accursed place. The little boy, meanwhile, on his arrival at his uncle's house in São Luís, was, as one might easily imagine, merely skin and bones. Lack of care had brought a sad expression of illness to his swollen little face; he was barely able to open his eyes. Weak and unkempt all over, his belly was grimy, his tongue coated, his body wasting away from rheumatism and convulsive coughing, and his blood predisposed to scrofulous anemia. Despite maternal instinct, which resists and conquers all, the slave woman had been unable to look after her child: Quitéria had been there to drive her away from him, to cut short her caresses with a whip. Therefore, when José had told her that Raimundo was going to his uncle's house in the city, the wretched woman blessed the separation with tears of despair.

However, the poor little fellow was to find in Mariana, his father's sister-in-law, the most affectionate and tenderhearted of protectors. This good lady, well aware that what little her husband possessed he owed to his brother's generosity, immediately felt bound to serve as mother to José's son. Ana Rosa, the only child of her marriage, was not yet born at the time, so that the energies of her maternal instinct were lavished on her protégé.

In a short time, within the tender shelter of those motherly wings, Raimundo, from the ugly child he had been, grew strong, healthy, and handsome.

It was then that Ana Rosa came into the world, initially very weak and almost without chance of survival. Manuel hurried about distressed, fearful of losing her. What a struggle, those first three months of her life! She seemed about to die at any moment, the poor little creature! No one in the house slept. The merchant cried constantly while his wife made vows and promises to her own saints.

It was because of this that the little girl would later pleasantly recall having played the Veronica angel in the Lenten processions.

And at the side of Mariana, who night and day kept a vigil at her sick little daughter's crib, was Mundico, the other child, who also called her mother and who had already forgotten his real mother, the black slave woman who had carried him in her womb.

The little girl pulled through, thanks to the talents of a Dr. Jaufret who had recently arrived from the University of Montpellier. From then on Manuel would hear of no other physician in his house.

At about that time the news arrived that Dona Quitéria had succumbed to a cerebral hemorrhage.

"It came on her of a sudden," the letter carrier explained, his leather pouch on his back. "It was the work of the devil, God help me!"

And shortly afterward José Pedro da Silva, in mourning, very pale, gray, and broken in spirit, showed up to liquidate his business and thereafter depart for Portugal. Manuel, who truly admired him, felt sorry to see him in that state.

All the preparations were made for his trip and José went to spend the last night in his brother's house. But he was unable to fall asleep. He was agitated, and the recollection of the terrible events that had recently taken place had never plagued him so much. He rose and began to pace about his room, talking to himself, nervous and delirious, seeing ghostly figures surge forth from all sides.

Around four in the morning Manuel became curious, for each time he had awakened he had seen light coming from the guest room and had heard the sound of shaky and vacillating steps. He could catch the muffled laments and the weak and doleful crying. Unable to restrain himself, he got up. "What can be wrong with José?" he thought, wrapping a sheet around himself and heading off in that direction. Finding the door unlocked, he opened it slowly and entered. The widower, sensing the presence of someone else, spun around terrified and confronted the ghost that had invaded his room. He drew back with his arms upraised, letting out a shout of terror. Manuel ran toward him, but, before he could make himself known, Quitéria's murderer had crumpled helplessly to the floor.

An immediate ruckus swept through Manuel's house, which at the time was located on Caminho Grande and in which the clerks were not yet living. The good Mariana rushed zealously to help: "A hot-foot bath! Quickly!" she said, groping for the tensed and bulky feet of her brother-in-law. Barley water and all kinds of remedies were suggested; home medicines flew into action and, an hour later, José regained consciousness.

But, unable to get up, he remained prostrated. After the attack, a violent fever took hold and lasted until evening, when Jaufret finally arrived.

It was a gastric fever, he explained. Furthermore, the sickness demanded a certain amount of care—especially a calm spirit, and no disturbances whatsoever!

Despite the doctor's orders, José wanted to see his son. Sobbing, he embraced him and told him he was about to die. And the next day, still confined to bed, he officially adopted him. They sent for a notary public, José made out his will and, crying, called Manuel to his side.

"My dear brother," he confided to him. "If I should depart this life, which is quite probable, send my little boy at once to Peixoto's home in Lisbon."

He ended by saying that he cared greatly for the boy and wanted him placed in a first-rate school. There was plenty of money left and Manuel should not hesitate to spend it on the boy. They should give him the best that money could buy. These efforts only caused his condition to worsen. Everyone wept, giving him up for dead, and, during the most critical days, while José suffered his delirious fever, the priest from Rosário appeared at Manuel's home. Highly concerned, he had come to inquire about the condition of his friend José, "his good friend," said he with great piety.

And from then on he did not forsake the house. He looked after everything, quite obliging and discreet. At times he would whimper because they forbade his entrance into the sick room. Manuel and Mariana did not shy from showing their appreciation for the good priest's solicitude and the concern with which he would come every day to inquire about his friend's condition. They bestowed a warm reception on him and found him kind, tactful, and likable.

"He's a saint of a man," said Manuel with conviction.

Mariana agreed, adding in a soft voice: "It isn't to flatter us, that's certain. Everyone knows that Father Diogo doesn't need anyone's table scraps."

"He's got enough to get by! And notice how well he gets along on what he has."

A lengthy summary of the praiseworthy episodes in the life of the saintly vicar followed: examples of self-denial were cited, as were sizable alms to needy souls, pardons for serious offenses, acts of friendship, and gestures of unselfishness. "A saint! A veritable saint!"

Thus Father Diogo got his foot into Manuel's house and made himself a fixture therein. They were already counting on him to be Ana Rosa's godfather and would await him every afternoon for coffee. In the evening, during family gatherings, both husband and wife missed no opportunity to relate the charming stories told by the vicar and to extol his religious virtues by commending him to visitors as an excellent friend and splendid patron. One day, when with his customary solicitude he asked about "his patient," he was told that José was out of great danger and that his recuperation would be complete with the trip to Europe. Diogo smiled, apparently satisfied. But if anyone had heard what he muttered while descending the stairs, he would have been astonished to hear these and other phrases:

"The devil! They're hoping he'll pull out of it, that cursed fellow! And here I thought I'd gotten rid of him!"

On the following day the scoundrel said to Manuel: "Well, now that our man is out of danger I can return more tranquilly to my parish. And it's time for me to go!"

So he took his leave, brimming with comforting words and angelic smiles and accompanied by the family's blessings.

"Vicar!" cried out Mariana from the stair landing. "Now don't you act like those doctors who only appear when there is sickness! Think of this as your house, too!"

"Do come from time to time, Father," Manuel added. "Put in an appearance!"

Diogo vaguely promised and on that same day crossed the Boqueirão River, heading toward his parish.

That night in Manuel's house the conversation centered on the admirable qualities and good deeds of the highly esteemed priest from Rosário.

To the general satisfaction of the family, José convalesced marvelously. Manuel and Mariana surrounded him with affection, eager to make him forget the rash occurrence of that ominous morning, which they supposed was the only cause of his sickness. About a month later the convalescent decided to return to his ranch despite the insistence to the contrary of his sister-in-law and the advice of his brother.

"And just what's there for you to do?" questioned the latter. "If it's on account of Domingas, what the devil! Have her come here!" Even better, in his humble opinion, would be to leave her where she was. A rural Negress who'd never been out of the backlands! . . .

"No, it isn't that," José answered. But he could not return to Portugal without setting his eyes once more on Rosário.

"At least don't go alone, José. I can accompany you."

José thanked him. But he was perfectly well. In case of need he could count on the canoemen, all of whom were dependable.

He mentioned his innumerable journeys inland and related episodes about the Boqueirão River. They should leave him alone. They shouldn't blow the trip up into something it wasn't! They would all see him before the month was up, sailing off to Lisbon.

He departed. He progressed at a snail's pace, as was customary at that time when Maranhão still had no steamships. Moreover, his ranch was quite distant, some five leagues farther inland from the village of Rosário. He was obliged, consequently, to stop there for a few hours before setting off into the brush. He ate, drank, took care of his animals, arranged transportation, and took on provisions.

Those few familiar with such areas always, as a precaution, take along a "page"—that being the romantic title given in those parts to the guide. And, as the road is good, the page, instead of guiding the traveler, serves more to dispel the fear provoked by fugitive slaves, wildcats, and snakes, of which the local residents speak with terror.

Such fright is not without foundation: the backlands of Maranhão are full of shanty villages where fugitive slaves live with their women and offspring, forming large families of renegades. Whenever these wretched souls cannot or do not want to live by hunting wild game, which is abundant in the area and easy to sell in the village, they plunder and attack travelers on the high roads. At times they wage veritable small-scale wars among themselves, leaving many victims.

In the village José da Silva bought what was necessary and set off, without a page, for his ranch. Ah! How well he knew the area! . . .

Numerous memories were awakened in him by the solitary carnaúba trees, the desolate and silent pindova palms, and the wavering horizons of verdure. How often, when pursuing a spotted cavy or a deer, had he not crossed, at a gallop, those hazardous gullies that branch off from the main road.

It distressed him now to leave all that behind, to abandon the untamed enchantment of the Brazilian forests. There the European felt like an American, attuned to the mysterious voices of the eternally lush verdant cannas, accustomed to the austere company of the age-old trees, the lazy afternoon naps at the ranches, the comfortable rural way of life: barefoot, shirt open, his hammock lulled by the fragrant forest breeze, and a slumber under the watchful eye of slaves.

And he had to part with all that!

Why deny it? It was sure to be painful, he pondered, halting his horse. He had progressed about four leagues and needed something to eat.

In the interior of Maranhão the traveler ordinarily rests and eats at the ranches he encounters along the way. This is so common that all of them, anticipating such visits, always have special quarters exclusively for chance guests. But for José da Silva, who had often spent the night at many of these houses and knew intimately the hospitality of his neighbors, the situation was now altered: he wanted above all to avoid anyone's company; he dreaded their questions about his wife's death. So he preferred to eat supper in the open air and continue immediately on his way.

Nevertheless, it was already getting dark; locusts chirred in a chorus and doves cooed mournfully while nestling together to sleep. Nature, yawning, was veiling itself in shadows.

Night fell slowly.

At that moment José da Silva felt more bleakly the loss of his wife; he experienced a great desire to reach home, but he wanted to encounter a well-laid table where he could relax, eat, and drink, just like before. He wanted his wide double bed, his pipe, or his informal clothes.

Ah, but he would find none of these! The room where for so many years he had slept happily would surely be a frightful and barren place by this time. The kitchen was probably cold, the cabinets bare, the orchard withered, the water jugs dry, and his bed without a woman.

How distressing!

Despite everything, he felt deep longings for his wife.

"Oh, how a man needs a family," he grieved in his isolation. "That priest! That accursed priest! And then, who knows . . . if I'd pardoned her perhaps she would have repented and become a faithful companion, upright and docile. But . . . and he? Oh, never! He would still be around! The misgivings would still continue. He, he's the one I should have killed!"

And after pondering an instant:

"No, it's better like this! It was for the best!"

This conclusion, which was settled on solely because of his respect for religion, was followed by a rapid digging in of his spurs. The horse bolted and careened off in a dizzying race during which José, bent fully over the saddle, seemed to sleep in the rhythm of the gallop. Then he suddenly pulled in the reins and the animal stopped short.

The horseman turned his head, cupping his hand behind his ear. From afar, a strange song reached him, a whisper of voices, and the disorderly clatter of horses' hooves.

The night air was fragrant with forest. The last streaks of daylight were still visible along with the gradually increasing shadows. The moon rose, gleaming with the pride of a young monarch inspecting his domains, and the sky was still reddened by the purple of the late sun, which was fleeing into the horizon, trembling like a king exiled and ashamed.

José da Silva, totally immersed in his torment, watched without appreciation the marvelous spectacle of a summer dusk in the far north of Brazil.

The sun sank toward the west, retouching everything that surrounded it in hot and vigorous tones with the precision of a Flemish painter. From one direction the hills and valleys were rimmed in gold; everything was red and flaming; at the same time, from the other direction, the moonlight insisted on the gentle contrast of its silvery and cool beams, outlining against the horizon the wavering and uncertain profile of the carnaúba palms and pindova thickets.

In these surroundings, amid the boreal conflict of those two opposing lights, a faintly perceptible but noisy group emerged and grew steadily.

A caravan of gypsies was approaching.

It moved slowly with the dull gait of a herd of cattle. In the sad and shadowy solitude of the forest voices of diverse tones little by little became audible and groups of men, women, and children, of all colors and all ages, astride magnificent horses, could be made out. Some were singing to the lulling and monotonous sway of their mounts; others strummed small guitars; one cradled her son; another, farther away, repeated lyrics that some young girl had taught her. Young men could be seen in trousers and light shirts, with long hair, an indolent air, pipes stuck in the corner of their mouths, and their eyes wandering and full of voluptuousness. Next to them rode robust young girls, burned by the sun, with very black and smooth long locks falling over their opulent shoulders. They were seated in the manner of odalisques on top of voluminous bundles, which served at one and the same time as saddle bags and saddle. Some of them carried children on their laps or seated behind them on the horse.

And, slowly and heavily, the gypsy caravan approached. José hid in the forest to watch it pass.

It was surely in flight from some ranch, because the leader, a hefty old man with lengthy white whiskers and deep-set, smoke-gray eyes, somber but restless and lively, from time to time held up his fist and threatened in the direction of the sunset.

"May alligators tear you to bits, you devil! May you be tied across the mouth of a blunderbuss!"

And the hoarse and husky voice of the old man lost itself in the forest.

Half stretched out across his legs, with her arm around his waist, a beautiful woman, her neck bare and fresh and her throat smooth and fleshy, sought with the soft mien of a humid, slavelike tenderness, to calm his wrath.

And the caravan went passing by, illuminated by the last rays of the lingering twilight. Gradually the murmur of the voices dissipated into the melancholy undertone of the forest just as the last shafts of glowing light vanished on the horizon.

Soon everything relapsed into primitive silence and the moon from on high drenched the solitude of the glades with its mysterious and sad light.

José remained motionless, pensive, lost in an invincible sorrow. The spectacle of that old vagabond embracing his attractive and doubtlessly faithful wife gnawed away at his innards with the sharp tooth of jealousy. That creature, a tramp, a poor wretch with no home, no money, no longer even young, nevertheless had a female in his life who cherished him and followed him like a slave, while he, alone in the countryside, companionless, utterly forgotten, wept there because everything had been torn away from him—his home, his wife, and his happiness! And then, through a natural association of ideas, he started recalling Diogo's pale face. Despite the hatred he felt for him, he thought the priest handsome, with his curly hair, his pious and tender smile, his eyes and lips with an expression at once sensual and religious. Such a contrast certainly should have pleased women, conquering them through its mysterious and unknown qualities. And José wept, and wept ever more!

"They must have really loved each other! How much pleasure they must have enjoyed!"

Instinctively he compared himself to the priest, and, filled with rage and envy, acknowledged himself inferior. All of a sudden, a new thought came to him:

"And if I were to kill him?"

He rejected it immediately, not wanting even to mull it over. But the idea would not vanish and took hold of his mind with the tenacity of a parasite.

Then there came into his memory, in a lucid and nostalgic reminiscence, his marriage, the happy surprises of his engagement, and his courtship of Quitéria. None of it had ever seemed so good, so alluring, as at that instant. Only now was he discovering virtues and fine qualities in his wife that he had never heeded before.

"Might I have been to blame for everything? Did I not fulfill my duties as a good husband? Was my affection insufficient?" he questioned his own conscience. The latter answered, counterposing doubts that were like accusations. He defended himself by explaining the circumstances, citing evidence in his favor, and recalling his dedication and deep regard for the deceased. But the accursed inner voice would not be convinced and would not accept his arguments. And José burst into tears like a lost soul.

He was astonished to find himself in such a state. Wanting to flee from himself, he jabbed his spurs into the horse. For some time he raced along with the reins loose, as if fleeing from his own shadow's pursuit.

"And if I were to kill him?"

It was that accursed idea which once again rose to the surface of his thoughts.

"No, no!" And again he repelled it, pushing it down to the depths of his fantasies, like the murderer who casts his victim's body into the sea: it would submerge at first, but quickly reappear, floating. "And if I were to kill him?"

"No, no!" he cried out, shattering the silence of the forest with a yell. "One death is enough!"

And remorse raged through him.

At that moment a cloud hid the moon. Specters loomed out onto the trail. José perspired and trembled in the saddle. The slightest stirring of the branches made his hair stand on end.

In the meantime, he galloped rapidly along.

His ranch was just a little farther, a little more, a paltry distance, and yet that short stretch was more painful than the entire previous part of his journey. He closed his eyes, allowing the horse to race along, galloping noisily over the earth dampened by the evening dew. He breathed heavily, hounded by ghosts. He saw his victim, with her mouth open wide, her eyes convulsed, muttering strange things to him in a moribund voice, her tongue hanging out, swollen black amid a gushing of blood. And he also saw that vile priest looming up, patting him on the shoulder, presenting him smilingly with a suggestion, proposing terms, and immediately proceeding to the brutal threat: "I have you in my grasp, you murderer! If you try to punish me I'll deliver you over to the law!"

And José shouted out insanely, sobbing:

"And I accepted, you fiend! I accepted!"

Suddenly, the horse balked. A shadowy form stirred behind the trunk of an inga tree, and a bullet, followed by the detonation of a shot, pierced the chest of José da Silva.

The blacks at São Brás saw the riderless horse appear all spattered with blood. They had heard the shot down the road and gone running in that direction, searching for the victim.

It was Domingas who discovered him, and, in a frenzy, threw herself on the body, kissing his hands and cheeks.

"Master! My beloved! My love!" she cried out, wailing convulsively.

But, taken by a sudden thought, she rose and shouted, pointing vaguely in the direction of the village.

"It was him! Wasn't no one else! It was that wicked one! It was that devilish priest!"

And she began to laugh and dance, clapping her hands and singing. Her madness was returning.

The murder was attributed to runaway slaves and José da Silva's body was buried next to his wife's tomb at the side of the chapel, which was beginning to crumble for want of the usual care.

Slowly the ranch fell into ruin, and legends and superstitions of all sorts sprang up to explain its decline. The local priest, an honest and discerning person, not only confirmed what others were saying, but also advised that no one go there. "That property is accursed!"

In later years they would relate that in the ruins of São Brás lived a black sorceress who in the dark of night would go out into the fields imitating the song of the nighthawk.

No one was daring enough to approach the place and the unheeding traveler, wandering into the area, would see, singing and dancing through the cemetery, the tall and thin form of a woman covered with rags.

José's sudden death was a great shock to his brother and an even greater one to Mariana. Raimundo was but a small child and scarcely understood; at the time he was five years old, if that. They dressed him in black serge and told him he was in mourning for his father. Manuel took care of the estate, accepting from the inheritance what fell to him and his wife. He deposited the orphan's share in the recently chartered bank of the province and, despite the favorable terms he proposed for selling or leasing São Brás, no one wanted it. Having dealt with all this, he immediately wrote to Lisbon to request information from Peixoto, Costa & Co. As soon as he received the details he needed, he dispatched his nephew to a preparatory school in that city.

It pained kindly Mariana to part from Raimundo. Her affectionate heart ached on seeing a motherless, sad five-year-old child sent out of the country. Even so, after being readied with every care, the little one, in tears, was placed aboard a ship and departed.

He traveled in the charge of the captain and wailed constantly during the voyage. When he arrived in Lisbon, he at first dreaded his surroundings. He was always well treated, however; his agent welcomed him like a relative and treated him like a son; later he placed him in one of the best preparatory schools. Raimundo donned the school uniform, was assigned a number, and attended classes. In the beginning, the minute they left him alone he would burst into tears. He was terribly afraid of the dark; at night he would hug the wall, clasping his pillows. He did not like the other children because they called him "Little Monkey." He became obstinate, full of capriciousness, and was resentful of the inferior culture the Portuguese had taken to Brazil.

At the school he was the only student with the name of Raimundo, and his colleagues ridiculed it: "Raimundo, Mundico, Nico!" they would call him, pulling at his shirt and rapping on his closely cropped head until he would slip away, not wanting to return to the playground, weeping and shouting that they should send him back to Brazil. But with time friends came along, and life then appeared better to him. He soon began giving short talks, and his companions rarely tired of asking him questions about Brazil. What were the Indians like? Could one encounter naked women on the streets? Had Raimundo ever been hit by a backwoodsman's arrow?

One day he received a letter from Mariana and for the first time thought about his own past. But his recollections did not go beyond his uncle's house. Still, it did seem to him that his real mother was not that lady. He realized that she was his aunt because she was the wife of his uncle Manuel. And if his memory were not mistaken, he had more than once overheard Mariana herself speaking about a mother, his real mother. But who could she be? What was her name? . . . They had never told him! . . .

As for his father, he must have been that bearded man who had appeared one night very pale and distressed, and for whom shortly thereafter they had dressed Raimundo in mourning. He recalled perfectly the scene on that night. He had already been tucked away when they brought him half awake from his hammock to sit next to that man. He remembered that on that occasion the man's whiskers held a certain gloomy moistness, which Raimundo now reckoned had been caused by tears. He had then gone back to sleep and thought no more about it. He also remembered, but without the same clarity, the occasion when the same man was sick, he recalled receiving many kisses and hugs from him, and only now did Raimundo understand that all those expressions of affection had always been hidden and timorous, done secretly, as if they were illicit, and almost always accompanied by weeping.

After these and other divagations into his past, Raimundo, although still quite young, set about thinking. The mysterious veils of his childhood were already casting shadows onto his heart with a vacant and obscure sadness, in a bewilderment filled with sorrow.

His greatest desire was to run to Mariana's arms and ask her to tell him for the love of God just who his father and, especially, his mother were.

The years went by, and he remained enmeshed in those same doubts. He concluded his preparatory studies, and qualified for entry into the university. And always there persisted the same uncertainty concerning his origins.

He enrolled at Coimbra University. From then on his life changed profoundly; his manner of observing and judging was completely transformed. He began to feel happy.

But then came a disheartening blow, which once again saddened him: the death of his adopted mother. He shed bitter and long tears over her death, not only for her sake but also very much for himself. In losing Mariana he lost everything that linked him to his past and to Brazil. Never before had he considered himself so totally orphaned. Yet with the passing of time the grief vanished and youth triumphed; the melancholy child became a young man brimming with life and good disposition. He felt comfortable in his romantic academic gown; he participated in merrymaking with his classmates; he gained new friends and, finally, noted that he possessed aptitudes and charm. He wrote satires, ridiculing the grouchy professors; he acquired enemies and admirers, and there were those who feared him and those who imitated him. In his second year he developed his skill at romancing: he flung himself into lyric verses and sang of love in all meters. Later he became receptive to revolutionary ideas, joined radical clubs, spoke quite a bit, and was applauded by his cronies. During his third year he turned into a dandy, spent more than the others, had lovers, but, in compensation, succumbed to a journalistic fever and wrote enthusiastically on all matters, from feature articles to theater criticism. In his fourth year, however, he distinguished himself academically and nurtured a taste for science. From then on he was a man, took responsibility for himself, and became very studious and serious. His academic discourses were esteemed, and his thesis was extolled. He graduated.

It was then that he had the idea of making a trip. In Coimbra it was rumored that he was rich, for he possessed a letter of credit. He readied his bags. His principal ambition was to acquire learning, a great deal of learning, and take in the largest possible amount of knowledge. He felt full of courage for this struggle and confident in his efforts.

At times, however, a nagging shadow of sadness would cloud his aspirations. He knew nothing with certainty about his forebears, nor just how or by whom the money that filled his pockets had been acquired. He sought out his agent in Lisbon and asked him for enlightenment in that regard—but nothing! Peixoto told him very dryly that his father had died before Raimundo's arrival in Portugal, and his uncle, who was his legal guardian, was in business in Maranhão on the Rua da Estrela with a wholesale fabric warehouse. As for his mother—not a single word, not one piece of information! . . .

It was enough to make one go mad! But, after all, just who could she be? The sister perhaps of that saintly lady who was a second mother to him? . . . But then, why all the mystery? . . . Could it possibly be some story so thoroughly shameful that no one dared reveal it to him? . . . Might he be a foundling? No, certainly not, because he was his father's heir. . . . And the more he tried to clarify his existence, the more Raimundo became lost in the labyrinth of such conjecture.

Of the letters he received from Brazil, not one mentioned his past, but, despite this, his zeal in deciphering it was such that, at times, with much effort on the part of his memory, he reconstructed and linked together the dispersed fragments of a few incomplete and vague recollections from his infancy. He succeeded in remembering his cousin Aniquinha who on many nights had fallen asleep at his side on the same straw mat, listening to Dona Mariana singing "Little calf from the corral, come nuzzle up to baby." He also recalled Dona Maria Bárbara, Manuel's mother-in-law, who used to appear amid much ostentation to visit her granddaughter for a few days. She would usually arrive at nightfall in her sedan chair borne by two slaves. She would come dressed in an enormous hoop skirt, surrounded by little black girls and boys, and preceded by a black slave charged with lighting the street with an eight-sided lantern having two candles in the center. And the devil of a woman was always scolding, always angry, beating the Negroes, and especially picking on Raimundo. Each time she would give him her hand to kiss, with the back of it she would whack him on the mouth. And he vividly recalled Maria Bárbara's gaunt face, already then half sagging. He could picture her light brown eyes, her triangular teeth which had been pared down with a knife, an extravagance the women brought up in rural Maranhão barbarously used to indulge in the old days.

On one occasion, while still in Coimbra, Raimundo inhaled the scent of burning lavender and felt the enchanting surge within his memory of many events that he had until then forgotten. Immediately he recalled Ana Rosa's birth: the house was completely silent and impregnated with that odor; Mariana moaned in her room and Manuel paced back and forth on the veranda, restless and bewildered. Then suddenly a fat mulatto woman, whom everyone addressed as "Inhá," appeared at the door of the room, excitedly summoning the master of the house aside to tell him something in secret, and shortly thereafter everyone was happy and satisfied. And from inside one could hear a nasal wailing that sounded like a mouth organ. At the time Raimundo understood nothing of all that. They told him that Mariana had received a little girl from France, and he piously believed it.

Other recollections passed through his mind in the same manner; for example, of the fragrant Macassar oil, then very much in use in Maranhão, with which Dona Mariana perfumed his hair every morning before breakfast. But above all what he remembered most were the old lamps that illuminated the city. There was still no gas there, nor kerosene. When the bell tolled the Ave-Maria, the lamplighter would appear, untie the lamp chain, lower it, open it, pour inside the turpentine mixed with alcohol, light the wick, raise it up into place again, and continue along. And what a bad smell on all the corners where there was lighting! Ah, unless it was quite transformed, his province must be simply horrible!

Even so, he wanted to go there. He felt an affinity for his native land, almost as unknown to him as his own mysterious birth. On the trip he would discover everything! But, first, he needed to travel through Europe.

So he went resolutely to the offices of Peixoto, Costa & Co., withdrew the necessary money, bid his friends farewell, and sailed off to France.

He passed through Spain, visited Italy, went to Switzerland, was in Germany, traveled the length and breadth of England, and, at the end of three years of travel, arrived in Rio de Janeiro where he met his old agents from Lisbon. He stayed for a year in the capital, took a liking to the city, made some contacts, mapped out some plans for his life, and decided to establish his residence there.

And Maranhão? Ah, what a nuisance! But he could not avoid going there. He could not set himself up in Rio without first going up to his native province. It was indispensable that he meet his relatives, liquidate his holdings, and. . . .

"True, true," he said, conversing with a friend to whom he had confided all his future plans, "the situation isn't as bad as it may appear, because after all with a short hop over to Pará and Amazonas I'll get to visit all the northern regions of Brazil, which I want to see. And I'll return back here rested, with my life in order, my conscience relieved, and the little I own turned into money. I can't complain about my luck!"

The journey through Europe had benefited not only his spirit but his body as well. He was much stronger, well disciplined physically, and had an enviable vigor. He prided himself on having acquired a worldly experience: he could converse freely on any matter, knew how to enter a reception room of the first rank, as well as how to chat with the young men in a newspaper editorial room or in the foyer of the theater. And, in matters of honor and loyalty, he would not, quite rightly, concede that there existed anyone more scrupulous than he.

It was in this happy spirit, positive and full of hope for the future, that Raimundo boarded the *Cruzeiro* and departed for São Luís, the capital of Maranhão.

4

Meanwhile, with Raimundo's arrival old family friends gathered in Manuel's house. The Sarmento girls arrived with their enormous coiffures. They were quite ugly young ladies, but with beautiful hair that was praised and renowned throughout the province. "Braids like those of the Sarmento girls'! Beautiful hair like the two Sarmentos'! Curls like the Sarmentos'!" Those and many other phrases had been converted into unvarying maxims. Everyone used the Sarmentos as a basis of comparison for hair, and the two girls, well aware of their fame, never failed to flaunt the object of all this admiration with startling hairdos of fantastic proportions.

"I regret," on occasion feigned Dona Bibina Sarmento (whose real name was Bernardina), "having so much hair! Untangling it is sheer torment. And if after my bath I don't comb it out right away, or if I let one day go by without applying oil. . . . Ah, you can't imagine what it's like!"

And she would stare wide-eyed and shake her mane as if describing a lion hunt.

In addition to Dona Bibina, the Sarmento family was composed of the other young girl and their aunt, fifty years of age, who was extremely nervous. The old lady talked of nothing but illnesses and knew cures for them all; she possessed a thick book of remedies, usually carried in her pocket. Back home was her immensely varied collection of flasks, bottles, and clay mugs. She always saved orange and pomegranate peels and tuturubá pits, about which she would pathetically declare: "After God, they are the sacred remedy for earaches!" Her name was Maria do Carmo, and her nieces addressed her as "Godmother." She was a highly apprehensive person but excelled at making sweets.

A widow, she had spent her youth in the Our Lady of the Annunciation and Consolation Retreat where she had conceived her first child by the man she later married, Lieutenant Espigão, an army officer, a blatant show-off who paraded constantly in his uniform and would unsheath his sword at the drop of a hat. It was said that one day, at a dinner party, after losing his patience with the roast turkey, which seemed disposed to resist his carving knife, he yanked out his useless old sword and tore the innocent bird apart with thrusts.

He enjoyed scaring little children by feigning to grab hold of them, or sharpening his sword blade on the floor bricks. He would also act highly flattered when they told him he looked like the Emperor Dom Pedro II.[1] He regarded himself as deeply cultured and told everyone that as a youth he had been a poet: he would allude to a half-dozen acrostics and poems that Dona Maria do Carmo had inspired in him during her years as a lay sister in the retreat.

The poor fellow! He died from a massive attack of indigestion on the day following a tremendous dinner during which he had imprudently eaten an entire cucumber salad, his very favorite dish. The widow was disconsolate and, in homage to the memory of Espigão, never again ate that vegetable. Her hatred overflowed implacably onto that cursed plant's entire family; she could never again bear to hear mention of gherkins, squash, or pumpkins.

"Alas, my precious lieutenant," she would lament whenever someone spoke of her husband. "What a true gentleman! The heart of a dove! Now his type of husband just doesn't exist these days!"

Dona Maria do Carmo's other niece was called Etelvina. An extremely skinny little creature, as nervous as her aunt, she had a thin, long, and ice-cold nose, bony and chilly hands, sensual eyes and rotten teeth. She was detestable; the young commercial apprentices referred to her as "Lizard." She tried to be very romantic, esteemed her frightfully pallid coloring, emitted sighs every five minutes, and knew enough to mutilate folk songs on the guitar. It was seriously rumored that at sixteen she had had a tremendous passion for an Italian voice teacher who had fled to Pará to escape his creditors, and that, since then, Etelvina had never eaten properly.

Also present at Manuel's house was Dona Amância Souzelas, an elderly lady with a great memory for events, dates, and names. She always remembered the birthdays of her innumerable acquaintances, and on those dates would inevitably cadge a dinner from them. She constantly spoke ill of other people's lives—in the shadow of which, however, she seemed to live: fifteen days at a friend's house, fifteen more at a relative's, the following month in the home of still another relative or friend, and so on. She was always, always, on the move. She went anywhere, whether wanted or not, and, in less than an instant, would make herself at home. She knew everyone in Maranhão and would relate without hestitation the scandals that she collected, and would even stroll unaccompanied in the street, twittering about the entire city in her shawl, poking her nose into everything. If a friend happened to die, there she was, dressing the body, cutting its nails, and repeating worn-out words of consolation, esteemed and referred to as very helpful, diligent, and worthy.

She was a chronic virgin but affirmed that when young she had refused many good marriage proposals. She devoted herself to churchly activities and knew how to dress angels for processions, tinting their hair with a black cosmetic.

She detested progress.

"In my time," she would say sourly, "young girls had sewing tasks lasting a specific number of hours, and they had to sit up and work! And if they finished early, would they go off to relax? Heavens! They would undo it, my good lady! They would undo it and sew it up again! And nowadays?" she would ask, giving a small jump with her hands on her hips: "Today it's that Machiavellian sewing machine! When a sizable task has to be done, it's just 'click-click-click!' and the work is finished! And so the young hussies are off to read the newspapers, delve into novels, or even take to the indecency of the piano!"

And she would swear that no daughter of hers would learn such an instrument, because the shameless young things wanted to play it only so they might secretly chat with their suitors without others noticing their trickery!

She also cursed gas lighting:

"In the olden days slaves had plenty to do! As soon as supper was served, off they went to prepare to light the lanterns, fill them with fresh oil, and hang them up. And today? All they have to do is touch the burning wood match to the black magic of the gas outlet, and then they're off having fun! There's no drudgery for them any more! You can't even call it slavery! That's why they go about so impudently. The whip! The whip, until they say 'enough!' That's what they need! If I had many slaves, I swear to you, by my godmother's blessing, I'd bloody their backs!"

However, Dona Amância Souzelas's specialty, the reason she was adored by certain young men and detested by many parents, who would turn up their noses on receiving her visits and displays of courtesy, was undoubtedly her old habit of relating low and coarse stories. She had always been quite foulmouthed, but some simpletons in her circle would say of her, in fits of laughter: "With Dona Amância one just can't be serious! The devilish old lady does have a certain charm!"

At Manuel's house there was also present Eufrasinha, widow of the infantry officer. All adorned with little bows of purple ribbon, she was dark-complexioned despite an overabundance of white rice powder. Her facial features were strongly delineated, and she had a silver nitrate beauty mark on the left side of her mouth, a disastrous imitation of that of a French ex-singer with whom she was friendly. The mark was meant to be the size of a flea, but ended up the size and shape of a bean. She sat swaying, full of the latest gossip, and would get up from time to time to go whisper a little secret in Ana Rosa's ear, while pretending to straighten her hairdo. During these jaunts she would look out of the corner of her eyes toward the rooms and the veranda, taking note of everything, and would return to her chair, stealing glances at herself in the living-room mirrors. Incessantly curious and fidgety, she tried to find a double meaning in everything that was said to her. She would offer expressive smiles and grimaces whenever she did not understand, in order to pretend that she had understood perfectly. Her voice was both sibilant and affected, and she would hiss her "s's" and pronounce each syllable carefully.

Freitas, in whose home Ana Rosa had suffered her most recent fit of hysteria, was also present, with his daughter, his beloved Lindoca.

Freitas was a man separated from his wife, "who had gone to the dogs," he would coldly explain; he stood very straight, thin, and tall, with his scrawny neck wrapped in a large starched collar. He never appeared without his white trousers and he bragged about his secret for keeping them clean and pressed for a week at a time. Despite the heat of the province, he always wore that stiff collar with a spotless shirt front, and, invariably, a black necktie. He cultivated an enormous nail on his little finger, and with it he habitually stroked his moustache, composed of smooth, long, dyed strands, which shrouded his mouth. Never would he allow any barber to "lay a hand on my face." He did his own shaving every other day. His baldness was hidden under extremely long wisps of hair, stretched out as if fastened onto his cranium with Gum Arabic. He possessed a prodigious memory that was lauded by the entire city; he had become an expert on ancient history. When speaking he would select specific terms, attempt a certain style, and, whenever referring to the Brazilian Emperor, would gravely affirm: "Our perpetual defender!" Many vouched for his talents. Over the years he had patiently compiled his family's genealogical tree and had had it lithographed in Rio de Janeiro. That accomplishment was widely appreciated and commented on throughout Maranhão.

He had been a civil servant for twenty-five years and had missed only three days of work: once after a fall, once on account of a large boil, and then on the day of his ill-fated marriage. All this he would proudly recite to everyone. Whenever he felt a cold coming on, he would cautiously whiff strong cognac fumes: "That's enough to make me dizzy!" he would declare with virtuous repugnance. He dreaded card games, knew how to play the clarinet but never touched it—because the doctor had told him "he didn't think it prudent." At one time he had smoked, but the doctor had spoken the same words of the cigar as of the clarinet. So he never smoked again. Nor did he dance, for fear of perspiring. He spoke with anger about women and, even if he were collapsing with hunger, he would never eat in the evening. "After late-afternoon tea, nothing else. Nothing!" he would protest steadfastly. And no matter where he happened to be, he would inevitably retire exactly at midnight. He wore polished dress shoes and never forgot his sunhat.

He had never ventured off the island where São Luís is located, so overpowering was his fear of the ocean.

"Not even to go to Alcântara," he vowed, conversing that night in Manuel's house. "From here to Gavião?[2] No, my dear sirs, I want to die in my own bed, calmly, and at peace with God."

"In complete comfort," observed Raimundo, laughing.

Quite devout, Freitas would help carry the litter every year in the procession for the miraculous Bom Jesus dos Passos. He was quite organized: "In his home, he has everything, just as in the pharmacy," his intimate friends declared. "The only thing lacking is money," Freitas would add with a discreet air of jesting. For the rest, he was a very steady fellow and had never been one for extravagances. Even as a young man he had always kept to himself, he disliked owing anything to anyone, collected old stamps, furnished free homeopathy to his friends, and was famous as the greatest bore in Maranhão.

His "beloved Lindoca" was a girl of sixteen, quite small, extremely fat, almost rotund, with beautiful features, slow wits, a good heart and an honest temperament. Etelvina had once remarked that even her brain was getting fat.

Lindoca Freitas did not conceal her desire to marry and was quite fond of her father, whom she addressed as "Nhôzinho."

"Oh, how I detest all this fat," she would lament to her companions when they praised her fatty exuberance. "If I knew of some medicine for losing weight, I would take it!"

And her friends would attempt to console her: "Among the fat and the round, that's where beauties abound!" "Stoutness signifies good health!"

But the plump young thing could not resign herself to her misfortune. She led a sad life. Her rolls of fat grew incessantly; she became flushed and tired after a mere five steps. It was a serious problem. She resorted to vinegar and practiced prolonged physical exercises on the veranda. But to no avail! The layers of fat continued to increase. Lindoca grew more and more rotund, like a ball. Their house shook more and more under her weight; her eyes vanished into the abundance of her cheeks; her nose took on the appearance of a tenderloin, and her back that of a huge cushion. She huffed and puffed.

Dias, pious and sweet Luís Dias, was also in attendance that night in his boss's living room. There he was, sitting off in one corner, fiercely gnawing his fingernails, his motionless gaze fixed on Ana Rosa at the piano, preparing to play something and trying out the keys.

Leaning on the sill of one of the front windows, Manuel and Canon Diogo listened to Raimundo's soft-voiced description of his trip from Paris to Switzerland. The ladies' whispers circulated through the rest of the room.

"Well then, have we made it to the Boqueirão River yet?" exclaimed Freitas, rising from the sofa and shaking his trousers to fend off baggy knees. And, turning around toward one of Dona Maria do Carmo's nieces: "Say something, Dona Etelvina!"

Etelvina raised her eyes to the ceiling and let out a sigh.

"For whom are you sighing?" old Amância, who was at her side, asked her in a strange falsetto voice.

"For no one," answered the Lizard, smiling in a melancholic way with the remnants of her teeth.

"He's not bad looking, don't you think, Dona Bibina?" whispered Lindoca to Dona Maria do Carmo's other niece as she sneaked glances toward Raimundo.

"Who? Ana Rosa's cousin?"

"Cousin? My good lady, I don't believe he is her cousin."

"Oh, really!" butted in Bibina, somewhat annoyed. "He is too her cousin . . . on her father's side! And, besides, over there is someone who knows the entire story quite well!"

And she stuck out her lower lip in the direction of her aunt.

"Humph," muttered fat Lindoca, turning to ponder the object of their discussion from head to toe.

At the same time, Maria do Carmo was confiding to Amância Souzelas:

"Well, it's just as I tell you, Dona Amância—a very good Negress. As black as this dress. You're speaking to someone who knew her!"

And she thumped her flat chest. "Many's the time I saw her getting the rawhide whip. Uggh!"

"Who would have imagined!" muttered Amância, pretending to

be unaware of Domingas's existence in order to hear more. "Something like that right here in Maranhão! Goodness!"

"It's just as I tell you, my dear lady . . . the little fellow was freed when baptized, and now, just look at that! He's full of boasts and bombast! Just ask the canon, there at his side!"

"Heaven protect me from this evil!"

And through force of habit Amância clapped her hands to her shriveled cheeks.

At that moment a hubbub was heard on the veranda.

"Hey there, Benedito! Black scamp! You pest! Are you asleep, you shameless creature?!"

This was followed by the sharp noise of a slap. "Get up, or you'll make me furious even with visitors in the living room!"

It was Maria Bárbara at odds with Benedito.

"Go set the table for tea, you black rascal!"

Manuel hurried immediately to the veranda, upset.

"Please," he said to his mother-in-law. "What a ruckus! Don't forget we have company here!"

Freitas came over to Raimundo's window and took advantage of the opportunity to spill out for his benefit a boring speech concerning the poor domestic services performed by the slaves.

"I recognize that we must have them, I'll admit it! But they're just about the most immoral things in existence. The Negresses, yes, above all the Negressees! They're a bunch of whores each family man has right in his home, sleeping under his daughters' hammocks and telling them dirty stories. Such immorality! Just the other day, in a certain home, a little girl, poor thing, turned up infested with revolting fleas she had picked up from a Negress. And I know of another case of a slave woman who infected an entire family with ugly rashes and eczema! And note, sir, that this is the least of it. What's worse is that they tell their white missies everything they do out on the streets. Our poor daughters end up with dirty bodies and souls in the company of such rabble! I guarantee, my dear sir, that if I do keep blacks working for me, it's because I have no other choice! All the same. . . ."

He was interrupted by Benedito who, naked from the waist up and pursued by old Bárbara, cut through the room with the agility of a monkey. The ladies, startled at first, immediately broke into giggles. The black boy reached the door of the stairway and fled. Then Dias, who until that moment had sat quietly in his corner, quickly jumped up and set off on the run after him. Both of them disappeared.

Benedito was one of Maria Bárbara's houseboys. He was a sly and coal-black little Negro who was quite devilish, with long legs, thick lips, and extremely white teeth. He was constantly breaking china and fleeing from the house.

Old Maria Bárbara stopped short in the middle of the living room, furious.

"Please everyone, don't pay any attention!" she shouted. "That damned rascal! That cursed black tramp! The shameless creature wanted nothing less than to come carry water to the living room without putting on a shirt! Scoundrel! Oh, if I get my hands on him! But just wait, you'll catch it yet, you dog!"

And running to the window: "If Senhor Dias doesn't catch you, tomorrow you'll have a hunter on your trail, you good-for-nothing!"

And she went out once again to the veranda, still quite worked up and shouting for Brígida:

"Oh, Brígida! Are you sleeping too, you devil, you?"

In the living room the visitors laughingly discussed the spectacle of the black boy and Maria Bárbara's evil temperament. But they had to muffle their voices because Ana Rosa began to play a polka at the piano.

In a short while there was a rustling of starched skirts, followed by the appearance of Brígida, a corpulent mulatto, her kinky hair tightly braided and full of flowers, wearing a calico dress with three hand spans of train smelling of coumarin. She had dressed in that style in order to go to the living room to serve water. And securing with both hands an enormous silver tray loaded with glasses, she went around one by one to everyone, swaying her voluminous hauches.

Besides Brígida and Benedito, Manuel and Maria Bárbara's household servants consisted of an elderly Indian-Negro halfbreed named Mônica, who had been Ana Rosa's wet nurse and who did the family washing, a black woman who only starched and ironed, still another who cooked, and a last one just to dust the furniture and run errands. But, despite these helpers, the housework was always slow and poorly done.

"These slaves have it soft nowadays," observed Amância in a low voice to Maria do Carmo, indicating with a glance Brígida's inflated form.

And they began to chat about the scandalous way the mulatto girls were doing themselves up just like white ladies. "They're no longer happy with short skirts and lace collars. Now they want long dresses and, instead of slippers, high lace shoes! What frauds!" They then conversed about the clerks who filched from their bosses in order to adorn their girl friends. And as a matter of course they extended their criticism even to carriage outings, festivals in the public squares, and dances for Negroes.

" 'Shindigs,' as my dear departed Espigão used to call them," cut in Maria do Carmo. "I sure do know about them. We used to have plenty of headaches because of them!"

"It's really a shameless thing! To see the slave women decked out in cambric, ribbons and bows, with perfumed handkerchiefs, their rear ends swaying in rhythm!"

"Oh, for a good whip," mumbled one of the old ladies at the same time.

"And do they dance properly?" asked Maria do Carmo.

"Why certainly they do! It's the housework they don't know how to do punctually! But they're always ready to go dancing!"

Indignation parched her voice.

"They even look like real ladies, God forgive me! All of them making like they were us! The Negro men address them formally. First it's 'ma'am,' then 'my lady!' It's a real disgrace, you just can't imagine! On one occasion I went to peep in on one of their shindigs, because someone told me my late husband was there, and I was astonished! But the worst is that the insolent things don't even address each other by their own names, they use their masters' names instead! Don't you know about Filomeno, the provincial president's mulatto?[3] Well, the others address him always as 'Mr. President!' Then there are those who are 'Mr. Judge,' 'Mr. Doctor,' 'Mr. Major,' and 'Mr. Colonel!' An outrage the police ferule ought to put a halt to!"

Ana Rosa finished her polka.

"Bravo! Bravo!"

"Very good, Dona Anica!"

All applauded.

"You played superbly!"

"No, sir, it was a simple polka by Marinho."

They all went over to compliment the pianist. Freitas immediately prophesized "that right in our midst is a creative genius!"

Raimundo was the only one who was unmoved. He was smoking at the window and remained there smoking. Without revealing it, Ana Rosa felt a slight disappointment over that. She had made a special effort to play well, and he gave no sign: "He seems to have noticed nothing! He's ill mannered," she concluded to herself. And, with a touch of pique, she sat down beside Lindoca. Eufrasinha immediately hastened to her friend's side.

"Well, what do you think of him?" she asked softly, showing marked interest as she sat down.

"Who?" said Ana Rosa, feigning inattention and wrinkling her nose.

Eufrasinha pointed vaguely toward the window with one of her thumbs.

"You know who."

And the merchant's daughter made a grimace of indifference. "Not that fellow!"

"He sure is handsome," ventured Eufrasinha enthusiastically.

"Goodness! What do you mean, Eufrasinha?"

"He's darling!"

And the widow bit her lips.

"Yes, he's not bad looking," replied Ana Rosa, losing her patience. "But let's not get carried away."

"What eyes! What hair! And his manners! Just look, girl! Look how he toys with his cigar! Notice how he's leaning on the window grille. The devilish fellow looks like a nobleman!"

Without unwrinkling her nose, Ana Rosa tilted her gaze toward her cousin and felt, more than her friend, how accurate were her comments about him. Raimundo was indeed elegant and quite handsome. But what could be wrong? Since his arrival he had yet to bestow a single word on her. Not even one gesture directed specifically to her, while all the time she was undeniably the most chic, the most attractive, and, above all—his cousin! (Ana Rosa had little or no certain knowledge of her kinship to him.) No! He had not behaved properly toward her. He had spoken to her as he had to the other girls, equally cold and reserved. He had not acted like the other young men of Maranhão, who, as soon as they approached her, melted with praises and protestations of love. Raimundo's indifference pained her as an injustice. She felt wronged and cheated of her rights as an irresistible young woman. "He's a pedant, that's what he is! A self-satisfied smug! He thinks he's so important, merely because he has a degree from Coimbra University and toured Europe! What a fool!"

At that moment two tardy young fellows noisily entered the living room: José Roberto and Sebastião Campos.

Both were shortly introduced to Raimundo and moved on to greet the ladies, giving each one a phrase, word, or gesture of friendly gallantry: "Dona Eufrasinha—still as beautiful as love itself. What a pity I'm all burned out already!" "And you, Dona Lindoca, where are you off to with all that fat? Share it with me!" "When are we to eat your wedding cake, Dona Bibina?" They always had on the tip of their tongues a jest or a saying to banter with the girls. Although rather insipid and risqué, such words at least made the girls break into smiles and giggles.

"God created those two and the devil united them!" old Dona

Amância let pop with a crackling sound from her mouth when the two went by her.

José Roberto, always referred to as "Mr. Casusa," was a young man in his early twenties, thin, dark, and spotted with acne. He had deeply black eyes and was toothless. His enormous head of hair was thick, completely curled, shining with fragrant oil, and quite black, parted carefully down the middle. He wore blue eyeglasses and sang to guitar accompaniment the sentimental songs he, as well as others, had composed. They were spiced up in the style of Bahia with the sensual Arabic aftertaste of wanton African songs. Whenever he played he would adopt the pleasure-loving air of a street-corner troubadour and drape himself over his instrument, plucking the notes with his nails. His fingers seemed like the claws of an insane crab. With his palm he would muffle the sound of the strings, which lamented and cried like real persons.

A typical northerner, quite frank and with a dread of money, he was proud, and wary of the Portuguese whom he belittled with his constant crude jokes, imitating their accents, manner of walking, and gestures. He possessed a bit of wealth and was known as a playboy. He adored serenades and merrymaking with the girls, and when at a dance he would miss neither quadrille nor jig. But on the following day he would stay in bed, worn out.

For quite some time José Roberto had been attempting to ingratiate himself with Ana Rosa. But she always rebuffed him, laughing. Few people took him seriously: "A crackpot" they would say; but everyone liked him.

Sebastião Campos was the widower of Maria Bárbara's elder daughter and, like José Roberto, a typical son of Maranhão. There was, however, no similarity between them except for their pride and antipathy for the Portuguese. When none were present he would refer to them as "sea dogs," "furrners," and "Galicians."

He was a plantation gentleman, owner of a sugar mill off toward Munim, where he would spend three months each year at harvest time; the rest of the year he would stay in the city. He was probably twice as old as José Roberto, quite short and very neat, but always wore poorly tailored clothes. His white trousers were too short—which permitted his ridiculously tiny and dainty feet to appear from the ankle down. He had a dense beard, still black, and close-cropped hair, birdlike eyes that were lively and lascivious, a child's nose, and an enormous forehead. His large head was disproportionate to his body, and his thick and reddish lips revealed tiny and worn dentures, which, however, were very well cared for, with a sweet herbal mixture that he used to freshen his mouth.

Provincial in every detail, he was an ardent nationalist. He would not trade his good and hearty sugarcane and cashew wine for any number of cognacs or Port wines, no matter what! Nor his delightfully fragrant special leaf mixture produced in Maranhão for the best foreign tobacco, or even for any imported from the other Brazilian provinces! Either you were from Maranhão or you were not!

He never let his slaves make a slip. On the plantation he was feared even by the foreman. He was somewhat religious and full of racial prejudices. "Negroes are Negroes, whites are whites! Black boys are black boys, children are children!" And he was always repeating that Brazil would have been much better off if it had lost the Guararapes War.[4]

"Our misfortune," he would intone, "was to have fallen into the hands of these foolish Portuguese! A bunch of snails! A people incapable of progress, who want only to stuff their craws and hoard money!"

Personal favors, no matter from whom, he would refuse to accept, "because I don't want to owe anything to any mother's son." But whenever he had a chance to humiliate some other person, he was relentless. In no sense mealymouthed! Nervous and energetic, he liked to read or converse, and would straddle his hammock for hours on end in his underwear, smoking his black bowl pipe made in Maranhão. On the street he would appear in an open frock coat, a small camel's hair waistcoat, an embroidered shirt garnished with three large cut diamonds. Around his neck he wore a long, thin chain of solid gold, an antique, fastened to his pocket watch. He adored strong colognes, jewels, and lively colors. But there was nothing, in his view, equal to a short trip out to his rural property. He would set off in the fresh early morning, swigging gulps of sugarcane brandy and smoking his Codó mixture. At home he was quite courteous. In all, he led a comfortable life.

With the arrival of these two men the gathering grew more lively. A guitar was brought in and Mr. Casusa, after much imploring, tuned the instrument and began to sing a selection from Gonçalves Dias:[5]

> "Shall I tell you, if you're curious,
> What enraptures me at times?
> It's the wings of thought that lift me,
> If they're set in pleasant rhymes."

At that point one of the guitar strings snapped.

"Goodness sakes," mumbled the troubadour. And then he shouted out: "Oh, Dona Anica, do you have an E string?"

Ana Rosa went rummaging around the house to see and returned with a middle string. "This is all I found." Casusa made do with it and continued, after repeating the lines already sung. At the window, in the meantime, Freitas discoursed to Raimundo about the author of that poem as well as other notable figures of Maranhão, the "Athens of Brazil," as he called it. The canon scurried rapidly toward the veranda like a coward, fearing such boring talk.

"I'm not a provincial, no sir," the tedious fellow was saying, "but our dear Maranhão *is* a privileged place!"

And he proudly cited "Cunha, Odorico Mendes, Pindaré, Sotero, et cetera, et cetera!"[6] His way of saying "et cetera" was splendid. "We have our pageantry, indeed we do!"

He then started off speaking about the beauties of his Athens: the Mercês Dam, "which is still under construction, but when finished will be a work worthy to see and appreciate," he, full of respectful gestures, assured everyone. He mentioned the Sagração Docks, "also yet to be completed," the barracks, "about to undergo repairs," and the Santo Antônio Church, "which they never finished, but if they did manage to, it would be a beautiful temple!" He praised at length the São Luís Theater. "The canon affirms it to be a smaller version of the São Carlos in Lisbon!" He recalled respectfully the Ramonda Lyric Company, and Remorini the tenor "who died of yellow fever after being highly applauded in *Gemma de Vergi*." Ah! Another company like that, he swore, would never again be seen in Maranhão! "But then, right here in the province there are highly talented young men." He was referring to a private amateur group. "They're quite adroit, yes sir!" And, his voice swelling with an authoritative tone: "They've presented the *Seven Princes of Lara, The Renegades, The Man in the Black Mask,* and other plays of equal merit! They have a knack for the stage, yes they do! You can't deny it!" And, blowing his nose, he shook his head with conviction: "Principally the leading lady. Ah yes, the fellow who played her role. He had all it took: the way he held the fan, the way he rolled his eyes, in addition to certain languishing looks, a certain coquetry! In short, gentlemen, he was perfect, perfect, perfect!"

Raimundo yawned.

But Freitas did not stop even to clear his throat. Raimundo was pelted with droll facts about the local theater. With scarcely a pause, Freitas unfurled endless anecdotes. Raimundo could no longer find a comfortable position at the window; he turned to the left, then to the right; he stood first on one leg, then the other, and, annoyed by the tedium of it all, he finally let his head droop and stared down at his feet. "What a bore!" he thought.

Meanwhile Freitas, shaking the coat sleeve Raimundo had soiled with the mortar on the sill, confessed that amusements were at a low ebb, and that his only diversion was gossiping a bit with his friends.

"Ah!" he exclaimed, "I'm wrong, I'm wrong. There's a new festival—the Santa Filomena celebration. But it won't be like the Remédios festival, just wait for that one!"

"Yes, of course," stammered Raimundo, pretending to pay attention.

And he stretched his limbs.

"The Remédios festival," repeated Freitas, snapping his fingers and letting out a long whistle like someone saying "That's something to behold!"

Raimundo shivered. He had grown chilled to the roots of his hair. By now fully aware of this great menace, he instinctively sized up the height of the window as if planning his flight.

"Our João Lisboa,"[7] declared Freitas, sinking his hands deeply into his trouser pockets, "our João Lisboa has an article published in number . . . now just what is the number of that issue of *Publicador Maranhense?* One moment!"

And he gazed up at the ceiling.

"1173—yes! 1173, on October 15, 1851. Well it's in that article that he describes in minute detail, and with great elegance and stylistic grace, our famous, picturesque Remédios festival.

Raimundo, panic-stricken, promised on his word of honor to read the article at the first opportunity.

"Ah!" replied Freitas implacably, "but nowadays it's something else! You can't even compare today's! There's much more pomp, much more!"

And taking hold of the lapel of Raimundo's coat with both hands, and staring up at him with his wide-open eyes, he added energetically: "Believe me, my good doctor, it pains one to see the piles of money spent for such a festival! It hurts to see the silks, the velvets, the lace petticoats, being dragged on the red soil at Remédios."

Raimundo nodded his head as if he more or less caught the idea.

"Nonsense, nonsense! Be patient, my friend, it isn't possible!" And Freitas forcefully pushed his poor victim backward. "Only by personally seeing and feeling it, Mr. Raimundo José da Silva!"

And he described minutely the color and trickiness of the soil: how the cursed stuff dirtied everything it touched, how it penetrated through the seams of the dresses, into the boots, onto hat brims, into the workings of watches, and how it invaded the nose, mouth, fingernails, and every pore.

"And that, my good friend. . . ."

Raimundo unexpectedly complained that he felt very warm.

Freitas led him by the arm out onto the veranda, had him sit in a canvas easy chair, handed him a Bristol fan, and mixed him a drink of sugarcane juice and lemon. After making him comfortable once more, just as used to be done for the condemned before the execution, Freitas, like a true hangman, stood relentlessly before his victim and poured out a complete description of the Remédios festival day. He drew on all the secrets of the torture chamber, selecting words and gestures, repeating sentences, underscoring certain terms, harping on whatever seemed most interesting to him, replete with body gestures as if he were discoursing before a huge audience.

He began by expounding in detail on Remédios Plaza, with its small white chapel, the benches around it, the numerous ouricury palms, the many flags, skyrockets, and ringing of bells. He described with wonder the exaggerated luxury in which everyone appeared, everyone! For the six o'clock and ten o'clock masses, he said discreetly, "gather the cream of our noble society!" Everything was brand new, the most expensive, the finest. On that day everyone would show off his wealth, from the rich capitalists down to the poorest store clerks; young and old, black and white, no one went there without first having gotten decked out from head to toe. Not only were there no old clothes, but no sad hearts, either!

"At four in the afternoon," added the narrator, "the plaza begins to fill. You, my friend, might think that perhaps they're wearing the same outfit from the morning."

"Naturally."

"Well, you're wrong. Everything is once more brand new! New dresses, new trousers, new. . . ."

"Et cetera, et cetera! But go ahead."

"Some foreigners affirm, and with this I'm saying the last word, that nowhere in the world is there a more luxurious festival!"

And the bore's voice took on the solemnity of an oath.

"What I can guarantee you, Doctor, is that there's not a single child on that afternoon who doesn't have a silver coin tied into the corner of his handkerchief. Thick bank notes appear, as well as old yellowed coins, money changes hands, expensive cigars are puffed in the bazaar—there is a bazaar, by the way—and the price of little gifts rises scandalously! And I can tell you even more: On that day there's no man, no matter how penny-pinching, who doesn't spend a good amount at the auctions, the booths, the sweets counter, or on games of chance. Neither is there any woman, lady or young miss, who doesn't do it up big, or at least put on her new little poplin dress. All around are enormous packages of dried sweets, coconut candy hearts, toy ships made of dough with sugar-coated mast work, golden eating turtles, tiny decorated agoutis inside small cages, doves covered with ribbons, glass jars of Barbados cherry, oranges, and muriti palm fruit preserves; in short, just everything, my dear sir! Black women, slaves or freed, are present to sell their gold, their thick rich tortoiseshell tiles, their lace tablecloths, their gorgeous velvet skirts, and their polished slippers, wearing rings on each finger, two or three on every one. And these people are jammed together, covered with shining luxuries, their stomachs full and their hearts happy. They stroll about on display, puffed up with pride, erroneously thinking they're attracting everyone's attention, when each individual in fact is thinking about and noticing only himself and his own clothing."

Raimundo laughed politely and stretched himself in the chair, yawning.

"At night," continued Freitas, "the entire plaza is illuminated. Gigantic and dazzling transparent arches are erected, each with the saint's likeness and the emblems of the commercial and navigation societies, because Nossa Senhora dos Remédios is the patroness of the commerical groups that sponsor the festival. But, at any rate, all the decorations are lit up: the Brazilian emblem, the decorative stars, the ornamental flower pots, the name of the patroness saint—everything is illuminated by gaslight, not to mention an infinity of small Chinese lanterns shining among the flags, floral pieces, ouricury palms, and bandstands. To sum it all up, everything is as light as day!"

Raimundo let out a deep sigh and changed his position.

"For the little black children there's also a Chinese tallow tree, some swings, and wooden horses. Of course, the good doctor knows what a Chinese tallow tree is?"

"Quite well. Please don't explain."

"Of course! If you don't know, just say so, so I can . . ."

"For God's sake! Please don't worry, I swear I'm impatiently awaiting the outcome of the festival. Continue!"

"All right, then, sir. When eight o'clock arrives . . . Oh, my dear friend, an endless avalanche of families surges out, made up of oldsters, young boys, children, little mulatto and Negro girls, packing the plaza, just like an egg! There are blacks of both sexes and every possible age, from street urchins to old uncles. They come trooping in, balancing immense stacks of chairs on their heads. And with those chairs they set up curving rows right in the open air of the plaza. And the families either remain seated there or, under the guise of strolling about, jostle and elbow one another among the throng. They form groups, laughing, discussing, criticizing, flirting, getting angry, scolding . . ."

"Scolding?"

"Why, yes! There was once a lady who punished a black boy with a whip, right there in the plaza!"

"With a whip?"

"Yes, with a whip! The whole affair, my dear doctor, is a kind of pilgrimage. The families bring along water jugs, couscous, roasted chestnuts, cookies, and the rest. And all this is accompanied by the whirring din of the percussion instruments of three bands, the shouts of the auctioneer, and the unspeakably loud uproar of the people!"

Raimundo wanted to stand up. But Freitas forced him to remain seated by placing his hands on his shoulders.

"We are at the height of the festival!" exclaimed the bore.

"Ah," moaned Raimundo.

"Thin paper balloons are cut loose, the young girls parade in pairs, the young dandies whirl about together. Chunks of sugarcane, ice creams, sugarcane juice, beer, sweets, pastries, and orange lollipops are sold. The smell of cinnamon cigars is all-pervading, the last excesses are unleashed, everyone's pockets are empty and, finally, with great elation, the yearly fireworks display is set off. Then all the bands break out playing at the same time. A cloud of smoke arises, large enough to smother a bellows. And in the midst of the popping of the fireworks and the crowd's unrestrained enthusiasm, the image of Nossa Senhora dos Remédios appears in the Castle, shining amid the lights. Streaking skyrockets fly up by the thousands through the air. The sky disappears. Everyone removes his hat out of respect for the saint and opens up a parasol, afraid of the falling fireworks. There's a storm of multicolored lights. Everything is lit up like a fantasy: all the groups, all the faces, all the nearby houses take on the different reflections of the prism. Throughout this apotheosis the people mass together in mystic contemplation, the end of which signifies the end of the festival!"

And Freitas caught his breath. Raimundo was going to speak, but he interrupted:

"Of a sudden, the people stir and try to leave! They run, spilling out in a mass onto the Rua dos Remédios, crowding together, squabbling over the public carriages, they curse, they rage! Each one wants to be the first to return home. Some crash to the ground and insults, shouts, giggles, and moans are heard. Horses whinny, trays of sweets are upset, dresses ripped, feet smashed, children lost, drunken men stagger. But suddenly, almost by magic, the plaza is deserted and the throng vanishes!"

"Really? Why?"

"A short time later they're all safely at home, already dreaming of next year's festival, planning how to save money, thinking about earning money, in order to cut an even greater figure the following year!"

And Freitas caught his breath, prostrate, his tongue dry.

"But why in the devil do they leave so fast?" asked Raimundo.

Freitas hastily gulped down three swallows of water and immediately turned around.

"It's because these low-class folk love fireworks so much—they're worse than monkeys around bananas! Take away the fireworks and no one will budge from home!"

"Indeed! And do you know if this festival is very old?"

"Quite. It's been in existence for some time. Just a moment." And the great memoirist immediately threw his gaze up to the ceiling.

"During the time of the Portuguese governors," he said, after a pause, "the São Francisco Monastery was located there. That was . . . it could be . . . in . . . in 1700 . . . and, yes, 1719! At that time the intersection that nowadays forms Remédios Plaza was called the Romeo Crossing. Well, the monks there deeded that property over to a certain Monteiro de Carvalho who erected the small chapel that, as well as can be calculated, was then out in the forest. On one occasion, however, a fleeing slave killed his master there and the pilgrims, who used to go there constantly, out of fear abandoned their devotions. It was only fifty-six years later that the governor, Joaquim de Melo e Póvoas, had a good road built that is nowadays our picturesque Rua dos Remédios. The chapel fell into ruin, but the hermit caretaker, Francisco Xavier, in 1818 ordered the construction of the chapel that's still there today. So the festival I've had the honor and pleasure of describing to you dates from that time."

"All in all," ventured Raimundo, "what really astonishes me is your memory: you, sir, indeed have the memory of an angel!"

"Well then, you haven't seen anything yet. Let me tell you about. . . ."

Freitas was heedlessly about to blurt out more, but, fortunately, everyone hurried out to the veranda. Raimundo felt better immediately.

"The devil," said Raimundo to himself, taking a deep breath. "What a first-class bore!"

Hot chocolate was served.

The canon came over to chat with Manuel in a secretive tone.

"Well, it's just as I tell you, my friend: you keep the houses and divide each into two units, that will yield more."

"You think then I'd be doing well to shell out four thousand milréis[8] for each one?"

"Certainly! That's like paying nothing. My good man, they're all of stone and cement, solid, old-style construction! It'll last centuries. Besides that, each one of the little houses has a nice backyard, a good well, and they're not encroached on by the surrounding neighborhood. . . . It does tend to get somewhat hot there, but . . ."

"You can open the windows facing east," the merchant concluded.

And, conversing thus, they reached the veranda where the others were already at the table.

José Roberto and Sebastião Campos were serving the ladies, accompanying each dish they offered with a jest. Raimundo asked to be excused from the tea, fearful of Freitas who had crowded into a place at his side.

The chewing of toast and the slow sipping of hot chocolate were heard.

"Doctor," exclaimed the canon, attempting to impale a slice of tapioca cake with his fork. "At least try some of our Maranhão cake. Around here they also call it 'poorman's cake.' Try it, there's nothing like it outside this area, it's a regional specialty."

"It isn't half bad," said Raimundo, helping himself. "Very tasty, but it seems a little heavy."

"It's to give you strength," added Maria Bárbara. "It's made of oven-baked tapioca and eggs."

"Dona Bibina," called out Ana Rosa, pointing toward the tapioca pancakes. "They're piping hot."

Amância, her mouth full, mumbled softly to Maria do Carmo: "Well, my dear, when you need a special mass, I tell you all you have to do is talk it over with the canon. He's very punctual and is happy with whatever you give him. Why, just the other day he got eighteen milréis from me for a sung mass, but then, you could see all the trouble he went to. Well, you've got to give each one his due, because it's so hard for many priests to earn anything. Around here there are many who start thinking about lunch and their lovers the minute they step up to the altar. God help us! It sure weighs on the conscience of a Christian!"

"Like Father Murta," the other woman prompted.

"Oh, don't even mention that one! At times, God forgive me, he's even come to funerals drunk!"

And Maria do Carmo chattered on. "I myself once saw him completely soused, committing José Carocho's body!"

"Goodness, nowadays it's enough to make you lose your faith. Those priests are so obvious about it! But the canon isn't like that. He behaves quite well. He conducts himself properly and fulfills his obligations. Zealously religious! Believe me, my dear, it's a pleasure to watch him. They even say that. . . ."

And Amância whispered some words to her friend. Maria do Carmo lowered her eyes and mumbled beatifically: "God have mercy on him, poor fellow."

There was a rumbling of chairs being dragged around. The guests arose from their places at the table.

"That's the end of a fine supper!" shouted out José Roberto, sucking on his stubby teeth. And he went off after the ladies, who were quietly moving toward the living room.

At that moment Dias entered, dragging Benedito by the waistband. Out of breath, his tongue hanging from his mouth, almost unable to speak, he related how he had pursued the thief to the end of the Rua Grande, from which point he had headed off toward the Praça dos Quartéis and almost reached Gamboa Forest. With this said, he himself led the black boy inside. "Get going, pest! Go get your hide in shape, because you're still going to get whipped today!"

Everyone was delighted by Dias's efforts, and they exchanged comments on that act of dedication, praising the zeal of Manuel's loyal friend and clerk. An hour later the young ladies all took their leave amid a noisy confusion of kisses and embraces.

"Lindoca," cried out Ana Rosa. "Don't stay away so long next time, do you hear?"

"Yes, my dear, I'll drop by. Listen!"

And she climbed two steps to whisper a little secret to her.

"Yes, yes! Goodbye, Eufrasinha! Dona Maria do Carmo, don't fail to bring those girls to the country house on St. John's day. We'll have crabmeat pie, just wait."

"Farewell, dearest."

"Etelvina, don't forget that thing there."

"Bibina, say goodbye to everyone. Take care now!"

"Just look," observed Sebastião Campos, "when these girls say goodbye to each other, they're awesome."

" 'If one ship could only hold them all,' " Freitas recited, scratching his moustache with his lengthy aristocratic fingernail, "and if I were the captain . . . an eternal triumph!" And after a dry chuckle, he turned toward Raimundo and pretentiously offered him "a place at my humble table."

"Come, Doctor, come to my small cottage," he said, "Come and relax awhile."

Raimundo, inattentive, promised that he would. He was yawning. Out of sheer politeness he inquired if any lady wanted an escort to accompany her home.

The Sarmentos immediately accepted his offer, with a flurry of courteous gestures. Raimundo, inwardly annoyed, took them to nearby Mercês where they lived. He returned shortly afterward.

"Do retire, Doctor, try to go to bed," advised Manuel, who stood there awaiting him. "Your body must be crying for some rest."

Raimundo confessed that this was so and shook his hand. "Good night, and thank you."

"Until tomorrow. Remember, if you need anything, call Benedito, he sleeps on the veranda. But everything should be in place. Brígida is quite thorough. Sleep well."

Raimundo closed the door of his room; he undressed, lit a cigarette, and got into bed. Through habit he opened a book. But after the first page his eyelids drooped. He blew out the candle. He then felt an infinite and deeply pleasant sense of well-being; he hugged the pillows close and, before any of the day's events could assail his spirit, dropped off to sleep.

Yet, just a short distance away, someone was lying awake thinking of him.

5

It was Ana Rosa. No sooner had she retired to her room than she had shouted for Mônica.

"Black Mammy."

This was how she addressed the mixed-breed woman who had raised her and who slept every night under her hammock.

"Black Mammy, wake up!"

"What is it, Missy? Don't you get upset."

"Goodness, you sleep like a stone!

She clicked her tongue.

"Help me undress."

And she stretched out lazily on a chair, abandoning her dainty and well-shod feet to her servant.

Mônica took them lovingly in her black and calloused hands; she carefully removed the high-laced shoes and tugged off her stockings. Then, with an almost religious solicitude, like a devotee disrobing a statue of Our Lady, she began to take off Ana Rosa's clothing. She untied the laces of her petticoat, loosened her corset and, when she had her down to just her chemise, Mônica said, rubbing her back:

"Missy, you're all heated up."

And she ran immediately to the trunk.

Ana Rosa sat meditating absentmindedly, lightly scratching her waist, the spot where the garters had been, and the other areas of her body that had been compressed for some time. Mônica returned with a sweet-scented nightgown, permeated with sedge. Holding it open with her arms, she slipped it over Ana Rosa's head. Ana Rosa stood up and allowed the chemise she had been wearing to drop down to her feet while she pressed the nightgown to her skin, caressing her virginal breasts in a dovelike quivering. She then sighed softly and trotted on tiptoe over to her hammock as if not wishing to touch the floor.

The servant woman zealously gathered the clothing scattered about the room and put away the jewels.

"Do you want anything else, Missy?"

"Water," said the young woman, already snuggling into the

lavender-scented sheets. Only her comely head could be seen, poking out disheveled from among the billows of white cloth.

The servant brought a pitcher of water, and the mistress, after drinking some, kissed the older woman's hand.

"Good night, Black Mammy. Turn down the light and close the door."

"May God make you a saint," answered Mônica, tracing a cross in the air with her open hand.

And she withdrew humbly, brimming with good words and kindly gestures.

Mônica was said to be some fifty years old. She was fat, healthy, very clean, and had huge and pendulous breasts inside her chemise. There was a string around her neck that held a metal crucifix, a small silver two hundred milréis coin, a tonka bean, a dog's tooth, and a piece of bloodwood mounted in gold. Ever since she had suckled Ana Rosa she had maintained an excessive and maternal love for her, an unselfish and submissive dedication. Missy had always been her idol, her only "truly beloved," for her own children had been snatched away from her and sold in the South. In the past she would never come up from the fountain, where she spent her days laundering, without bringing the girl both fruit and butterflies, which was the greatest pleasure in life for the small child. Mônica called her "my daughter," "my captivity," and every night and every morning gave her her blessing, always using the very same words: "May God make you a saint, God protect you, God bless you!" If at home Ana Rosa committed any devilry that displeased her black mammy, she would reprimand her immediately and with authority. If, however, the accusation or the rebuke originated with someone else, even from the girl's father or grandmother, she would stick up for the child and defend her against the others.

She had been emancipated now for six years. Manuel had given her her certificate of freedom at his daughter's request, an act of which many people had disapproved. "You'll end up paying for it," they warned him. But the good Negress had remained in her master's house and continued to watch by Missy's bedside more zealously than before, more a captive than ever.

Scarcely was Ana Rosa alone in the secret protective shelter of her hammock, with the intimate stillness of her room softly illuminated by the dying light of an oil lantern, than she began to review all the day's events. Raimundo stood out among the multitude of happenings like a misplaced capital letter; his ardent face, his melancholy eyes the color of the blue sea on stormy days, his reddish and strong lips, and his teeth whiter than a jungle beast's—all this affected her deeply. "What kind of man might he be?"

Persistently she tried to remember him from some episode of her childhood—to no avail! Yet she had been told that he had played with her when very tiny, and that they were friends, crib companions who were raised together like brother and sister. And all of this produced a strange and singular effect on her spirit. The half shadows, reservation, and reticence with which they timidly spoke to her about him made him even more interesting in her eyes. "But, after all, just who is this handsome young man, really?" They had never explained him to her; they would stop at certain details and skip over others as if they were hot coals. And all that, those blank spaces that they left vacant concerning Raimundo's past, all those veils within which they had enveloped him like a shrouded statue, all this lent him a magnetic attraction, an irresistible and dangerously mysterious charm, a deeply romantic fascination.

It dizzied her to think of him. The hybrid figure that he cut, in which the urbanity and nobility of his bearing mingled capriciously with the rough and haughty frankness of a savage, produced in her mind the effect of a potent wine, but of an irresistible and treacherous sweetness. She was bewildered and totally vexed by the memory of the contrast between his countenance and the contradictory expression of those eyes, entreating and dominating at the same time. She felt defeated, humiliated in the presence of that mythlike being. She recognized a certain force, a certain supremacy in him that she had never found in anyone else. The more she compared him with others, the more she found him superior, unique, exceptional.

And Ana Rosa allowed herself to be slowly overcome by that rapture, forgetting herself, estranging herself from everything, not wanting to think of anything but Raimundo. Suddenly, she caught herself saying: "How good his love must be." And she continued musing, making conjectures, and sizing him up minutely from head to toe. She stopped at his eyes: "How many treasures of tenderness are hidden in them?" . . . Eyes shaped like almonds, bathed in benevolence and circled by crisp and black lashes like the fur of a poisonous beast. Those eyelashes reminded her of the bristles of a crab spider. She shuddered, yet she felt the desire to touch them with her lips. "How good it would be to hear 'I love you' from that mouth and that voice!" And she became frightened, as if in fact, in the silence of her alcove, close to her face, the voice of a man were whispering words of love to her.

But she was soon awakened from her meditations by the idea of Raimundo's cold and austere bearing. That indifference, while simultaneously stinging and tormenting her pride, excited in her feminine vanity a nervous craving to see subdued at her feet that mysterious creature, that unalterable and somber specter, who had seen her and contemplated her without the least reaction.

And among a thousand reveries of this sort, with her blood hurriedly traversing her arteries, she finally fell asleep, overcome with exhaustion. And anyone observing her throughout the night would have seen her from time to time embracing the pillows and tremulously extending her half-open and avid lips like someone searching for a kiss from out of nowhere.

The following morning she awoke pallid and nervous, like a bride on the day of her wedding. She lacked the energy even to dress and leave her room, and remained lying in her hammock, brooding wearily, with her eyes half-closed.

She seemed to still feel on her cheek the heat of Raimundo's face.

Two hours flew by and she remained in the same irresolute state; her eyelids languid, her nostrils dilated by her hot and feverish breath, her lips dry and rough, and her body crushed by a general lassitude that left her shuddering and feeling ill. And prostrated thus, she lingered between the sheets, numb from vexation, perplexity, and the delirium of the night.

The clear voice of Raimundo, who was conversing on the veranda as he ate breakfast, awakened her. Ana Rosa shivered but in a flash jumped up, washed, and dressed. Looking at herself in the mirror, she felt unsightly and askew, though she was no worse than on other days. She straightened herself up, dabbed rice powder on her face, arranged her hair better, and brushed on a smile.

She appeared on the veranda with great shyness and gave Raimundo a cold "good morning," her eyes lowered. She was unable to face him. Maria Bárbara was already there toiling, taking care of the house, whirling about and shouting at the slaves.

"Look, a note from Eufrasinha," she said, upon seeing her granddaughter. And she handed her a piece of paper artfully folded into a bow with a sprig of rosemary stuck through the center.

Ana Rosa made an involuntary gesture of annoyance. Without knowing why, the widow's friendship now bored her. Until then she had been her confidante, her closest and best friend; of her other friends Ana Rosa had grown weary a long time ago. Her one desire at that moment was to be alone, completely alone, some place where no one might disturb her.

She helped herself to a cup of coffee, giving the impression of being indisposed.

"Are you feeling unwell?" Raimundo asked politely.

Ana Rosa was nearly startled; she raised her eyes, met those of the young man, lowered hers immediately and, with a slight smile, stammered: "It's nothing. Nervousness."

"That's what it is," retorted Maria Bárbara who had come to a stop in order to hear her granddaughter's reply. "Nervousness! Just look how these young girls nowadays are busily inventing all kinds of new things! First it's some nervous malady. Then it's that so-called migraine! It's stomach gas! It's conniptions! Ah, for the good old days!"

Raimundo laughed and Ana Rosa shrugged her shoulders, feigning indifference to what the old woman was saying.

"Don't pay any attention, young man. She's been like this for quite some time, and no one can convince me it's not the evil eye."

Raimundo laughed once again, and Ana Rosa straightened up in the chair on which she had just sat down. "That granny," she thought, embarrassed. "Imagine what kind of impression he's forming of us!"

"Don't you laugh, *nhô*[1] Mundico. Don't you laugh," continued Manuel's mother-in-law, "because here's someone," and she pounded on her chest, "who's already had the evil eye and been at death's door!"

And removing from her bosom a gold chain with a large shiny amulet mounted in gold: "Ay, my precious charm, I owe it to you. I owe it to you, freeing me from that evil eye!"

"But, Dona Maria Bárbara, tell me, what's this story of the evil eye?" asked Raimundo.

"What! Then you don't know that the evil eye, if it seizes onto one of God's creatures, dooms it? My heavens! Just what were you learning out there where you traveled?"

"Do you, cousin, also believe in the evil eye?" the young man questioned, turning toward Ana Rosa.

"Foolishness," murmured the latter, with a superior air.

"Oh, then you're not superstitious?"

"No, fortunately not. Besides that," and she lowered her tone and laughed, "even if I did believe in it, I'm in no danger. . . . They say the evil eye in general only attacks beautiful individuals."

And she smiled at Raimundo.

"Well, in that case it would be prudent to be on your guard," he replied gallantly.

And, as if Ana Rosa had called his attention to her own beauty, he began to consider her more closely, while the old lady jabbered:

"My dear Mr. Mundico, nowadays no one believes in anything! It's because of that the times are as they are, everyone with fevers, gall bladders, consumption, and palsies, so that not even professional doctors know what's wrong. They say it's beriberi or who knows what. The point is, I've never in my life seen such a wave of sickness, and that whatchumyacallit kills suddenly, just like some work of the devil. Heavens, it even seems like a punishment. God forgive me! But everything is headed down the road to a republic! And there'll surely be one: a republic that'll make people gnash their teeth! And why not, indeed, sir, if there are no God-fearing people left! There are hardly any who still pray. . . . Today, may the Saintly Virgin pardon me," and she clapped her hand to her mouth, "even priests! There are even priests who are worth nothing!"

Raimundo continued laughing.

"And what's more," he observed good-naturedly, to get her to talk, "if you, my dear lady, were to get to know certain peoples of southern Europe, then you'd be truly astounded."

"Heavens above! Just what inferno is passing through this vast world of heretics? It's because of all this that we're now seeing what we see, God bless me!"

And, crossing herself with both her hands, she asked them to permit her to go take a look at the kitchen.

"If I'm not there the work right away gets behind. They start dawdling, those devilish scourges!"

She went off, shouting out from the veranda for Brígida that it was approaching nine o'clock and she hadn't seen the least sign of any preparations for lunch!

Raimundo and Ana Rosa remained alone, facing one another; she, eyes lowered, confused, had an almost dejected appearance; and he, a happy expression on his face, sat observing her with interest, pleasurably contemplating from so close that simple and well-disposed provincial girl from whom he had been absent since childhood and who now seemed to him like a sister. "She must surely be an excellent young lady," he reckoned. "Her entire being seems to say she is naturally good-hearted and honest. And besides that, quite pretty."

Yes, for until then Raimundo had not realized that his cousin was attractive. But now he noticed the freshness of her skin, the purity of her mouth, and the abundance of her hair. He judged her well groomed; her hands were fresh, her teeth sparkling, her complexion very clean, delicate and bright, with its charming pallor of a northern flower.

After some moments of silence they began to converse with much ceremony. He continued to address her formally, which made her rather ill at ease. He inquired about her father.

The latter had gone down to the warehouse as usual and would come up only for lunch and supper. She then complained about the solitude in which she lived within the general tedium of that house: "A sad place, like a cemetery." She lamented being an only child, and, in reply to his question, said she read for amusement, but that reading often fatigued her as well. Her cousin, if he had a good novel, might perhaps lend it to her.

Raimundo promised to look among his books as soon as he opened his packing box, which was nailed shut.

With the mention of novels, the conversation moved to travel. Ana Rosa regretted never having left Maranhão. She wanted to experience other climates, other customs; she became enthusiastic over his description of certain places. She spoke with sighs about Italy. "Ah, Naples!"

"No, no," objected Raimundo. "It's not the way you think. The poets have exaggerated greatly. It's good not to believe everything they say, the liars!"

And, after a brief summary of his impressions gleaned in Italy, he asked his cousin if she would like to see his sketches. Ana Rosa replied yes, and Raimundo, very solicitous, ran to get his album.

As soon as he got up Ana Rosa felt a great sense of relief; she breathed as if a weight had been removed from her shoulders. But she was already less nervous and even seemed disposed to laugh and banter. For Raimundo, in the middle of their conversation, had unassumingly said that he sympathized greatly with her, that he found her interesting and attractive, and just that alone had immediately improved her disposition and restored to her face her natural expression of good humor.

He returned with the album and opened it wide in front of the girl.

They began to look at it. Ana Rosa paid close attention to the drawings, while Raimundo, at her side, turned the pages with his dark and roundish fingers and explained the mountainous landscapes of Switzerland, the buildings and gardens of France, and the regions of Italy. And he recounted the trips he had made, the meals while traveling, the serenades in the gondolas, telling everything the drawings recalled to his memory: how he had reached a certain lake, how he had gone over this particular bridge, how he had been served in such and such hotels, and what he knew about that little green chalet, which the watercolor portrayed hidden among mysterious and somnolent trees.

Ana Rosa listened in an envious silence.

"What's this?" she asked, seeing a sketch that showed two bishops already in shrouds in their individual coffins, as if awaiting the moment of burial. One was lying flat, his hands crossed and eyes closed. The other, however, was sitting halfway up and seemed about to return to life. At their side was a priest.

"Ah," he exploded, laughing, and explained: "This is copied from a painting I saw in the sacristy of the old Convent of St. Francis, in Paraíba.[2] It's worthless, like all the other paintings there, and there are quite a few, painted on the wood with impossible color schemes, the figures poorly designed and very rigid. This is one of the oldest, that's the reason I copied it. Purely a historical curiosity. Do you see that shield in the hands of the priest? If you'd be so kind as to turn the page, you will encounter a sonnet written with the brush." Ana Rosa turned the page and read:

> These painted figures, reader, faithfully depict
> A mouldering bishop rising from his grave,
> And how Saint Francis intervened to save
> A man whom neither guilt nor wickedness convict.
>
> Now mark the facing image. Here the derelict
> Is *in extremis,* which becomes the knave,
> For he, the friars to deprave,
> Invented countless lies, their Order to afflict.
>
> Seeing therefore, O reader, how these two
> have met contrasting destinies, reflect
> Which of their walks of life is right for you.
>
> The first adored the Order: he is resurrect;
> The second hated it: death is his due.
> Each has the fate his words and deeds pursue.

"Grandma would love this . . . she's very devoted to St. Francis."

"Look, my lady, there you see one of the most beautiful spots in Paris. It's a sketch by a painter friend of mine—quite well done! Those ruins in the background are of the Tuileries."

And they began conversing about the Franco-Prussian War, which had recently ended. Ana Rosa, without taking her eyes from the album, saw and heard everything, and was quite attentive. She asked for explanations; nothing escaped her notice. Raimundo, leaning over the back of her chair, had to lower his head from time to time to explain the drawings, and involuntarily brushed his face against the girl's hair.

On turning one page they suddenly came across a loose photograph, the portrait of a woman smiling mischievously in a theatrical pose. Her cambric skirt was extremely short, forming a diaphanous cloud around her hips. Her neck was bare and her legs and arms were covered by stockings and long gloves.

"Oh," uttered Ana Rosa, astonished, as if the picture were some strange person who had intruded into their conversation.

And she automatically diverted her eyes from that expressive face, which smiled at her from the photo with a vivid insolence and daring mockery. She immediately declared her detestable.

"Ah, that's right. She's a Parisian dancer," Raimundo explained, feigning disregard. "She does possess some artistic talent. . . ."

And picking up the photograph carefully so that Ana Rosa would not glimpse the dedication on the back, he slipped it among the already turned pages of the album.

After they finished with the album, he spoke extensively about Europe, and, since the subject of music had entered their conversation, he asked Ana Rosa to play something before lunch. They went to the parlor where, quite timid and somewhat dissonantly, she performed various Italian pieces.

Benedito appeared at the door, bare-chested.

"Missy, the master's calling everyone to the table."

The lunch passed swiftly, amid jokes and jests. Canon Diogo had come at Manuel's invitation, intending to go to São Pantaleão with Manuel and Raimundo to have a quick glance at the cottages.

The clerks noisily trotted upstairs, after their meal was served.

When the three men appeared on the street, each formed a striking contrast with the others: Manuel with his heavy and dull merchant's appearance, his canvas trousers, and alpaca coat; the canon, imposing and very aristocratic in his shining cassock, displaying his scarlet silken stockings and dainty feet, which were squeezed into polished shoes; Raimundo, totally European and elegant, wearing a light cashmere suit appropriate to the climate of Maranhão, raising eyebrows in the commercial district with his sunhat covered in light-colored linen, its crown lined on the inside in green. They formed, Raimundo commented, bantering, without taking his cigar from his mouth, an honorable philosophical trio in which the canon represented theology, Manuel metaphysics, and he, Raimundo, positivist philosophy; the sum of which, applied to politics, translated into a prodigious alliance of the three types of government: papal, monarchical, and republican!

Ana Rosa peered out and followed them with her curious eyes from the half-closed shutters of a window.

Wherever they went Raimundo was the object of everyone's attention. Little Negro girls scurried inside their houses, shouting for their young mistresses to come see the "handsome young man" passing by. On the street the busybodies came to a halt with dumb expressions, the better to scrutinize him. Their stares measured him rudely from head to toe as if in challenge. The groups he passed on the sidewalk interrupted their conversations.

"Who's that fellow there with the light suit and straw hat?"

"That's a good one! You still don't know?" responded a man called Bento. "That's Manuel Pescada's guest."

"Oh, then that's the so-called doctor from Coimbra?"

"He's the one," declared Bento.

"But Brito, come over here," said the other in a mysterious tone, like someone about to make an important disclosure. "I've heard he's a mulatto!"

And Brito's voice carried the astonishment of someone denouncing a crime.

"What do you expect, my dear Bento? That's the way these slick-haired Brazilian birds are! And they still get angry when we want to bleach out their race without charging them a thing!"

"He's a Brazilian-style white guy! Bento, they're the very type who really make my blood boil," said Brito, mixing up terribly his *b*'s and *v*'s, which gave away his Galician origins.[3]

Elsewhere they were saying:

"Olé, a new face? What a find!"

"It's that doctor, Raimundo da Silva."

"Is he a medical doctor?"

"No, he's a law school graduate."

"Ah, then he's a lawyer? What does he do?[4] How does he earn his living? What does he own?"

"He's come here as his own advocate. He's taking care of what does and doesn't belong to him!"

"What are you saying, man?"

"Just a few facts, my friend. These would-be doctors think rich marriages are to be had everywhere around here!"

And in one family home:

"Do you know what? That Raimundo passed by here!"

"Raimundo who?" they asked in a chorus.

"That mulatto who says he's a doctor and who's living off Manuel Pescada's hospitality."

"They say he's worth a tidy sum."

"He's a skunk, my dear. All these adventurers who put into port here think they're top dog!"

"And why does Pescada put him up in his home?"

"What do you mean! Old Manuel disposed of him as best he could, but the dandy stayed on."

"There always are plenty of shameless people."

Elsewhere they were gossiping that Raimundo was Canon Diogo's illegitimate son, back from school. In other places they viewed Raimundo as a stalwart of the Conservative Party. The editor of the newspaper *Maritacaca* said to a colleague: "Just wait a bit, until the elections, then you'll see this fellow lock, stock, and barrel with the provincial president. Look, they're sure to get along perfectly because they each have the face of a scoundrel!"

And thus Raimundo went about, unaware of being the object of a thousand remarks and stupid conjectures.

That night he concluded the business of the cottages and decided that as soon as the weather was good he would go to Rosário with Manuel to resolve the problem of the ranch there.

The following day Raimundo took a stroll to the Alto da Carneira; the day after he went as far as São Tiago; on another he strode about the market square. He went three or four times to Remédios Plaza. After repeating all his visits to those places, he had nowhere else to go. He shut himself up indoors, intending to cultivate his uncle's acquaintances and to go out to visit them from time to time, for amusement. But, although everyone insistently repeated to him that Maranhão was a very hospitable province, as it in fact is, he noticed resentfully that everywhere and always he was received with awkwardness. Not a single invitation for a dance or a simple soiree reached his hands. Conversations would often cease when he approached; people were hesitant to speak in his presence about matters that were innocent and common. In short, they isolated him, and the unhappy fellow, convinced that he was gratuitously disliked by the entire province, buried himself in his room and went out only for exercise, to attend some public gathering, or when one of his business dealings demanded his presence. Nevertheless, one circumstance intrigued him: while parents closed their homes to him, their daughters certainly did not close their hearts. In public they all snubbed him, that was true, but in their daydreams they summoned him to their bedrooms. Raimundo found himself pursued by several women, single, married, and widowed, whose folly reached the point of sending him flowers and messages, which he pretended not to receive, because he, with his refined upbringing, found the situation ridiculous and foolish. On many a day he would not budge from his room other than to eat or, as frequently happened, to go out to the veranda for a friendly talk with his cousin.

These chats took place during the hottest hours at midday, and often, as well, in the early evening, from seven until nine. Always courteous, the young man would sit in front of the machine where Ana Rosa sewed, and, with a book in his hands or doing a sketch, they would converse calmly and at great intervals. On occasion he would ask for explanations about her sewing; with a childish and kind-hearted interest, he would want to know the technique used for finishing a hem, or removing the basting. At other times, they would speak absentmindedly about religion, politics, and literature, and Raimundo with good humor would in general agree with everything she said. But when the whim took him, he would disagree, slyly, so that the girl would grow excited, hold forth on a certain point and rebuke him, with great seriousness attempting to get him to accept the true faith, telling him he "ought not to be such a Mason and ought to fear God."

Raimundo, who, once grown up, had never experienced the intimacy of family life, was delighted with all that. Dona Maria Bárbara, however, would almost always come and break into that happy idyll with her mean disposition. The devilish old lady was growing progressively more unbearable! She would bellow for hours at a time; she suffered fits of rage, and was unable to go for long without knocking the slaves about. Raimundo had often plunged his hat on his head and stomped out, threatening to move away.

"What a harpy!" he would grumble on the staircase, going down four steps at a time. "She gives drubbings for the fun of it, and amuses herself by making the whip and ferule sing!"

And that barbarous and cowardly punishment revolted him deeply, depressed him, and made him feel like doing something outrageous in his uncle's house. "The ignoramuses!" he would indignantly mutter when alone. But, since moving out was not so easy, he contented himself with spending a part of each day in the billiard room of the province's only restaurant, but not without regret at giving up the innocent chats on the veranda.

In a short while he established a reputation as a gambler and drinker.

For all these reasons, in fact, a dulled repugnance against the province and the accursed old hag was undermining his spirit.

Whenever the snap of the whip or the slap of the ferule sounded in the backyard or the kitchen, Raimundo would toss aside the pen with which he sat writing in his room.

"There's that old devil! She doesn't let me get a thing done! Damn her!"

And he would go angrily out to the billiard parlor.

Now, Ana Rosa was also against punishment, and her grandmother's behavior was a pretext for her first experience of solidarity with the viewpoints of her cousin. The two would speak in low voices against Maria Bárbara, and this conspiracy was drawing them ever closer, uniting them. But one fine day when Benedito got a more prolonged trouncing than usual, Raimundo approached Manuel and spoke to him resolutely about moving out. He knew he was inconveniencing Manuel and did not want to impose on him. Could Manuel be patient and arrange him a small furnished house with a servant?

"What do you mean!" Manuel protested immediately. That his guest would move before settling the purchase of the ranch was unsuitable. "Do you think you're in Europe or Rio de Janeiro? A furnished house with a servant is not something one finds around here. Now just put that out of your mind!"

And when his nephew insisted, he went on, declaring that such a request, in addition to being unfeasible, carried for him, Manuel, a certain odiousness. What wouldn't they say around here? . . . They'd say that Raimundo had been so mistreated by his father's family that he'd preferred to bury himself inside four strange walls rather than endure his own relatives!

"No sir," he concluded, patting Raimundo's shoulder, "you just remain here at home, at least until the dry season. In August we'll go together to see the ranch—and, as by then all your transactions will be finished, you can either go back to Rio de Janeiro or set yourself up right here in the province, but properly! Doesn't that seem reasonable to you? Why do things in a shoddy manner?"

Raimundo finally consented and from then on awaited the month of August with the impatience of a famished person. It was not so much the desire to get away from Maria Bárbara that made him wish so feverishly for that journey to Rosário. Rather, it was his anticipation, his old thirst to once again see the place where, so they curtly told him, he had been born and had lived his first few years. And, then, who knows? Out there he might decipher the mystery of his origins.

He waited, and while he waited he was occupied every day with Ana Rosa, so much so and with such satisfaction that by early June he was already forgetting his regret at not moving. On the contrary, he even foresaw some difficulty in making the trip without suffering the absence of the snug comfort of that family, without feeling a strong nostalgia for that sister, that sincere and gentle friend who had allowed him for the first time to taste the extremely tender pleasure of family intimacy.

Indeed, Manuel's daughter was already quite attached to Raimundo. The formal terms for addressing one another had disappeared as something unnecessary between two relatives who regarded one another highly. The fears, alarm, and misgivings that before had assailed her in the presence of that austere young man who was apparently so uncommunicative, were replaced, thanks to measures taken by Manuel concerning Maria Bárbara, by pleasant moments replete with tenderness, during which Raimundo would first relate amusingly the unexpected happenings of a journey; then sketch in pencil caricatures of those in the house; then sing some German melody or Italian verse; or at the very least would read to her selected poems and short stories.

Ana Rosa experienced in all this an immense but incomplete delight: Raimundo, judging by his manner, seemed to feel for her nothing but the respectful friendship of a brother; and this did not satisfy her. Rare was the day when the young woman, under some pretext, would fail to give him a disguised caress. She would say, for example: "This veranda is quite nippy . . . don't you think so, cousin? Just look, see how my hands are cold. . . ." And she would offer him her hands, which he would fondle limply, afraid of being indiscreet. Other times she would pretend to notice that the young man had very long fingers and would come to him whimsically to measure them against hers, or she would complain of fever symptoms and ask him to feel her wrist. But to all of these dissimulations of fondness, and timid pretenses of love, he would submit coldly, with indifference and at times inattention.

That disregard distressed her; she was pained by his lack of enthusiasm, that absence of affection for one who sought so diligently to merit his tenderness. On certain days Ana Rosa would appear without saying a single word to him, her eyes red and weary. Raimundo attributed it all to some nervous disturbance and would attempt to distract her through chats and music, without mentioning the sad and dejected mien he noticed in her. He feared exciting her, but succeeded only in distressing her even more, for Ana Rosa, getting up from her hammock and seeing her own pallor, would struggle to maintain that expression of grief intact on her countenance, hoping to move him or to be questioned by him so that she would finally have an opportunity to confess her love. But Raimundo kept a coldly deferential air and asked measured questions, frozen with delicacy, as he inquired about his cousin's health. The medical nonchalance with which he spoke of her depression, her insomnia, her lack of appetite, and, the stiff complaisance which he affected, like a favor granted a poor convalescent who was not supposed to be upset, filled her with anger and shattered her hopes of having her sentiments reciprocated.

On one occasion when she appeared to be much more upset and pallid, Raimundo called Manuel's attention to his daughter's health.

"Be careful," he told him, "that age is a very dangerous one for single women. Perhaps if you arranged a trip. . . . At any rate, there'll be no cure without a diagnosis. You would do well to consult a doctor."

Manuel scratched his head in silence. Jaufret had already explained the true cause to him; but because Raimundo again brought up the matter and painted the case as exceedingly grim, insisting on the necessity of doing something, the good-natured Portuguese that same afternoon held a meeting with the canon and with his clerk Dias, to whom he promised a business partnership with the proviso that within the following month his marriage to Ana Rosa would take place, as decided.

"But will Dona Anica be pleased?" asked Dias, lowering his eyes with the best hypocritical smile in his repertory.

"Naturally," answered Manuel, "because the last time I touched on this with her, she gave me reason for hope. . . . Now it's probable she'll give some certainty!"

"Of not marrying perhaps," reflected the canon.

"What do you mean, 'not marrying'?"

"What do I mean? I'll tell you."

And the canon presented his reasons, put forth strong arguments, established premises, drew conclusions, cited Latin proverbs, and stated that lodging the young mulatto in the bosom of the family had never been to his liking, and, if Ana Rosa's marriage was to be arranged, the first thing to do was get him out of the house.

But the merchant, who placed his pecuniary interests above all else, wagged his ears at his friend's words and described Raimundo's respectful and detached behavior in Ana Rosa's presence. He spoke of the zeal with which his nephew had wanted to move away, his aversion to the province, and his enthusiasm for Rio de Janeiro. And Manuel recalled that it had been Raimundo himself whose concern had instigated this meeting of the three men. He finished by saying that he himself feared nothing. Besides, he had full confidence in his daughter's good sense. No, on this score they could all relax. There was nothing to fear.

"We'll see, we'll see. . . . Until I attend Dias's wedding to my goddaughter, I'll stick with what I've said. Cui fidas vide!"

And the canon blew his nose with a roar.

That same evening Manuel, taking advantage of his guest's absence, led his daughter to Maria Bárbara's room. The old woman was resting in her hammock, drinking in the smoke of her pipe and staring at an old oratory of holywood. Ana Rosa, intrigued with the situation, leaned against a chest of drawers. Her father, after discoursing about various unimportant things, said that on the following day the Vilarinho Shop would deliver samples for the bride to select the fabrics for her trousseau.

"Who's getting married?" the girl asked with a start.

"You're pretending ignorance, my wily daughter. Now, which of us seems the most like a fiancée; certainly not I or your grandmother."

And Manuel tickled his daughter's chin.

"Marry! Me? But with whom, Father?"

And Ana Rosa smiled, for she guessed that Raimundo had asked her hand in marriage.

"Now just who could it be, my clever little one?"

And this time it was Manuel who laughed, deluded by the warm reception his daughter had given the news.

"I don't know," she answered with the air of one who knows perfectly well. "With whom?"

"Oh, get on there, you sly one. You know for sure!"

And while Ana Rosa appeared quite occupied in scraping with her fingernail some drops of old wax scattered about the dresser top, the merchant continued: "But why didn't you speak to me frankly some time ago, you capricious girl? You were making the poor fellow suppose you didn't want him?"

And Rosa grew serious.

Her father added:

"There he was, poor thing, going around so dejected—it sure made one pity him!"

"What?"

"Oh, then you don't know how our Dias was behaving?"

"Dias?!" Ana Rosa asked, turning pale.

And she fell silent, brooding, and revived only with these words:

"Now both of you, you're joking!"

"Joking, no, my dear. You said you'd accept him as a husband.

Now what the devil does this change mean? . . . Something is very odd here, just as the canon was telling me!"

"I don't know what godfather said to you, but all I have to say, Papa, is, once and for all, I will not marry Dias. Never, do you understand?"

"But Anica, if you no longer want him, it's because you've your eye on someone else."

"I don't know."

And she lowered her eyes.

"Well, look now. This is already smelling fishy. First you say one thing, now another! Last month on the verenda you told me 'perhaps' and now, a moment later, you're saying no! You know I only want your happiness. . . . I'll not go against you. But at the same time you shouldn't take advantage. . . ."

"But, just what is it I've done?"

"I'm not saying you've done anything. I'm only warning you to pay close attention to your choice of a husband. . . . I don't even want to imagine you might choose someone unworthy of you!"

"But what do you mean, Papa? Speak clearly."

"This should strike home. I don't know if you understand me! . . ."

"One moment, Manuel," exclaimed Maria Bárbara, getting up and placing her enormous bamboo pipe from Pará on the floor. "At times you have spells that seem like forgetfulness. Well, then, that a young girl brought up by me should even gaze on," and she shouted even louder, "at just whom, my dear Manuel?!"

"Well, well. . . ."

"As if it weren't enough to provoke a person."

"Well, well, I'm not saying this to offend anyone," the merchant apologized, "but it's just that we have here a handsome young man who. . . ."

"A nigger!" screamed his mother-in-law. "And it's fitting that something like this should happen, so in the future you'll be more careful who you take in as a guest! It was that head of yours that dreamed up the insane idea of having a mulatto full of boastful airs stay in the house! Nowadays they're all like that! A gang of thugs! Give them your foot and they grab your hand! Rabble! And just be happy your daughter hasn't pulled a fast one on you! Remember you owe what she is to me. I'm aware of the upbringing I gave my granddaughter! I'll answer for her! . . . And as for the nigger, you're to send him on his way now, and I mean now, unless you want to get into even hotter water later!"

"All right, all right! I'll take care of this tomorrow. Oh!"

Manuel at once thought of going to the canon for advice.

Ana Rosa restrained her tears.

"I'm going to my room," she said brusquely.

"Listen here," countered her father, detaining her. "You . . ."

"Don't say any nonsense," cut in the old lady, pushing her granddaughter outside. "Go on now, and pray to the most holy Virgin to watch over you and give you common sense!"

Ana Rosa shut herself into her bedroom, prayed intensely, refused to have tea, and sobbed until four in the morning.

The following day, after reaching an understanding with the canon, Manuel advised Raimundo to get ready to go to Rosário.

"I'm at your disposal, but you said we'd go in August."

"That's true. However, the weather is dry, and next week we'll have a full moon. We can go Saturday. Does that suit you?"

"As you wish. I'm ready."

And a little later Raimundo went to his bedroom to see to his belongings for the trip: a rubber bag full of sugarcane brandy, riding boots, spurs and whip—all were ready for him. But he thought it strange to find all his things freshly disturbed, as if someone had used them. This was not the first time he had noticed this sort of thing; other times it had seemed to him that some ill bred and curious soul had had fun by rummaging through his papers and clothing. "It's perhaps the meddling of that black boy."

But the following day, upon lying down, the found on his pillow a tortoiseshell comb pinned to a black velvet bow. He immediately recognized those objects as belonging to Ana Rosa. But how in the devil did they end up provocatively there on his bed? This was certainly some crazy mystery which he should clear up. Then he remembered having once been quite piqued at discovering in his hairbrush and comb some long strands of hair, a woman's hair—without doubt a white woman's.

By now quite irked, he decided to carry on a minute search within his room and came across the following evidence: two hairpins, a dry jasmin bough, a button from a dress, and three rose petals. Now then, these objects belonged to her, just like the little tortoiseshell comb and the velvet bow. . . . It was Benedito who cleaned and straightened up his room. He certainly didn't use bows or hairpins. Well, just as he had thought, someone was amusing herself during his absences by ransacking his things; and that someone could only be Ana Rosa! But what the devil did she come here to do? . . . How could he decipher the reason for those fanciful visits? Might it be simple curiosity or could there be behind all that some Maranhão-style intrigue against him? Or, perhaps, who knows . . . maybe against Ana Rosa herself? Whatever the case, it was necessary to put a stop to such nonsense.

From that day on, Raimundo paid careful attention to all the objects he left in his room; he marked not only his place in the album but also the alarm clock, a book, his shaving kit, and anything the boy would not need to move while cleaning. And by means of these experiments he became more and more convinced of the mysterious visits. The shocking evidence popped up again and again. Once he found fingernail scratches on the face of the dancer whose photograph he had carefully hidden from his cousin because on the back of it was the dedication *"A mon brésilien bien-aimé, Raymond."*

Beyond a doubt, all the evidence implicated the beautiful daughter of the owner of the house! The irony, however, was that Raimundo, despite his dislike, as a serious and honest man, of anything that smelled of subterfuge and deceit, nonetheless felt a certain vain pleasure in so occupying the imagination of an attractive woman. This interest, along with that style of timid and discrete revelation, flattered him; he enjoyed noting that among all the objects his own portrait was the most violated, and, like a good detective, he eventually discovered on it traces of saliva, signifying kisses. But whether propelled by curiosity or by the misgiving that all was the work of some rogue, or, finally, because the occurrence repelled his honest character, the truth was that he planned to take advantage of the first opportunity to end those goings-on.

A few days later, upon stepping out of the house and tarrying to converse with someone near the door, he saw from the street the shutters of his room closing cautiously. He did not hesitate—he climbed the stairs two at a time, crossed the empty veranda, and went directly to his quarters.

6

Ana Rosa had indeed for some time been visiting Raimundo's room during his absences.

She would enter secretively, close the shutters and, because she knew he would not soon return, would begin to leaf through the books, poke through his open drawers, experiment with the locks, read the calling cards and all his written papers that she could get her hands on. Whenever she came across a used handkerchief on the floor or on top of the chest of drawers, she would take it and sniff it avidly, as she would also do with his hats and the small pillow on the bed.

This meddling would leave her in a sensual and morbid swoon, with her body shivering feverishly. Once she found a gray glove misplaced behind one of his trunks. She eagerly and quickly slipped it on and stood staring at it, questioning it with her eyes, opening and closing her hand, and absentmindedly rubbing the wrinkles of the kid leather. And this glove wrenched from her conjectures about Raimundo's past; it made her imagine the ostentatious balls in Paris, the parties, the outings, the railroad stations, the crisp mornings on ocean crossings, dinners in hotels, horse races—an entire life of excitement, bursts of laughter, and luncheons with women. This existence unfolded in her mind's eye as a broad panorama based on the drawings in Raimundo's album, and there, striding across the foreground, was he, laughing, smoking, arm in arm with the dancer in the photograph who, in a theatrical show of love, declared *"Raymond, mon bien-aimé!"*

It was during one of those daydreams that Ana Rosa unthinkingly dug her nails into the face of the portrait, in the same rage with which at school she used to scratch the poorly sketched Jews in her manual of Christian doctrine.

Those visits were now her sole preoccupation; her happiest moments were spent there, body and soul absorbed in her secret. The remainder of her waking hours served only to await the moment of this beloved pleasure. And when for some reason she was unable to carry out her design, she would become intolerably frantic and nervous. By now she wanted nothing to do with her girl friends; she had not repaid a single visit of theirs and had taken a strong dislike to Eufrasinha. And not in the remotest way did mention of parties and entertainment interest her—her sole entertainment, her only festivity was to be there, in the forbidden room, alone, at ease, in that intimate conversation with Raimundo's possessions, reading his papers, prying into everything, throbbing with a new and unfamiliar delight that was secret, full of unexpected twists, and almost criminal! Little by little, in measured sips, like an excellent wine, she savored these strong, even violent, delights as she sensed herself becoming intoxicated, consumed, and absorbed by that folly of pursuing a nothing, a hope that tormented and slipped away from her, but that was nonetheless better and more entrancing to her than the best and most seductive pleasures of society.

On the day that Raimundo returned, on tiptoe, up the stairs to his room, Ana Rosa had entered shortly before and, as usual, had shut herself inside. The surroundings had taken on a listless and dubious tone in which a mixture of light and shadow hovered. After sweeping her gaze about, she had sat down on the bed and absentmindedly picked up from a nearby chair a physiology treatise that Raimundo had been reading sleepily the night before and had left next to the candlestick, his place marked by a tiny box of matches.

Opening the book, Ana Rosa let out an embarrassed cry: she had come upon a drawing in which the author of the book, with a scientist's cold lack of ceremony, exhibited to the reader a woman in the act of giving birth. The unseemly and grave accuracy of the print produced a strange effect of respect and chagrin on the young girl's feelings. Without understanding fully what was before her eyes, she stared fixedly at the page and moved it from side to side, attempting to fathom it better. She turned some pages and, with the little French she knew, tried to grasp the meaning of what was written about the various phenomena of gestation and birth. On reaching one of the prints, however, she slammed the book shut and glanced about as if to verify that she was completely alone. Unprepared, she had glimpsed a spectacle that her senses had barely formulated through instinct: the act of fecundation. She turned the color of pomegranate and pushed the indiscrete volume away with a rapid and spontaneous gesture of modesty, but shortly thereafter, pondering the situation and becoming convinced that the book had not been produced with malicious intent but, on the contrary, for study, she worked up her courage and confronted the page.

The drawing opened before her like a small door into a vast, cloudy, and unknown world, populated with pain but at the same time irresistible, a strange paradise of tears that simultaneously intimidated and attracted her. She studied it with great attention while within her there raged the battle of desire. Her entire being was in revolt; her blood cried out, demanding its food of love; her whole organism protested in exasperation against its idleness. And she then felt vividly the responsibility of her womanly duties before nature, she understood her destiny of tenderness and sacrifices, and perceived that she had come into the world to be a mother. She concluded that her very own existence imposed on her, as an impeccable law, the sacred mission of producing many healthy, handsome children, nourished on her milk, which would be good and abundant and would create a handful of strong and intelligent men.

And before her eyes she could already picture her beloved little children, naked, soft and plump, their heads well formed, their darling pink feet, almost imperceptibly small noses, and tiny toothless mouths, which nursed at her breast with the charming irrational greediness of small infants. And, thinking of them, she fell listlessly into an indolent posture—her arms stretched across her thighs, her head limp and inclined toward her breasts, her exhausted gaze immobilized on the book resting on her knees between her benumbed fingers. And she mused: yes, it was necessary to marry, to have a family, a husband, a man solely hers who would love her vigorously! And she pictured herself as the lady of the house with a ring of keys at her waist, scolding, watching over their interests, burdened with obligations, avoiding whatever might annoy her husband, giving orders so that he would find his dinner ready. And she wanted to satisfy all his whims and fancies, to become passive, to serve him like a loving, docile, and submissive slave who confesses her weaknesses, fears, and cowardice, happy to discover her inferiority to her man, and delighted at being unable to do without him. And she brooded at length about her husband, and this husband appeared to her imagination as the slender figure of Raimundo.

Just then the drapery around the bed parted behind her with the slight rustle of starched lace.

Ana Rosa spun around with a start and came face to face with Raimundo, staring censoriously at her. She let out a cry and tried to flee. The book fell to the floor, opening wide at a page on which the drawing of the interior of the womb, full of a tangle of yellow and pink innards, was visible.

Raimundo did not give her time to leave and placed his body between the bed and the wall.

"Please wait," he said gravely.

"Let me go, for the love of God," she pleaded, turning her head to avoid Raimundo's eyes.

"No, my lady, you must hear me first," he responded with delicate authority. And, after a pause, he added with a certain mark of paternal superiority: "It pains me, but I must admonish you, all the more as I am in your father's house, which is also yours. You, however, have committed a misdeed and I would be committing an even greater one if I were to say nothing."

"Let me go!"

"You will leave this room promising not to return to repeat what you have been doing! . . . If they discovered your secret visits, what would they not think of me? Of me and of you—which is far more serious! What would they not say? And with reason! Is the reputation of a lady a thing to be risked in this way? Is this fitting? And even if it were, if through some unpardonable aberration you, Cousin, felt that it was fitting, could you cheapen your reputation without sullying your family as well? Let me tell you, young lady, that the duty each of us has to look after our own good name is based not only on self-respect, but on the consideration we owe to those who vouch for our reputations! A lady has no business in the room of a young man! It is unseemly! You, Cousin, are thereby committing an ingratitude to the one to whom you owe everything: your father!"

The girl's nervous weeping, held back until then with difficulty, burst from her throat and eyes like a brook overrunning its banks. Her hot tears streaked down her cheeks and dripped in thick beads on the white and palpitating flesh of her breast.

Raimundo was touched, but he attempted to conceal his perturbation. And moving to one side to offer her passage, he added with his voice somewhat altered: "I ask you to leave and not return under such circumstances."

He wanted to take her to task further, to reprimand her more, but his brows unfurrowed in the presence of that honest little calico dress, those simple auburn braids, those innocent tears.

Ana Rosa listened to him without a word, her head bowed and her face buried in her handkerchief. When Raimundo finished speaking, she sobbed loudly and sighed like an inconsolable child.

"Well, what foolishness is this? Now you're sobbing like that! . . . Come now, don't be a child."

Ana Rosa wept still more.

"Really, if you go on like that they'll hear you from the veranda!"

And Raimundo became flustered with emotion and fear; he was no longer certain what he meant. The words were not on his tongue; he felt foolish. The situation began to frighten him.

"Come now, my friend," he stammered nervously. "If I offended you, excuse me, pardon me, but it was in your own interest."

And he moved closer to her, to soothe her; he was regretting having been so harsh. He had been brutal! After all, he well understood that Ana Rosa was not responsible. . . . Feeling remorseful, he sought to diminish the blunt effect of his initial words:

"Well then, come now, I'm your friend, tell me why you're crying."

Ana Rosa, continuing to sob, did not answer. Raimundo could not contain a gesture of impatience and scratched his head.

"Look, things are getting out of hand!"

By now he was sincerely repenting having surprised her. If only his patience would hold up! His sole fear was that they might hear her from the veranda. They would discover everything! Surely they would!

And, bewildered, not knowing what to do, he went to the door, returned, and once again paced, distressed and anxious.

"Well then, Cousin, do you intend to remain here? Don't cry! How imprudent you are! Just remember you're in my room. Please be so good as to leave. Don't be offended, but go, because we could compromise ourselves quite seriously!"

She redoubled her weeping.

"You have no reason to cry."

"Yes, I do," she responded from behind her handkerchief.

"Well then, what is it?"

"It's because I love you so, so much, do you understand?" she declared between sobs, her eyes closed and dripping. And slowly blowing her nose, she clasped the tear-soaked handkerchief in her hand. "Since I first saw you, from the first moment! Do you understand? And in the meantime you, Cousin, never even. . . ."

And confused and impassioned, she burst into tears even more.

Raimundo lost all hope of terminating the scene in an appropriate manner. He nevertheless sensed that he liked Ana Rosa quite a bit, more than she perhaps realized, more than he himself might have expected. But if this was the way it was, what the devil! They should get married like anyone else. He should lead her to the church decently and in broad daylight, at the family's side, and not have her there romantically shedding tears on the sly in his room. No, he would not permit this! It was ridiculous! And he blurted out:

"Fine, my lady, but I don't have the right to detain you here in my room. Please leave! The time and place are highly improper for such delicate revelations. We'll speak of it later."

Ana Rosa continued crying, immobile.

Raimundo even thought of going out to the veranda, calling for someone, causing an uproar, and telling everything. But he had pity for her. It would only injure her, offend her, and it would be brutal and scandalous besides. Oh! A formidable scandal! . . . What the devil should he do? . . . Yes, after all, it would be stupid to turn against the girl! She loved him, she was twenty years old and wanted to get married, nothing wrong with that! And he decided to change his approach, to employ gentle and affectionate means to resolve the situation. It was the shortest and safest path. So he approached Ana Rosa tenderly, and, after wiping the perspiration from her forehead and straightening her disarrayed hair, affectionately said to her:

"But, my dear cousin, the fact that you love me is no reason to cry. On the contrary, we should be quite happy. Look how satisfied I am, I'm smiling. Follow my example. And do you know the best thing we could do? Not cry, certainly. We should marry! Don't you think so? Doesn't it seem the most sensible thing to you? Won't you accept me as your husband?"

On hearing this Ana Rosa immediately removed the handkerchief from her face and did what she had not yet done: she faced Raimundo, fearlessly, happy, smiling, her eyes still red and wet, her breathing still in sobs, and unable to articulate a word. And then, with a self-assurance that astounded her cousin and of which she normally would never have thought herself capable, she warmly and expansively embraced him, resting her head on his shoulder, and extending her lips to him in an entreating eagerness.

There was nothing else the young man could do—he planted a timid kiss on her mouth. She immediately responded—ardently—with two more. Then Raimundo, despite all his moral composure, became flustered: he was crumbling, a flame was rising into his head, his temples were pulsating and, on his flushed and burning face, he felt Ana Rosa's cold nose breathing rapidly. He, however, contained himself: gently and tenderly, he freed himself from her arms, respectfully kissed her hands, and asked her to leave.

"Will you go? They may see you. This isn't worthy of either of us."

"Are you annoyed with me, Raimundo?"

"No, what a thought! But go now, won't you?"

"You're right. But, look, when will you ask Father?"

"At the first chance, I give you my word. But don't come back here, all right?"

"Yes."

And she left.

Raimundo closed the door and began to pace about the room, quite agitated. He was satisfied with himself: despite all of his twenty-six years, he had behaved faithfully and generously toward a poor girl who loved him.

And, elated, he sang with his voice still somewhat shaky: "Sento una forza indomita."

But two knocks sounded at the door.

It was Benedito.

"Master had me ask you to visit his room.

"I'm coming at once."

The trip to Rosário was to be postponed for a month because Manuel had come down with a severe case of mumps on the very day Raimundo had surprised Ana Rosa in his room.

That night the house filled with friends. Freitas came right away, bringing a homeopathic dose. The sickness was discussed and appropriate information related. Each one had had a case much worse than Manuel's.

Suggestions for remedies showered in from every side.

"Seville oranges, Seville oranges!" cried Dona Maria do Carmo. And she guaranteed that, "except for God Himself, there is no better remedy for this illness!"

"No, no! Remember that linseed poultices have served quite well," reflected Amância.

"Well, the thing I found effective was the caladium leaf," observed the older of Maria do Carmo's nieces.

"And I," said Etelvina with a sigh, "when I wanted to put an end to the case I had, I resorted to sweet almond oil!"

Ana Rosa lit a candle to St. Manuel do Buraco and Maria Bárbara promised a shipment of wax to St. Rita dos Milagres.

Eufrasinha appeared and immediately prescribed janaúba milk.

"You cut the vine and a white sap trickles out, so thick it's an oil," she explained with gestures. "You catch it in a cup, then soak cotton in it thoroughly and plant it on the face of the sick person. It takes just once, my dear."

On the veranda they were chatting about the patient's despondency.

"He's quite discouraged," protested Maria Bárbara. "Any little thing makes him think he's dying. He's all the time saying 'Woe is me, this time I'm dying.' Just a tiny fever makes him like that."

And Maria Bárbara, to demonstrate vividly how her son-in-law acted, tugged on her cheeks with her fingers and hideously pried open her eyes.

"Gracious!" exclaimed Amância, and then recounted the death of an acquaintance of hers.

Maria do Carmo pathetically began to tell about the passing away of Espigão. "That was a real death, just seeing it. . . ."

A series of funereal anecdotes followed.

In the parlor, Freitas, with patriotic thoroughness, examined some lithographs perched on the console. They were poorly drawn episodes from the Paraguayan War: the taking of Paissandu, the forcing of Humaitá,[1] and others, printed in Rio de Janeiro. There was General Osório on horseback, readily visible with his black moustache and white beard. Lindoca's father from time to time took his eyes from the pictures and scanned the room, looking for a victim for his boring talk. Raimundo, as soon as he had caught a glimpse of him, had hidden in his room out of fear.

Ana Rosa kept her promise not to return to Raimundo's room, but instead she spoke to him every day about the marriage. After the agreement with her cousin, she went about impeccably happy, humming merrily while sewing or prancing about the veranda under the pretext of helping her grandmother with the household arrangements, something that now held more interest for her. Maria Bárbara, on the other hand, cursed the devil for Manuel's mumps and the consequent postponement of the journey to Rosário. That nigger's delay in the company of her granddaughter knotted up her stomach! She wouldn't be able to relax until she'd seen the last of him.

In the meantime St. John's day was approaching. In Freitas's and in Maria do Carmo's houses, just as in Manuel's, they spoke about the festival. The celebration would be held, as it was every year, at Maria Bárbara's country house. It was an old custom, dating back to the time of the deceased colonel, Ana Rosa's maternal grandfather. The old lady would not let up concerning St. John's festival. Nothing would keep her from sponsoring the customary party on that day. For her, that date represented the anniversary of the most notable happening of her life: on that day her João Hipólito, the never sufficiently lamented colonel, had been born; also on that day he had asked for her hand in marriage, and, one year later, again on St. John's day, she had married; on the same day her first daughter, the deceased wife of Sebastião Campos, had been baptized: and, finally, on that day Mariana had become Manuel's wife.

A gathering took place in the merchant's house, made up of Amância, Maria do Carmo and her nieces, and presided over by Maria Bárbara. They spoke at length about the roast pork, lamb, and turkeys, and discussed types of stuffing: whether with manioc meal or the bird's own intestines. The majority decided it should be manioc meal, "in the style of Pernambuco,[2] explained Etelvina. They placed elaborate orders for dozens of eggs, and planned on serving the less common sweets. Several extremely difficult culinary processes were prescribed: they consulted the *Imperial Cookbook*. There were offers of china, compotiers, silverware, and black boys and girls to help with the preparations. Individuals exceptionally skilled at making various desserts were mentioned; they spoke about Bahian fish stew and cold sliced hams.

The following day they ordered a mason to whitewash the house in the country; slaves were sent out to clean up the grounds, sweep off the footpaths, water tanks, and dovecotes. Lamparinas, the priest who sang the St. John litany there every year, was contacted. There would be a dance and fireworks. It was to be a wonderful and massive feast. "The devil," thought Maria Bárbara, "is just that the nigger will only be leaving Maranhão next month!"

In the meantime Raimundo was quite bored. The province seemed ever uglier, ever more narrow-minded, more foolish and scheming, and less sociable. To cheer himself he wrote and published a few pamphlets; they pleased no one because they were too serious. He then started turning out short stories in prose or verse. They were realistic observations worked up in a certain style, cleverly depicting the ridiculous customs and characters of Maranhão, "our own Athens," as Freitas used to say.

These caused a flurry! People shrieked that Raimundo was attacking public morality and satirizing the most respectable persons in the province.

And that was all it took: the Athenians leaped into action, writhing in anger at the novelty. They criticized him bitterly and called him names everywhere—"Stupid ass! Pushy nigger!" The shopkeepers, government scribes, and clerks who attended the literary clubs where for years and years they had been discussing the immortality of the soul, and the innumerable grammarians, incapable of composing an original sentence, all declared that what was called for was—to beat him up! "We'll give him such a drubbing that he'll think twice before being impudent and disrespectful of those things most sacred to our life here: the innocence of our damsels, the virtues of our married ladies, and the sorrow of the widows of Maranhão!" At the doors of the pharmacy, on the corners of Carmo Park, in the rear of the small stores where white wine was sold, and inside all the private homes, they swore they'd never witnessed such scandalous language in pamphlets. The newspapers spoke constantly of such famous native figures as Gonçalves Dias, Odorico Mendes, Sotero dos Reis, and João Lisboa. Anonymous attacks on Raimundo appeared in the papers, obscenities directed at the "new poetaster" were scrawled on the walls with chalk and cheap paint. And for many days he was the talk of the town. Fingers pointed at him; behind closed doors it was whispered that a new little newspaper was going to be published, entitled *The Half-Breed,* just to expose that shoddy fellow's rottenness to public view! Black boys would shrill such vile things at the persecuted man that he could not even understand them.

And unaware of the true meaning of the insults and cutting remarks, he swore, in astonishment, never again to publish anything at all in Maranhão.

"Damn them all!" he would say.

And in fact he developed an overwhelming sense of nausea for that province so unworthy of him; he grew impatient to carry out his marriage to Ana Rosa and depart from that pigsty of pretentious and evil people.

"Good God, what a stupid little place," he would mutter to himself, smoking cigarettes and lying stretched out in his room.

Yet the worst still awaited him in the month of June.

7

June arrived, with its very bright and very Brazilian mornings.

It is Maranhão's most beautiful month. The first trade winds appear, gusting through like a wild band of mischievous and prankish demons, reveling about the city, whistling at passersby, whipping pedestrians' hats into the air, turning parasols inside out, and lifting the women's skirts, impishly exposing their legs.

Joyful mornings! The sky is swept clean on these days as if for a celebration; it is clear, completely blue, and cloudless; nature prepares and adorns itself; trees preen as the trade winds sing to their dry leaves and shake their fronded greenish crowns. Roads are scoured; the grass of the fields and meadows is scrubbed; water throbs and becomes clearer and fresher. The turbulent band of winds never ceases as it moves forward, constantly eddying, buzzing, singing, flicking up everything it encounters, awakening the low-lying and lazy little plants, allowing not a single flower to remain asleep, and shooing from their nests the entire chirping winged republic. And the butterflies, in multicolored throngs, flit here and there crazily; clouds of bees soar mischievously, truants to their daily tasks, and also the dragonflies—what a lazy bunch!—playing in the sun above the ponds, dancing to the sound of an orchestra of locusts.

Experienced people on those mornings awake cheerfully, after a hearty and complete sleep that has been swallowed in a single gulp like a glass of cool water. They cannot resist the invitation of the devilish band as it leaps in through the window to invade the room, tossing papers from the table to the floor, ripping paintings from the wall, and unfurling curtains, which flutter in the air like gay floating flags; they don't resist—they dress, humming, and go out to the street and into the country, put flowers in the lapels of their cutaways, shake their canes, speak incessantly, laugh, feel like running, and eat lunch on those days with a savage appetite.

The morning of St. John's Eve was one of those days. Before dawn broke, Raimundo was already up and on his way, along with Maria Bárbara, Manuel, and Ana Rosa, to the country house where the great traditional feast reminiscent of the deceased colonel's era would take place. The old woman was repenting not having waited for the horse-drawn trolley at six o'clock and, exhausted, she sat down with her son-in-law on a bench in front of one of the villas on Caminho Grande. Raimundo continued walking distractedly, with his cousin on his arm.

The weather was clearing up. To the east, the horizon began to be tinged with red for its dazzling daily rebirth; the sun was about to appear. There was a huge ruby-red elation about the golden and purple womb, which finally ripped apart in a swirl of flame, spewing light throughout the earth and sky. A chorus of warbling broke from the forests; nature in its entirety sang out, hailing its monarch!

Raimundo, ecstatic at Ana Rosa's side, could not contain his enthusiasm.

"How beautiful it is! How beautiful it is!" he exclaimed, pointing toward the east.

With the agitation of a painter, crumpling his felt hat between his fingers, he seemed avidly to imbibe, through dazzled eyes, that marvelous birth of a southern sun in June. Then, still enthralled, he took his cousin's arm and, without removing his gaze from the scenery, called her attention to the wondrous effect of the light filtering among the leaves in the thickness of the trees, to the drops of dew that sparkled like diamonds, to the reddened vegetation of the distant plain, to the luminous areas around far-off country homes where cattle grazed and carts stood heaped with huge sheaves of fresh forage.

And from the country to the city market came enormous trays of vegetables, dripping from the last watering, pyramids of tiny bouquets of flowers to sell to the mulatto girls, and wicker baskets of fruit that spread an appetizing perfume in the air. On poles slung over their shoulders backwoodsmen carried spotted cavy and agoutis that had been caught in the forest. Rural carts passed with their immense one-piece wooden wheels creaking. Men from the country, followed by their women and large bands of children, streamed in at a steady pace from Vila do Paço and São José de Ribamar, loaded down, having stomached mile after mile on bare feet to appear at the top of Caminho Grande and sell their fish, caught and roasted the previous evening, their piping-hot tapioca flapjacks, sesame seed oil, baking dough, sweet cassava, and manioc cakes.

Ana Rosa seemed a different person than she had been lately: she was lighthearted, unconcerned, as if she had returned to one of her school days. It was as if the trade winds had lifted the veil of her maidenly melancholy and breathed new life into her heart with a gust of wind.

"Forget about the scenery, Cousin, and give me your arm!" she said, out of breath, having gone at a run to buy tangerines from a rural fellow. "Oh, I'm tired!"

And, unable to speak, she hung on Raimundo's arm. After contemplating her at length, he leaned toward her.

"Do you know?" he whispered to her, "today you're prettier than ever, Cousin. Your cheeks are like two roses!"

"You're just teasing. . . . If you really found me attractive, you'd have already asked Father for me."

"I confess, I've never seen you so beautiful!"

"It's the trade winds! They've cleansed your eyes!"

"Now don't joke. Shall I confess something to you? I'm not sure what extraordinary effect this morning is producing in me. It's very peculiar, but I don't even know myself. I feel transformed. The very idea, for example, of my habitual dignified manner, my exaggerated seriousness, which you've complained about to me on more than one occasion, it all seems now as childish and ridiculous as Freitas's style and the great pride of Sebastião Campos. That's right! Believe me, at this moment I lament not being more expansive and happy, more of a youth. I regret having wasted so many sunrises studying, killing myself with work, falling asleep exhausted at daybreak, when others were getting up comforted and rested. Frankly, all the labors of an entire generation of scientific investigators and everything the best academies can teach are not worth the wonderful lesson that nature, the great teacher, is offering me in this short time as I stroll at your side. With this one lesson the youth I stupidly strove to suffocate is reborn in me. I feel eager for happiness, I feel capable of loving you, my dearest friend."

Ana Rosa lowered her head, flushed with modesty and contentment, not wanting to interrupt him so as not to miss a single one of those words that were so dear to her. What Raimundo said made her feel like crying and falling gratefully into his arms, translating into kisses all the affection that her bashfulness prohibited her lips from uttering.

They had stopped next to one another. The rising sun was striking them fully. They were speechless. Raimundo took her hands and the two gazed at one another with a promise in their eyes, and they spoke no more of love as they awaited Manuel and Maria Bárbara, who once again had started walking.

A half hour later they reached the country place. Raimundo was astonished by his good spirits; he recognized that moment as the happiest of his life. He even became frolicsome and, on entering the house, clamped Dona Amância in an embrace as she came to greet them at the door. The old woman backed away, crossing herself:

"Heavens! Get on with you!"

For some time, since the previous evening, Amância had been there preparing everything, straightening things up, giving orders, scolding, threatening punishment, as if she were at her own ranch surrounded by her own slaves.

Maria Bárbara's grange, like almost all the others in Maranhão, was pleasant and rustic. An old iron gate, with the usual lamp suspended on a chain, opened onto two lengthy rows of ancient mango trees that ended in front of the house, forming a shady and cool gallery that the sun penetrated only horizontally among the thick, gnarled, and rough tree trunks. Off in several directions, without any particular symmetry or order, were planted fields, for the most part productive and well tended. Bright green stood out from the vegetable beds, which gave off a fresh smell of parsley and coriander. Toward the inner portion of the estate were massive water tanks, green with algae. Winding troughs branched out, suspended on wooden poles, carrying water in all directions. Extensive trellises sagged under the weight of squash, pumpkins, and a multitude of different passion fruits, ranging in size from that of the orange up to the melon. Even further inside, on any day of the year the dark and lustrous green of the colossal jackfruit and breadfruit trees stood out, both with their large and whimsically scalloped leaves, contrasting with the dusky masses of the petite foliage of the timeless tamarinds, the golden tones of the young plum trees, the haughty marmalade genip, the comely pitomba, and the flowery fragrance of the guava tree groves. Elsewhere the location of cold-water springs could be surmised by the heavy growth of assai palms. Thousands of species of clinging vines with their wild and beautiful blossoms decorated the trees and dovecotes, in an amazing variety of colors. And everywhere tiny birds were trilling and flitting and doves skipped about, hunting worms and insects in the grass.

The front of the house looked out onto the two rows of mango trees that were sagging downward over its verandas, completely open and fast becoming overgrown with plants from the surrounding garden. It was one of those picturesque, low-level dwellings, quite common in the rural areas of the island where São Luís is located. A large and square tile roof, without a ceiling underneath, formed a sharp point at the top. It was supported on its four sides by columns made of pikes painted green and anchored into heavy blocks of stone and lime that formed a kind of wall, high on the outside and low on the inside. In the middle, some twenty firm paces inward from the heavy blocks, was the house with its solid walls, whitewashed from top to bottom. The floor was paved with red tiles. At the entrance was a wooden half-door, three stone steps, Italian jasmin plants, wooden benches, and a jumble of creeping plants that had twisted around the columns and climbed onto the roof, victoriously shooting out their new sprouts there on top, greedy for sunlight.

This grange was the apple of Maria Bárbara's eye. There she had enjoyed great happiness during the time of the colonel. It was still quite sturdy and in excellent condition, but for ten years now, since the old woman had gone to keep her granddaughter company, it had been entrusted to the care of a Portuguese, Antônio, and to the labor of three old black men who went to the city daily to sell vegetables, flowers, and fruit.

At six-thirty in the morning the horse-drawn trolley arrived with the guests.

They brought musicians. It was a surprise arranged by Casusa, who perched on the running board of the trolley and, wild with enthusiasm, shouted, "Long live St. John! Long live the beautiful ladies of Maranhão!" as well as hurrahs to the music.

The musicians struck up the national anthem.

Casusa, completely beside himself, already hoarse and somewhat tipsy with cognac, a bottle of which he carried fastened by a tiny piece of wire slung over his shoulder, jumped about, came and went, plowing into everyone, pulling the still-seated women across the trolley benches and forcing them to get off, frightening them with his shouts, bruising the fingers of the passengers against the wooden backs of the trolley benches, provoking groans, protests, and making them laugh at the same time. He planted a kiss on Dona Amância who furiously called him a brandy drunk, maniac, and devil. He thumped the belly of Manuel who admonished him for having gone to such trouble, spending money to contract musicians.

"My pleasure, my pleasure, Manuel. Don't worry! This is going to be a hot party, with all this merrymaking!"

And the guests jumped off the trolley. The first one down was Freitas, all decked out in white drill from Hamburg that was spotless, had a row of fancy buttons, and an enormous braided chain holding his watch from a gold ring on which the word "longing" was enameled. Because of the dust he wore large blue spectacles, virtual windowpanes, which provided his imposing countenance with the picturesque tone of a rural mansion. He also had on his shaggy white felt hat, which the street urchins of the province referred to as the "sheep" and about which the owner would relate marvelous attributes. What a contraption! One could mash it at will without harming its nap, that's how good it was! It had cost twenty thousand milréis, but it was easily worth fifty! And, with his unicorn walking stick under his arm, he assisted his fat Lindoca as she with difficulty descended from the trolley. The Sarmento girls, accompanied by their aunt and by Eufrasinha with a small furry white puppy in her lap, alighted, bursting with commotion, much giggling and yelping, amid the lively colors of their hats and parasols. They flaunted more than ever their famous hair with its castellated clusters, redolent of aloe. The canon, smiling discreetly and always dapper, arrived, followed by a scrawny little priest who throughout the province was renowned for his skill at chanting litanies; he bore the nickname "Friar Lamparinas." Sebastião Campos, dressed in white like Freitas, but with a panama hat and coat, jumped down, holding a huge basket of firecrackers, Roman candles, pinwheels, and small cherry bombs.

"It's our supplies," he responded to the curious stares.

He was crazy about fireworks.

"I'm hopeless when it comes to this," he was saying, showing off the thick leather glove with which he lit the formidable firecrackers.

On Holy Saturdays he permitted himself the luxury of burning a Judas doll in front of his house. He also never missed the opportunity for fireworks during the country festivals, and he knew how to produce ladyfingers, pinwheels, and skyrockets.

Two new guests from outside the usual circle were also introduced: one brought by Manuel and the other by Casusa. The first was Joaquim Furtado da Serra, a respected merchant, a close friend of the family, as simple as an egg, which, nevertheless, had not prevented him from becoming wealthy. He understood and conversed only about business, but he liked doing good and was a member of several philanthropic societies. He led a contented life with plenty of friends and admirers, and was always laughing and talking about his three daughters. "They couldn't come to Manuel's, poor things! They stayed behind to look after a sick woman." He wanted neither honors nor grandeur and told everyone how, barefoot and with a barrel on his back, he had got his start in Brazil; and he prided himself, between chortles, on his present independence. The other guest was a boy of twenty-two who at first glance seemed sixteen. He was thin and fastidious in appearance, well combed, and very nearsighted; his fingernails were polished, he wore a high collar, and his feet were squeezed into shiny shoes. He studied at the provincial lycée, had a metal-plated watch chain, false diamonds on his shirtfront, and clasped a thin walking stick, between the index finger and forefinger of his right hand. He kept a collection of acrostics and poems that he had penned, some unpublished and others already sold to newspapers, which he regarded with great vanity as his "treasure!" His name was Boaventura Rosa dos Santos, but he was known as "Dr. Sparky," and he liked to enact and guess charades.

They entered the house like a mob, impelled by the music—a smashing polka by Colás—and by an ill-timed pinwheel that Sebastião had let loose. There was an uproar. Casusa, despite the tempestuous disorder, was making Dona Amância dance a half-dozen quick turns around the veranda. Chased by Joli, Eufrasinha's little dog, they both ended up collapsing onto a bench of paparaúba wood.

In the frenzy of the dreadful dance, Amância's topknot had flown off and come to rest in the garden. Joli sprang on it and tore it apart frantically with his teeth.

"Look, Mr. Casusa!" shouted the old lady, almost breathless, "don't you make me lose my bearings, you penny pincher! When you get on these binges, you go to the devil! Heavens! What a worthless lush! Go take your liberties with someone who doesn't give a hoot, you shameless man!"

The topknot was yanked away from Joli and returned to its owner.

"Just look! Look at the wonderful condition of my hemp topknot! It looks more like a swab for cleaning pots! Darn their foolish pranks! Instead of causing such a brawl, it'd be better if everyone minded his own business—which would be a lot of work for them!"

And turning around to Sebastião:

"But you're the culprit, Mr. Sebastião. You're the one I'm going to take care of. I just can't lose my new topknot!"

"What do you mean, *new?*" contradicted Casusa. "I saw a spider jump from it."

"It's new, and I want another one right here and now!"

"Come now, my friends, let's forget about this," intervened Manuel, "and have some coffee, it's getting cold."

"And my topknot? We can't just let it go at that!"

"You shall have another, don't worry."

No sooner had they served coffee with cream and tapioca cakes with butter, than a group was formed in which Casusa was paired off with Eufrasinha to perform a step he called "paint the priest." Those words strongly offended the specialist in litanies, who launched censorious glares at him over the top of his glasses.

This Friar Lamparinas was an ugly, tight-lipped little man, a native of the interior city of Caxias.[1] He had never been fully ordained because of his extreme stupidity. He still had to spell out the litanies he had been chanting for twenty years; he had never even begun his study of Latin. The young boys at the lycée used to tease him and would throw green lemons at him over the wall of the Carmo monastery whenever the unhappy soul passed by on the other side. He could tell an amusing life story, full of nonsense, and everyone said he was good-hearted and would harm no one.

"The folk song, bring on the folk song!" they shouted from the rear of the veranda, clapping their hands.

And the little musical group, with no further coaxing, moaned out a languid and sensual Brazilian dance tune.

Suddenly Casusa and Sebastião jumped into the middle of the room and began nimbly and noisily to stomp, snap their fingers, and suggestively move their entire bodies. They soon dragged out Serra, Sparky, and Freitas. The girls, beckoned for, joined in the irresistible merrymaking. They spun about on the tips of their shoes, their steps tiny and light, their arms folded and heads tilted, first to one side then the other, clicking their tongues on the roof of their mouths with an original and charming sensuality.

The older folk stood gaping.

"Shake a leg!" Casusa was shouting enthusiastically. "Shake a leg, my dear!"

And he vigorously moved his feet.

The folk song had finally reached its phase of greatest intensity. Those unable to dance watched, keeping time to the music with rhythmic and spontaneous clapping and body movements.

"Bravo! That's the way, Casusa!"

"Hop, hop!"

Suddenly there was a heavy crash and a shout: it was Sparky who had been tripped up by Casusa and had fallen at the feet of Maria do Carmo. Everyone laughed.

"Heavens!" cried out the old lady. "Wasn't that man trying to grab my leg? Goodness, the scamp!"

"Don't exaggerate, my dear lady, it was the ankle, that little bone in the foot!"

"But I'm very ticklish, and, other than the deceased Espigão no one else has ever touched my body!"

A little later they were called to lunch, and the merrymaking continued without interruption.

On St. John's day Manuel's warehouse was always closed. This year the eve had fallen on a Sunday. "Two complete days," as Vila-Rica said, satisfied.

Since the night before, Benedito and a black girl had been going back and forth to the grange, loaded down with fireworks as well as with the ornaments necessary to set up an altar. That morning Brígida went out, accompanied by Mônica. Dona Amância was there to take charge of everything. All the firm's employees were to go also; consequently, there was no need for any slave to remain at the house in the city.

The clerks' quarters by then had taken on the usual Sunday appearance. There were freshly polished boots on top of trunks, cashmere clothing carefully draped over chairbacks, starched shirts lying here and there awaiting use, and the keen smell of handkerchief perfumes. The young clerks were dressing. At the latest, it was eight o'clock in the morning.

Despite the festive appearance of his colleagues, Dias remained in his underclothing, sweeping the floor.

"Aren't you going to get ready, Dias?" asked Cordeiro, busy slipping on a pair of beige trousers. "Aren't you coming with us to the country?"

"Go on ahead, I'll soon be on my way."

Exchanging no further words, the three left, and Dias, resting his chin on the broom handle, stood lost in thought. As soon as he heard the click of the street door latch downstairs he tossed the broom into a corner and cautiously descended to the veranda.

The house exhaled the nostalgic tranquility of a deserted place. Only the thrush warbled in its cage.

Manuel's trusted clerk closed and locked the heavy polished wooden door that separated the veranda from the hallway, and, after glancing about, headed toward Raimundo's room to sniff out, not even he knew precisely what. He set about scrutinizing what was in the room, not with the tender curiosity of the amateur snoop, but coldly and calculatingly, with the prudence of one who realizes he is committing a vile deed. He opened drawers, read the manuscripts he encountered, searched through the pockets of clothes on hangers, leafed through books, examining everything and burrowing into every little corner. In one of the suitcases he found a green-covered pamphlet and stashed it in his pocket after reading the title page. And, finally, when there was nothing else to check out, he sneaked away, leaving not the slightest indication of what he had done. From there he headed to Ana Rosa's quarters, but immediately encountered a setback: the door was locked. He rummaged for the key on the veranda, then in the corners, and, not finding it, went hurriedly up to the next floor from where he returned with a piece of wax to mold into the keyhole. Next, he scurried to Maria

Bárbara's room and tried the door; it too was locked. But there was a transom, and Dias squeezed through it and managed to enter the room.

The old woman's quarters corresponded to her character. On top of an ancient chest of drawers made of holywood, with metal knobs and covered by a dusty and tattered oil cloth, perched a wooden oratory, whimsically constructed and filled with an extremely varied collection of saints. Among them were some made of cajá skin, plaster, red clay, and porcelain. The specially ordered St. Anthony of Lisbon with the Christ child in his lap was present, quite ruddy and gleaming; a St. Anne, teaching her daughter to read; a St. Joseph in crude colors, execrably painted, a St. Benedict dressed as a priest, very black with reddish lips and glass eyes; a St. Peter, whose size made him look like a child next to the others; some trifling lesser saints, tiny and grotesque, which one could not look at without laughing, concealed among the pedestals of the larger ones, and, finally, a huge St. Raimundo Nonato, totally bald, bearded, ugly, and with a chalice in his right hand. At the rear of the oratory shoddy lithographs portrayed St. Philomena, the flight of St. Joseph with his family, Christ on the cross, and other religious subjects. From the group of saints was missing St. John the Baptist, who had deserted them for the villa. On the dresser there were still two brass candlesticks, decorated with lace-trimmed papers and half-spent wax candles. A group of porcelain figurines depicted Our Lady of Sorrows and the Christ child, sealed in a glass tube because of the flies. Leaning against the wall was a holy pindova palm branch, which, according to popular sayings, possessed the virtuous quality of pacifying the elements on stormy days. Two other garish palm branches, adorned with cloth and bits of mica, decorated the sides of the oratory. In every direction there were also framed illustrations and poorly produced colored lithographs with which the clever printing houses of the province exploited the sanctimoniousness of the old women: one of Mount Serrat, one of the divine birth, one of the Virgin, and others.

On the wall, contrasting with all of this, there hung a formidable ferule for beatings: It was black, frightening, and quite shiny from use.

In front of the oratory were two frames with glass, each of which exposed a cross-stitched canvas teeming with samples of the diverse woolen embroideries that young girls learn in school: "tapestry cloth," as they say in Maranhão. In the center of one were the initials "M. R. S." and "Trinity School—1838," and on the other, which was in better condition, "A. R. S. S." and a far more recent date. Judging by the initials, the two works had been embroidered by Mariana and Ana Rosa, mother and daughter. All of this was minutely taken in by Dias. He read a specially printed prayer to Our Lady, probed through Maria Bárbara's clothing, put his tongue to the tip of the roll of special tobacco with which she "mulled over past vexations," and, afterward, when there was nothing else to scrutinize, he began to reflect, thinking about what he should do. Finally he was struck by an idea, which gave him a contented smile; he immediately lit one of the thick wax candles, picked up the statue of St. Raimundo by its legs, and scorched the head and bald spot with the wick. After the operation the poor saint looked like a coal miner; he had become as black as the odd-looking St. Benedict, his companion on the oratory.

Dias contemplated his labors and laughed, calculating the wondrous effect it would produce, and then put the statue back in its place, and left hurriedly, thinking he had heard a noise at the street door. He was mistaken.

Half an hour later, dressed totally in black, as was his usual custom, Manuel Pescada's highly trusted clerk took the trolley to Cutim, heading for the country house of his employer's mother-in-law.

8

It was five o'clock in the afternoon.

Maria Bárbara's celebration continued on its lively way; everyone was in good spirits. The men had been sipping small glasses of cognac throughout the day and now puffed smoke from their hefty cigars with the imposing air of important persons. The ladies had daintily sweetened their lips with a liqueur of roses and peppermint. They had danced a great deal. They played at parish priest, catch the ring, and tug of war. Finally, everyone went outside to savor the afternoon, seated on the benches in front of the house. The gathering was augmented by Manuel's four clerks and a rustic backlander who entertained them with his ballads. Lamparinas had gone nearby to the villa of an acquaintance but had promised not to miss the litany.

The sun had taken refuge. The beautiful afternoon, with its crimson sunset, reddened the men's perspiring faces as well as the wrinkled dresses of the women who went off for fresher air under the trellises of passionflowers and Italian jasmine. The matrons, comfortably seated, made little mannered gestures, subtle movements filled with social significance, repressed laughter, glances from beneath lowered eyelids. Each held a fan to her lips and her little finger elegantly raised.

The group's hearty appetite for dinner prevailed; some stomachs growled indiscreetly. But all the gazes and attention converged, so it appeared, on the backlander, who, standing by himself at a certain distance, held up his head with a rustic aggressiveness, his leather hat cocked backward and tied at his neck with a strap. His crude cotton shirt hung out of denim trousers rolled up to his knees, his feet were bare and flattened like a hiker's, his chest smooth and cedar colored, his bare arms hairless. He was enthusiastically plucking the metallic strings of a small folk guitar and, with an original style of strumming, was accompanying the verses he improvised as well as others he knew by heart:

"Toward the backlands the heron flies
Moving swiftly, straight as a dart!

Holding Maria in his beak,
Carrying Teresa in his heart."

At the end of each stanza a chorus of laughter would burst forth, during which everyone would hear the stomping of the backlander, beating the ground in a dance.

"Everyone's scared of wildcats,
But they don't frighten me!
I'm not scared of you,
But Micaela, where is she?"

And the country fellow, after his dance, sang to Ana Rosa:

"Tell me, my lady:
(I ask, and I want to know),
If I leave here now
Where am I to go?"

"That was a sentimental one," reflected Etelvina with a gesture of approval.

"I enjoyed it, I did," Freitas affirmed in a patronizing tone.

And the backlander fastened his gaze on Ana Rosa:

"Missy, if I asked you . . .
But don't you laugh at me. . . .
For a flower from your hair,
What would your answer be?"

"Bravo!"

"Yes, sir!"

There was a merry ripple.

"Dona Anica, give him the flower!"

Ana Rosa hesitated.

"How about it, child?" Manuel admonished in a soft tone.

Ana Rosa removed a jessamine from her hair and passed it to the minstrel, who immediately put into verse:

"God bless you, my fair lady,
Your charms are wondrous great;
But never I'll deserve them,
In my poor wretched state."

And placing the flower behind his ear, he continued, after staring directly at Raimundo:

"Oh, my lady sorceress,
You have me in your power!
But don't let jealous passions rage,
For the sake of a mere flower."

Then he removed his hat and extended it to them one by one.
They dug into their pockets, dropping in pennies and little silver coins. The troubadour, his head uplifted with an air of expectation, sang:

"Keep those pennies coming,
Each of you give me at least one;
I take money from the men folk,
But from women I'll accept none!"

And, when he got to Manuel:

"Little Manuel, red carnation,
I'm impertinent, I know;
If you can pay, I'll take it,
If not, away I go."

Between bursts of laughter they filled his hat with coins. When Sparky's turn came, instead of money he tossed in his cigarette butt. The backlander, as usual, scorned the prank and shouted angrily:

"Mr. Lancer from Bahia,
Pretty top coat from Pará!
The kick I receive is as hard,
As the size of the beast in the yard."

The laughter increased, and Sparky became furious, even threatening the backlander, who sneered at him with an air of mockery.
"I'll throw something yet in that devil's face," the student muttered, livid.
"Let's stop this," he was admonished, "you ought to know those people are like that, why get mixed up in that?"
"Here, take this," Manuel said to the backlander, "have a drink and be on your way out of here."
And Manuel passed him a glass of wine which he gulped down. After clicking his tongue, he sang out:

"Wine is the blood of Christ,
And also Satan's soul;

It's blood when you take a few drops,
It's the devil when you drain the bowl!"

And, saluting them with his hat:

"Ladies and gentlemen,
I'll be on my way;
God grant you long life,
And many a happy day!"

And, turning his back on them, off he went, dancing and singing a passage from "Bumba Meu Boi":[1]

"Please, not that, it just can't be,
Oh no, not that, it just can't be,
My master's daughter, wed to you, not me!
The backlander has done me in,
 Oh, my love!
It was such a sure thing,
 Oh, my heart!
Now we must part. . . ."

And in the deep shadows of the mangroves, the backlander's voice and the sound of the guitar faded away.

They were discussing his style and poetic talent when, from the house, Manuel, Maria Bárbara, and Amância, all three at once, called them to the table with kindly authority.

A murmur of pleasure spread through the group.

"Look here, child, my stomach was already telling me it was time," whispered Dona Maria do Carmo, passing by Ana Rosa.

They all went up to the veranda and proceeded quickly to take their places at the table amid a jumble of voices discussing a thousand topics.

"Man!" exclaimed Sebastião Campos, "it seems they've taken on new life just with the smell!"

Freitas pestered Raimundo about popular poetry and spoke in wonder about Juvenal Galeno.[2]

"Very original, very original."

"He's from Ceará, isn't he?"

"He sure is! Ah, you just can't imagine what a place that province is for popular ballads!"

And before Raimundo could take any measures against the bore, Freitas was already reciting into his ear:

"When you pass by on the street,
Cough and spit, so I can hear.
As I sew by the light of my lamp,
I can't tell if you're far or near!"

"Well, there's nothing like a party out in the country," Sebastião was saying at the other side of the table, "it's either a real lark or it's nothing."

But Freitas persisted:

"Missy, give me any old thing,
A banana, any piece of fruit.
My belly takes whatever he's given,
He's such a crude and stupid brute!"

Raimundo was no longer listening to him; he was paying attention to a conversation among Bibina, Lindoca, and Eufrasinha.

"Did any of you draw lucky lots tonight?" Eufrasinha asked.

"Of course," the fat girl said, "however, I didn't see anything, or at least I couldn't make out whatever appeared."

"Well, not I," the widow stated. "I drew a very attractive lot."

"What was it, what was it?"

"A white veil and a bridal wreath!"

"Marriage!" several voices shouted out.

"I drew a tomb," said Bibina from the corner of the table, sighing lugubriously.

"Goodness!" exclaimed Amância, passing around a watercress salad, which she had just finished preparing.

Raimundo, seated against his will at Freitas's side, spoke nostalgically of Portuguese customs on the eves of St. John and St. Peter; he related how young girls burned artichokes and put them in vases by the window so that they could see their fortunes sprout along with the plant. He cited the custom of placing beans on top of their pillows, and quietly holding water in their mouths at midnight to try to hear the name of any future sweetheart. He also mentioned the bonfires of dry thistle and, finally, that custom of glasses of water about which the girls were chatting.

"An old custom," Freitas explained, chewing some pieces of bread. "It consists of leaving out in the night air, on St. John's Eve, a glass of water with an egg yolk in it."

"And the egg white, too," protested Dona Maria do Carmo, who was following the conversation with great interest.

"Well, have it your way . . . the yolk and the white. And they say that on the following day, early in the morning, the fate of the individual will be represented inside the glass. All nonsense!"

"It's not nonsense!" the old lady retorted, sitting down with her nieces. "Here's someone who received the news of Espigão's death long before the fatal day!"

And she drew her napkin to her eyes in a pathetic gesture.

"There are other customs," Freitas continued, passing a bowl of soup. "The St. John bath, for example."

"Imitations of Portugal. . . ."

"Whoever doesn't bathe tomorrow at dawn, will have a foul soul! That's what they say."

"Well now, Mr. Cordeiro, Mr. Dias, and you there, boy, why don't you all find a place to sit?" Manuel urged.

"We were waiting for the other table," Dias responded shyly. "There aren't any more places. . . ."

"What do you mean, the other table! No, sir, sit down right here, Mr. Dias."

And the merchant made space for him at his daughter's side.

Luís Dias, all flustered, went and sat down, smiling, next to Ana Rosa who made an immediate gesture of annoyance and repugnance.

"And you, gentlemen? Mr. Cordeiro, Mr. Vila-Rica, and that young man! Come over here!"

"We'll wait. . . .They'll set another table later."

"And you'll wait? No, you don't. And you, my dear mother-in-law? Dona Amância! Where shall we put them?"

"There's a place here, ma'am," Raimundo said, getting up and offering her his chair.

"My friend," Manuel cut in, "none of that now. Remember, we're out in the country now. This isn't the city where one stands on ceremony!"

"It's not a party in the country unless something's missing," Serra ventured, stirring and then blowing on a spoonful of soup.

"No, no," Freitas contradicted. "I want my comfort, even in hell!"

"Well now, everything is arranged!" shouted Amância who had finished setting up another table. "We'll sit here. We're few in number, but worthy!"

"And those over there?" questioned Vila-Rica, counting the people at the large table in the following order starting with the head of the table: "The boss, one, the canon, two, Dona Maria do Carmo, three, the nieces, five, Dr. Raimundo, six, Freitas and his daughter, eight, Dona Eufrasinha, nine, Mr. Serra and that young man"—this

was Sparky—"eleven, Dias and Dona Anica, thirteen altogether!"
"Thirteen?!" Dona Maria do Carmo bellowed, spitting out some of the noodles in her mouth. "Thirteen!"
"Thirteen!" all the ladies repeated, frightened.
"Someone must leave!" they demanded.
Not a soul stirred.
"Or someone else must sit down," reminded the canon, putting down his spoon. "We can't just leave it at thirteen."
The dinner came to a halt.
Freitas immediately started to explain to Raimundo what that meant, even though the latter had at once stated that he understood perfectly well.
"Isn't there anyone else around here?"
Maria Bárbara got up and went inside to get a little three-year-old black girl.
"Here we are!"
"That's right—and Casusa!"
"That's right everyone, Mr. Casusa!"
"Let Casusa come out!"
Casusa was sleeping. He had taken a bath and gone to bed tired. The little girl was again taken back to the kitchen.
"Hey, black boy, go to Mr. Casusa's room and call him!"
Casusa appeared, yawning and stretching his arms.
"Why have dinner so early? I'm not at all hungry," he muttered, opening his mouth.
"Early! It seems early to you, but it's already past five o'clock!"
"You were almost left in the lurch," added Sebastião, laughing.
"But that wouldn't have been a loss!" scorned Amância, with a scowl of disdain.
"If you want to quarrel with me, my dear, go ahead. You'll be sorry! . . . But at any rate, where do I sit? I don't see a place. Ah!" he exclaimed, turning around toward the small table: "I have one right here and with good company!"
"Get over there, then," countered Amância, offended.
"Come on over here, my good fellow! You're needed here."
And with some difficulty a chair was arranged at Sebastião's side.
"Well, finally," said Manuel, sitting down slowly.
"Tollitur quaestio!"
And the canon sipped a large spoonful of soup.
There was silence for an instant; the only thing that could be heard was the scraping of spoons on the bottom of soup bowls and the smacking lips of those who slurped their noodles.
Cordeiro showered Amância and Maria Bárbara with attention,

delicately attempting to accentuate this by using the diminutive forms:

"A tiny thigh of chicken, my dear little Dona Amância?"

"He's a perfect gentleman," she whispered to Maria Bárbara. "Just compare him with that pest Casusa!"

"No, it's that the young fellows from Portugal are all gentlemen, that's for sure."

"They have a sedate manner those here haven't got."

"Could you pass me the dish of olives, Mr. Serra? If you please."

"Do you want more manioc, Dona Lindoca?

"Yes, much obliged. That's enough, just a tiny bit."

"Goodness, do you use that much pepper, Dona Etelvina?"

"That's enough, oh! I don't want to drown in broth!"

"Could you please give me more elbow room, my friend?"

"Don't stuff your mouth like that," whispered the old Sarmento lady to one of the nieces. "That was Espigão's problem: he would eat like a horse, but no one thought anything of it then."

"Just look, you're dropping grease on me, Mr. Casusa! What a devil of a fellow!"

"Well, who's going to mix the salad?"

"The salad," judiciously proclaimed Freitas with a smile, "should be mixed by a wild person."

"Well then, take charge, Casusa!"

"How much does the little guy want for that joke? If I had a penny, I'd pay you, 'Mr. Poet'!"

That spat was between Casusa and Sparky.

"Doctor, don't let the lantern go out," Manuel warned Raimundo.

"A slice of pork, please, Dona Maria Bárbara."

"A bit less, my dear. That's it exactly!"

"Dona Etelvina, you're thin from not eating."

"Ah!" she sighed, staring at the silverware crossed on her plate.

"Hey, Sebastião, don't you want some rice?"

"No, I'll stick with the manioc meal."

"A toast!" shouted Casusa, getting up and holding the glass as high as his head. "To the beautiful womanhood of Maranhão that honors us today!"

"Hip-hip, hurrah!"

"Ladies and gentlemen, allow me to thank you for the kindness offered to my mother-in-law and to me by your presence at our traditional family gathering."

Manuel was speaking. A torrent of exclamations and hurrahs followed, which turned into frightful shouting. The merchant's clerks, already somewhat excited by the wine, yelled in a friendly manner: "Long live Manuel!"

One indiscreet voice shouted, "Manuel Pescada!"

But order was soon reestablished, and, except for the noise of silverware and chewing, all that was heard was the tipsy voice of Cordeiro who shouted to his neighbor on the right with an exaggerated solicitude:

"Drink up! Drink up, my dear little Dona Amância! Drink it all the way down, it's the best thing in life!"

And he whacked her on the shoulder, rolling his eyes in which the alcohol flashed.

"Gracious, do you want to get me drunk?"

And since Cordeiro insisted on serving Lisbon wine to her, Amância pulled her cup away and it spilled out over her plate, the table, and her legs.

"Ooooops!" she went, leaping up suddenly from the chair and crying: "What savagery, Holy Mary!"

"Manioc, dry manioc, Dona Amância! Dry manioc!" chanted everyone from all sides.

Cordeiro promptly picked up the manioc flour bowl and emptied it smack onto the poor old lady, who, choking, began to cough. There was a general and prolonged burst of laughter.

"Good heavens! God help me! The devil!" shrieked Amância, all covered with flour, when she was finally able to talk, shaking herself thoroughly. "Darn! I'll not sit here anymore!"

"Come over here next to me, my lost soul!" said Casusa, inviting Amância amid the smiles of the entire table.

"If flour is the antidote for wine, you're now cured," advised Raimundo, jokingly.

"Even you?!" screamed Amância, blind with rage. "Just look at yourself! Do you want a mirror?"

"I would prefer a brush, my lady, to clean off your clothing."

The guffaws again resounded without pause, contagiously. Nothing more was needed to provoke them.

"Spilled wine, a sign of happy times," affirmed Freitas, busily picking the meat off a chicken leg without soiling his moustache.

Dessert was served and a new round of drinks brought out: port wine in cups.

"To your health!" yelled Cordeiro, scarcely able to stand up.

Suddenly there was a silence, during which these phrases were overheard:

"It's sure bad! We have a real drunken spree here!"

"Young men are so weak!"

"That brute insists on drinking! Out of pure spite!"

"The devil of a man can't be trusted anywhere!"

"This is going to turn out bad!"

"Shhhh . . . shhhh. . . ."

"Ladies and gentlemen—of both sexes! I'm going to drink to the health of the best . . . yes, the best, why not? Of the best boss we've ever had, the one looking at me: Manuel Pescada!"

There was a murmur of reproof.

"I mean Manuel da Silva!" corrected the speaker. "He's a steady fellow! He's first-rate, yes sir! For any task . . . I mean, when one needs him, you can speak up and he listens. But . . ."

The whispers increased.

"Shut up!" Vila-Rica said softly, tugging on Cordeiro's coat. "Shut up, you idiot! You're acting like a fool!"

"But!" shouted the blabberer, heedless of his colleague's admonitions, "What I can't stand is the great number of nasty tricks and insults he constantly plagues me with. . . ."

The murmur was transformed into a chorus of protests that drowned out the orator's shouts. The young girls tossed little balls of bread at him. Manuelzinho, very red-faced, grew oddly gleeful. Vila-Rica yanked on Cordeiro's coat with both hands.

"Let go of me!" Cordeiro snorted. "Let go of me, you devil, or I'll punch your face! Mind your own business and leave me alone! I want to get it off my chest! Damn! I won't shut up, I don't want to! I won't!"

"Yes," he continued in a calmer tone, "I won't put up with his insults. Why, just the other day. . . ."

"Long live Manuel!" someone shouted.

"Long live!" answered everyone in a chorus.

"To your health, Mr. Manuel!"

"To you!"

"Hip-hip, hurrah!"

"Hurrah!" yelled Cordeiro and smashed his glass on the table. "It's time to smash things!"

"Only if it's your head, you big drunkard," muttered Serra, very much annoyed.

"Attention! Attention please, everyone!"

It was the voice of Sparky, accompanied by hand claps.

"Attention!"

And he pulled a piece of paper from his pocket.

There was something of a silence and Sparky, after adjusting his cuffs, began to speak in his flutelike voice, full of affectation and with the minute mimicry of myopic persons; his tiny twitching head was cocked, his eyes bulged, straining to see as far as the lenses in his spectacles; his mouth was opened wide and his nostrils were dilated.

"My friends, on a day such as this, I could not fail to create . . . some poetry!"

"It's a poem, a poem," declared Bibina, clapping her hands happily.

"Yes, I believe you're right, it's a real poem in verse!"

"And because of that," continued Sparky, pressing upward his spectacles, which perspiration had made slide down, "resorting to the muses, I venture to raise my weak voice to offer to Manuel, a worthy man of commerce established in our city, as a token of esteem and consideration, this humble sonnet, which, if it's outstanding. . . . Yes, if it's not outstanding. . . ."

"Make it outstanding!" yelled Cordeiro.

Sparky, all flustered, was searching for a word.

"Bring on the verses!"

"Where's the poetry?!" they demanded.

" 'Son of Camões's ancient land,' " Sparky began to recite, wavering.

" 'Son of Camões's ancient land,' " Cordeiro repeated, aping his voice.

"Sir, can't you be quiet?" reprimanded Manuel.

The performer carried on:

> "Son of Camões's ancient land,
> And our brother in heart and company . . ."

"Heart and Company?" pondered Serra in his serious manner, meditating. "Say, that firm's name sounds familiar to me. Wait now, might it be J. Heart & Company from the state of Piauí?"

Sparky continued, quite nervous:

> "Let me salute you on this venerable day,
> When real friends sit in harmony!"

"Bravo! Bravo!"

"Notice everyone, he rhymed it!"

"Shhhhh . . . shhhhh!"

"Recite another, Sparky?"

"Recite another verse!"

"Make one up about rapture," suggested Etelvina with a sigh.

"Quiet!"

But the poet couldn't continue because, in one of his flustered gestures, his pince-nez had dropped into a compotier filled with sweet syrup.

"A toast," requested Casusa. "A toast!"

"Quiet!"

"Hold it there!"

"Order!"

"Ne quid nimis!"

And after those words the voice of Maria Bárbara was heard, commenting to Dona Maria do Carmo:

"My dear, have a little chunk of melon."

She passed her the plate.

"Ah, my dear, I don't know if I can even begin to eat it," Espigão's widow lamented sadly, recalling the protest she had made against cucumbers and related vegetables. "Doctor," she inquired of Raimundo, "could melon be of the same family as cucumbers?"

"Yes ma'am, both belong to the cucurbitaceae family."

"What?" asked the old lady, her mouth full of rice pudding.

"He means," explained Freitas immediately, glowing at the opportunity to show off his knowledge, "that it's a cucurbitaceaen, of the important dicotyledon family, according to Jussieu, or of the calicifloras, according to De Candole."

"I'll stick with the so-called califorchon family."

"What family? What family? What did they do? Some scandal, I'll bet," sniffed Amância, excitedly believing that she detected a hint of intrigue. "I've said it before: there's just no one you can trust nowadays! But just who are those cursed people? What family is it?"

"That of the cucurbitaceaens."

"Ah, they're foreigners! . . . I've got it, I know who you mean! It's that family of beefeaters living in the Boavista Hotel! That's right, now I remember, just the other day a red-haired young thing . . . she must be the wife or daughter of the fellow . . . just what's his name?"

"Who, Dona Amância? You're making a muddle of everything!"

"That English guy!"

"What English guy? No one here spoke about Englishmen, or even Frenchmen."

And Maria do Carmo tried to explain to her friend that they were talking about cucumbers and melons.

Casusa continued to hold forth with a toast to Serra (he had designs on one of Serra's daughters); he had already referred to him as a genius and was now comparing him to a lily bravely growing along the road. The good man listened to him, smiling, but not understanding, while Raimundo, his head almost in his plate, was enduring Freitas and pining for the end of the meal so that he might escape him. The bore, with his customary vanity, was praising his own memory:

"You haven't seen anything yet," he confided to Raimundo. "I know entire discourses, lengthy ones I first heard ten years ago. I know by heart, my dear doctor, extensive poetry that I've read only twice. Don't you think it extraordinary?"

"Certainly. . . ."

And as proof the unfeeling man started off reciting the poem "The Jewess," by Tomás Ribeiro,[3] which at that time in Maranhão had the lively fragrance of novelty:

> "The night flowed softly, the Tagus was serene. . . ."

"Louder!" demanded Cordeiro at the small table. "It doesn't reach us over here! We want to hear the recital!"

And since Raimundo had finally succeeded in shutting Freitas up, Cordeiro jumped to his feet precipitously and began to mutilate a coarse ditty:

> "Carolina, what time is it now?
> Nine in the morning by the clock tower. . . ."

"Why don't you sing the song 'I Don't Want Anyone to Catch Me?' " advised Eufrasinha with a loud laugh.

"Goodness!" chorused the other girls, shocked at the widow's lack of restraint.

Cordeiro obeyed, and, clambering up on a chair, grabbed the neck of a bottle, held it aloft, and blattered out what at that time was the drunkard's song in the province:

> "Get your hands off me,
> Wahoo!
> When I'm on a spree!
> If you go out at night,
> Wahoo!
> Carry a bottle, that's right!
>
> Mr. Cop, get your hands off me,
> Don't cart me off to a cell!
> I came to fetch my woman,
> Not to raise any hell!
> Wahoo!

When I'm on a spree!
If you go out at night,
  Wahoo!
Carry a bottle, that's right!"

Little by little, they all, with the exception of Dias, began yelling the frightful "Wahoo!" and, along even with some of the women, struck their knives against their plates. In no time it turned into an uproar in which not a word could be understood.

Finally, the confusion reached a climax. Toasts were made with arms intertwined; glasses were shared; different wines were mixed together; noisy guffaws broke out; projectiles of wadded bread flew about; glasses were smashed, and, amid all that turmoil, Casusa's hoarse voice stood out, insisting on his toast to Serra whom he now referred to with a shout as "The Poet of Commerce! The Colossus of Business!"

The ladies had already left their places and were sticking toothpicks into their teeth, propped up in their respective chairs and sluggish from their stuffed stomachs. Night was falling. Maria Bárbara went off to see to the lighting of the lamps. A voice was heard discussing grammar with Sparky; Cordeiro, who had finally quieted down, had collapsed, prostrate, in his chair with his legs extended out onto the one Amância had vacated. Meanwhile, Freitas, still erect and with not a single wrinkle in his starched linen suit, begged their indulgence as he offered a modest toast.

He wiped the surface of his lips with his folded napkin, which he then rested deliberately on top of the table; he ran the long nail of his little finger through his lackluster moustache, and fixing his gaze on a compotier of banana sweets, his right hand held up in the pose of someone about to take snuff, declaimed with emphasis:

"Illustrious gentlemen and most highly respected ladies!"

There was a pause.

"We would not, perchance, be able to terminate satisfactorily this family party, as small as it is perennial and traditional, without toasting a person who is quite respectable and worthy of our total . . . respect! Because of that . . . I! I, ladies and gentlemen, the most insignificant, the most inadequate among us all! . . ."

"Not so! Not so!"

"Just so!" said Cordeiro, his eyes glassy.

"Yes, I whose voice has yet to be honeyed by the sacred talent of eloquence! I, lacking the divine words of Cicero, Demosthenes,

Mirabeau, and José So and So, et cetera, et cetera! I, ladies and gentlemen, propose a toast . . . to whom?"

And he unfurled an endless repertoire of mysterious formulae suitable to the situation, finally exclaiming with a torrent of hisses:

"It is unnecessary to mention the name!"

They all queried one another, asking for whom the toast might be intended. Arguments broke out; bets were made.

"It's more than pointless to mention the name," the orator continued, savoring the effect of his impenetrable allusion, "it's more than pointless to mention the name, for you all know quite well that I'm speaking about that excellent lady, Dona . . ."—another pause—"Maria Bárbara Mendonça de Melo!"

There was a hubbub of exclamations.

"Dona Maria Bárbara! Dona Maria Bárbara!" shouted many voices.

And everyone turned around toward the rear of the house where she was last seen.

"Mother-in-law, dear!"

"Mother-in-law!"

"Dona Babu!"

"Dona Maria Bárbara!"

Finally she appeared, carrying a lighted lantern in her hand.

"Here I am, here I am!"

And, all smiles, she placed the lantern on the table and drank from the first glass they handed her.

A hearty "Hip-hip! Hurrah!" followed, and the band launched into the Brazilian anthem.

"Our hymn," Freitas mumbled secretively to Raimundo, tapping him on the shoulder. "One of the most beautiful I know."

"Darn! The devil!" Dias sputtered, getting pallid and lifting his hands to his head.

"What is it? What is it?"

Everyone turned around to him.

"Nothing, nothing," he pretended, not parting his lips again.

For just then, at the sight of the lantern, he had remembered leaving the candle burning in Maria Bárbara's room.

Coffee was served and liqueurs brought in: cognac and backland sugarcane brandy.

Dias grew ever more worried. "Oh, darn, to forget to blow out that cursed candle! What the devil! A fire could break out and everything would go up in smoke!"

Sebastião Campos disappeared with Casusa, carrying his basket of fireworks. Everyone else, more or less aroused by the libations, went over to the ledge of the veranda. Night had now closed in completely; fireflies could already be seen, dancing in the shadows of the garden. Another table was set, for the musicians, who were still playing. Cordeiro, hardly able to stand up, tapped out a popular tune to the sound of the national anthem. Serra, rubbing his impressive belly, was challenged by fat Lindoca, and they both danced. Serra got Manuel out on the floor, and, with their boss in the lead, Vila-Rica and Manuelzinho both stepped out to dance, disregarding the rigorous commercial etiquette. Sparky, who was weak-headed and queasy of stomach, on the verge of ostentatiously bursting into tears, complained about his anxiety and cold sweat; he claimed to feel a tremendous disappointment with life, a steadfast resolve to commit suicide, and a stupid desire to vomit.

Just then a firecracker, tracing spirals of shooting sparks, landed along the edge of the veranda right next to Amância.

"Goodness!"

An explosion sounded. The old lady jumped backward, coughing and choking, and Cordeiro guaranteed that just as Amância was about to take a breath, she had swallowed a live firecracker. Ana Rosa, frightened, scurried to the opposite side of the veranda where the light did not reach, and fell trembling into Raimundo's arms. He, in violation of all his training as a serious young man, planted two expert kisses on her lips.

The firecrackers continued exploding without interruption. All the lanterns were finally lit, and wax candles illuminated the rear of the left side of the veranda, the colorful altar where, in the midst of an effulgence of lights and golden paper flowers, stood St. John the Baptist, resplendent with a tiny lamb in his arms, brandishing a silver shepherd's staff.

Everything had become bright and cheerful. The musicians went off to dine and Manuel distributed fireworks among the guests. The younger girls were burning Roman candles and the men pinwheels, skyrockets, and tiny bombs. In front of the house a large bonfire of small kegs of black pitch arose, and then others, and the veranda, in the midst of all those tiny explosions, aglow with the red flashes, spewed forth bright and multicolored missiles and seemed like a war-ravaged bastion.

Dias, removed from all this, paced back and forth, absorbed in his worries. Those long, white Roman candles irritated him especially, because they looked like wax candles.

After their dinner the group of musicians left, playing a merry tune.

"Mr. Freitas," said Bibina, "light this pinwheel for me!"

"Ooooh!" cried out Eufrasinha at just that moment, attempting to ignite a Roman candle. "I'm afraid this will singe me!"

"Hold it with a handkerchief," the Sarmentos' aunt advised.

"My dear young man, light this for me, please."

Sebastião and Casusa continued downstairs, busy with the fireworks, which flew wildly through the air.

Raimundo, at Ana Rosa's side, with the end of his cigar lit the fireworks she held and spoke to her softly about marriage.

"At the first opportunity I'll talk to your father."

"Why don't you speak with him tomorrow? My mother's hand was asked for precisely on St. John's day."

"All right, then, tomorrow."

"You won't fail me?"

"I won't. And you, tell me, do you really care for me? Remember, marriage is a very serious thing."

"I adore you, my love."

"The priest is here!" shouted Sebastião from downstairs.

"The priest has arrived! The priest has arrived!" repeated a chorus of voices.

Friar Lamparinas was in fact coming in to chant the litany. He was accompanied by four ragged-looking fellows. Their faces were reddened from sugarcane brandy, their hair was as long as that of biblical characters. They wore poorly cut jackets and weary glances; and altogether conveyed insomnia and the reserved gestures of people who don't know their host personally. They were contracted musicians, carousers who were accustomed to late-night serenades and shindigs of all types. Their stomachs, subjected to handouts at odd hours, had rebelled by causing bilious splotches on their cheeks. One was carrying a guitar under his arm, another a flute, another a cornet, and the last one a fiddle. They entered like a flock of sheep, their footsteps muffled, and went over to sit down on the veranda railing, smiling humbly, whispering to each other, and gazing with gastric sorrow at the leftovers on the table.

Only Casusa, who had followed them up from downstairs, greeted them individually, calling each by name and in turn being addressed by them with the familiar "thou" form. He immediately ordered a bottle brought and served them in a friendly manner, laughing and reminding them of their other sprees together. Manuel came over, too, offering them food and urging it especially on Friar Lamparinas, who himself confessed that he had not yet dined. They all refused but promised to dine after the litany. Then they would be able to eat more at their ease.

"Well then, let's get on with the litany!"

And everyone got ready for the new party about to begin. Sebastião Campos remained in the garden, throwing around his firecrackers and formidable little bombs, which roared like cannons. Ah! He would allow no one else to light his fireworks. He had no confidence in those other sissies who set off fireworks. Small kegs filled with wood, watched over by Benedito, crackled into flame. Everywhere there was a reddish shimmer and a martial odor of burnt gunpowder. In front of the house the trees loomed like apotheoses of hell. Hands were soiled, and clothing was singed by sparks. Some people jumped over the bonfires. Others, their hands joined and arms upraised, paraded around solemnly, arranging partners.

"Would you like to be my partner, Dona Anica?" asked Casusa.

"Fine!"

And the two went down to the garden. There, with the bonfire between them, they held hands and made three rapid passes around the flames, their arms uplifted, repeating each time:

"For St. John! For St. John! For St. John! And for all the saints in heaven!"

On the veranda Lamparinas, in the midst of a group, tranquilly related the news that a fire had occurred in the city.

"Where?" they asked, frightened.

"On the Praia Grande."

Without a word Dias threw himself, at a dash, into the garden and vanished immediately into the row of mango trees.

Freitas explained to Raimundo the great drawbacks of such dangerous playing with fire. "Almost always, on the days of St. John and St. Peter, there are fires in the city. Businessmen in financial straits often take advantage of the opportunity and burn their stores." In the meantime, Serra, pointing to the spot where Dias had disappeared, whispered into Manuel's ear: "He's a first-rate worker, my dear fellow. Believe me, I'm envious of you. He's worth his weight in gold."

Lamparinas attempted to calm the minds of the two businessmen by declaring that the fire was on the Praça do Comércio and had not attained great dimensions. "By now it's possibly been extinguished."

The entire veranda was then swept from wall to wall; woven mats were spread about on the floor tiles in the places where the women devotees were to kneel. More candles were lit on the altar where Friar Lamparinas was about to chant his "thousandth litany," according to what Freitas had just at that moment asserted.

"His thousandth? . . ." asked Raimundo, astonished.

"You're surprised, eh?" replied the man with the long fingernail. "Just look, in this house alone, judging by the quick calculation I've taken the trouble to make, he's uttered no less than 657 litanies!"

And, in that connection, Freitas described in detail the old and proper celebration of St. John's festival.

"Nowadays they do nothing, in comparison with what used to be done," he said. "We had huge feasts in the colonel's time, and there were religious celebrations honoring St. John for nine and sometimes thirteen straight nights! And we would dance the entire night without letup! My friend, it was a spree that invariably provided at least half a month of real merrymaking!"

And with a mysterious air, like someone about to make a revelation of major importance:

"Do you want me to say it, just between us? Today's young girls don't measure up to even the old ladies of those days!"

And the lout chortled a laugh, as if he had said something witty.

The fires were still burning and everyone's spirits continued high when, unexpectedly, the door of one of the rooms opened, and Friar Lamparinas appeared, all decked out in his new surplice, a prayerbook in his hands, his eyeglasses mounted on his hooknose, his steps solemn, his demeanor replete with religion. He planted himself on the altar steps, announcing that the litany was about to begin.

There was a prolonged rustling of skirts as the women knelt in front of the priest.

From on high, against the light of the wax candles, flickered the scrawny shadow of Lamparinas's angular form, his arms lifted toward the ceiling in routine ecstasy. The men all drew closer, except for Sparky, who was sleeping. A few also knelt. They tossed away their half-smoked cigars and put aside their firecrackers and tiny bombs. Silence prevailed. And Lamparinas's lugubrious voice wheezed indistinctly through the *Tua Domine*.

"Well, aren't we to have an ejaculatory?" asked Amância, offended.

Lamparinas tossed an admonishing glance at her and concentrated once again on his prayers, concluding with:

"We present, oh Lord, this offering on Your altar to commemorate this festival honoring the birth of the saint who, in addition to announcing the coming of Our Saviour into the world, showed us as well that there had been born this same Jesus Christ Our Lord, who reigns and lives with us in harmony."

"Well said!" shouted Cordeiro.

A murmur of indignation broke out. Nevertheless, amid coughs, dry phlegm, and a few dispersed sneezes that were betrayed here and there, Lamparinas continued in a nasal drone:

"Gratiam tuam, quoesumus, Domine, mentibus nostris infunde, ut qui Angelo nuntiante Christi Filii tui incarnationem cognovimus, per passionem ejus et crucem ad ressurrectionis gloriam perducamur. Per eumdem Christum Dominum Nostrum. Amen!"

"Amen!" they repeated in unison.

And Lamparinas's voice twittered, accompanied by the music:

"Kyrie eleison!"

The devout answered, chanting in many different tones:

"Ora . . . pro . . . nobis!"

And they stretched out the final "—bis."

"Christe eleison!"

"Ora pro nobis!"

Cordeiro's coarse wine-soaked voice stood out, always lagging a few words behind in the singing, and dragging out the "—bis" shamefully.

"The devil of a heretic," muttered Amância without disturbing her sanctimonious pose.

"Pater de coelis, Deus, miserere nobis."

"Ora pro nobis!" persisted the chorus.

"Fili Redemptor mundi, Deus, misere nobis."

"Ora pro nobis!"

And after a quarter hour of this chanting, poor Friar Lamparinas felt squarely in his element and became enthusiastic, singing excitedly, tapping out the rhythm with his foot, and practically dancing. He no longer awaited the "Ora pro nobis," but shouted out:

"Santa Maria!"

"Santa Dei genitrix!

"Santa virgo Virginum!

"Mater purissima!"

And the chorus and music went racing after him, at full steam.

But the specialist in litanies was forced to quell his enthusiasm, because around Maria do Carmo a buzzing arose.

"What's wrong with my aunt!" exclaimed Etelvina, aflutter.

"Dear stepmother! Lord's sakes, God help me!"

"What is it?"

"What's the matter?"

"What's wrong with her?"

"What happened?"

No one knew. Meanwhile, Maria do Carmo, kneeling and rigid,

with her chin stuck into her collarbone, had an appalling immobility in her stare.

"Heavens!" shrieked Amância, crossing herself.

The two nieces immediately began to cry loudly; Ana Rosa, Eufrasinha, and Lindoca instantly followed suit.

Everyone dashed to the grim scene: the musicians with their instruments under their arms, and Lamparinas with his right index finger marking his place in the prayer book.

Mario do Carmo's belly was rumbling oddly. Raimundo pushed his way through, reached her, lifted up her head, and, as he let her go again a gush of putrid vomit spurted over the old woman's body.

"It's an intestinal obstruction," he said, turning his head.

"The Latin is *volvulus,*" Freitas, having following him there, whispered in his ear.

Maria do Carmo was carried to the bedroom. They stretched her out on a settee. A copious and cold sweat dripped from her entire body; her belly was as hard as stone. Raimundo had them give her some sweet oil and instructed them to buy some electuary of senna as soon as possible. Someone went off to call the doctor in the city.

The sick woman regained consciousness, but she had horrible stomach spasms and a strong itching over her entire body; she complained of an intense thirst and turned delirious from one moment to the next. A half hour later the vomiting again returned; her agony grew, and the intestinal attacks increased. The poor old woman writhed in pain, clawing at the cane of the settee, sinking her nails into the wood.

There was a terrifying silence around her. Finally, the reaction struck: she was shaken from head to foot by a convulsion and then immediately became motionless.

Raimundo asked for a mirror, placed it before Maria do Carmo's mouth, then observed it and said dryly:

"She's dead. . . ."

There was a chorus of shrieks. Etelvina fell over backward, writhing in a hysterical fit. Manuel hustled his daughter out. Everyone in the house came on the run. Their spirits, which the wine had benumbed, revived as if by magic. The situation immediately turned doleful.

Cordeiro, his wits perfectly restored, helped carry the body, pushed back chairs, dragged away a chest of drawers, and prepared for the laying out. Everyone invaded the room. The house Negroes approached fearfully, terror stricken, muttering guttural monosyllables, dumbfounded, their mouths agape.

In less than two hours Maria do Carmo was stretched out on a couch, illuminated by wax candles, washed, dressed in a clean dress, and with her hair combed. On top of the dresser, near her, sat the unchanging statue of St. John the Baptist, while, kneeling on the tiled floor, his gaze fixed on the saint, the canon, with arms stretched out, babbled a prayer.

Manuel sent messages throughout the city; his clerks all left. Maria Bárbara had shut herself in her room and begun to pray with the desperation of a seriously devout old lady. Agitation prevailed. Only Amância kept her head; she was in her element—coming and going, giving orders, making arrangements, advising, scolding, crying when necessary, consoling the dejected, uttering prayers, recalling events, directing, reprimanding those who were not obeying, and putting into practice her own orders.

At ten o'clock at night, a cotton hammock, strung across multicolored bamboo poles whose ends were carried on the shoulders of two sturdy Negroes, conducted the body of Maria do Carmo to the two-story house on Mercês Square, followed by a large retinue of men and women. Benedito led the way, illuminating the mournful procession with the reddish light of an enormous tar torch held above his head.

Lamparinas trotted along behind, in a rage, making the loose gravel of the road fly before his feet, and complaining like the devil about the nonobservance of that old and comforting proverb: "Where the priest prays for the sinner, there he stays for his dinner."

9

Soon after the removal of the body, Maria Bárbara and Ana Rosa left the country house in a private coach. They headed directly to Mercês Square. Manuel and Raimundo followed on the trolley, and went straight home. But the young man, despite his fatigue, could not rest. Needing fresh air, he changed his clothes and went out again.

It was already past midnight. The city had that special look of St. John's Eve: the remains of bonfires could be seen smoldering in the distance at various locales; from time to time a sharp crackling was heard. Raimundo set off toward Mercês. Was it possible, he thought while walking, that he was really so bewitched by his cousin? Or might it all be one of those fleeting turns of fancy that the pretty face of a girl produces in us on our good days? The truth was he had never felt so absorbed in any other woman.

"At any rate," he concluded, "it's better to bide my time! No rash haste."

Reasoning thus and already looking forward to his probable marriage to Ana Rosa, he reached the Sarmento home.

By that time many acquaintances of the deceased had gathered around, having been notified at once of the sad event by Manuel's employees. The burial would be held that same afternoon. Several business acquaintances sent their clerks over to help prepare the letters of invitation and to keep vigil. An undertaker was soon summoned to arrange the house in accordance with the custom in the province. Someone spoke with an artist concerning a portrait of the body. Measurements were taken and the coffin ordered. They debated the garment Maria do Carmo was to wear and decided on the costume of Our Lady of the Conception, for hers is the prettiest and most eye-catching. Amância quickly volunteered to make the clothing. "It's not worthwhile to order it from the undertaker, since not only wouldn't it be properly cut and sewn, but it would cost a fortune besides."

"I just don't know," she said. "All these things for a funeral always cost four times more than they're worth! It's highway robbery! That's why those undertakers get rich so fast! The devilish thieves!"

For once the old woman was right.

They ordered pink, blue, and white satin, petite dance-style shoes, lace and tulle for the veil, which would be fringed in gold. Some insisted that the dead woman hold a bouquet of carnations in her hands; others were opposed, pointing out not only the age of the deceased but also that she was a widow.

Further suggestions rained down from everyone:

"Why just the other day Dona Pulquéria das Dores, despite her sixty years, held an enormous branch of red roses in her hands. And besides, she was married."

"And what does that have to do with it? Dona Chiquinha Vasconcelos went in an open coffin, but she didn't hold a bouquet, and let me tell you, it was done without a holy palm branch, and not even a chapel! Moreover, she was an old maid and half the age of Dona Maria do Carmo."

"But her cheeks were painted carmine, which is much worse! Goodness! . . . And, furthermore, we all know what everyone said about Chiquinha. God forgive me!"

An obese mulatto woman sliced through the Gordian knot of the question, declaring that the bouquet might easily be hidden under her garb. They all immediately agreed.

The clock struck one in the morning. Several clerks had already departed, carrying packets of announcements that would be delivered later in the morning. A few families, dressed in black, took leave of one another with a round of kisses and apologies for not staying until the funeral. The undertaker hammered away in the parlor. Again, the night closed in silently. Here and there a delayed firecracker popped. On the street, reveling groups passed, bantering on their way to the St. John's bath. From the Alto da Carneira came the distant chanting of "Bumba Meu Boi." The first roosters crowed; far away dogs howled protractedly; in the blue and tranquil sky a slice of moon appeared, sad and drowsy, as if performing its duty, while a man with a ladder on his shoulder went about extinguishing the street lamps.

Raimundo had stopped for a moment to gaze at the ocean in front of the Sarmento home. At the front door was a large black velvet drape with a cross of gold braid. He contemplated the building: it was a massive old house, one of those typical old-fashioned two-story homes of Maranhão, which were already becoming rare. It was fifty hands high and about the same in width, with a tar-covered foundation showing fragments of dry plaster at several spots. There were five windows with sills set in a row above four flat doors that had between them an imposing front entrance with a stonework frame. It all gave off an odor reminiscent of construction in colonial times when stone and hardwoods were readily obtainable, and walls six feet thick and stairs of holywood used to be built on leased lands.

He entered the house. The hallway emitted a funereal quality. He climbed an unsightly staircase, holding onto a black banister that was shiny from use. On the walls, despite the inadequate light cast by a dingy lantern, he could make out greasemarks from the hands of the slaves, and on the ceiling were patches blackened by smoke.

The stairs had two flights, running in opposite directions. Suffocating, Raimundo reached the end of the first flight, then strode rapidly up the second, consigning to the devil that damnable custom of closing up an entire house just when, because a dead body was within it, air was most needed. In one of the front rooms, by then covered with the undertaker's old carpet that was so spotted with drops of wax that one's foot slipped, there was a large tray of paparaúba wood, covered with ornamental candles and enormous lanterns of wood and tinplate, painted yellow. On one of the walls, draped from top to bottom with black velvet and trimmed with gold braid, an altar jutted out. Although not yet lit, it was completely studded with sequins and loaded down with ornaments. There was a lace cloth in the middle, on top of which perched two brass candlesticks, speckled with flies. Between them was a crucifix made of the same metal and extremely tarnished. In front stood the bier, decorated like the rest of the room and awaiting the coffin, which was then being prepared in Manuel Serigueiro's shop.

Perched on a ladder and with a hammer in his fist, a man in shirtsleeves nailed embroidered curtains above the doors.

"What time is the funeral?" Raimundo asked.

"At four-thirty," replied the undertaker, not turning his head.

A murmur of voices could be heard from the veranda. Raimundo headed toward them.

The veranda was wide and high, whitewashed, and entirely opened toward the backyard. It had an unlined ceiling that revealed its irregular beams, from which gloomy spiderwebs hung. In one of the corners a very dark bench of purpleheart wood held, in rounded holes, two enormous big-bellied red clay pots. Along the sill of the veranda, water was cooling in a row of small jugs. A crude and immense wardrobe cabinet stood open against a wall and right at its feet was a trapdoor set into the floor, protected by a grating that showed a dark stairway descending.

Propped over the grating, a fat bespectacled fellow, with no moustache but a small beard under his chin, said to another of similar appearance, pounding his foot on the wide floorboards:

"Nowadays nobody fiddles around with woodwork like this! Just look, it's all trumpetbush wood, holywood, satinwood, bacuri, rosewood, and souari nut tree! That wood's just like iron, even a hatchet couldn't scratch it!"

Around a table ten men, under the guise of keeping vigil over the deceased, were playing cards, conversing in low voices, and partaking of endless cups of coffee and glasses of cognac, amid whispered jokes, muffled laughs, and the thick smoke of cigarettes.

As Raimundo entered, one of them was confiding to the man next to him:

"I'm no longer up to these things. . . . I just can't miss a night's sleep any more. No matter how much coffee I drink, I feel sleepy. But I couldn't pass up the opportunity, it was a chance to see the girl. I've never before set foot in her house."

And he yawned.

"Did you know the old woman who died?" the older man asked him.

"No, but I do believe I met her once at Manuel Pescada's house. I've already been to look at her—it's awful!"

"Well, I'm furious at being here. My boss told me to come, but any minute now I'm taking off. There's a party going on in Cutim, and I'm not going to miss it!"

"Why couldn't the old thing have picked a better day to die!"

"Right on St. John's Eve! What a bother!"

And they both yawned.

"Who's that guy?" one of the card players asked, seeing Raimundo enter. "Cut me in with the three of spades."

"It's that Raimundo fellow, a guy Pescada is putting up in his house out of pity."

"Well, what does he do?—Queen!"

"They say he's a doctor. My turn."

"He doesn't seem like a bad guy. . . ."

"Watch out!"

"Why, has he already pulled one on you? Tell us about it!"

"I won't say another word. Trust in the Virgin and keep your eyes open!"

There was a pause while cards were dealt onto the table, accompanied by the tapping of feet on the carpet.

"But what does he live on?" asked the curious fellow who was trying to find out about Raimundo. "I need an ace!"

"What do you mean, what does he live on? . . . Don't you have any hearts? . . . Ask all those who have no employment and are supposedly living off 'commissions,' and then you'll find out."

"I won!"

"But what is he to Manuel!"

"They say he's his cousin," the other responded, shuffling the cards.

"Ah!"

"Deal."

Raimundo greeted them and asked about the family of the deceased.

They were attending the wake. He could enter through there, the men said, motioning toward a door.

The minute Raimundo turned his back, the gossiper raised his arm and made a crude gesture at him.

"I really love those types," he said, and then added loudly so the entire group could hear: "They're all big shots on the outside, 'Because I did this,' and 'Because that happened to me,' and 'Because this is just a village' here! 'It's a pigsty!' But in the meantime they butt into the pigsty and won't budge from here!"

"My friend, there's no place like our Maranhão."

"I've heard, however, that the nigger's loaded," ventured a third fellow.

"What do you mean? . . . You still fall for those stories! They all say they own the world. I like our little Maranhão because it's so hard on these guys who flock here full of airs. That fellow, who wants to look like more of a wise guy than the others, is going to get a licking that'll teach him not to be such a pedant! What the devil! If he knows anything, he'd better keep it to himself because no one around here needs him or asks him anything. He'd better not start scribbling pamphlets and newspaper articles—that's ridiculous! . . . Lopes, my boss, sure knows how to deal with these types. Why, just a little while back he needed some kind of document, for his nephew who had arrived from Porto. And he goes off and asks an acquaintance of ours, who'd been to university, to take care of it for him. Well now, what do you think the rascal said to the boss?"

No one knew.

"Well, he told him to go to the devil! He called him a nincompoop, and said that what he wanted was absurd."

"Oh, yeah?"

"In exactly those words, just like I'm telling you! Well, my friend, my boss really taught the fellow a lesson! You know Lopes, when he's got the whim, he thinks nothing of spending his pennies."

"Yeah, like that time with the medal . . ."

"Right. Well, Lopes went over to some brainy fellow and paid him to write a first-class attack!"

"And so?"

"So, the other guy wrote it down even better than the boss suggested! Now, hang on! What was that other fellow's name? It was . . . I've the devilish thing right on the tip of my tongue. . . . Ah! He was anonymous!"

"Oh, anonymous!"

"A dressing-down that knocked little doctor Melinho out flatter than the ground!"

"Ah, this happened to Melinho?"

"That's right. You read about it, huh?"

"Damn, but Lopes went too far that time. He really made the young guy lose face."

"I don't know. But it sure was done right!"

"And from what I gather, not everything the anonymous guy wrote was the truth."

"I don't know. But for sure it really rubbed Melinho wrong."

"Yes, but you can't deny that Melinho really is an intelligent and honest fellow."

"Much good it'll do him! May he eat off his intelligence and drink from his honesty! Look, kid, let's face facts! Everything nowadays is pure money! Forget about honesty and intelligence!"

And he rubbed his fingers together to indicate money.

"If I've got my dough safely stashed away in my pocket," he added, "I don't care what anyone says! Just take a look at our society!"

And he cited well-known names, told frightening stories of smuggling, major robberies, counterfeit bills, the whole works!

"Yes, yes, that's old hat. But what happened to Melinho?"

"How should I know? He took off for the south! He can go to the devil!"

"Now watch it, I like that guy!"

"Well, I wouldn't brag about your taste!"

Raimundo, after passing through another spacious room, entered the parlor and found himself facing a circle of ladies of various ages, most of them dressed in mourning, who were sitting and staring with weary and somnolent eyes at the lifeless body of Maria do Carmo. In a hammock hanging at one corner, Etelvina sobbed, hiding her head among some pillows; at her side a fat mulatto woman bedecked in gold, wearing a black camel's hair skirt and a lace shawl on her shoulders, was mechanically repeating words of solace. Seated on the wooden floor on a woven mat, Amância was cutting and shaping the dress of Our Lady of the Conception in which the deceased would go costumed to the tomb as if to a masked ball. On the walls, the family portraits were covered by vast pieces of black crepe. The one of Lieutenant Espigão, appallingly painted in oils of a crude and garish coloring, exhibited a hardened, red-lipped smile through the veil. In the middle of the room on an ancient sofa with a varnished cane back, the old woman's body lay decomposing; her face was covered by a lace handkerchief soaked in toilet water. Her hands were crossed over her chest and bound tightly with a blue silk ribbon; her legs were stretched out, her hair well coifed and pulled sharply back. Her entire body lay rigid and shriveling, twisted slightly out of shape by muscular tension. Atop her swollen belly was a plate filled with salt.

At the head of the settee, on a small table covered with lace, stood a brightly colored statue of Christ hanging from the cross, with arms spread, and two wax candles melted away at the feet of the good and bad thieves. Nearby was a small vessel of holy water containing a twig of rosemary, and, close to the front, a tiny Virgin Mary made of painted clay.

Amid the dry crackle of the candles, unobtrusive sobbing could be heard.

Raimundo approached the body and, merely out of curiosity, uncovered the face. It was livid, its few teeth showing, the half-closed eyes exhibiting a tallowy ashen white. From the chin a handkerchief was tied upward to the top of the head and knotted to hold the jowls in pace. A bad odor was beginning to disperse.

Just then a little Negro girl with a tray of coffee cups appeared in the room.

The women helped themselves.

Raimundo carried a cup to Ana Rosa, who sat among the ladies.

"No, thank you," she said tearfully, "I just had some a moment ago."

From time to time a distinct sigh and the nasal sound of the young girls blowing their noses could be heard. A group of women in skirts and blouses conversed in gloomy tones about the good character and many virtues of the deceased. Their voices were timid, as if fearing to awaken someone or to be overheard by the object of their conversation.

"She was a really good person," declared one of them, contritely. "I owe her so much, and I'll repay her with a paternoster. Why, just the other day when pneumonia struck my little girl, who came right to my aid? Those doctors with diplomas didn't know what to make of it! And now, my dear? There she is fine and dandy, so happy . . . while poor Maria do Carmo . . . God forgive me, but it seems just like witchcraft!" And she pointed to the cadaver with a grieving gesture: "At least she's at rest, the poor soul."

"We just ain't nothin' in this world," sighed a thin woman blinking her eyes, who, hand in chin, had until then maintained a pitiful immobility.

And she related the story of a friend of hers, who, thirty years earlier, had died in the flower of her youth.

That story provoked others. A lengthy string of funereal anecdotes followed. The obese mulatto woman closed the recital, narrating, grief stricken, the story of a beloved pet parrot she used to own who, one fine day while singing—poor thing!—"Maria Cachucha," had fallen over backward—dead!

"Goodness!" exclaimed Amância. And turning around to the mulatto woman, her eyeglasses on the tip of her nose:

"Miss Maria, is this lace trim just for the veil, or do the bows have to come out of this piece too? . . . "

After the burial, when Maria Bárbara, on returning home, entered her room, she immediately noticed the wax candle burned down to a stub and the black mask of her beloved St. Raimundo. Terrified, not knowing what to think, she threw herself down on her knees in front of the oratory and, in her superstitious blindness, began to pray fervently.

That night, despite her exhausted state, she could not get to sleep until dawn approached. But mulling over the case, she ended by perceiving a miracle in it. Yes, a miracle, exactly as the catechisms taught in school explain, and, as her own teacher had taught her—an incomprehensible mystery. There couldn't be any doubt: God our Father had employed that ingenious ruse to warn her of present and future calamities! . . .

In the meantime, she took heart and confided the event only to the canon, and even asked him for secrecy, because if her son-in-law were to learn about it, he would stir things up too much. She could already hear him mutter with that unbearable snicker of a faithless man: "My mother-in-law's nonsense!" Besides, if St. Raimundo wanted to make his sacred warning public, he would have used some other means!

"Now, what should be evident, Canon, is that the cursed nigger Mundico has something to do with all this! I hope to God I'm wrong, but the thing smells like he had a hand in it!"

"It may be, it could be. . . . Davus sum non Aedipus!"

"And what should I do?"

"Offer a mass to St. Raimundo. Sung, that wouldn't be a bad idea . . . a small sung mass."

That was what they decided; but, alone again, the old woman was unable to calm down. It seemed to her that everywhere about her great transformations were taking place. The truth was that Maria do Carmo's death had succeeded in disturbing the daily routine of Manuel Pescada's small circle. One week after her passing, a brother of the deceased arrived from Alcântara, and after the Seventh Day Mass, he took the two disconsolate nieces away with him. Etelvina, wrapped in her black wool dress, had begun to exaggerate her habit of sighing deeply; Bibina, with considerable self-denial, kept her hair concealed in a hairnet made of silk. Dona Amância Souselas, in order to grieve more comfortably over the loss of her friend, had gone to spend a few weeks at the Our Lady of the Anunciation and Consolation Retreat, in the restful warmth of the prayers and thick soup of the refectory. Eufrasinha, noticing Ana Rosa's coolness, decided to be offended and ceased visiting her. For some time before, she had been noting a certain annoying little air of constraint and tedium.

Anica was just no longer the same! She didn't know why the girl was so out of sorts: Eufrasinha held the firm conviction that someone was staying up nights plotting against her, but, then, she was big-hearted and willing to look the other way. Roly-poly Lindoca had likewise retired, but the poor creature did so out of misery over her lard. Quite ashamed, she was no longer willing to show herself to a single soul. Following her father's advice, she had begun to take lengthy morning strolls when there were few people on the street—to see if her fat would diminish. But to no avail! The flood of fat continued, making her limbs ever more rounded. The poor girl no longer had a shape; whenever she went out she was forced to stop and rest from time to time, thus attracting people's attention, which in turn irritated her. She could no longer wear boots and was condemned to a type of flat-soled, almost round, cloth shoe; her hands had lost the ability to touch her hips; she always held her arms open; her neck displayed frightful layers and coils; her eyes, nose, and mouth were threatening to disappear, drowned in her cheeks. And, with all that, she developed a taste for straight lines, became fond of anything that was neat and smooth, and gazed enviously at skinny people. Freitas spent his leisure time consulting medical treatises to see if he might discover a cure for that malady. The good man became exhausted. The chairs in his house were all coming apart. If things went on this way, his entire salary wouldn't be enough even for furniture. And, clever man that he was, he ordered a special chair with strong screws and very hard wood constructed for Lindoca. They both led sad lives.

And all this, all this silent sorrow burrowing into that little clique, was chalked up by Maria Bárbara to Raimundo. She complained bitterly about him to everyone; she would repeat that ever since the arrival of that creature the house seemed cursed: "Everything now comes out awry!" She went so far as to request that the canon bestow a blessing on her room and, in addition to the promise to pay for a mass, she offered ten pounds of fresh wax, to be sent over to the rector of the cathedral on the day the nigger would be sent packing.

But, a short time later, Manuel's mother-in-law had a private visit with the canon, and told him, radiant with triumph:

"Guess what? I've discovered everything!"

"What do you mean, everything?"

"The reason all these misfortunes have been happening to us lately."

"And what is it?"

"The nigger's a Protestant!"

"A Protestant! How do you know?"

Maria Bárbara put her mouth near Diogo's ear and whispered, her flesh creeping:

"He's a Mason!"

"Really, what are you saying!" exclaimed Diogo, feigning great indignation.

"It's just as I tell you, Canon! The nigger's a Protestant!"

"But this is serious. . . . How did you find this out?"

"Of course it's serious! Look here!"

And, brimming with revulsion and mysterious grimaces, she removed from her skirt pocket the little booklet with a green cover that Dias had filched from Raimundo's drawer.

"See this witchcraft, Reverend! Just look, and then tell me whether the damned creature does or does not have a pact with the devil! And didn't I sense something like this!"

And she pointed, aghast, at the brochure on whose title page were drawn two columns supporting two earthly globes, and other emblems. The canon seized the pamphlet and read from the first page: "Masonic Legend, or Master of Regular Lodges, in accordance with the Reformed French Rite."

"Yes, ma'am, you're quite correct, this is the final proof of his knavery!"

As he read from the introduction to the work, a partisan rage overcame him: "Masons, let us be imbued with our own dignity! The rectitude of our vows, the union of our labors, the harmony of our hearts, unceasingly nourish the sacred fire whose resplendent brightness illuminates the interior of our temples!"

"Yes, ma'am! He's got this talent too," he muttered, handing the booklet back to the old woman: "Besides being a nigger, he's a Protestant!"

And without a transition, coldly:

"We must get this man out of here."

"And as soon as possible!"

"Is Manuel there now?"

"I believe so, in the warehouse."

"Well, I'm going to make him see the light. Good day."

"Try to do your best, Reverend. Look, I even think it would be better to forget about buying that ranch! This type of folk, if he doesn't turn everything into soot, he at least dirties it! You can't imagine how it needles me just to see him every blessed day at the dining table next to my granddaughter. . . . I just never expected anything like this from my son-in-law! We've got to get the man out of the house! This can't go on! Those Limas women have already gossiped a lot; Brígida said that out at José Xorro's grocery stand they asked her if it was true he was about to marry Anica! Now that's intolerable! Everyone's talking about it! Does that whatever-you-call-him need someone to shout in his ear that he should know his place? . . . After all, how many are there of us? No, it has to end! We must put a stop to such goings-on! Speak to my son-in-law, Canon. . . . Speak frankly to him! Look, you can even tell him if he doesn't want to deal with this, I'll take charge of throwing this vermin right out into the street! The door of the house is always at our service! Don't you know that no one in my family can stand to be in a room that smells of someone with a trace of Negro blood! What filth!"

"All right, all right! Don't get worked up, Dona Babu! Everything's going to come out fine, with God's divine aid."

And the canon went off to have it out with the merchant.

"My dear man," answered Manuel, having heard his friend's arguments, "as far as sending him back to the devil, I agree! After all, it's dangerous for the head of a family to have him within the house. . . . But as for forgetting about the ranch, that's what I'm against! It would be assinine on my part. It's a good deal. Cancela has written me and wants to talk business. I could put a sizable little commission in my pocket without risking any capital and with almost no work. Am I to hunker down, leave the poor boy spinning, and risk his falling into the hands of some shrewd fox? Look here, my friend, even putting aside my financial interest, who except for me could poor Mundico entrust with this deal? We have to take care of these things, you know."

The trip was planned for the following Saturday.

Much to everyone's surprise, Raimundo welcomed the news with obvious satisfaction. He was finally going to visit the place where everyone said he had been born.

"Look," he said to Manuel, "I have something important to ask you."

"If it's within my power."

"It is."

"What is it, then?"

"Something very serious. We'll talk it over on our trip to Rosário."

Manuel scratched the nape of his neck.

10

On the agreed upon day at six o'clock in the morning Manuel and Raimundo boarded the steamboat *Pindaré,* belonging to the new Maranhão Coastal Navigation Company.

The weather was scorching and quite dry, the light exceedingly strong. The trip was uncomfortable owing to the considerable number of passengers, who, in the seditious saying of those on board, were packed "like sardines in a container."

Even so, all of this was much better, reflected Manuel. Now one could at least travel easily to the interior of the province. In the old days navigating the Itapicuru River certainly had its drawbacks.

And he began to narrate in detail the primitive conditions of the trek to Rosário. "So, you see, the Navigation Company, despite everything, has lent immense services to the province. Let people say what they will, the only inconvenience is the stopover and transfer at Codó! That, indeed, still is a problem, and the sooner it's resolved, the better."

"Fortunately," he concluded, "Rosário is the first stopping point and we'll not have to suffer that cursed nuisance!"

By nightfall they had alighted at the village of Rosário and were met by an old acquaintance of Manuel's, who had been residing there for a good many years. He was a stubby little Portuguese fellow, middle-aged, talkative, lively, by now Brazilian in his manner and as dark as a backwoodsman.

"Come stay at my house and then at daybreak you can be on your way," he suggested to the merchant. "I've always wanted to show you my palace!"

The invitation was accepted and the three set off walking, each carrying his case in his hand.

"Do you remember," the little man was saying, "all that low area belonging to Bento Moscoso? Well, that's now my own backyard! I took possession of the ranch from the widow for a trifle and nowadays it's producing like you've never seen! My plan is to set up a mill near there, where the Ribas River channel is located; I want to see if I can plant the low areas in sugarcane, you follow?"

And he lectured at length about the freshly cleared land and his hopes for prosperity, criticizing the ill-advised measures taken by his neighbors; finally he steered the conversation to the topic of Barroso. Barroso was the name of Cancela's ranch, where the other two were headed.

"They're sure good lands, that they are! Well cleared, blessed in every way. I wonder how Luís Cancela did so well in life? Yes, if I'm not mistaken, he told me once upon a time that you'd leased him these lands, isn't that so?"

"Exactly," answered Manuel.

"Ah, then they're yours?"

"No, they belong to my friend here."

And Manual pointed toward Raimundo who was meanwhile negotiating with a man he had summoned about horses for the next day's trip.

"That really is good land," insisted the little Portuguese. "Luís Cancela has wanted to buy it on several occasions."

"He can buy it now."

And they reached the house.

"Everyone else is away," said the planter. "However, it doesn't make any difference, we've got plenty to get along on. Hey there, Gregório!"

"Yessuh!"

An old Negro man appeared, to whom he gave orders in a soft voice.

The night, in contrast to the day, turned cool. After supper each man stretched out lazily in a hammock. Raimundo complained of the insects and gnats. Manuel, ruminating on his business dealings, nodded off to sleep; and the little Portuguese fellow didn't give his mouth a moment's rest: he spoke about the terrain with increasing enthusiasm, relating its agricultural marvels, and revealing his utter devotion to the village of Rosário.

And, drawn on by the heat of the conversation, he began lying, exaggerating everything he described.

Raimundo interrupted him to ask if he were familiar with the ranch at São Brás.

"São Brás!"

And the little man jumped up from his hammock with a start.

"São Brás! Have I heard about it! Why around here, sir, you won't find anyone who *doesn't* know its story!"

Raimundo burned with curiosity.

"Would you kindly relate it to me?" he asked, settling himself in his hammock. "Because I'm going in that direction . . ."

Manuel had fallen asleep.

"So, you, sir, don't know the story of São Brás? . . . God help you, my good sir, you could fall under some evil spell. But I'll teach you the prayer we learned from our blessed vicar. Look, when you stumble onto a cross along that road, dismount and pray, and then afterward continue heading down the road, saying over and over again:

São Brás, alas!
Sweet Jesus, alack!
Here I pass
With no cross on my back!

Then, when you catch sight of the mango trees by the Barroso Ranch, you can continue to the riverbank without a worry, because the hex doesn't reach that far."

"But why take such precautions?"

"Now there, that's where the shoe pinches! It's because of an evil and mean person who's contaminated that area. I'll tell you about it."

And the little man, swallowing hard, related at length how São Brás, or Ponta do Fogo, as it had been called formerly, had in days of yore been a locale of excellent and fertile lands of multiple plantings and harvests, so blessed it was by the hand of God. But then who should show up but the infamous killer Bernardo, the terror of Rosário and the dread of the ranchers. After a life spent wandering in the backland, looting and killing, he had set up camp at Ponta do Fogo and there fizzled out. And from that time on, at that accursed spot, never again did fruit flourish without the rancid taste of poison, nor did plants thrive free of blight. The water there would leave ashes in your mouth; the earth, if you gathered it in your hand, turned into saltpeter, and the flowers smelled of brimstone. And whoever ate that fruit, or lay down on that earth, or bathed in those waters and sniffed those flowers, would get so bewitched that there was no way to uproot him from the spot, because the devil himself had daubed the fruit with honey, perfumed the flowers, and softened the grass to entice the unwary traveler.

"That," he continued, "was what happened to poor José do Eito when he poked his nose around there: he ended up bewitched! I was very young at the time, but I well recall having seen him often, the wretched fellow! So yellowed, whiny and weary, that right away you could guess the devil had socked him a good one! And he always went around like that! One day his wife up and died on him suddenly, and a short time later he himself was pierced by a bullet, and no one ever found out where it came from! From then on São Brás became a dilapidated ruin. On the spot where José died a cross was erected, and all those who venture near there pray for the wretched fellow's soul so that, after a set number of prayers, it can rest in peace. As if that weren't enough, there's a poor tormented soul who wanders about the ruins by day just like an enormous black bird, singing to the dead, and at night it turns into a witch, dancing and singing, laughing like a fox. Whenever a careless person passes nearby, the witch will pursue him in such a way that if the unfortunate man is not well mounted, she'd surely nab him!"

"And if she does nab him?"

"If she does? Ah, it's better not to even speak about that! If she nabs him, well she'll turn immediately into a sack of bones and fall on top of him with such furious blows that she'll leave him dead!"

"And then?"

"Then his soul will come back for penance, having lost, for every blow she gave him, at least twenty paternosters. When you leave tomorrow, you'd better carry a twig of common rue on the saddle, and then, after praying at that cross, go on your way shaking it constantly as far as the mango grove at Cancela's, without once stopping that prayer I taught you!"

"Yes, yes, but tell me something, this José do Eito, his real name wasn't José Pedro da Silva, was it?"

"The very same! Did you know him?"

"Only by name."

"Well, I knew him quite well."

And at Raimundo's request, the little fellow described the kind of man José was, and reported what he knew about his life. Raimundo listened to everything with rapt attention; he did not want to miss a single word. But he had to interrupt the narrator often, to ask him questions which the other answered in rapid asides.

"Well, Dona Quitéria Santiago died shortly before her husband. I went to see her! And, imagine, instead of the attractive woman she had been, she ended up horribly. She was more purple than an eggplant!"

"She never had children?"

"No, never."

"And her husband? Yes . . . he could have had some illegitimate child. . . ."

"No, as far as I know, he had none."

"Isn't it known if any female relation might have lived on the ranch with José?"

"Search me, but. . . ."

"Some sister of Dona Quitéria, or perhaps some woman friend? See if you can remember. . . ."

"What do you mean? On the contrary, they lived quite isolated. Dona Quitéria's only relative was her mother. She was always at odds with her son-in-law, so she never left her own ranch, the one where Cancela lives nowadays, the old Barroso Ranch. That's right! You know who can tell you a lot about these things? The vicar! He still lives in the city and nowadays he's a canon. Well, he was a real buddy of José do Eito."

"Canon Diogo?"

"Exactly! He's the one who was vicar of this parish. Let's see now, how long has it been? . . ."

"Oh, then Canon Diogo was the vicar of this parish and a regular visitor of the Santiagos'?"

Yes, sir! And he's always ready to tell anyone willing to listen about his efforts to remove the hex from São Brás! Poor fellow, he had no success at all and was almost the victim of his own good will!"

"Did he believe in witchcraft too?"

"Did he believe in it! Whenever he saw any signs of it, he'd say so! And just note, sir, the canon is not the type to lie. He declared that there was a cursed soul at São Brás, and he didn't want anyone talking about it. In fact, he expressly prohibited it, under threat of excommunication. Did he believe in it? That's a good one! Then why did he abandon the parish, even though he was born here, was held in the highest esteem, and received—and he really did—an endless flow of gifts from the entire parish? Cattle, sheep, geldings, all kinds of livestock! He's there in the city now, so let him tell it all!"

Raimundo jumped from one conjecture to the next.

"Then he was quite a friend of José da Silva? The canon?"

"Was he ever! A friend, and a very good one! . . . When the poor man was murdered, the vicar didn't even want to sprinkle holy water on him, so he called in the sexton! He couldn't even look at José's body. And you see, sir, he locked himself up in his house and hardly appeared until one day he up and left the village for good! We all felt sorry at such a loss; we were used to him. . . . At the time I was working over on Colonel Rosa's property. I was well into my twenties and still single; I saw everything that went on. I recall it as if it were just yesterday! The ranch was abandoned right away; no one even wanted to hear anything about it, for every night anyone passing by there would hear blood-curdling shrieks, enough to cause goosebumps on your skin!"

"But, besides José and his wife, who else lived on the place?"

"Well, now, the slaves and the foreman."

"No, I mean the masters."

"No one else."

"Well, was José happy with his wife? Did they get along well?"

"What! Haven't I told you those lands belong to the devil? Why, those two got along just like cats and dogs! It was the canon who kept them together, giving them advice and beseeching God in their favor."

And Raimundo was lost once more in conjecture. Constant shadows . . . always the same doubts about his past. . . .

The conversation died down. The little Portuguese man stretched out and, after a few vague and yawning comments, fell asleep. Raimundo dreamed throughout the night.

At four in the morning they were all up, the horses saddled, their knapsacks packed for the trip, and the guide mounted.

They departed at five o'clock.

As soon as the two men and the guide were well on their way, Raimundo attempted to broach the same subject he had discussed the night before with the rancher. He wanted to see if he could wrench from Manuel some sort of clarification about his parents. He got nothing. The merchant's answers were, as always when his nephew touched on the issue, obscure, vague, and interrupted by pauses and silences. Manuel spoke to him about the canon, his sister-in-law, his brother José, and no one else. As for Raimundo's mother—not even the slightest reference. "So much for that! It always ends up this way," Raimundo concluded, and struggled to think about other things. And yet, despite his artistic temperament, he had not a word to say about the beautiful scenery unfolding before his eyes. He rode along dejected and preoccupied.

They journeyed in silence for hours on end. From time to time the guide, with his backlander's sad air, would lead them to a ranch or a roadside cabin where the three would relax and eat, and then at once continue to ride amid the melancholy carnaúba and pindova palms along the road. Raimundo felt dispirited and was growing impatient for the trip to end. His burning desire was to visit São Brás. He even proposed that they go there first, but the merchant declared that it would be impossible. "There's no time to waste!"

"On the return trip, Doctor, on the return," he added, "we'll set off quite early and stop by there. Remember, Cancela is waiting for us, and it wouldn't be right to disturb his family at a late hour."

Raimundo agreed, cursing with clenched teeth, annoyed and filled with boredom. What a great nuisance! That devil of a ranch straight from hell seemed to be fleeing before their eyes!

"Now don't worry yourself, sir. It's just up ahead," said the guide unhurriedly, stretching out his lower lip. "Give your horse some spur, and perhaps we'll arrive in daylight."

"Ah," sighed Raimundo, discouraged at seeing the sun still high and realizing he had to ride on until nightfall.

And he let himself lapse into a wretched state of lethargy, staring at his mule's ears, which rolled and pitched with the monotonous regularity of a bird in flight.

"Here it is!" exclaimed Manuel two hours later, arriving at a shaded place on the road.

"What is?" the young man was going to ask, when he in turn noticed a wooden cross, quite crude and dilapidated. "Ah!"

"This is where José was killed."

They all stopped, and the guide dismounted and went to pray on his knees at the cross.

"Pray for your father's soul, my friend. In this place he was pierced by a bullet."

"And the killer?" inquired Raimundo after a silence.

"Some runaway slave . . . to this day no one knows for sure . . . but some say politics had something to do with it. Others attribute the event to the devil. Nonsense!"

Raimundo dismounted and asked whether his father was buried there.

Manuel, already on his feet, answered no. He had been laid to rest in the ranch's cemetery, at his wife's side. The cross, he explained, was an old custom in the backlands; it was to show the traveler the spot where someone had been killed and to urge him to pray for the victim's soul, just as that man was then doing.

And he pointed toward the guide, who, finished with his prayers, stood up and went to pick a branch of myrtle, which he placed at the foot of the cross.

Raimundo was overcome with emotion. Manuel, on his knees, his head bowed and his hat hanging between his clasped hands, prayed devoutly. Upon finishing he was surprised to notice that Raimundo did not intend to do likewise.

"What's this? You mean you're not going to pray?"

"No. Shall we be off?"

"Now, just a minute there! Just what is your religion, sir? How do you worship God?"

"Come now, Mr. Manuel, never mind that; let's talk about something else!"

"No! I just want you to tell me how you worship God."

"Forget about it, man, leave God in peace! Now, why should you care?"

"But, if that's the case, then you have no religion?"

"Yes, yes, I do. . . ."

"Well, it doesn't seem that way! You should at least pay more heed to prayers, which, after all, were taught us by the apostles of Our Lord Jesus Christ!"

Raimundo was unable to stifle a laugh, and, because his uncle took offense, he added in a serious tone that he did not actually disdain religion, that he even judged it to be indispensable as a regulating element within society. He declared that he admired nature and worshipped at its cult, attempting to study it and to understand its laws and phenomena, keeping up with men of science in their investigations, and doing everything possible, in short, to help his fellow men, and always taking honesty as the basis for his own acts.

They mounted once again and set off down the road. A tense conversation ensued between them concerning religious beliefs. Raimundo behaved indulgently toward his companion but was growing bored, inwardly repelled at having to put up with him. From religion they proceeded to other things, to which the young man responded out of courtesy. Slavery finally came up for discussion, and Manuel attempted to defend it. Raimundo lost his patience, grew angry, and railed against it and those who practiced it, in words so firm and sincere that the merchant fell silent, rather irritated. In the meantime, the guide trotted along in front, inattentive, singing to pass the time.

"Love doesn't hurt, you say,
From the bottom of your heart. . . .
Just love and go far away,
Then see if it hurts or not!"

They traveled along in silence for half an hour. Day was waning; the first symptoms of night arose from the earth like a dark perfume. Birds took refuge in the fragrant depths of the forest. The refreshing late afternoon breeze ruffled the palm-tree leaves, filling the atmosphere with a sweet and sensual murmur.

"I've been jabbering so much," Raimundo said finally with a certain perplexity, "but I've yet to touch on what concerns me most."

"How so?"

"Do you remember the other day, I requested a meeting with you in your office, and, either because you forgot or because it was really not opportune, we never did get to talk, and yet the matter is of the utmost importance for us both."

"And what might it be?"

"It's a great favor I must ask of you."

Manuel lowered his head, repressing the embarrassment he foresaw.

"Is it about some financial problem?" he asked.

"No, sir, it has to do with my happiness."

"Is it my daughter's hand you want to request?"

"Yes."

"Then, please withdraw your request."

"Why?"

"To spare me the pain of refusing you."

"What!"

"It's natural that you're surprised, I agree. And I don't blame you, you're within your rights. You're a fine gentleman, you're intelligent, you've your learning, which no one can deny, and without doubt you'll obtain an excellent position, but. . . ."

"But? But what?"

"Excuse me if my refusal offends you, but please believe me, even if I wanted to, I couldn't comply with your request."

"Then she's already promised to someone else, perhaps? . . . Well, in that case, I'll wait. There's still hope for me!"

"No, it's not that. . . . But I do ask you not to insist."

"Is it that you don't want to lose her?"

"Oh, how you torment me!"

"That's not it either? Then what the devil! Might there be, without my knowing it, some debt on my father's part that may one day explode like a bomb?"

"What an idea! If it were that, I'd be criminal in never having warned you. What you own is clear and safe. You can look at the books whenever you wish!"

"Oh, now I know," replied Raimundo with a sudden awareness, laughing. "You don't want to give your daughter to a man with such revolutionary ideas?"

"No, it's not that! Let's leave it there! I realize you have the right to an explanation, but please believe that, despite my good intentions, I can't give you one."

"But, why not?"

"I can't say a thing, I repeat. And I ask you again not to insist. This position is extremely painful for me, believe me!"

"Then you refuse me your daughter's hand? Once and for all?"

"I'm very sorry, but . . . definitively."

They both fell silent and exchanged no further words all the way to Cancela's ranch.

11

When they reached the gate of the ranch the moon was already glowing brightly, casting along the path the broad shadows of the rustling giant macaw palms. The weather was splendid—dry, cool, and clear; one could have read by the moonlight.

The guide shook the bell vigorously and shouted:

"Anyone home?"

This was greeted by the howling of dogs. A black man arrived to open the gate, holding a tiny torch that he shook constantly to keep it lit.

"Good evening, old man," Manuel said.

"Good ev'nin', white sir," answered the Negro.

And taking the horse's reins, he led both the horse and Manuel up to the house.

Raimundo and the guide followed along behind. From a distance they glimpsed a misshapen plastered wall, which in the moonlight took on the appearance of a lake surrounded by trees. But closer up, the lake became a two-story house, and the travelers could make out a door where the manly form of Cancela holding back two formidable sheep dogs stood outlined.

"Greetings!" shouted the owner of the house. And, turning around toward the dogs, who persisted in barking: "Scram, Cloud-Breaker! Get out of the way, Chain-Breaker!"

The dogs growled in a friendly way, and the rancher with his strong voice and powerful lungs shouted to Manuel:

"Well, you came after all! Look now, I've arranged that this visit should be like the others. So there! How goes our friend?"

"Oh, more or less . . . a little weary from the trip," said Manuel, handing his horse over to the black man and shaking Cancela's hand. "How are your folks here doing?"

"Just fine, thanks to God. They're in singing the Ave Maria, but they shouldn't be long."

And, indeed, a muffled chorus of voices singing prayers came from the interior of the house.

Raimundo, having dismounted, approached.

"This is Mundico, the one I was telling you about," declared Manuel, pushing his nephew forward.

Raimundo was astonished by the rustic introduction, and even more so when the farmer, instead of greeting him, placed his hands on his haunches and began to look him over from top to bottom, as if examining a child.

"What the devil!" he exclaimed, letting out a laugh. "You and the canon spoke about a child!"

"Twelve years ago!"

"Just look at the devil! Well, little Mr. Mundico, squeeze the hand of an old friend of your father's, and don't fret if you don't find the genteel manners of the city around here! This here is still the country! But remember the saying, 'a little bit of generosity is worth more than a whole lot of stinginess!' "

He led his guests to the veranda, minus the guide who had already taken up his lodgings in the Negroes' quarters.

"Men, you go ahead and sit down in those hammocks. Oh Pedro, bring out the pipes! Shall I have him bring the rum and coffee, or do you want wine first?"

"Anything you have."

"We've cognac here," motioned Raimundo, offering a flask he carried at his belt.

"You can have your fill of it!" said Cancela scornfully. "It's something you'll never see going down my gullet!"

Three small glasses of rustic sugarcane brandy were readied.

"To our health! And now go and take off those heavy clothes before supper!"

And he conducted them to a room, kept exclusively for guests.

The house consisted of the old Barroso Ranch where in the distant past José de Silva's mother-in-law had lived and died, and a new addition made of stone and lime, whose careful construction revealed the tenant's prosperity.

The "new house," as the latter section was called, was made up of a building surrounded by a huge veranda where hammocks, sometimes serving as chairs, were strung up in every corner. In the center, traditionally the place of honor in rural Maranhão, was a spacious and well-ventilated room. The rest was simply unpainted walls and unlined ceilings, red clay jugs, brooms of carnaúba wood leaning here and there, and saddles spread along the sill of the veranda. As for furniture, there was nothing but a rough table and some long wooden benches. The storage room for manioc flour was under the house, where there were also enormous leather-covered trunks containing some seventy hammocks for the use of guests. A wine-cellar was off to one side. Outside, the lazy grunting of the pigs could be heard from the pen, and from the rear of the yard, blown in by the night wind, came the fragrant smell of Cayenne jasmine, Peruvian lilies, mignonettes, and sweet marjoram.

When the three men returned from the room, the rancher's wife and daughter had already finished their prayers. Manuel appeared, dressed comfortably in a gray canvas jacket and a pair of wooden clogs. Raimundo had not changed his clothing, but had merely washed his face and hands and combed his hair. Cancela's wife set the table for supper. The daughter had run and hidden in her room, peeping at the visitors from behind her door, too embarrassed to appear.

"Come here, Angelina!" shouted the farmer. "You're acting like a wild animal! Haven't you ever seen people, my girl?"

He went to her room and made her leave her hiding place.

"Come now, speak up! Don't go hiding your face, you've nothing that needs to be hidden. Come on!"

Angelina appeared timidly and was greeted by the men.

"Well," scolded her father. "Can you answer only with your head? Ah, you're acting more and more like a hillbilly. Now what harm did that new pinafore do you for you to mistreat it like that? Watch it, it's going to rip, silly girl!"

Angelina, very much upset, had lowered her dark face, which was more flushed now in a fit of laughter at the embarrassment that overcame her.

"Well, what are you laughing about, you ugly thing?"

These last words were an injustice Cancela was doing to his daughter. Raimundo, upon shaking her loose and unkempt hand, immediately realized that he was face to face with a beautiful and foolish backland girl, as innocent and strong as a field animal. She was eighteen years old and a woman—a woman because her body was already fully formed, with ample shoulders, a rounded bosom, and arms well developed from work in the open air. "A good woman for bearing children," he thought.

"What you're seeing here, my friend, is a sly one," said Cancela, well satisfied with Raimundo's flattering gaze. "Why, she could turn this house upside down and make it seem like she hadn't broken a single plate! Look how the dizzy creature hasn't even asked my blessing since she finished her prayers. It seems she's become entranced with the visitors. Get on with you, you wild critter!"

The girl went to kiss his hand, and he then dealt her a slap across the sturdy cushion of her hips. "You trickster, get away! May God keep you white!"

Manuel, meanwhile, was chatting with Cancela's wife, a typical small Northeasterner who was squat, full of life, with beautiful teeth and dark curly hair. Her entire being gave off the modest air of someone who likes to do good; she was always looking for something to straighten up, was highly diligent, quite tidy, and very much the worker. In the kitchen she could hold her own against the best. She knew how to wash better than anyone, and helped the black slaves work the gardens without falling ill. "She can do anything," the slaves would say about her. Her name was Josefa, and she had been to the city only twice.

"Well, now!" complained the rancher, "is our dinner coming or not? Remember, these men's stomachs are probably wrapped around their spines by now. And I don't want them to jabber away without sinking our teeth into something."

His wife was already in the kitchen by the time he finished his complaint.

"Now, why don't you just take off those fancy duds?" Cancela asked Raimundo. "Around here no one pays any attention to them. If you like, make yourself right at home."

"Thank you, I know that, but I'm fine like this."

And they conversed while Angelina set the table. Cancela felt pleased, and garrulous. He loved to talk and, whenever he could latch on to guests who could put up with him, he couldn't be stopped.

Meanwhile, Josefa was bringing out appetizing dishes, and the men sat down, ready to eat heartily. A white linen tablecloth shone brightly in the light of a rickety kerosene lantern, and the china shimmered, bursting with freshness. White bottles, full of cashew fruit wine, scattered golden reflections about; the egg crust of a shrimp pie crackled; a huge roast chicken lay resigned and immobilized like a patient; a gourd of dry manioc flour stood next to one containing moist manioc; in the center, a large platter of fluffy white rice was heaped up like a pyramid, filling the air with its fragrant aroma.

The two felt quite at ease there, with that spruced-up atmosphere and Cancela's rustic and forthright manner.

"Olé!" their host shouted, removing the lid from a steaming tureen of fish. "Do we have marinated fish? Bravo!" And examining the other dishes: "Bravo! Bravo! Mussel stew! Stewed fish! This one isn't from our river, you see, so you can't get your hands on it just any day! It's got scales, Mr. Manuel!"

And they filled their plates.

"Wonderful! It's wonderful!" he repeated, stuffing his mouth with huge spoonfuls.

"And aren't the ladies going to keep us company?" said Raimundo, turning toward them.

"What!" the rancher retorted quickly. "They're not accustomed to outsiders. Let them be! Let them be, 'cause afterwards they'll eat and be more comfortable! Look, my wife over there says she can't enjoy fish unless she eats it with her hands. Those are a woman's tricks! Don't you worry about them!"

Nevertheless, Josefa came to preside over the table at her husband's side and to gauge the success of her tasty food.

"Now, don't you get up without trying that mussel pie, it'll really fill your craw!"

"Give us time, we'll get to it. Let's have some more peppers!"

"My friend, drink it down! Don't be afraid, the wine's somewhat weak. Mr. Manuel, Mr. Mundico: let's drink one to the memory of my old friend, José da Silva!"

The three downed their wine and Cancela, after resting his empty glass and wiping off his mouth with the back of his hand, added respectfully:

"He was a second father to me. When I settled in these parts, in the days of my deceased employer, Dona Úrsula Santiago, I had nothing but my health, strength, and willingness. So, José, who at the time was courting her daughter, Dona Quitéria, set me up here as foreman and told me: 'Look here, young man, stick around here, and if you get on the good side of the old lady and the parish priest, you might even make your fortune! She's got a favorite goddaughter with a fine character and a good head on her shoulders.' I go, I stay on working at the place and, thanks be to God, I earned the trust of Dona Úrsula. At night I'd come up to the veranda to chat with her and my Josefa, who at that time was an eyeful, you should have seen her. The result was that after two years Father Diogo married us, and a good thing it was, too! I've been happy, praised be the Lord!" He took a mouthful and continued: "I was the one who built this house here where we're eating. I put up the mill, hacked fields out of the forest, planted cotton, which wasn't even grown here then, and I intend to make other improvements next year, God willing!"

"Might they want coffee now?" asked Josefa, touched by her husband's story.

After coffee they had some pineapple liqueur and lit their long-stemmed clay pipes. When half an hour had been spent chatting, Manuel groaned that he was no longer the man he used to be and needed to rest his weary bones.

"Well, we'll save the rest for tomorrow. Pedro!"

"Yes, sir!"

"Take these two to the guest quarters and show them the room your wife prepared."

"Understood, yes, sir."

"Well, a very good night to you!"

"Until tomorrow."

Manuel and Raimundo were settled into a room in the old house, originally the residence of José da Silva's mother-in-law. This section, unlike the other, was a silent and sad two-story house, which exuded only abandonment and decay.

The merchant was soon snoring, whereas Raimundo, stretched out in a hammock, gazed through the window at the sky flooded by moonlight and mentally reviewed what had happened during the day. The events paraded through his mind in a dizzying and outlandish procession: first came his request for Ana Rosa's hand, arm in arm with the refusal; close behind followed the tiny Portuguese from Rosário, marching along with a rue branch in his hand, singing:

> "São Brás, alas!
> Sweet Jesus, alack!
> Here I pass
> With no cross on my back!"

And in his wake followed an infinity of fantastic images: the blackbird singing to the dead, and the witch who changed into bones; then followed Canon Diogo, youthful once more, showering solicitude on José da Silva's mother-in-law, who in his imagination, was modeled after Maria Bárbara.

And, unable to lure sleep close, Raimundo began to dwell on totally haphazard things: the guide, lazy, glum, and singing in his feminine falsetto; a ranch they had come upon, where there was a fat man who was an idiot; the ruins of a house, which from a distance seemed to him at first glance a demolished fortress. And in the same fashion a thousand other vague and uninteresting subjects moved through his memory with a tedious persistence. Finally, sleep approached, but Manuel's refusal popped up yet again and sleep, ever skittish, fled. Why should the man so formally deny him his daughter's hand? Well, certainly for some foolish reason. It wasn't even worthwhile worrying over such futile things. Tomorrow, yes, tomorrow, he reckoned, he would find out everything. And he even felt like laughing at the grave manner in which his uncle had answered him. Well, after all, it was nothing more than some childishness on Manuel's part. Or, who knows? Perhaps some intrigue? . . . Of course! That could well be it. In Maranhão the spirit of meddling knew no bounds. It couldn't be anything else! Some plot. But what kind of plot? Well, he would unravel it. He would get to the bottom of it all. No losing heart! And without knowing why, he realized that he was now even more committed to that marriage; he wanted it much more after the resistance that his request had encountered. Manuel's refusal provided him with a measure of the true esteem in which he held Ana Rosa. Until then he had supposed that their marriage depended on him alone, and he had readied himself coldly, without enthusiasm, almost as if making a sacrifice. And now, after his unsuccessful request, now, he desired it passionately. That unexpected refusal was for Ana Rosa what a dark-colored pedestal is for a marble statue: it set out in relief the harmony of the lines, the whiteness of the stone, and the perfection of the contour. And Raimundo, attempting to gauge the depth of his love for her, stumbled from surprise to surprise, from shock to shock, astonished at what he uncovered in himself, and frightened by his own thoughts as if they were being laid bare by a stranger. At times he reached the point of not understanding them well and fled from scrutinizing them too closely, fearful of concluding that he truly was in love. In this duplicity of feelings his spirit groped blindly in his brain like someone wandering in the dark in a strange and unknown room.

"And so what?" he soliloquized. "Haven't I been thinking about this for two hours?"

He could not convince himself that he attached such great importance to that marriage and even attempted to persuade himself that he had intended it as a kind of compassionate indulgence toward Ana Rosa; yet his whole being rebelled at the thought of failing to carry it out. But wait, neither would he die of disappointment because of this! There was no lack of good matches for making a family! The trick was to be willing to search out another fiancée. Yes, it wasn't seemly to insist on his plans to marry his cousin. After all, that brutal and dry refusal offended him. . . . Certainly, it offended him! No, he shouldn't think about such folly, not in the least. He would never, ever marry Ana Rosa. Anyone else, but not her! Nothing doing. Definitely not, for it was by now a matter of self-respect. But with this resolution his considerable admiration for the young girl's charms returned to him in a clearer and more positive fashion, and he felt a secret unspoken regret, a hypocritical grief that he could not possess her.

A few feet away Manuel snored with irksome persistence. After twisting and turning for some time in his hammock, Raimundo got up, fatigued, lit a cigar and went out on the veranda. A bat, on the curve of its flight, grazed his face with the tip of its wing.

Unimpeded, the moonlight shone in as far as the door of his room and extended a white light along the floor. Raimundo leaned against the sill of the veranda and, with his tired eyes, gazed across at the dense countryside, which was shaded in half hues from the horizon, like a pastel drawing. The silence was complete; suddenly, however, there was a melodious contralto note, followed by others, prolonged and melancholy, ending in little moans.

Raimundo was startled; the song seemed to come from a tree in front of the house. It seemed to be a woman's voice and had a strange and monotonous melody.

It was the song of the nighthawk. As the bird took flight, Raimundo saw it clearly, its white wings open, carrying its trilling off into space. He reflected that the backlanders were fully justified in their legendary fears and fabulous beliefs. He, if he were to hear that sound in São Brás, would certainly at once be reminded of the bird that sings to the dead. According to the guide's instructions, he continued thinking, the bewitched ruins of São Brás were situated precisely in the same direction that the nighthawk had taken. They must be in that low-lying area visible from where he stood. They couldn't be too far off, and he could even make it over there alone. He was distracted from these reflections by a weak, mysterious noise, which reached his ears as a vague and almost imperceptible mumbling. He lent it his complete attention and was sure that someone near by was softly conversing or engaging in a monologue. Immobile, he stood listening. No doubt about it! This time he had heard it distinctly! He had even caught a word here and there! But, where the devil might it be? . . .

He went to Manuel's room, but the good man was sleeping like a child, now wheezing instead of snoring. He crossed the entire veranda on tiptoe—but discovered nothing; he returned along the side opposite the moonlight—still nothing! Could it be downstairs? He descended, but once there failed to hear the whispering. Well then, it was upstairs after all! But upstairs there were no other guests besides Manuel and himself; Cancela had told him so! He went up again, but this time by the back stairs. Oh, now it was even clearer! Raimundo made out entire sentences, moans, laments, random words, some furious, others tender sounding. It was enough to drive anyone crazy! Who the devil could be out there talking? . . .

"Who's there?" he cried out, on the last step to the veranda, his voice somewhat agitated.

No one answered and the mysterious murmuring ceased immediately. Raimundo nonetheless stood still, already overcome by a certain nervous impatience, his ear still enthralled by the strange effect of his own voice questioning the silence: "Who's there?" A pause that seemed infinite ensued, and finally the murmuring began again, now, however, more distant and coming from the area opposite where he stood. He made his way as silently as possible in the direction of the mysterious voice and was satisfied to note that it gradually grew louder.

"Oh!" Raimundo said to himself in amazement. He had clearly heard his name and his father's: "José do Eito." He doubled his attention. Might he be dreaming? The infernal voice spoke hesitantly about São Brás, Father Diogo, Dona Quitéria, as well as other people he did not know. Surely he would hear something about—his mother! It would be the first time! Oh, at last! He held his breath and listened. Standing there tremulous and cold, he had never before felt such trepidation.

The voice kept on speaking, referring to the major events at São Brás, making revelations, and mentioning, one by one, all the characters except Raimundo's mother. In the dark, with a heavy heart, Raimundo stretched his head forward and opened his eyes wide, his chest heaving. Not a word about her. Impossible! But the voice continued, and he stood there listening. Suddenly, however, complete silence fell, and nothing was heard other than the distant chirping of the night birds.

Motionless but impatient, Raimundo waited—two minutes, four, five. It was in vain; the voice did not return. Not a single word about his mother. This damned conspiracy! . . . After half an hour he once again traversed the veranda; he did not know what to make of it all, nor what he ought to do, but he vowed to discover the truth. Oh, whoever had spoken was perfectly acquainted with the story of São Brás and would surely know something about her life! He went to his room, picked up the lantern, lit it, and then inspected the various sides of the veranda, entered the open rooms, went downstairs, groped about because it was all cluttered with objects, went up again, and, weary and frenzied, having accomplished nothing, returned to his room, turned the light low, and lay down without removing his boots.

He had intentionally not closed the door; it was open—at the first sound he would jump up. Nonetheless, his eyelids dropped, fatigued from the journey, and his body cried out for rest; it was nearly dawn. He was falling asleep.

Then, a slight and muffled noise awakened him. Raimundo shrank back into his hammock and automatically remembered the revolver at his side; outlined against the light of the doorway was the most unimaginably squalid, ragged, and scrawny figure of a woman. She was a black woman, tall, cadaverous and tragically ugly, with hesitant and ominous movements, shrunken eyes and fleshless gums.

Despite his presence of mind, Raimundo felt a shudder of nervous anxiety. But he did not budge, still hoping to hear some revelation. The specter, however, looked about, spied him, smiled, and silently began to leave.

Raimundo leaped up and rushed after her as she fled before him like a shadow. They hurled down the first flight of stairs, the second and the third.

"Wait, stop!" he shouted, beside himself. "Wait, or I'll kill you, you devil!"

The phantom disappeared through the rear door. With much difficulty, Raimundo kept up with it and, upon reaching the ground floor, caught sight of it already on the patio, still fleeing from him. He was hampered by his lack of familiarity with the terrain; but, groping and colliding, he managed to get across the ground floor of the house. Outside, the fleeing shadow was already lost to sight. Raimundo glanced about, walked aimlessly from one side to another, nervous, restive, and spinning around rapidly at the least stir of the branches. Finally, aided by the moon, he glimpsed the sinister shape at a distance, moving steadily away and about to vanish into the halftones of the night. At once he set out after it, his healthy legs flying dizzily along. But the figure penetrated the woods and disappeared completely.

In the meantime, the first signs of daylight reddened the horizon, and the slaves in their rude huts were already rising for their day's labor in the fields. The few hours during which Raimundo laid his head down for a bit of rest were filled with dreams.

When he got up, at about seven in the morning, he felt dispirited and almost doubtful whether he had dreamed throughout the night, or if indeed he had seen and heard the extraordinary specter. Even so, at breakfast the incident was discussed at length, and Cancela explained that the phantom was surely one of those numerous old Negresses, a hanger-on at one of the huts on the ranches nearby, who, naturally, had been drunk. And he told how on the nights when the drums beat the women usually slept anywhere, at the first shack they found along the road. Around here there was always a gang of that vermin; they would drop in and out without anyone asking where they came from or where they were headed.

"Are they runaway slaves?" inquired Raimundo.

Cancela answered that they were not. Fugitive slaves formed a separate group; they never appeared publicly, lived hidden in their own settlements, and showed themselves on the open road only to assault travelers. But these hangers-on were freed blacks, usually liberated at the death of their master, but accustomed since childhood to captivity. With no one to oblige them to labor and not wanting to leave the backlands, they wandered aimlessly, living from hand to mouth, begging at the ranches for a handful of rice to appease their hunger and for a plot of covered ground to sleep on. They were simple vagabonds who harmed no one.

"Just look," he continued, "at the beginning we had three here from São Brás, and they went about doing nothing. Two died and I buried them; as for the third, I don't know if she's still about, but she's an idiot Negress. Perhaps she was the one you saw last night, Doctor."

And since Raimundo requested more facts, he added that at times she would spend entire months on his ranch; the blacks liked to listen to her singing and see her dancing. A raving lunatic! She was always muttering to herself; but for some time she hadn't appeared in the area, so it was quite possible that the poor devil had already kicked the bucket somewhere off in the woods.

They also talked about the nighthawk. Cancela told some old stories about outsiders who vanished in the forest, pursuing the singular call of that bird. The three then dealt with their business; the negotiations concerning the ranch were concluded. Raimundo agreed to everything, provided it not delay his departure—he was burning with impatience to visit São Brás.

Nonetheless, Cancela entreated his two guests to remain for a week, or a few days at least.

"What an idea!" Manuel blurted out. As if he could spend days there, far from his warehouse!

"Well then, leave tomorrow morning."

"No, sir, it has to be this very evening. Why the devil put up with the sun along the way when we can have moonlight bright as day?"

The meal dragged on and Raimundo could scarcely contain his annoyance. It was already three in the afternoon when they finally packed up to leave.

"Take us to São Brás," Raimundo ordered the guide, as soon as they were beyond the main gate of the ranch.

"To São Brás? God help me!"

And the half-breed Indian, after crossing himself, asked why the devil they were headed to São Brás.

"Now, see here, that's none of your business! Just take us!"

"I won't go to São Brás!"

"That's perfect! You won't go! Well, what did you come for, if not to guide us?"

"Yes, sir, but it's just that I won't go to São Brás, not even tied and bound!"

"Go to hell then! We'll go ourselves. Mr. Manuel, you know the way, don't you?"

"Of course, of course, but the fellow does have his reasons! After all, what the devil are you going to do at that ramshackle ruin?"

"That's a good one! See the place where I was born!"

"Well, you're right, but. . . ."

"If you don't want to go, I'll go by myself!"

"But you realize that . . ."

"They talk about the hexes at the place, and there are those who believe in them. . . . I'll do you the justice, however, of supposing you're not one of them."

Their horses reached the main road.

"Look," said Manuel, "I do know the route, and that guide, since he doesn't want to come, could wait for us at the foot of that cross, but . . . I confess . . . I have some misgivings about the runaway slaves. Besides that . . . anyone who heard, as I did, my brother's last words . . ."

"My father's?" Raimundo exclaimed intensely. "Tell me about it!"

"You're going to laugh. . . . They are things that sound like rubbish. Nowadays, young men don't believe in anything. But it's just that certain words, heard from the mouth of a dying man, disturb a person, don't you think? They cause a fellow to kind of wonder. Look, my friend, I'll tell you, just between the two of us, and don't you get upset, but your father didn't lead a very peaceful life there. After his marriage, he couldn't get along with a soul, and even his own mother-in-law didn't want anything to do with him. He lived like an outcast! At that time I was just getting started in business and could hardly get away from my work. However, I did come here three times—but, believe me, I didn't like coming here. It was such a sorrowful place. . . . It pained me to see José so neglected, so sad, as if he were serving out a sentence. Not a single traveler would accept hospitality at São Brás; they preferred sleeping out in the open with the snakes. It was rumored that in the middle of the night horrible screams were constantly heard from the ranch, and for hours on end the striking of blows, and chains being dragged. Slaves would die off, and no one knew why! In short, Canon Diogo, who was the vicar of this parish, confesses that he could never get to the bottom of it. And look, poor fellow! He got it into his head to bless and protect São Brás, and he almost ended up the victim of his own dedication! He even became a bit like those moonstruck types! And he was so hexed around here that the poor man had to abandon his parish! Even today when I touch on all this, he crosses himself all over. Well, just keep in mind he was my brother's closest friend and possibly the only one who would visit his house toward the end. Who knows why, but in his last days your father didn't even want to see anything of him! When he was delirious with fever, he would constantly see spooks and shout like a lunatic that he wanted to finish off the priest! 'I want to kill that priest! Bring me that priest! He's the one to blame for it all!' That so-and-so priest was the canon. I never dared mention those things to him because he's so distrustful and might get riled at me."

And, after a pause:

"Well, my friend, you see that though I don't believe in souls from the other world, I've my reasons for . . ."

Raimundo tried to disguise the anxiety Manuel's words had provoked in him and remarked that if Manuel weren't up to going to São Brás, he could stay with the guide, and he, Raimundo, would continue on alone.

"But you realize," Raimundo said, "that I don't blame the backlander for his fear, because after all he's not up to certain truths, but as for you . . ."

"I've no fear of anything at all, I've already said so! But it's just that . . ."

"You're still afraid the devil might leap out at you, I presume."

And Raimundo pretended to chortle slightly, to intimidate his uncle.

"No, but . . ."

"Aw, forget those stories! You aren't acting like a real man!"

Manuel finally gave in, and the two set off toward the abandoned ruins.

They traveled the entire stretch in silence, Raimundo because of his heightened emotions, and Manuel out of pure dread.

Instinctively, they halted a respectable distance away.

"I believe we've arrived," Raimundo ventured.

And, proceeding a few paces, he said to Manuel: "There it is."

"Is anyone at home?" shouted Manuel.

Only the echo answered.

They advanced further, and Raimundo took his turn at a shout, with the same result.

"Let's get a move on, Manuel! We're dawdling. There's not a living soul here."

After a few more paces they were in front of the ruins.

It was the remains of a one-story house, lacking its exterior plaster but with a hardwood frame that had resisted the years of utter abandonment.

Night was arriving. The sun was sinking, going under in an ocean of fire and blood. The sky shimmered like the hood of a furnace; the countryside seemed to be ablaze.

Wanting to take advantage of the waning daylight, the two travelers at once dismounted and tied up their horses. They entered the veranda of the house through a breach cutting the outside layer of the wall from top to bottom. This section was totally in ruins and teeming with weeds; chameleons, lizards, and tiny opposum scurried about, frightened by Raimundo's feet, which went springing over the clumps of nettles and wild grass.

From the inside the ruin had a hard and repugnant look. Long spider webs hung dejectedly in every direction like curtains of rotting crepe. Along the walls rain water, tinged with reddish soil, had left long, bloodlike tears, which snaked amid the wasp and lizard nests. In one corner on the brick floor sat an abominable instrument of torture: stocks made of black wood, whose rounded holes for imprisoning the legs, arms, or neck of the slaves still displayed sinister purple stains.

The two went on, moving into the interior of the house. As they passed through each door, a black cloud of bats and swallows would flit away before them. The floor, caked with bird and reptile excrement, was sticky and damp; the roof was open at various points, and a sorrowful and listless light seeped through. A dungeonlike atmosphere pervaded everything. From a quagmire near the house, the hoarse croaking of frogs throbbed as monotonously as a clock. Cuckoos flew from tree to tree, breaking the afternoon silence with their prolonged and extremely sharp cries. From the gloomy depths of the forest came the periodic yelps of foxes, and the sensual cries of monkeys and marmosets. The evening concert was already under way.

Manuel, emotionally on edge, slowly contemplated the ruins surrounding him, attempting to recognize in those mute and filthy remains his brother's former residence. There was nothing to remind him of a single sign of life from the past.

"Let's have a look around here," he said, leading his nephew toward a room whose unfastened window shutters were ready to collapse. "This was José's room."

And he began to ruminate.

Raimundo contemplated everything with a sorrow that was deep, borderless, and infinite, but still closed in like a foggy horizon. What had his father been like? he wondered silently. What could he have been like, that good man who had never neglected poor little Raimundo's upbringing? How many times, in that very room, perhaps near one of those windows, while staring out at his garden, had the unhappy man not thought of his beloved son who was so distant from his affection? . . . And his mother? . . . His poor unknown mother, might she have been there at his side? Or, who knows? Perhaps she had been in hiding, ashamed, sobbing over her errors in some humiliating exile?

"Here," said Manuel, tapping his nephew's shoulder, "you were born and spent your first years."

Raimundo felt a frantic desire to inquire about his mother but did not have the courage. He now feared an unexpected disappointment, some unprecedented anguish, which might completely crush him. He dreaded some merciless truth, solid and cold as steel, which might slash him from side to side like a sword. Until then no one had ever spoken to him about her. Surely there was some sort of family secret in all that, some shameful passion, some horrible misdeed, perhaps an abominable crime that no one dared reveal! And yet all the while Raimundo was certain that the man at his side, within range of his voice, knew everything, and could, if he wanted, wrench him forever out of that accursed uncertainty! . . . Who might she be, that strange and mysterious mother for whom he felt a confused love? . . . Some lady, certainly beautiful, for she had been the cause of crimes; herself a criminal, out of love, driving his father to follies by kindling a fatal and romantic passion, full of dread and remorse! And from that secret and criminal life, from that adultery which had surely brought on his father's death, he had been born! . . . But why wouldn't they tell him all this frankly? Why wouldn't they tell him the whole truth? . . . Ah! It must be some hellish secret for it to be hidden with such zeal! And, despondent at these thoughts, humiliated by doubts about himself, wretched and sad, Raimundo roamed through the house in silence.

Manuel's voice awoke him once more:

"Let's head for the chapel before night closes in completely."

They passed first through the cemetery. It was wrecked. Manuel pointed toward an old grave, and said respectfully:

"There lies your father."

Raimundo approached the tomb, removed his hat, and tried to

make out on its face some inscription that might tell him about the dead man. Absolutely nothing! Time had erased even his father's name from the stone. All that remained was a decayed and blackened slab of marble. It had ceased being a marker and was now just a lid. Raimundo felt then, more than ever before, the entire mystery of his existence weighing on his soul like a bar of lead. He realized that a silent and black stone lay over his own life as well, and that his past was nothing other than one more grave without an epitaph.

A mass of sobs coiled within his throat, and Raimundo felt the need to kneel before the silence of the tomb.

Manuel withdrew discreetly, coughing to disguise his emotion. Raimundo wiped his tears, by now abundant and heavy; he then moved toward another grave sheltered by a leafy mango tree. It was already empty, its gravestone out of place. Relatives of the deceased had obviously removed the bones from there to some churchyard in São Luís. The location of the tombstone and some foliage had served to protect the epitaph. Raimundo wiped his handkerchief over it and was able to read the words: "Here lie the mortal remains of Quitéria Inocência de Freitas Santiago, affectionate daughter, exemplary wife. Married 15th of December 1845 and deceased 1849. Pray for her."

"There's no doubt that in addition to being a bastard child, I was the result of a tremendous disgrace. My birth coincides more or less with this date."

And, finishing this monologue, he reached the back of the cemetery and found himself in front of a chapel. Climbing over three dilapidated steps, he entered. An owl fled, terrified. The moon's sad light was already seeping through the openings in the roof, but through the windows the hot and hazy twilight crept in. Raimundo, approaching the vestry, stopped short and shuddered all over: the skeletal ragged phantom of the night before was standing there in that dim light, dancing with a strange swaying movement, her scrawny arms raised above her head. Raimundo felt a cold sweat freezing his forehead; he stood motionless, in near disbelief that the thing in front of him was a human figure.

Nonetheless, the mummy came hopping up to him, snapping her long and bony fingers. Her white and gumless teeth were visible, her eyes writhed convulsively in their deep sockets, and her skull seemed to poke angularly into her flesh. First she raised her hands, lowering her head; then she spun around, stamping her feet and leaping into the air.

Suddenly she noticed Raimundo and hastened toward him with open arms. His first reaction was to withdraw in repugnance, but, coming to his senses, he approached the madwoman and asked her if she knew anyone who had lived on that ranch.

The lunatic stared at him and laughed, without answering.

"Didn't you know José da Silva, known as José do Eito?"

The Negress continued laughing. Raimundo persisted in his interrogation, but to no effect. The crazy woman contemplated him fixedly, as if attempting to recognize his features. Suddenly she hurled herself at him, trying to embrace him. He had no time to flee and could not avoid contact with the repugnant body. Then, with a sign of exasperation, he brusquely repelled her. She fell over backwards, her bones snapping against the floor tiles.

Raimundo fled at a run to find Manuel, but the idiot woman caught up to him, already in the cemetery, and again flung herself onto him.

"Don't touch me!" he shouted, in a rage, raising his whip.

Manuel came running:

"Don't strike her, Doctor! Don't strike her, she's crazy! I know her!"

"But she won't leave me alone. Go! Scram, you devil! Watch it or I'll hit you!"

Manuel seemed both anguished and astonished.

"Right now!" he said, frightening the madwoman. "Get inside right now."

The Negress withdrew meekly.

"Who is she?" Raimundo asked once outside, as he was getting ready to mount. "You said you knew her."

"That poor Negress," answered Manuel hesitantly, "was your father's slave. Let's go!"

And they set off down the road.

12

They both returned deeply affected by the abandoned ruins. Twice Manuel had tried to strike up a conversation, but it had not succeeded in taking hold of his companion's troubled spirit; Raimundo responded mechanically to his words, and rode along preoccupied and dejected. With his doubts about his origins and the certainty of his illegitimacy, a strange sensitivity now came over him; he did not know precisely why, but he felt he urgently needed a full explanation of what had led Manuel to refuse him his daughter's hand. Certainly the key to the mystery lay there!

What he wanted was to penetrate his past, search through it, study it, get to know it thoroughly; until then he had encountered all the doors shut and mute, like his father's tomb. In vain he had knocked on them all: no one had answered. Now it seemed that a trap door lay revealed by Manuel's refusal, and he had to open it and enter, whatever the cost, even if the trap door opened onto an abyss.

And so dominated was he by his resolution that, on reaching the cross at the main road, he failed to notice either it or his uncle who had at once set off down the road.

"Hey there, my friend," Manuel shouted after him. "Pull out of it! Forget about that place!"

And he dismounted in order to place a myrtle branch at the foot of the cross.

Raimundo came up behind and, after a long silence, fixed his eyes on Manuel and, giving voice to the single thought that held sway over him, asked:

"Is she by chance my sister?"

"She, who?"

"Your daughter."

The merchant understood his nephew's concern.

"No."

Raimundo immersed himself again in the quagmire of his doubts and conjectures, once more searching out the motive for that refusal, like someone searching for an object in deep water; and his mind, at other times so lucid and discerning, turned impotent and blind, darkly groping about in desperation, almost snuffed out by the muddy and mysterious depths of the swamp.

And, from all this, a great uneasiness afflicted him. After Manuel's denial, Ana Rosa seemed to him indispensable for his happiness; he could no longer envision any existence without the sweet company of that uncomplicated and lovely young woman who, to his aroused desire, now appeared to him a thousand times more seductive. And in his enamored fantasy he still nurtured the idea of possessing her, an idea that, as he only now realized, had slumbered with him every night, but now, like an ingrate, wanted to slip away from him with the banal and commonplace excuses of a weary lover. Oh, yes, he desired Ana Rosa! Imperceptibly he had grown accustomed to regarding her as his; little by little and without perceiving it, he had been linking her to all the aspirations of his life. He had dreamed of himself at her side in the happy intimacy of a home, watching her manage a house that belonged to them both, and that Ana Rosa would fill with the happiness of an honest and fruitful love. And now, wretched, he looked on all that happiness like the criminal who stares through the prison bars at the fortunate married couples parading down the street arm in arm, laughing and conversing, with their children at their side. And Raimundo perceived perfectly that Manuel's zeal in denying him his daughter, far from separating him from his love, was pushing him more and more toward her, linking her forever to his destiny.

"Might your daughter have some hidden physical ailment which would cause the doctor to prohibit her marriage? Might she have some organic defect?"

"Oh, indeed! Your questions torment me! . . . Believe me, if I were able to tell you the reason for my refusal, I'd have done so at once!"

Raimundo could not restrain himself and, bringing his horse to a halt, blurted out:

"But you must understand my persistence! One just can't talk like that to a man who honestly and respectfully requests the hand of a lady who has authorized him to do so. 'I'll not agree because I don't want to!' Why don't you want to? 'Because! I can't tell you the reason!' Really! Such a denial is a direct affront to the man who made the request! It was an attack on my dignity! You must agree that you owe me a reply, whatever it may be, an apology, even a lie! What the devil, some explanation is necessary!"

"That you deserve, but. . . ."

"If you told me: 'I'm opposed to the marriage because I seriously and instinctively dislike your personality,' then fine! It wouldn't be a plausible reason, but you'd be within your rights as a father. But you. . . ."

"Pardon me, but I couldn't say such a thing after having praised you repeatedly and having declared myself, as I do again, your friend and admirer."

"Well, then? If you're my friend, what the devil! Tell me frankly the reason! Deliver me once and for all from this accursed state of doubt! Explain to me the secret of your refusal, whatever it may be, even if it's a crushing revelation! I'm willing to accept anything, anything! Except the mystery, for this has tormented me my whole life! Come now, speak! I entreat you on behalf of . . . the one who was murdered!" And he pointed in the direction of the cross. "He was your brother and, so it's said, my father. Well, then, I ask you for his sake to speak to me frankly! If you know anything about my forebears and my birth, tell me all. I swear to you I'll be grateful for it! Or, who knows? Am I so despicable in your eyes that I don't even merit such a paltry show of confidence?"

"No, no! On the contrary, my friend. I'd be delighted to see you married to my daughter, if it were possible. . . .I just pray to God that a husband possessing your good qualities and wisdom can be found for her. But believe me, as a good father, I could in no way whatsoever consent to your union. I'd be committing a crime if I were to allow it!"

"Then there must certainly be some close kinship between Ana Rosa and me!"

"Careful, you're offending me. . . ."

"Well, defend yourself by clarifying everything once and for all!"

"And do you promise not to be outraged at what I say?"

"I swear it! Tell me!"

Manuel shrugged his shoulders and then muttered as if conveying a secret:

"I denied you my daughter's hand because you are . . . you are the son of a slave woman."

"I!"

"You're a colored man! . . . And that, unfortunately, is the truth."

Raimundo turned livid. Manuel, after a short silence, continued:

"You surely see, my friend, that it's not for my own sake I denied you Ana Rosa's hand but for all these other reasons. My wife's family was always quite scrupulous in that regard, and all of Maranhão is like them. I agree it's a gross stupidity, I agree it's a silly bias. You can't imagine how deep the prejudice against mulattoes is around here! They'd never forgive me for such a marriage; besides, in order to carry it out, I'd have to break the promise I made to my mother-in-law not to give her granddaughter to anyone other than a proper white man, either Portuguese or the direct descendant of Portuguese. You're a very worthy young man and quite deserving of esteem, but you were freed at your baptism, and everyone here is aware of it."

"I was born a slave?"

"Yes, it pains me to tell you and I would not do it if I hadn't been forced to, but you are the son of a slave woman and you too were born enslaved."

Raimundo lowered his head. They continued their journey. And there in the rural landscape, in the shade of those colossal trees through whose gaps the moon sadly filtered, Manuel went on to narrate his brother's life with the Negress Domingas. When, at one point or another he would hesitate, embarrassed to tell the whole truth, Raimundo would urge him to proceed in all frankness, maintaining his appearance of feigned tranquility. The merchant recounted everything he knew.

"But whatever happened to my mother, my real mother?" the young man asked when Manuel had finished. "Was she killed? Did they sell her? What became of her?"

"Nothing of the sort. I found out just recently that she's alive. . . . She was that poor lunatic at São Brás."

"My God!" Raimundo cried out, wanting to return to the ruins.

"What's this? Come now! Stop this folly! You can return some other time!"

They both fell silent. For the first time Raimundo felt unfortunate; an incipient ill will against other men began to take shape in his soul—until then honest and unblemished. Disillusionment placed the first stain on the purity of his character. And in his desire to react, a revulsion was taking hold of him. Confused ideas, soiled and muddied with hatred and vague desires for vengeance, were coming and going, hurling furiously against his strong principles of honesty and morality, as when a storm in the ocean incites the huge, black, white-capped waves to beat against a rocky cliff. One word alone floated to the surface of his thoughts: "mulatto." And it grew and grew, expanding, transforming itself into a terrible cloud that cloaked his entire past. A parasitic idea, it was strangling all his other thoughts.

"Mulatto!"

That single word now explained all the petty suspicion with which the society of Maranhão had treated him. It explained everything: the coolness of certain families he had visited; the conversations abruptly cut off the moment he approached; the reticence of those who spoke to him about his forebears; the reserve and caution of those who, in his presence, discussed questions of race and blood; the reason Dona Amância had offered him the looking glass and said "Just look at yourself!" and the explanation for why they avoided calling the street urchins "black boy" when he was present. That simple word revealed all he had desired to know until then, and at the same time denied him everything; that cursed word swept away his doubts and cleared up his past, but also robbed him of any hope for happiness and wrenched from him his homeland and future family. That word told him brutally: "Here, you wretch, in this miserable land where you were born, you shall only love a Negress of your own sort! Your mother, remember it well, was a slave! And so were you!"

"But," retorted an inner voice, which he could scarcely hear within the storm of his despair, "nature did not create captives. You should not bear the least blame for what others have done. And yet you are punished and damned by the brothers of those very men who introduced slavery into Brazil!"

And in the whiteness of his immaculate character a mass of destructive worms burst forth and seethed, carrying hatred, vengeance, shame, resentment, envy, sadness, and evil. Into the circle of his now relentless and profound loathing entered the image of his native land, and of those who first colonized it, and who then and now governed it, and of his father, who had caused him to be born a slave, and his mother, who had participated in that crime. Was there no value, then, in having been well raised and educated? Did being decent and honest count for nothing? . . . For in that hateful province his countrymen would forever look upon him as a despicable creature whom all would repel from their bosom. And then with great clarity, in the raw light of his despondency, he finally perceived the utter abject malevolence of Maranhão; the gossiping at the pharmacy door, the paltry intrigues that reached his ears by means of idle and contemptible beings at whom he could never glance without scorn. And all that misery, all that squalor, which until then had been revealed to him little by little, now became an immense black cloud in his spirit, for, drop by drop, the tempest had finally formed. And, in the midst of that gale, one desire, and only one, grew: the desire to be loved, to have a family, a legitimate haven where he might forever take refuge from all men.

But his desire only demanded, only wanted, and would only accept Ana Rosa, as if the entire world had once again vanished around that pallid and tender Eve who had offered him a taste, for the first time, of the entrancing venom of the forbidden fruit.

13

The return seemed much longer than the journey out to Rosário. Raimundo scarcely uttered a sound during the entire trip; he was bursting with impatience to be alone, completely alone, to think things through, to converse with himself and convince himself that his mind could rise above those small social trifles.

As soon as he arrived at the house, he went straight to his room and shut himself up inside, to the harsh noise of the lock that was seldom put to use. Night fell. He stopped in front of his desk, in the dark, and lit a match, which went out; then a second, a third, and finally a fourth, which flamed well. But Raimundo stood staring abstractedly at the blue flame, twisting the tiny sliver of wood absentmindedly between his fingers until it burned down and singed his nails. He then sat in the dark for a long while meditating, lost in his concerns. And, by careful reasoning, he reached the heart of the problem: Should he give up or fight? But his mind was unable to decide anything; it balked like a horse facing a chasm. Raimundo jabbed the spurs, to no avail.

"The devil!" he exclaimed, regaining his senses.

And he lit the candle. He sat down at his desk without even removing his hat, and began to think, twitching his leg nervously. He inattentively picked up a pen, dunked it repeatedly in the inkwell, and scrawled on the margins of the newspapers closest to his hand. With unconscious apathy he sketched out a star of David, and, as if taking the greatest care with his drawing, he corrected and emended it. Then he drew a new one similar to the first, then another, and still another, filling the entire newspaper margin.

"The devil!" he exclaimed once again, with the despair of someone unable to find the solution to a problem.

And he began to stare with utmost attention at the candle's flame. Then he picked up a pack of cigarettes that had been left on top of the table and began to use it to break the stalactites of spent wax until the packet, thoroughly soaked in tallow, burst into flame and fell to the floor.

"The devil!"

And he impassively repeated Manuel's words: " 'I denied you my daughter's hand because you are the son of a slave woman!—You're a colored man!—You were freed only at your baptism, and everyone here is aware of it! You can't imagine how deep the prejudice against mulattoes is around here!"

"Mulatto! And I, who never dreamed of such a thing! I might have remembered everything, but not that!"

And he berated himself for having been weak, for not having given stronger replies at the time, for not having reacted with a tough spirit and demonstrated that Manuel was making a mistake, and that he, Raimundo, did not attach the least importance to such . . . trivial things! Magnificent replies now paraded through his mind, veritable rays of logic with which he would blast away his adversary. And, debating now with the replies he had earlier lacked, he recreated the entire situation in his mind, endowing himself with a new role as brilliant and energetic as the earlier one had been feeble and passive.

He pushed the chair back and leaned over the desktop, burying his face in his folded arms. Thus he stayed for nearly an hour; when he finally lifted his head, he noticed for the first time a lithograph of St. Joseph, which had always been there on the wall of his room. Raimundo minutely examined the saint, with his vivid coloring, the baby Jesus in his left arm, and a palm branch in his right hand. He was surprised to see it in that spot: during his carefree days he had never noticed it. He went on to recall having seen in Germany the operation of one of the most up-to-date lithograph presses; then he thought about the various procedures of design, about the diverse styles of the artists he knew, and, finally, about St. Joseph and the Christian religion. And, moreover, a number of entirely irrelevant things scurried through his mind: he remembered a red and sweaty man he had seen the previous week, talking about Napoleon Bonaparte with a shop owner on Nazaré Street. They both blabbered much nonsense; and the image of the shopowner popped perfectly into his memory—extremely scrawny, with long moustaches, affecting the delicate manners of a Lisbon tailor. Raimundo had heard his name but was now unsure. "Moreira? No, it wasn't Moreira." And he searched his mind insistently for the name. "Pereira? No. Nogueira . . . yes, it was Nogueira." That name immediately made him recall an occasion when he was chatting with Nogueira Penteeiro and a crazy woman had walked by and lifted her skirt to exhibit her body. Suddenly, Raimundo shuddered: it was that idea returning, that original idea, the principal one. It was coming back; it had made a false retreat; it had remained at the door of his brain, peeping inside. And he let out a sigh at the troublesome and vexing presence of that idea, lurking in his mind like a policeman who awaits a criminal in order to carry him off to jail. And Raimundo's thoughts lingered, not wanting to move on; but the relentless idea laid claim to them. And the prisoner finally held out his wrists for the manacles.

"Hell! What the devil do I have to do with all this? What I came to do in this stupid province was to look after my financial holdings. Now that they're liquidated, I have nothing more to do here. I'll disappear! I'll get out of here. Farewell to them all!"

And he began to pace about his room, agitated and feigning great pride, his hands in his pockets, while he continued his monologue:

"Yes, of course, once I'm away from here, I'm not somebody freed at baptism! The son of a slave women! I'm Dr. Raimundo José da Silva, esteemed, liked, and respected. I'll go away, why not? What could stop me?"

And he halted, then paced once more, and finally sat down on the bed, ready to retire. He removed his jacket, hurled his hat and vest away.

"Yes! What could stop me?"

He was about to pull off the first boot when the memory of Ana Rosa struck him. An insistent voice shouted from his heart: "And I? And I? And I? You forgot me, you ungrateful soul? Well, I don't want you to go, did you hear? You shall not leave! I'm the one who's going to stop you."

And Raimundo, astounded for not having thought about Ana Rosa in all that time, undressed rapidly and, as though wanting to flee from this new thought, fell face down onto the bed, sobbing.

At six in the morning there was still a light in his room.

On the following day, at two in the afternoon, Raimundo, extremely downcast, descended to Manuel's office and stiffly requested that he hasten his business dealings so as to allow him to depart as soon as possible, for he could no longer tarry in Maranhão. He needed to be off as soon as possible.

"Come now, Doctor, you shouldn't hold it against me that I. . . ."

"Ah, of course, of course! Let's not even think about that," Raimundo interrupted, attempting to deflect the conversation. "You're entirely right. . . . Let's proceed to what really matters. Please tell me when I'll be free to leave."

"But you're not angry at me! Isn't that correct? Believe me that. . . ."

"Oh, sir, how can I show you I'm not? Angry! What do you mean! Really! I've already forgotten all about it. I even came to ask you a favor."

"If it's in my power. . . ."

"It's quite simple."

And, after a pause, Raimundo continued, his voice somewhat agitated, despite the effort he was making to appear calm: "As I told you yesterday, I was authorized by your daughter to request her hand in marriage. However, in view of what you revealed to me about myself, I must present Dona Ana Rosa with some sort of explanation. You understand that I can't leave this province just like that, out of the blue, having already assumed such a delicate pledge."

"Oh, of course . . . but don't trouble yourself about this. . . . I'll arrange some sort of excuse.

"An excuse, exactly. She has to be given an excuse, and the best thing would be to tell her the truth. Explain everything to her. Tell her what happened between the two of us. There's no one more suitable for that than you."

Manuel scratched the nape of his neck with one hand while the other played with the tip of a writing pen stuck in his teeth, with the annoyed attitude of someone who, through pure chance, must take an interest in a situation that has nothing to do with him. But when Raimundo spoke about moving out, he cut in immediately:

"As you wish. But our humble dwelling is always at your service."

"Well," Raimundo concluded, thanking him for the offer with a gesture, "may I count on you, my friend, to explain all this to your daughter?"

"You can rest assured."

"And when will I have my business taken care of?"

"Before the arrival of the coastal steamer you'll be completely free."

"I thank you."

And Raimundo went back up to his room.

It was extremely hot. The clear sky, with its rounded clouds, seemed like a vast blue carpet where enormous shaggy and lazy dogs were sleeping. Raimundo thought of going for a walk, but lacked the spirit: "There goes the son of the slave woman!" He was about to open the window, but hesitated; since Manuel's revelation, he felt an immense lethargy, a growing uneasiness, a dull rancor toward everything and everyone. At that particular moment, for example, he was irritated by the shrill voice of a street vendor, haggling outside the house with some vagabond. Raimundo opened his sketchbook intending to draw, but pushed it away immediately;

he picked up a book and inattentively read a few lines; he got up, lit a cigarette and, with long steps, paced about the room, his hands in his pockets.

On one of his turns he stopped in front of the mirror and studied himself closely, attempting to discover in his pale face some thing, some sign, that might give way his Negro blood. He looked carefully, pushing back the hair at his temples, pulling the skin taut on his cheeks, examining his nostrils, and inspecting his teeth. He ended up slamming the mirror down on the dresser, possessed by an immense, cavernous melancholy.

He felt an impatience that was vast but vague, insinuating, and purposeless, a feeble wish for time to run faster so that a certain day would arrive—although he was unsure which day that might be; he felt an ill-defined desire to go once more to Rosário and search out his poor mother, the poor Negress who had been his father's loyal slave, and bring her back with him and say to everyone: "This idiot black woman here on my arm is my mother, and woe to anyone who does not treat her with respect!" He would then flee the country with her, like someone escaping from a lair of evil men, and put down roots in some other land where no one knew about his past. But Ana Rosa kept returning unexpectedly to his memory, and the unhappy man collapsed into a deep despondency, defeated and humiliated.

Sobbing, he let his head fall into his palms.

At about that time Manuel was finishing explaining to his daughter the absolute necessity of forgetting Raimundo.

"After all," he said, "you're no longer a child, and you're quite capable of judging what is right and not right for you. There are plenty of decent fellows around, from good families . . . capable of making you happy. Come now, I don't like seeing that sad little face! Just wait, later on you'll thank me for the favor I'm doing you now."

Ana Rosa listened to her father's words with her head lowered, apparently resigned. She trusted absolutely in her love and Raimundo's promises, and hence feared no obstacles. Only now had she learned about her bastard cousin's origin, and yet, whether because her mother's last counsel still sprouted in her heart, or because her love was of the type that resists everything, the truth was that the story of his past, which had provoked exclamations of scorn from so many others, which furnished a subject for juicy gossip in pharmacy doorways, which was commented on, amid scornful guffaws and disdainful spitting, throughout the entire province, in settings ranging from the most pretentious of salons to the cheapest of vegetable stalls, this story that closed numerous doors to Raimundo and surrounded him with enemies, this story that was so scandalous and repugnant to the people of Maranhão, did not alter in any way the sentiment Ana Rosa bestowed on him. Manuel's words had not the slightest effect on her; she continued to love and desire the young mulatto with the same faith and the same fervor. She was convinced that he possessed an abundance of worthy qualities and was sufficiently attractive to reward the full attention of all who might contemplate him—without it being necessary to drag in the question of his ancestors. She drew comparisons between the special pleasures of Raimundo's love and the possible embarrassments that might result from it, and concluded that the former quite justified the sacrifices involved in the latter. She loved him—that was all.

On the heels of his advice Manuel proffered some unfavorable comments concerning the moral character of mulattoes, but this served only to further stimulate his daughter's desire by appending to the handsome youth's attributes an additional one, equally strong: that of prohibition. While he, exploring the inadmissible hypothesis of such a disastrous marriage, unfolded a frightening tableau, prophesying, with the dark colors of his own experience and the fever of his fatherly love, a future replete with humiliations and regret, and even going so far as to threaten to withdraw his blessing from her, Ana Rosa stared straight ahead inattentively and answered mechanically, "Yes," "No," "Of course," "Naturally." She paid not the least attention to his wise words, for the very topic under discussion drew her thoughts far afield and brought to her, through an association of ideas, her favorite reveries, in which she dreamed of herself at Raimundo's side in complete conjugal happiness.

"After all," said Manuel, attempting to terminate the conversation and feeling satisfied by his daughter's attentive and resigned air, "we have nothing to fear. He's going to move soon and will leave for good on the first coastal steamer to the South."

That news, presented at point-blank range and in such a firm tone, violently aroused her.

"Eh? What? He's leaving? He's moving? Why? . . ."

And she stared at her father, caught by surprise.

"Yes, he's moving. He doesn't want to stay with us even until his departure."

"But why?"

The merchant found himself facing a sizable complication: it wouldn't be suitable to tell the complete truth and say that Raimundo was moving to spare himself the torment of seeing Ana Rosa daily without hope of possessing her. And, failing to find some reply, some way out, the poor man babbled:

"That's right. The young fellow was annoyed at what I told him and, since he's his own boss, he's moving! How do you like that! You perhaps believe he is very sorry about all this? Well, you're fooling yourself, my child! He appeared nonchalantly in my office and asked me to apologize to you on his behalf, to say that you should forget there was ever a promise! That he needed a change of air, that he was terribly bored by the province, by the hamlet—as he calls it."

"But why didn't he come himself to explain to me?"

"My dear child! It's perfectly clear you don't know Raimundo. Is he the type of fellow for such things? He's the type who doesn't attach the least importance to respectable behavior. He's an atheist who believes in nothing! Why, he even acted satisfied after my refusal. He seemed to be dying for any pretext so as to call off his commitment to you."

"Oh, I understand!" exclaimed Ana Rosa, convulsed and covering her face with her hands. "It's that he doesn't love me. He never loved me, the wretch!"

And she burst out crying.

"Say, now there, what do you mean by this? Oh, my God, what have I done! Ay, this business of women, no one understands them."

Ana Rosa fled to her room, upset and sobbing, and threw herself into her hammock.

Her father followed her, frightened:

"Well, my girl, what's all this? The devil of a fellow!"

And the girl wept on.

"Really, what folly of yours, Anica! Look here, listen."

"I don't want to listen to anything! Tell him he can go whenever he likes. He can go, it would even be a favor!"

"You're not losing anything of value. Well, come now, stop that foolishness!"

Ana Rosa continued sobbing, more and more distressed, with her face hidden in his arms; the sleeves of her dress and the pillows in the hammock were already soaked with tears. For some time she remained like that, not responding to what her father was saying. But suddenly she suspended her crying, raised her head, and let out a quick and sharp wail. It was hysteria.

"The devil," muttered Manuel, flustered and scratching the nape of his neck. He immediately called for the others: "Dona Maria Bárbara! Brígida! Mônica!"

The room filled at once.

Canon Diogo, who had lingered in the anteroom, awaiting the result of Manuel's talk with his daughter, also entered, attracted by his goddaughter's cries.

"Hoc opus, hic labor est!"

At that moment Raimundo was asleep, stretched out on a divan. He was dreaming that he was running away with Ana Rosa, and that in flight they were pursued by three enraged fugitive slaves armed with machetes. A nightmare. Raimundo wanted to run, but could not: his feet sank into the soil as if in a bog, and Ana Rosa was as heavy as if she were made of lead. The three black men approached, brandishing their knives, about to reach them. Raimundo was in a cold sweat, immobile, unable to act, his tongue stuck.

The real cries of hysteria coincided with Ana Rosa's screams in his nightmare as she was knifed by the three fugitives. Raimundo leaped from the divan with a start and, half asleep, looked about. Then he set off on the run toward the veranda.

The canon, hearing his footsteps, came out to meet him.

"Attendite!"

"Well, we finally meet again!" Raimundo said.

"Shhhhhh!" motioned the canon, "she's calmed down now. Don't go in there or the attack might return! You're the cause of all this!"

"I must have a few words with you, immediately, Canon!"

"My good man, wait for some other occasion. Don't you see the uproar this house is in?"

"But I tell you I must speak with you immediately! Come! Let's go to my room!"

"What the devil do you have to tell me?"

"I want to clear up some things concerning São Brás, do you understand?"

"Horresco referens!

And Raimundo, with a considerable shove, got himself and the canon into his room and closed the door.

"Now, you're going to tell me who killed my father!" he exclaimed, fixing his stare on him.

"How should I know!"

And the canon blanched. But he held his ground in front of the other man.

He folded his arms:

"What do you mean by all this?"

"It means I've finally discovered my father's murderer, and I can take vengeance at this very instant!"

"But this is an outrage!" stammered the priest, his voice choked with shock.

And, struggling to control himself, he added in a more assured tone:

"Very well, Doctor Raimundo, very well. You're carrying on admirably! So this is the way you ask for information about your father? This is how you thank me for the faithful friendship I devoted to your poor father in the past? I was his only friend, his only support, his final consolation! And here's his son who shows up now, twenty years later, to threaten a poor old man who's always been respected by everyone! It seems you were just waiting for my hair to turn completely white to insult this cassock, which always used to be received with hats in hand! Very well, very well! I had to live seventy years to see this! Fine, so you want your vengeance? Well, take it, who's stopping you?! Am I the guilty one? Let the hangman come! I'll not defend myself, if only because I now lack the strength to do it! Well, then, why aren't you stirring?"

Raimundo, indeed, remained motionless. Could he have been mistaken? The sight of the canon's serene countenance caused him to doubt the conclusions of his reasoning. Was it credible that this gentle old man, who exuded nothing but religion and holy things, was guilty of so odious a crime? And, not knowing what to decide, he threw himself into a chair, covering his face with his hands.

The priest realized he had won ground and pressed on, in his unctouous and resigned voice:

"Of course, you must be right! Naturally, I was your father's murderer! It's a generous and proper deed on your part to unmask me and shower me with abuse, here in this very house where they've always kissed my hand. You're certainly within your rights! Look, just grab that cane and strike me with it. You're young, you can do it! You, with your twenty-five years, are in full possession of your strength! Come now, flog this poor defenseless old man! Punish this decrepit body, which is already useless! Go ahead, strike without fear, no one will ever know! You can rest assured I'll not shout—before my eyes is the image of Christ who with resignation suffered far more!"

And Canon Diogo, his arms and eyes upraised, fell to his knees and, with clenched teeth, sobbed:

"Oh, compassionate God! You, who suffered so for us, cast your benevolent eyes upon this poor confused creature. Take pity on this poor sinful soul, driven only by blind and mundane passion! Don't permit Satan to overpower this unhappy lad. Save him, Lord! Pardon him for everything as you forgave your torturers! Grant him grace! Grace, I beg of you, my Lord and Father in heaven!"

And the canon looked entranced.

"Get up," Raimundo said to him, wearily. "Stop that! If I did you an injustice, excuse me. You can rest assured that I won't persecute you. Go!"

Diogo arose and put his hand on Raimundo's shoulder.

"I forgive you for everything," he said. "I fully understand your agitated condition. I know what has happened! But console yourself, my son, for God is great and in his love alone you will find true peace and happiness."

And he left with head down and a humble and penitent air. But, while descending the stairs to the street, he muttered:

"That's all for now, but you'll pay for this, my uppity little nigger!"

14

One week later Raimundo was residing in one of his cottages on São Pantaleão Street. He lived a wearisome existence, awaiting only the day of his departure for Rio de Janeiro. The province had never seemed so tedious, nor its isolation so burdensome and sad. He almost never went out in public; he sought no one, nor did anyone visit him. It was rumored that he had taken to his bed as the result of a healthy drubbing his sweetheart's father had arranged. "Well done! That will teach him not to chase after white girls!"

The scandalmongers poked their noses into Raimundo's life as if he were a politician on whom their salvation or misfortune depended. They wagered that the crook was quietly hatching some plot.

"Just remember," exclaimed one of them to a group, "all these types who act so sanctimonious, whose personal lives no one knows anything about, are the most dangerous. For my part, I never trust anybody! When I see a fellow, I right off think the worst of him. Then, if the rascal pulls something, it doesn't surprise me in the least!"

"And if he doesn't pull anything?"

"Well, I keep in mind that a lot takes place on the sly here in Maranhão! But, as for trusting in the fine qualities of an adventurer, not even with a knife at my back!"

Raimundo, meanwhile, was leading the life of an outcast, with neither friends nor affection of any sort. In his exile, his only company was an old black woman who had undertaken to look after him. Scrawny, ugly, and superstitious, she would drag herself limping about the veranda and through the deserted rooms, smoking a horrid pipe, constantly talking to herself, mumbling interminable monologues.

And this seclusion bored him and filled him with nostalgia for those happier days he had passed at Ana Rosa's side, basking in the snug warmth of the family. He now spent little time studying, and was lax and lazy, preoccupied solely with his recent troubles. After lunch or supper, he would remain absentmindedly at the table for many hours, staring idly out into the barren backyard, his legs crossed, his head listlessly fallen to his chest, smoking one cigarette after another in an overpowering lassitude.

He had developed an aversion to everything and was physically wasting away.

At night, the kerosene lantern was lit, and Raimundo would sit down next to the desk, absently reading some novel or looking over the pictures in an illustrated magazine. In one corner of the veranda the servant sat muttering, mending old rags. Raimundo would feel a deathlike boredom as he sat limp with fever, his body overcome by a general collapse. He could not get used to the black woman's cooking—everything was always miserably prepared. It disgusted him to drink out of the poorly washed glasses. Repelled, he would bathe his face in the basin coated with grease. "My God, what a life!" And he became progressively more nervous and frantic. He counted the minutes until the day of his departure. Yet, despite everything, he sensed a dull and deep desire not to leave, a secret hope of still being legitimately loved by Ana Rosa.

"Impossible," he would always conclude, gathering up his courage. "Let's not be ridiculous."

And he wondered what she would not be thinking of him, and the judgment she would form regarding his character. They had never again had the opportunity to exchange a word or glance; he received news of her only through that idiot servant, who didn't even know how to relate it. But after all, what good was it to plague himself that way? The best thing was to let things happen on their own! He could not, and should not, by any means, marry such a woman. Why, then, still think about it?

In Manuel's house, too, things were not going well. Ana Rosa was suffering a heavy grief, barely disguised from her father, grandmother, and the canon. The poor girl was struggling to forget the unfaithful lover who, like a coward, had abandoned her. And in her disillusionment she conjured up rash forms of vengeance and felt absurd desires: marry right away, just to find any husband before Raimundo departed from the province. She wanted to prove to him that she didn't attach the least importance to the episode, and that she would give herself with pleasure to some other man. She thought about Dias and was on the point of speaking to him.

Manuel, prompted by the canon, turned his daughter's spirit more and more against Raimundo. He would tell her outrageous stories about him, invented by the canon. He was now very kind to her, giving in to all her whims, to all her fancies of a sick girl, with the sympathetic solicitude of a cheery male nurse.

Ana Rosa would nod her head, resigned. The evident fact that

Raimundo consented, without a struggle and perhaps through his own desire, to abandon her, at the same time that it provoked her desire to reconquer and possess him, furnished her pride with an abundance of energy to conceal her love from everyone. She felt herself the victim of a disillusionment; she had judged her lover to be more ardent and more forceful, and, in view of the passivity with which he had immediately surrendered to the circumstances, in view of his timid and bourgeois acquiescence—for Raimundo had not felt emboldened to speak or write a single word to her after Manuel's refusal—she felt disenchanted and deceived. "He never, never loved me!" she would say to herself, despairing. "If he loved me, as I imagined, he'd have reacted! He's a fake! A fool! A vain man, who only wanted one more amorous conquest!"

And a strong desire came over her to cry and utter evil things against Raimundo. She now thought he was the worst of men, the most despicable of creatures. At times, however, a sharp jab of remorse wounded her conscience: she remembered that it was she who had taken the initiative in their love affair. And then, with a pang of embarrassment, more favorable recollections of her cousin came to her; she even regretted having formed such a negative opinion of him. "Yes," she thought, "it's true, it's true, if it weren't for me, he'd perhaps never have spoken to me of love! . . . I was the one who provoked him, who cast the first spark into his heart!" And along these lines Ana Rosa discovered thousands of rationalizations, which somewhat softened her ill will against the unfaithful young man.

But her grandmother would immediately jump on her:

"Well, it seems you're a bit grieved over what's happened! But, remember, if I had to witness your marriage to a nigger, I swear, by the light that shines on us, I'd rather see you dead and buried! Because you'd be the first in the family to soil our blood! God forgive me, by the most sacred wounds of Our Lord Jesus Christ!" she would shriek, throwing her hands up in the air and rolling her eyes, "I'd feel like twisting the neck of any girl in our family who'd even think of such a thing! Heavens! Better not even speak about that! And I beg God to just carry me off as soon as possible, if someday I'd have to see, with my very own mortal eyes, a descendant of mine scratching his ear with his foot!"

And, turning around to her son-in-law, in a growing rage:

"Mark my words, Mr. Manuel, if such a misfortune occurs, you'll have only yourself to blame, because, after all, whose idea was it to set up, right here in our house, a nigger full of airs like that so-called know-it-all doctor? They're all like that nowadays! Hold out your foot and they'll grab your hand! These scoundrels no longer know their place! Oh for the good old days! In my time it wasn't necessary to discuss and contrive like this. If they were pesky, out into the street with them! The front door was the way we'd solve it! And that's what you ought to do, Mr. Manuel! Don't be a dunce! Send him once and for all on his way South with all the devils in hell! And try to marry your daughter to someone who's white like she is! Darn it!"

"Amen," said the canon, beatifically.

And he took a pinch of snuff.

The break between Raimundo and the Pescada family was the talk of the town. Each person commented on the event as best he understood it, altering it, of course, as he saw fit. Freitas seized on the event to state haughtily to the colleagues at his office:

"The same thing happens, my friends, to a rumor that runs the gamut of the entire province as to a stone swept along by a torrent of rain; as it rolls along from street to street, alley to alley, and ditch to ditch, it picks up all kinds of junk and filth from its dizzying rush, so that by the time it reaches the drain pipes, you can no longer recognize its original form. According to the same pattern, when a rumor is about to be forgotten, it's already so disfigured that there's nothing left of its original self but the source!"

And Freitas, satisfied with this tirade, thunderously blew his nose without unfastening from his audience that penetrating smile of a great man who, with no concern for who the recipient may be, squanders the precious jewels of his prodigious eloquence.

During those days Raimundo was the sole subject of conversation.

"He's discredited the poor girl forever," said a barber in the midst of the conversation in his shop.

"That's exactly what he tried to do," someone answered him, "but she never trusted him in the least! That I have from a reliable source."

In a house on the main square a naval commander affirmed that Raimundo's exit from the house was due simply to the theft of some money from Manuel's strongbox. And Manuel, it was said, had already gone to complain to the police, and the chief had begun an inquiry.

"Well done, well done!" roared out a pale mulatto with close-cropped kinky hair, who was well-dressed and wore a huge diamond on his finger. "Quite well done, you just can't let those negroes move in on us!"

A rapid exchange of knowing smirks occurred among his audience, and the conversation changed course, finally settling on famous figures of the dark race. Incidents involving racial prejudice were related; important persons were mentioned from Maranhão's high society who had a suspiciously dark tinge; all the distinguished mulattoes of Brazil were discussed; the famous incident concerning the Brazilian Emperor and the engineer, Rebouças,[1] was narrated with great emphasis. One fellow jumped up from the group and excitedly mentioned Alexander Dumas, and vouched his word of honor that Byron was of mixed blood.

"Well, why is that a surprise?!" said some idiot. "Here we've had a provincial president just as black as any of those porters going by over there with casks of brandy!"

"No, no," snorted a self-assured middle-aged man whose opinion among the commercial people was highly respected. "That they have ability, especially for music, is undeniable."

"Ability?" whispered another, with the secretiveness of someone revealing a prohibited thing. "Talent! I tell you, that mixed race is the craftiest in all Brazil! Pity the white if these types pilfer a little book learning and go out and raise hell! That's when everything will come crashing down! Thank goodness they're not given much of a chance!"

"That," commented Amância, gossiping on the same topic at Eufrasinha's house that very day, "just can't have any other outcome! Right here is one person who won't show up there any more if that simpleton Pescada lets that nigger in his family!"

"Now, it's not that bad," objected the ardent widow. "I know certain people who dress up in silk, but then continue to sponge supper off well-to-do niggers. It's simply a matter of hearty tables."

"What?" bellowed the old woman, putting her hands on her hips. "Is that a sly dig? Was it meant for me?"

And a purple color rose to her cheeks.

"Tell me!" she shouted. "Well, tell me! I want you to tell me the name of any Negro whom Dona Amância Diamantina dos Prazeres Sousela, legitimate granddaughter of a Brigadier Cipião Sousela—known as 'Corisco' during the Guararapes War—has ever flattered with her attention! Me? I'll shout it to the heavens! When have you ever seen me at table with a nigger?"

"I wasn't referring to you! Oh, for heaven's sake!"

"Oh, well then, speak up!"

"I'm speaking in general terms!"

And Eufrasinha gave some examples, cited some names, mentioned a few episodes, and ended by declaring that, "despite everything they're saying in this old Maranhão, Raimundo is a distinguished gentleman with an excellent future, a little money, and . . . in short . . . for goodness sake, let them say what they want, he'd be a husband who'd really fill the bill!"

And the widow's eyes opened wide and she bit her lip, draining the air with a sigh.

"Much good may it do you!" concluded Corisco's granddaughter, already in the doorway holding her shawl, about to leave. "It takes all kinds of people in this world! Gracious!"

And she set off at once, straight as an arrow, for Freitas's house.

"You want to hear a really good one?" she said upon arriving there, without stopping for breath. "That flirt Eufrasinha says she wouldn't mind marrying old Mundico!"

"He's the one I doubt would accept," yawned Freitas, lethargically stretching his scrawny long legs in the chair, and crossing his feet with a happy and untroubled air. "She's dying for a husband—everyone knows that. And she has a point, poor thing."

They all laughed.

"Gracious! Heavens!" grimaced Amância. "That's no way to talk! . . . In my day . . ."

"It was precisely the same thing then, Dona Amância: the poor single girl prayed to heaven for a husband, like . . . like . . ."—he obstinately searched for a comparison—"like I don't know what! Now, I'm counting on you to stay for supper."

"If there's fish, I'll stay," she said, stimulated by the odor of oil frying, which was coming from the kitchen.

"Well now, Auntie Amância, just remember we've plenty and it's quite good," observed Lindoca, tottering about the veranda.

"Say, girl!" the old woman shouted to her, "where you going with all that fat? Enough already! Ugh!"

"She won't go far," said Freitas, cheerful as usual. "She'll get tired quite fast."

"Now, have a look," protested the young woman, stopping a slave girl as she passed by with a tureen of fish. "It's really inviting! Nice and hot like a fire!"

"Oh, my dear, that's my passion! A well-prepared fish, piping hot, with manioc meal! But watch out," she shouted to the servant, getting up immediately, "don't set it down there, girl! The cat's likely to go after it. Better put it on that cupboard."

And, as if she were in her own home, she grabbed the tureen and stowed it up on one of the shelves. "You just can't trust those cats.

They're needed on account of the mice, but what a nuisance, my Lord!" Why just the other day her cat, Prankster, got into her pantry and, without a sound, tore into the dried beef that was hanging there for lunch, because she was taking a purgative. That darned cat! "But then, I taught him a lesson that made him look like this!"

And Amância, attempting to show how the cat had ended up, snarled with the remains of her worn-out dentures and stretched out the skin on her neck.

It was already past three in the afternoon. The government bureaucrats were filing from their offices, heading toward the shade with a methodical and never-changing saunter, their hats dangling from the left arm as if from a hanger. They had the untroubled and indifferent air of men paid by the month who never hurry, who never need to hurry.

The afternoon sea breeze began blowing, and the temperature cooled.

Lindoca, to a great heaving of the floor, dragged herself as far as the window to see Dudu Costa pass by. Dudu was a trainee at the customs house who was wooing her. A serious fellow, thin as a rail, and well off—he would be quite a catch for marriage. Freitas looked on this courtship with favorable eyes and only hoped that the young man might this very year take over a post in his bureau: a senior employee there, who was very sick, would without doubt kick the bucket during the next three months, and, since Dudu Costa had a friend whose father was in good standing with the provincial president, his promotion was in the bag. So certain was it that Dudu was already thinking about his outfit for the wedding, setting aside a small portion of his salary, and inviting his best friends to the big day when he would tie the knot. Freitas was quite aware of all this. "The devilish thing is the girl's accursed fat, which is increasing every day and transforming her into a sack!"

"Let's hope to God it isn't some hex!" observed Amância. "There are plenty of jealous people in this world, my dear!"

"My dear lady, 'it's God who sews your wedding dress and funeral clothes,' " recited the great man, sacrificing meter to rhyme.

At about the same time Sebastião Campos and Casusa bumped into each other at a corner.

"Hello! Well, Casusa, what are you up to here?"

"What's the latest word?"

"What? You have no idea! I'm undone by a toothache! The devil of a thing won't stop bothering me!"

And Sebastião opened his mouth wide to show his molar to his friend.

"An epidemic," muttered the latter. "Give me a cigarette."

Sebastião quickly handed him an enormous yellow rubber pouch and a packet of rolling paper.

"Well, what's new around here?" he asked.

"Same old news. Are you heading home?"

"Uh-huh," affirmed Campos with a guttural sound. "Did the steamer arrive from Pará?"

"Yes, and it leaves tomorrow at nine in the morning for the South. For sure! Do you know Mundico's going on it?"

"Yes, indeed! I heard that he'd fought with Pescada."

"He did, eh?"

"They're saying it was on account of money, that Raimundo asked him for a certain amount as a loan and, when Manuel refused him, he started ranting and raving!"

"Man, I'm not sure it's money he asked for. Pescada's daughter—I have it from a good source that's what he asked for!"

"And the Galician?"[2]

"He refused! They say because the guy's a mulatto."

"Yes, partly," said Sebastião, approvingly.

"Come now, Mr. Campos! It could be because I have no sisters, but let me assure you I'd prefer Dr. Raimundo da Silva over any of these stuffed sausages from the commercial district!"

"Now, that I don't agree with! . . . Black is black, white is white, don't confuse the two!"

"Then I'll say more: he'd be an ass to get roped into this marriage, because that nigger has a good sense of what's proper!"

"Yes, that's true," confirmed Campos, occupied at breaking fragments of dry mortar off the wall with the brim of his sunhat. "That fellow is wasting his time around here. He's a big-city man. Look, maybe he has a future in Rio de Janeiro. Don't you remember that. . . ."

And he whispered a name into Casusa's ear.

"Certainly! Why not? I often gave him five or ten cents to eat on, the poor guy. And nowadays, well?"

"Right, he was lucky. But, want me to tell you? I just don't believe this Raimundo has a future, on account of those republican ideas of his. Because everyone should get one thing perfectly straight: a republic is just fine on paper, just fine, yes sir! But it's not for the likes of us at this point! A republic here would provoke anarchy."

"You're exaggerating, Mr. Sebastião."

"It's not for the likes of us at this point, I repeat! We're not ready for a republic. The people have no education. They're ignorant! They're stupid! They don't know their rights!"

"But hold it there," replied Casusa, grasping the air with his pallid cigarette-stained hand. "You say the people don't have the education, very well. But how do you expect people to get educated in a country whose wealth is based on slavery and whose system of government owes its very life precisely to the ignorance of the masses? In such a situation, we'll never get out of this vicious circle. There'll never be a republic as long as the people remain ignorant, but, as long as the government is a monarchy, it will maintain the people in ignorance for its own convenience; in short, there'll never be a republic!"

"And that'll be for the better."

"No, I don't believe that any more. I think it should come, and the sooner the better! I hope a revolution breaks out, just to see what would come of it. I do think that only when all this finally boils over will this mess be washed away! And it's going to be a bloody affair, Mr. Sebastião! Believe me, my dear friend, there's nothing like our Maranhão! It'll never cease being a Portuguese colony! . . . The Imperial government in Rio pays no attention whatever to the northern provinces. This so-called centralization is swindling us! Whereas, if we up here were given some autonomy, each province could look after itself and surely progress, because it wouldn't have to contribute to the Imperial court, that insatiable courtesan."

And Casusa gesticulated indignantly.

"But what can we do about it? The governing group has its own relatives, its own godchildren, its retinues and hired-hands, its big shots—the whole works! And for all that they need lots of dough! Lots of dough! There the people are, so let them pay! Sock them with taxes and let the people manage on their own."

And, putting his mouth to the other's ear: "Remember, Sebastião, here in Brazil you're better off being a foreigner than a native son! Don't you see our compatriots being persecuted and scorned every day, whereas the Portuguese are grabbing up everything, getting richer and richer, and little by little they're becoming landed colonels, barons—everything! Oh, for a revolution!" he exclaimed, pushing Campos with both hands. "A revolution is what we need!"[3]

"What do you mean a revolution! You're just an overgrown kid, Mr. Casusa, and you still don't take life seriously. Just wait, and in time you'll see things the way I do, because here in this region . . . how old are you?"

"I just turned twenty-six."

"Well, I'm forty-four. In this region what you constantly see is that everything here begins with a roar and ends with a meow. Do you think a republic is really suitable for Brazil? Well then . . . oowwww!"

"What is it?"

"My tooth, the devil!"

And, after a pause.

"Goodbye, see you soon," he said, covering his face with a handkerchief and drawing away.

"Wait, Mr. Sebastião!" shouted Casusa, engrossed in the conversation and wanting to go on.

"Not now! I'm heading to Maneca the barber to cure this damned thing!"

And they separated.

Meanwhile, that same evening, as the clock struck eleven, Raimundo finished readying his trunks.

"At last!" and he shook his shirt sleeves, which were sticking to his arms with sweat. "Tomorrow at this hour I'll be far from here."

He then sat down at his desk and, from his briefcase, removed a sheet of paper that was covered from top to bottom with a tiny and at times shaky handwriting. He attentively reread it all, folded it, put it in an envelope, and addressed it to "Senhora Dona Ana Rosa de Sousa e Silva." Then he remained staring at the name, as if contemplating a photograph.

"Let's not get weak now."

And he stood up.

The streets were heavy with silence; far away a dog barked sadly and, from time to time, echoes of distant music could be heard. And Raimundo, there in the discomfort of his room, felt more lonely than ever, like a foreigner in his own land, despised and persecuted at the same time. "And all this, for what reason?" he mulled. "Just because it happens my mother was not white . . . What good is it for me to have so diligently pursued an education? What good are my exemplary conduct and moral integrity? . . . Why have I kept myself undefiled? Why the devil have I aspired to become a useful and honest man?" And Raimundo grew disgusted. "For, no matter how high my ideals, everyone here has avoided me, simply because my wretched mother was black and had been a slave. But, what fault is it of mine for not being white and not being born free? . . . They won't allow me to marry a white girl? Fine! Perhaps they're right! But why insult and persecute me? Oh, a curse on that damned race of smugglers who brought the African to Brazil! Damned, a thousand times damned! How many unfortunates, besides myself, have suffered the same rage and hopeless humiliation? How many others have shrieked in the stocks, under the lash? And to think that there are still beatings and unpunished murders on ranches as well as in the cities! To think that some are still born in captivity, because many landowners in conspiracy with the parish priest are baptizing the guileless as if they were born before the law of the free womb![4] To think that the consequence of such perversity will be a generation of misfits who'll have to suffer the same inferno where I now struggle in defeat! And still the government has qualms about abolishing slavery once and for all; they still say without shame that Negroes are property, as if the theft of their freedom for later purchase and resale, whether for the first, second, or thousandth time, legitimized their status as property and removed the stima of outright thievery on the part of their masters!"

And continuing to ponder the same terrain, greatly agitated, Raimundo got ready to sleep, impatient for the following day, eager to distance himself from Maranhão, that miserable province that had caused him such disenchantment and sorrow. That narrow-minded little land of petty intrigues and overblown jealousies! He wanted to wrench himself away forever from that poisonous and treacherous island, but he was assailed by the immense grief of losing Ana Rosa forever. He loved her more and more.

"Damn!" he interrupted himself. "And here I am thinking about this! . . . I've everything liquidated and ready . . . tomorrow the steamer is coming and . . . farewell! Farewell, dear Athenians!"

And, feigning tranquility, he lit a cigarette.

Just then, a letter was slipped through the shutters of his window and dropped into the room. Raimundo picked it up and read the phrase: "To Dr. Raimundo." He felt a tremor of pleasure, imagining it was from Ana Rosa, but it was simply an anonymous letter.

> Illustrious Scum:
>
> So you're getting out tomorrow? If it's true, I thank you in the name of the province for such a good deed. Be aware, dear sir, that it will be perhaps the first sensible act practiced by Your Excellency in your life, for we already have plenty of adventuresome fops here and need no more of your type. Honor us with your absence and do us the special kindness of remaining away as long as you can. Whoever told Your Excellency that ours is a land of cretins where any pedant can arrange a choice marriage, was mocking you, honorable sir, mocking you roundly. The days when people were so naive are gone. In the meantime, if you see your cousin, give her my best wishes.

It was signed "The Disguised Mulatto."

Raimundo smiled, crumpled the piece of paper, and threw it on the floor.

"Ignorant devils," he said, and went to lean out the window.

There he remained for a long time, draped over the sill, gazing into the darkness of the night where the gas lamps were glowing sadly, quite distant from one another. São Pantaleão Street was as silent as a cemetery.

A bell tolled in the distance.

"It must be two-thirty."

Raimundo closed the window and went to bed. He then rose once more, picked up the letter and reread it. Only the signature irritated him.

"Those dogs!" he said.

And he blew out the candle.

Then the rains began. The wind blew fiercely, whistling through the roof slats. Shortly thereafter the sky drizzled a thin and fleeting rain. Nevertheless, on the street corner a troubadour sang as he played his guitar:

> "In vain I've tried to tear you from my mind,
> Expunge your name from my despairing heart.
> I'll love you always . . . torment is my part. . . .
> This passion slays me. . . . Death would be more kind."

The following morning Manuel arose before his clerks, dressed in the half light of the dawn, and headed for Diogo's house.

"Hello, you're up early," the canon said to him from the window, where he was shaving in his shirtsleeves.

"That's right. I've come to take you to Mundico's embarkation."

"We've got time. Come in and I'll give you a cup of fresh coffee."

And turning around toward the kitchen:

"Get moving there, Inácia! We have to leave somewhat earlier," he shouted, while with a towel he slowly gathered together the soap foam he was removing from his chin.

"Come, make yourself at home and tell me the latest."

The servant entered with a tray containing coffee, a bowl of porridge, a bottle of liqueur, and some small glasses.

"Will you have a little porridge?"

"No, thank you. But I would like some coffee."

"Well, I can't get along without it, or my coffee, or my Chartreuse liqueur, either. Have a little glass of it, Manuel! Why not? This time you didn't come on business, right?"

"Of course, go ahead and serve me. Indeed, it's delicious!"

"Well, how about another? The first shot hardly goes to your head."

"And it does no harm. . . ."

"Correct! Now, how about a sip of coffee? And what do you say about the coffee?"

"Superb! It's from Rio, isn't it?"

"What do you mean Rio? It's good coffee from Ceará. Remember, the best coffee in Brazil is from Ceará. That black woman who brought it in is an expert at preparing it. I've never seen anyone like her. For coffee and an arrowroot porridge with eggs, she has no match!"

And the canon started dressing, stretching his scarlet silken stockings up his legs and, with his tortoiseshell shoehorn, putting on his oiled and well-polished shoes with sparkling buckles. He then slipped into his lustrous merino cassock, patting his round and fleshy belly, wiggling all over, shaking his fat little legs, and going to the vanity mirror to fasten his white lace collar about his neck. He was clean, perfumed, and well combed. With his smooth-shaven face and curly white hair, he had the lively air of an old nobleman-philanderer. The glass of his spectacles augmented the gleam in his eyes, and his new three-cornered hat, dashingly tilted a little to the left, gave his distinguished head and smooth face the picturesque and noble look of a seventeenth-century courtier.

"Whenever you're ready, I'm at your orders," he reminded Manuel, who stood at the window pensively smoking a cigarette.

"Then let's be off. The fellow is perhaps already awaiting us."

And they left.

A beautiful morning had dawned. The first rays of the sun were drying up the humidity of the night on the stonework sidewalks. The heels of the priest's shoes clicked against the stones. Laborers passed on their way to work: the breadman with a sack on his back; the washerwoman heading toward the fountain with a bundle of dirty clothing balanced on her head; black women shouting "corn porridge!"; slaves coming down to the butcher's with baskets or purchases looped in their arms; vegetable vendors arriving from the surrounding truck farms, their huge trays laden with greens and legumes. All of them greeted the canon with respect, and to each one he replied: "Good morning to you." A few children on their way to school came up with their caps in hand to kiss his ring.

"You say he's already waiting for us?"

"It would be natural," responded Manuel.

"Have no fear. It's still quite early," and the canon consulted his watch. "We can slow down. He'll only arrive an hour from now. It's not yet seven o'clock."

"I'm eager to see the last of him."

"It won't be long now. And the little one, how did she take it?"

"So so, but not as hard as I expected. I think she's gotten over it."

"And the other fellow?"

"Dias?"

"Yes."

"For the time being . . . not a thing."

"It'll work out, it's sure to work out," affirmed the canon with a practiced air. "Labor improbus omnia vincit!"

"What?"

"He's a highly suitable husband for Anica."

Conversing thus, they approached the ramp near the government palace, side by side. There were still only a few people on the streets.

"A boat, boss!" shouted an attendant, straightening up in front of Manuel and removing his hat with a fancy gesture.

"Wait, let's see if Zé Isca is here, he's one of my customers."

The boatman moved slowly away, swinging his torso in time with his wide-legged walk. The two men descended to the wharf. Isca appeared and the trip was arranged.

"Boss, can we be off?"

"Wait for the doctor. We must wait for him."

The priest remarked that they were too early. Manuel in the meantime drew the letter *S* several times on the ground with the tip of his umbrella.

"Well, the steamship made a fast trip this time," said the priest, striking up a conversation.

"Fifteen days."

"So, then, when did it leave Rio de Janeiro?"

"On the second."

"Then in another two weeks it'll be back there," calculated the canon.

"No, it'll take even less time. Going south the winds and currents are more favorable. Eleven, twelve, thirteen days at the most."

After a while they grew annoyed with waiting. Manuel had already finished four cigarettes. Raimundo was late.

"It must be eight o'clock already! What time do you have?"

"A quarter past eight. Raimundo's surely being careless. Say, Manuel, does he know the steamer leaves at ten?"

"Why shouldn't he? Just yesterday afternoon I sent him a message about it!"

"Then it must be some drawn-out farewell," ventured the canon with the laugh of a scoundrel. "Fugit irreparabile tempus!"

"That's right, but it's getting a little too hot."

And Manuel wiped and rewiped his large beet-red face, casting toward the ramp an entreating look that seemed to beckon his nephew.

"Let's go over to the customs inspector's," advised the canon, shielding himself from the sun.

An obsequious employee immediately offered them two chairs.

"Your Excellencies, why don't you sit down? Kindly make yourselves comfortable."

"Thank you, thank you, my friend." And they sat down, impatient.

"Your Excellencies have come to Dr. Raimundo's send-off?"

"Yes, has he come down yet?"

"I still haven't seen him, no sir. But, he'll certainly be here soon. The hour is fast approaching."

A piercing whistle gave the first boarding signal, calling the passengers. Manuel immediately got up, went to the door, devoured the wharf with a glance, and eagerly consulted the ramp in front of the government palace. "No one!" He looked at the clock whose hands pointed to nine. "Darn! To hell with trying to deal with such people!"

The ramp, which had been filled, was now already emptying. Lingering groups on the shore still waved their handkerchiefs at the small boats receding into the distance. Some people were crying, their faces hidden in their hands. Others were politely taking their leave. Besides the usual protestations and formal goodbyes, warm and sincere phrases, painfully drawn out, could be heard. Kind words were repeated, advice given, and endearments exchanged. There in the open air, in public view, love and despair were revealed as if in the privacy of home and family. The launches cast off to a deep roar from the dock workers. There was a hubbub of voices. Porters passed on the run, their backs bent under suitcases, trunks, and parrot cages. There were thumping collisions. At the end of the ramp a little mulatto slave girl screamed wildly, her feet in the water, waving her arms and sobbing because they were carrying away her older sister who had been sold to someone in Rio de Janeiro. The crew members were cursing; the skiffs tumultuously filled, and the tiny launch from the *Portal* squealed deafening whistles every few seconds.

As for Raimundo—no sign of him!

Little by little the groups thinned out. Eyes were dried; handkerchiefs were put away, and the friends and relations of those departing soon went off at a slack pace in groups, faces still flushed with emotion. The port policeman returned from his tour of the steamer. Only the slave dealers remained, leaning against the gate to the wharf, to see the last puff of the monster to which they had consigned a sizable shipment of Negroes.

The ramp finally lapsed into its customary tranquility, and still Raimundo did not appear.

Manuel was sweating.

"And now what?" he asked the canon, furiously. "What do you say about this?"

The canon did not answer. He was brooding.

At that moment a carriage arrived, rolling along dizzily. Those awaiting Raimundo rushed up and stretched their necks.

"It must be Raimundo," ventured the canon.

"The devil!" snarled Manuel as he saw a man jump out and nimbly enter the customs office.

It was not Raimundo.

The steamer whistled, insisting with piercing and impatient shrieks. The recently arrived man dragged a small suitcase out onto the street and handed it to the first boatman who jumped forward from a group.

"Get a move on, fellow! Here, take those!" and he pointed to the other bundles. "Fast! Quick!"

The boatman threw the baggage onto a skiff, shouting at a black boy who was helping him:

"Move, get hopping! Otherwise we'll miss the steamer!"

These last words set Manuel beside himself. The poor creature was sweating like the bottom of a soupbowl.

"And now what?! Now what?! What do you say about this?"

The canon said not a word, absorbed in private contemplations, his lips superficially forming a bitter smile.

"Well, well, well," and the merchant paced with giant strides into the customs office. "Well, well, gentlemen! This had to happen to me!"

The canon tapped his sun hat on the ground.

"Astutus astu non capitur!"

The employees of the customs house, dressed in their uniforms, and the idle curious who were there for entertainment, asked Manuel questions concerning Raimundo, pleased with that scandal-promising episode.

They were already wagering comments and opinions.

"Man," said one, "just among ourselves, he never seemed like much to me."

"Me too," added another, "to tell the truth, I never could stomach that false face of his!"

"Well, I always knew he wouldn't go!"

"He won't go, either. He's glued here and won't leave now!"

"Oh, what a great scoundrel! Yes, sir."

"Darn that son of a bitch!" muttered Manuel, swinging his immense sun hat in the air.

But they all ran toward the door because another carriage, driven at great speed, raced toward the pier with a clatter of hooves.

"It's him for sure!" shouted a fellow. "Just in the nick of time!"

An anxious silence assailed the group. The coach stopped abruptly in front of the customs house. But even this time it was not Raimundo.

15

The steamship had arrived the previous day at two in the afternoon, shooting off its cannon upon anchoring, to which the entire side of the city along the water's edge responded with the merry shout: "The ship's arrived!" And from that moment on a heavy dread had taken hold of Ana Rosa, making her ill. She knew the ship would take Raimundo away—forever. Raimundo, whom she had loved and desired so much! Yet she had to let him go, with not a single complaint, not a single recrimination, because everyone, even that ingrate himself, expected it to be that way. And what madness for her still to be thinking about those things! . . . For wasn't everything, indeed, completely over? . . . Why, then, continue to torment herself with such folly?

Nevertheless, she preferred to forgive him everything before he departed once and for all. She had suffered through a wretched night, attempting to find any reason, any pretext, to absolve her lover; she felt a strong inclination to play the role of a resigned victim, capable of moving the least human of hearts. No longer did she want him; no longer could she count on him for anything; for God's sake, she could not count on him! But she did want to see him repentant for his immense ingratitude, humiliated, saddened and suffering, and admitting his guilt and cruelty for tormenting her as he had.

"Oh, if he'd only given me courage," she murmured to herself sadly, "what wouldn't I have done? . . . for I loved him greatly, greatly! Yes, I have to confess I loved him madly! But that silence. . . . Silence? What am I saying? . . . Scorn! That insulting scorn for me—so much like him—it now lowers him beneath other men! That he, so honorable toward everyone else, should act that way toward me? To abandon me at such a time, knowing perfectly well I needed his strength and stability more than ever before! Could he possibly doubt that I loved him? No, I spoke to him with such frankness. Ah, and of course he knows one can't fake what I told him, what I cried out to him! Yes, yes, the ingrate knew quite well. What was missing was love! He never had any regard for me. Or might he have imagined I'd be capable, just like other girls, of sacrificing my heart to social prejudices? . . . But, then, why didn't he speak to me frankly? Why didn't he at least write me? Why didn't he tell me that he too was suffering and try to raise my spirits? Because, I swear, if I had him, if I possessed him completely as a husband, as a slave, as a master, I'd scorn everything else! I swear I would! What could anything else mean to me? And what wouldn't I be capable of doing for that ingrate, that mean, proud man?"

And Ana Rosa sobbed, unable to fall asleep.

At six in the morning she was in her room, up and dressed. Manuel had left to accompany the canon to Raimundo's embarkation. Maria Bárbara, still in her hammock, was preparing her silken curls, peering at herself in the mirror that Brígida, kneeling in front of her, held with both hands.

The entire house had the sad ambience of a funeral day. Ana Rosa, appearing on the veranda, had dark circles under her eyes, pale coloring, a general air of fatigue about her entire body, and two red spots of fever on her cheeks.

A small mug of coffee was served to her.

"Where's Grandma?" she asked in a weak voice.

"She's there inside," answered the black boy, folding his arms.

"Look, Benedito. Tell her that . . . I guess it's better you don't tell her anything at all."

And sluggishly dragging the train of her cambric dress, and with her heavy and thick chestnut braids undulating like those of a lazy serpent, she started to return irresolutely to her room, but then stopped, frightened at the idea of remaining there alone with the impetuosity of her love and the femininity of her reasoning. Her loneliness now terrified her. She dreaded not having the courage to put a decent end to that affair; all the energy, with which she had pretended until then, waned completely; contrary to the previous night, at that moment she needed to hear bad things said about Raimundo so that she could consent to losing him without having her heart shatter completely. She realized she needed someone to persuade her once and for all that the wretch had never deserved her, that he had always been unworthy; someone who would compel her to detest him scornfully as a nauseating and malicious being. She needed, finally, some charitable soul who would extract that love from within her, just as the doctor extracts a baby with forceps.

But, in the meantime, no matter how vigorously she protested her condition, and no matter how strongly reason cried out, her heart wished only to forgive and to draw her loved one back, telling him frankly that, despite everything, she still loved him as always, more than ever! Reality was present as well, demanding, out of respect for her pride, that everything be allowed to end without any protest on her part; demanding that Raimundo depart, that he go away once and for all, and that Ana Rosa remain safely under her father's wing. But a voice sobbed to her from within, the weak voice of a forlorn orphan, of a tiny motherless child, pleading with her secretly and fearfully not to let them strangle that first love, which was the best thing in her entire life. And these new-born whimpers, so weak in appearance, supplanted the heavy and terrible voice of reason. Oh, she would have to hear many, many accusations against that ingrate to withstand such an ordeal without succumbing! The logic of a burning iron would be needed to convince her that Raimundo had never loved her and had never deserved her!

She sent the slave boy to call her grandmother. Benedito went to fetch Maria Bárbara; and Ana Rosa remained alone on the veranda, leaning against the frame of a door, containing and stifling with sobs the impulses of her violated desires as if she were restraining a band of wounded lions.

The clatter of rapid footsteps coming from the stairway startled her. She was about to dash away, but Raimundo, appearing unexpectedly, entreated her, his voice choked with emotion, to listen to him.

Ana Rosa stood motionless.

"We will not see each other any more, ever again," he stammered, growing pale. "The ship leaves a few hours from now. Read this letter, after I've left. Good-bye."

He handed her the letter and, sensing that his courage was fleeing him completely, began to descend, quite flustered, when he remembered Maria Bárbara. He asked after her, she immediately appeared, and he bade her good-bye, stammering, without knowing what else to say. Ana Rosa, facing them both, remained immobile and dazed, not uttering a single word, neither answering nor objecting.

"Good-bye," Raimundo repeated.

And, haltingly, he took the limp hand Ana Rosa held out, squeezed it avidly in his and, without heeding Maria Bárbara's presence, brought it repeatedly to his lips, covering it with rapid and eager kisses. Then he hurtled down the staircase in one long leap, bumping against the wall and stumbling down the steps.

"Raimundo!" Ana Rosa screamed.

And she clung to her grandmother, shaking all over with convulsive sobs.

Raimundo left and found himself in the middle of the street, distracted, stupefied, not quite knowing which direction to take. Oh yes, he still needed to buy some things. He went off to obtain them; there was no time to waste. He hurried to the shops. But, independent of his will and discernment, a vague hope was growing within him, on its own, that his trip would not materialize. He was counting on finding some sort of obstacle that would impede it; he was relying on one of those blessed mishaps that opportunely come to our rescue when, despite our heart's desires, we proceed blindly to fulfill a duty. He longed for a pretext, but a pretext that would satisfy his conscience.

Raimundo went into various stores, purchased cigars, a pair of slippers, a cap; but he was doing all this for the sake merely of formality, as if to justify himself in his own eyes, ever more distracted, not paying the slightest attention to anything. He went to the storage house where at daybreak he had ordered his trunks taken. As he entered, he was hoping to receive word that they were no longer there, or that someone had laid claim to them, or had stolen them, and that this occurrence would prevent his sailing on that steamship. But nothing of the sort! All his luggage was there intact, carefully guarded. He ordered everything carried to the ramp and followed along behind, expecting still that the agency would notify him the departure had been postponed to the following day.

Indeed! . . .

There was no way out other than to leave. Everything was ready, everything concluded, all he had to do was embark. He had bidden farewell to all those to whom he owed that courtesy; he had nothing more to do on shore, his trunks were already heading toward the wharf—he had only to depart!

He felt a terrible sorrow as he approached the ocean, but nevertheless it was there that he headed, feeling unsteady and oppressed. He looked at his watch, the hands indicated a little past eight o'clock, and they seemed to him eager as never before to push forward. After this Raimundo completely lost his courage to draw the watch from his vest pocket; that inflexible diminution of time tortured him deeply. "I have to go on! The devil! All I have to do is get onto the boat out to the ship. I have to go on! In a short time I'll be on board, the steamer will soon journey away, farther and farther, without turning back. I have to go on. That is, I must renounce forever my only complete happiness—possession of Ana Rosa! I must vanish, leave her, never to see her again! Never again to hear her, embrace her, possess her! Hell!"

And as Raimundo approached the ramp, he felt a precious treasure slipping further away through his hands. Afraid to proceed, he stopped, taking deep breaths and delaying as if he wished for a few seconds longer to hold onto a beloved object which thereafter would never again be his. But reason pelted him with a throng of arguments. "Move on, go ahead!" reason screamed coldly at him. And he obeyed, his head down like a criminal. And all the while never had Ana Rosa appeared so beautiful to him, so adorable, so perfect and indispensable as at that moment! He even felt jealous of her and condemned her from within his innermost grief, because the haughty creature had not run after him to prevent their separation. And he was leaving her helpless, exposed to the love of the first ambitious fellow who might appear, and to whom she would surrender in complete abandon, faithful, quivering, and pure, because her sole ideal was to become a mother! "Hell! Hell! Hell!"

Raimundo awoke from these contemplations standing in the middle of the street like a fool, being observed by the pedestrians. He glanced about and hurriedly set off walking, almost running, toward the embarkation ramp. As he approached the ocean the number of baggage porters at his side increased; black men and women passed by with trunks, leather and tinplate suitcases, all types of wicker baskets, containers made of pindova palm leaves, boxes of fur hats, and little cages with birds. Raimundo continued running. All that travel gear affected his nerves. Suddenly, he halted, face to face with a piece of reasoning that injected a flash of hope into his eyes: "What if Manuel doesn't come here to the wharf? Yes, that's quite possible since he's always so loaded down with work, the poor fellow. So busy as to be unable to come here. And it'd be a devil of a trick for me to go away like this, without saying goodbye to him." And, as if to answer the objection made by someone else, his mind added: "Oh! Of course. It'd be a devil of a thing. The fellow might take it as an act of pure spite! . . . It would make me look ridiculous! And, besides, it'd be an unpardonable rudeness, even an ingratitude! He came on board to meet me when I arrived, welcomed me into the bosom of his family, and always surrounded me with a thousand kindnesses! . . . No, after all, I'm highly beholden to him! . . . It isn't proper for me to depart now without saying good-bye!"

An empty carriage passed by. Raimundo glanced rapidly at his watch.

"Rua da Estrela, number 80!" he shouted to the driver, jumping up on top of a cushion. "Hurry, as fast as you can! There's not a moment to lose!"

And, impatient inside the coach, he felt a nervous happiness that caused a shudder to pass through his entire body. In the meantime, a fingernail of remorse continued to scratch away at his conscience. "Oh, but it would be a great failing on my part," he replied to the importunate thought. "Was I supposed to leave here forever without saying farewell to my father's brother, the only friend I found in this province? . . . I vow that as soon as I arrive there, I'll say goodbye and return immediately."

And the carriage flew, propelled along by the hope of a good-sized tip.

Ana Rosa, when she had recovered from the shock into which Raimundo's visit had thrown her, wept copiously and then shut herself in her room with the letter he had given her. She opened it quickly but without any hope of consolation.

The letter, however, said:

My dear friend,

No matter how strange it might seem, I swear I still love you madly, more than ever, more than I imagined one could ever love. I'm speaking to you so frankly now because this declaration can in no way harm you, for I'll be quite far from you when you read it. So that you do not regret having chosen me as a husband and do not censure me for having stood silently and like a coward when faced with your father's refusal, please understand, my beloved friend, that the worst moment of my wretched life was when I saw it was inevitable that I should flee from you forever. But what is the alternative? I was born a slave, and I'm the son of a Negress. I pledged my word to your father that I'd never attempt to marry you, but the promise mattered little to me! What wouldn't I have sacrificed for your love? Ah, but it's just that my very devotion would be your misfortune, transforming my beloved into my victim. Society would single you out as the wife of a mulatto, and our offspring would suffer discrimination and be as miserable as I! I realized then that in fleeing I'd give you the greatest proof of my love. And I go, I leave, without taking you with me, my adored wife, the dearly beloved companion of my dreams and happiness! If you were able to appraise how much I'm suffering at this moment, and how painful it is for me to be strong and fulfill my obligation, if you knew how the idea of leaving you weighs on me, without any hope of returning to your side—you would bless me, my love!

So farewell. May destiny carry me where it wishes, you will always be the pure archangel to whom I shall dedicate my life. You will be my inspiration, the light of my path. I will be good because you exist.

Farewell, Ana Rosa.

Your slave,
Raimundo

On finishing the letter, Ana Rosa arose transfigured. An enormous change had taken place in her, as if a new spirit now flourished, overflowing, within her. "Ah! He loved me so much and was fleeing with the secret, the ingrate! But why didn't he tell me all this right away, in complete frankness?" And she jumped about the room like a child, giggling, her eyes filled with tears. She went to the mirror, smiled at her dejected figure, and then, devil-may-care, straightened her hairdo, clapped her hands, and let out a laugh. But suddenly she remembered that the steamer might already have left, and she shuddered with alarm, her heart throbbing wildly, like a dilated artery about to burst.

She ran to the veranda.

"Benedito! Benedito!" Oh, Lord! Where could that black boy be?

"What is it you want, Missy?" asked Brígida, her voice very calm and measured.

"What time does the steamer leave?" asked the girl, without taking a breath.

"What was that?"

"When does the steamer leave?"

"What steamer, Missy?"

"The devil! The steamer to the South!"

"Oh yeah, it's already gone, Missy!"

"What! My God, it's not possible!"

And, trembling from the horrible certainty, she ran to her grandmother's room.

"Do you know if the steamer has already left, Grandma?"

"Ask your father."

Ana Rosa felt a frightening and hellish impatience; she descended the first few steps of the staircase, intending to go down to the store, but came back up right away, went to the kitchen, and asked Brígida to find out from Manuel if the steamer had already cast off.

The maid returned to say, very calmly, that "the master had left quite early in the morning for Master Mundico's send-off."

"You go to the devil!" shouted Ana Rosa, enraged.

And, dashing to the window of her room, she abruptly flung it open. The tranquility of the Rua da Estrela benumbed her, like a dowsing of cold water over a feverish person.

Then her reaction set in. She had a nervous longing to cry out, bite, claw, and scratch. Thinking she was about to become hysterical, she backed away from the window to be more secure. She beat on her head with heavy, delirious blows, and felt a mortal rage at everything and everyone; at her relatives, her home, her society, her girl friends, and her godfather. And suddenly a powerful force, a strange feeling, a despotic desire came to her: with pleasure she contemplated having some sort of responsibility; she wanted life with all its tasks, its thorns, and its carnal delights; she felt an imperative and absolute necessity to come to an understanding with Raimundo, to pardon him for everything with ardent kisses, with wild and impassioned caresses, to seize hold of him, gritting her teeth, and say to him face to face: "Marry me! Forget about the outside world! Don't worry about the others! Here you have me! Come! Do with me what you will! I'm all yours! Make use of what is yours!"

Just then a carriage rolled down the Rua da Estrela.

Ana Rosa ran to the window, frightened and quivering. The coach stopped at Manuel's door. The girl shivered with fear and hope, and, greatly excited, convulsed and impassioned, she saw Raimundo jump out.

"Come up, come up here!" she called to him, already in the hall. "Come up, for God's sake!"

Raimundo felt her cold hands grasp his. He stammered:

"Your father? I didn't want to leave, without . . ."

"Come, come in here. Come, I must talk with you!"

And Ana Rosa pulled him forcefully. Raimundo allowed himself to be dragged, supposing he would encounter Manuel.

"But . . ." he babbled in confusion, slowly noticing he was entering his cousin's room. "Pardon me, my lady, but where is your father? . . . I came to take my leave of your father. . . ."

Ana Rosa ran to the door, shut it abruptly, and threw herself on Raimundo's neck.

"You're not leaving, do you understand? You're not to go away!"

"But. . . ."

"I don't want you to go! You said you love me, and I shall be your wife, come what may!"

"Oh, if only it were possible!"

"And why not? What have I to do with other people's prejudices? What fault is it of mine to love you? I'll be your wife only, no one else's! Who asked Papa not to heed your request? Am I to blame that they don't understand you? Is it my fault my happiness depends solely on you? Or, who knows, Raimundo, are you an imposter who never felt anything for me?"

"If only that were so. I swear to you that's what I've wished! But can you imagine I'd by chance be capable of sacrificing you to my love? That I could possibly condemn you to your father's hatred, the scorn of your friends, and the ridiculous gossip of this stupid province? No, let me leave, Ana Rosa. It's much better for me to go. And you, my beloved guiding light, stay, stay peacefully at your family's side; follow your honest path; you're virtuous, you will be the pure wife of a white man who'll deserve you. . . . Don't think about me any longer. Farewell."

And Raimundo attempted to tear away from Ana Rosa's hands. But she, clinging to his neck, with her head bent back, her hair loose and hanging down, fixed her gaze on him closely and asked:

"Then, just what in your letter was sincere?"

"Everything, my love, but why did you read it before I left?"

"Then I'm yours! Look, let's leave here, right now! Let's flee! Take me wherever you want! Do with me whatever you think best!"

And she let her face fall to his chest and embraced him warmly.

Raimundo, fearful of succumbing, stood still, dragged into a profound turmoil.

"Make up your mind," she demanded, letting go of him.

He, breathing hard, did not answer.

"Well then, if you don't want to flee, I'll make my father believe you're a vile creature! You're afraid, aren't you? Well, I'll tell him anything that comes to my mind. I'll call down on you all the hatred and all the responsibility for my love! Because you're an evil man, Raimundo, and my father will easily believe that you abused the hospitality he offered you. You're deplorable. Get out of here!"

Raimundo rushed to the door. Ana Rosa again threw herself at his neck, sobbing.

"Forgive me, my love! I don't know what I'm saying! Pardon me for all of this, my beloved, my master. I realize you're the best of men, but don't leave, I entreat you as the one you love most! I know it's your pride that makes you cruel—you're entirely right, but don't abandon me! I would die, Raimundo, because I love you so much, so much! We women don't have, as you do, any ambition other than to love the man we idolize! You can see that! I'll sacrifice everything for you—but don't leave, have mercy! Sacrifice something for me, too! Don't be selfish! Don't flee! And your pride! What does anyone else matter when we possess each other? I see only you, I respect only you, I'll attempt to please only you! Go! But take me with you! I'll throw away everything else, but I must be yours, Raimundo, I need to belong exclusively to you!"

And Ana Rosa fell to her knees, without releasing his body.

"I'm a slave who weeps at your feet! I'm a miserable soul who needs your compassion! I'm yours! Here you have me, my master. Love me! Don't abandon me!"

And she sobbed, cupping her hands over her face. Raimundo,

attempting to lift her up, bent deeply over her. And the sensual contact with the white flesh of the girl's arms and neck, the pressure of her burning lips, and his fear of touching all that forbidden treasure, made his blood throb and set his head to spinning giddily.

"My God! Oh, Ana Rosa, don't cry! Get up, for the love of God!"

As Ana Rosa continued to cry, a nervous quiver shot through Raimundo's entire body. It was then that the small launch at the port let out its first whistle, calling the last passengers. And that penetrating and impertinent shriek reached his ear, there in the sweet seclusion of that room, like a note broken loose from the chorus of imprecations with which the society of Maranhão, milling about like ants in the streets outside, applauded his departure from the province. In a flash he sized up the situation, calculated the ridiculous consequences of his weakness, remembered Manuel's words, and his pride finally burst out with the vehemence of a tempest.

"No!" he shouted, brusquely pushing her away.

And he plunged toward the door.

Ana Rosa half fell down, supporting herself on one hand, but got up immediately, blocking his way. And with a haughty gesture, she placed herself against the door, her arms spread, disdainful, noble, her fists clenched. She was livid and disheveled; her mouth contracted in a painful expression of sacrifice and despair. Her nostrils were dilated and her eyes flashed terribly, full of menace.

Raimundo remained still for an instant, perplexed at confronting that unexpected energy.

"You shall not leave, because I don't want you to," she said, her voice curt and muffled. "You'll not leave my room as long as we are not fully committed to one another."

"Oh!"

There ensued a silence that was anguishing for them both. Raimundo lowered his eyes and, quite distressed, began to reflect. He seemed repentant and humiliated by his weakness. Why had he returned? Ana Rosa went to him and gently placed her arm around him. Once again she was the tiny dove, timid and emotional.

"Everything good that I could do to marry you, you're quite aware I have already done," she murmured, now without the courage to face him. "Papa did not consent, in the hope of giving me to another, and I won't subject myself to that! . . . I shall exhaust every possible measure to continue to belong to you alone, my friend! It's with this intention that I keep you here at my side. This may seem bad and dishonest, but I vow to you that I have never defended my pride and virtue as I'm doing at this moment. To save myself I shall absolutely have to become your wife—and there's only one way to force them to allow it: to render myself lacking in virtue in the eyes of everyone else, while remaining chaste and pure in your eyes alone."

And she lowered her eyelids, completely overwhelmed with shame. Raimundo made not the least movement, nor did he utter a word.

Ana Rosa burst into tears.

"Now . . . , you can leave whenever you wish," she added, letting go of him. "Now you can abandon me forever. . . . I'll have a clear conscience because I did try everything to marry you. . . . Go away! What I never imagined was that even in this final trial, the cowardly one would still be you! Go away once and for all! Leave me alone!" And she sobbed loudly. "Even if I must later repent, it's best as of right now to finish all of this! I'm an unfortunate soul! A poor wretch!"

And she wept.

Raimundo pulled her close to him tenderly. He caressed her, drawing her head to his chest.

"Don't cry," he said. "Don't torment yourself like this."

"But isn't this how it's to be?" she lamented, her face hidden in his neck. "For someone else, who might deserve you more, you would do anything. I was a fool to confess I loved you so much, ingrate! . . . You don't merit even half of what I did for you. You're a fraud!"

And, like an injured child, she wept on and on. Raimundo silently embraced her and kissed her repeatedly.

"Don't cry, my flower," he whispered to her at last. "You're completely right. Pardon me if I was brutal with you! But what do you expect? We all have our pride, and my position in relation to you was so false! . . . Believe me, no one could love and desire you more than I! But if you only knew what it cost me to hear face to face: 'I won't give you my daughter's hand because you are unworthy of her. . . . You are the son of a slave!' If they'd said, 'It's because you're poor!' then, what the devil, I'd work! If they told me, 'It's because you've no social standing!' I swear I'd obtain it, no matter what! 'It's because you're vile, a thief, a miserable wretch!' I would endeavor to turn myself into the finest example of a reputable man! But an ex-slave, the son of a Negress, a—mulatto! How am I to transform my blood, drop by drop? How will I wipe out the recollection of my past in all these people who detest me? . . . As you know, my love, I do have some status, and I don't lack the means to live wherever I please. I have never performed even the smallest impropriety that might shame me. And, yet, I will never be happy because you alone are my happiness, and I should expect nothing from you! Oh, if you knew, Ana Rosa, how these truths hurt . . . you'd fully pardon my pride, for each honest man's pride is always linked to the scorn that others direct at him!"

Ana Rosa took it all in, word for word.

"Nevertheless," he continued, completely subdued, "I no longer have the courage to leave you!" And they embraced. "How, from this day on, will I be able to live without you, my friend, my wife, my life? Say something, speak! Please give me advice, for I can no longer think."

Another whistle from the steamer interrupted him.

"Do you hear, Ana Rosa? The steamer is calling."

"Let it go, my love! You will remain. . . ."

And the two held each other even more tightly, clasped in one another's arms, their lips united in the silent and nuptial bliss of a first love.

Manuel and the canon, meanwhile, were still waiting in the customs house after the disappointment of the last carriage.

"The dog!" exclaimed the merchant, fierce with rage, pacing back and forth, threatening the ceiling with his enormous umbrella. "The great swindler!" And stopping in front of Diogo: "He made fools of us! He tricked us, the shameless fellow! I swear by the cross he'll never again set foot in my house! Let me make that clear right now: never again!"

Three consecutive whistles were heard.

"It's the final signal," said the customs employee. "The steamer is going to cast off. They've drawn the gangway up."

Manuel, with his hands crossed behind him, his hat sloping toward the nape of his neck, his body wavering on his stubby little legs, his coloring quite red, interrogated the canon:

"So, what do you say about this? Well, what do you say? Have you ever seen anything like it?"

"Stop it," censured the canon, and he directed his steps toward the door, opened his eighteen-spoke parasol, and, ready to leave, added: "Let's be on our way. My good men, best wishes to you, and thank you all."

The two men began climbing slowly up the ramp.

"Now, how a man can get involved with a guy like that!" muttered the merchant, knocking the brim of his rain hat against the pavement stones. "Worthless fellow! A dandy! At any rate, he can get in with whomever he wants. But he'd better not count on me any more! Scum!"

And, in a verbose rage, he continued cursing. The canon interrupted him after a short time:

"Suaviter in modo, fortiter in re!"

Manuel hushed up immediately and paid him close attention. For a good hour they conversed in low voices, standing on the corner of the Largo do Palácio, deciding what was the best thing for them to do.

"Farewell," the canon said finally. "Don't forget, right? And observe carefully whatever she answers."

"Will you come by later?"

"Just after lunchtime."

And, head down, each went his own way.

The event was already the subject of gossip on the Praça do Comércio and the Rua de Nazaré.

Manuel arrived home and went through the warehouse.

"Has Dr. Raimundo been upstairs?" he asked Cordeiro.

"Yes, sir, he has, but he's already left. He was getting into a carriage just as I arrived from collecting the bills."

"How long ago?"

"About half an hour ago, more or less."

"Have you all had lunch yet?"

"Yes, sir."

"Fine. Tell Mr. Dias, when he comes, not to forget to take care of those accounts from the backlands. And you go to the customs to see if those bales of rough cotton, numbers 105 to 110, are on the cargo list of the steamer *Bragança.* Get the information."

And he handed Cordeiro a piece of printed blue paper. Then he started up the stairs but came down again.

"Oh, now I remember! Mr. Vila-Rica!"

"Sir?"

"Is the little fellow about?"

"No, sir, he went to the treasury."

"Have those orders from Caxias been dispatched yet?"

"Two crates of chintz are already packed up. The steamer only leaves the day after tomorrow.

"Good. . . ."

And Manuel thought for a moment. "Ah! Do you know if Mr. Cordeiro sent the matches off yet?"

"Not yet, sir, because the checker, who's up to his ears in shipments, couldn't get them ready yesterday."

"Well, tell Cordeiro to take care of it today."

The merchant finally went up the stairs.

The veranda was deserted. Maria Bárbara was praying in her room, thanking God and the saints for Raimundo's presumed departure. Manuel took a glass of cognac from the sideboard and then headed toward the kitchen.

"Where is Anica?"

"She's in her room, lying down."

"Sick?"

"Yes, sir, with a fever."

"What's wrong with her?"

"I don't know, sir."

Manuel knocked at the door of Ana Rosa's room. She herself, looking very pale, came to open it, then turned around at once to get into her hammock again.

"What's wrong with you, Anica?"

"I wasn't feeling well . . . nerves."

But she would not face her father, and sighs burst from her throat.

Manuel sat down heavily in a chair next to her, wiping off his face, neck, and head with his handkerchief.

"Greetings from Mundico," he said after a silence, dissimulating.

"What?!" exclaimed Ana Rosa, straightening up with a start and clamping on her father the strangest and most painful of stares.

"He's gone," Manuel explained. "The steamer should be departing at this very moment. And there he was on board. Poor fellow. Perhaps he'll be happier in Rio de Janeiro."

"The scoundrel!" she shrieked, with a cry of despair. And she fell backward into her hammock, writhing.

"Good God! Ana Rosa! What is it, my dear?" Manuel shouted, attempting to restrain her spasmodic movements. "Dona Maria Bárbara, Brígida, Mônica!"

The room filled rapidly. The door and windows were flung open; salts and burnt cotton were brought in. But only after a lengthy struggle did the hysterical girl's strength wane, and she began to weep, exhausted and gasping. Manuel, thoroughly distressed and unable to calm down, paced back and forth on tiptoe, speaking in a soft voice, going now and then out to the hall to see if the canon had already arrived, and constantly scratched his neck—which in him indicated extreme perplexity.

"Do you want lunch put on, sir?" Brígida asked him.

"Go to the devil!

At noon, the canon finally arrived with the tranquil air of one who has eaten well, a toothpick in the corner of his mouth.

"So?" he inquired of Manuel, leading him secretively off to a corner of the veranda.

"It was bad. As soon as she heard the fib, she had an attack, and now you can see for yourself. She cried out and floundered about for a long time until the weeping came on her. It was an inferno!"

"And now? How is she?"

"A little more peaceful, but I suppose she's going to have a fever. I didn't want to call the doctor without speaking to you first."

"You did well."

And the canon withdrew, meditating.

"The devil," he muttered finally. "The affair was much farther along than I imagined."

"And now?"

"Now, we tell her the truth. What I wanted was to know just how the matter stood. She thinks herself betrayed, so consequently, she must have agreed on some plan with the cunning fellow. . . . That's exactly what we must put an end to as soon as possible."

And, after a pause:

"Her indifference to Raimundo's departure was most certainly due to her knowledge of the opposite."

He grew silent, and then, a moment later, inquired:

"Did she right away believe what you said?"

"Yes, she immediately cried out 'scoundrel' and, bang, collapsed with her attack!"

"It's quite odd."

"What is?"

"Her believing it so easily. But, at any rate, let's tell her the truth!"

"No, no, wait just a minute, because . . ."

"No sir, Manuel, I'll do it. To me perhaps she'll tell everything more frankly."

And, inspired by an idea, he again turned to Manuel:

"Look! The best thing is for you to pretend you know nothing at all, do you understand?"

"How so?"

"Don't let on that you know. Pretend you're really convinced about Raimundo's departure."

"What for?"

"It's just an idea. . . ."

And the canon, donning a comforting and respectful air, entered Ana Rosa's bedroom with soft steps.

The hysteria had finally passed. She was sobbing lightly, her face buried between two pillows. Faithful Mônica, kneeling at her feet, watched over her with the docility of a gentle dog. Dona Maria Bárbara, seated near the hammock, calmly reproached her granddaughter for such immoderate sorrow over an event that was in no way regrettable.

"Well then, my goddaughter, what's all this?" the priest asked her, gently stroking her head.

Without turning around, she continued crying, inconsolable, from time to time blowing her little nose, which was quite red from so much weeping. She could not speak, and her dry and gasping sobs continued, almost without pause. The canon motioned to Maria Bárbara and Mônica to go away, and, putting his thin lips near his goddaughter's ear, he poured into it the following words, as sweet and unctuous as if they were anointed with holy oils:

"Calm youself. . . . He has not left. He's still here. Rest awhile."

"What do you mean?" And Ana Rosa turned around immediately.

"Now don't make a fuss. It's best your father know nothing at all. Calm youself! Rest! Raimundo did not depart, he's still here."

"You aren't deceiving me, are you?"

"Now, why would I do that, you suspicious girl?"

"I don't know, but . . ." and she began to sob once more.

"Very well! Don't cry, pay attention to what I'm going to say. When I leave here I'll look for the fellow and have him stay away awhile, until things return to normal. He'll appear later and then we'll do everything we can. . . . Nec semper lilia florent!"

"And Papa?"

"Leave him to me. Trust in me completely. But we must have a thorough chat, alone, in some safe place where we can speak freely. To help you two I must be up-to-date on the situation. Place yourself in my hands, and you'll see that everything will be arranged with God's divine protection. Don't despair! Don't do anything hasty! Be calm, my dear! Without calm nothing worthwhile is accomplished."

And, following an affectionate pat: "Look, come some day to the cathedral and confess to me. Your grandmother requested me to sing a mass. There couldn't be a better occasion. I'll hear your confession after the mass. Is that settled?"

"But, why?"

"Why? That's a good one—for me to help you, my dear goddaughter!"

"But. . . ."

"No? Well then, the two of you should reach an understanding, but I rather doubt you two alone will be able to accomplish anything. If you do have confidence in your godfather, go to the mass, confess, and I promise that everything will be arranged!"

Ana Rosa's expression was already expansive; she even felt like hugging the canon, that guardian angel who had brought her such good news.

"But don't fool me! Tell me seriously: he really didn't leave?"

"I've already told you he didn't, my goodness! Calm yourself, and come see me at the church! Everything will work out just the way you want."

"You swear?"

"Now, what a demand! How childish!"

"Then I'll not go."

"All right, I swear."

And the canon kissed his forefingers as they outlined the form of the cross on his lips.

"And now, are you satisfied?"

"Yes, now I am."

"And you'll come to confession?"

"Yes, I will."

"Fine!"

16

Manuel Pescada's residence had, in appearance at least, relapsed into its former state of peace and lassitude. Neither there nor throughout the city were they speaking of Raimundo any longer.

He, upon leaving his lover's room, had changed his life's plan. That same day he set off for Rosário to visit his mother, in the hope of bringing her back to the capital and living there with her. But Domingas did not let herself be caught, and Raimundo unhappily had to return alone.

He set himself up on Caminho Grande in a small old house and remained hidden like a deadly criminal. From that house, with much difficulty, he wrote a letter to Ana Rosa to confide his plans to her. The letter ended:

> The best way is for us to allow everything to calm down and all of them to forget about us completely. Then I'll come to you on the night that we decide, and we'll carry out the plan elaborated at the beginning of this letter. As for your father, I'll never reach an understanding with him until that stubborn man decides to pardon his son-in-law and daughter. Farewell. Don't lose heart and do have complete confidence in your devoted fiancé.
>
> Raimundo

With this missive Ana Rosa was so reassured that she tried to dissuade the canon from the business of her confession. After all, if she were a sinner, she had become one on purpose and would not repent of it. Her conscience told her that marriage would redeem her misdeed. The canon, consequently, would have to be patient, because she didn't see any need for forgiveness! Rationalizing in this manner, she spoke frankly with the priest and withdrew her promise. But the canon replied by threatening to denounce her to Manuel. She began to suspect that her godfather knew about everything, and she took fright.

"But, Godfather, you're so insistent on this business of confession!"

The canon looked up to the ceiling, for want of an open sky, and, falling back on the theatrical ploys of his profession, he unwound a little sermon that terminated:

"Malos tueri haud tutum! Do you, by chance, not know—sinner that you are, innocent victim of a diabolic temptation—that I owe to both my conscience and God a double accounting for what I do here on earth? Don't you realize, my goddaughter, that every priest in this vale of tears walks between two penetrating and discerning eyes, two austere and inflexible judges, one called God and the other Conscience? One of them looks from the outside inward and the other from the inside outward. The second is a reflection of the first, and, if the first is satisfied, the second is satisfied as well. Don't you realize that one day I'll have to render an accounting of my worldly acts, and that, seeing how a lamb is now straying from the flock and risks swerving from the path of light and purity, it is my obligation as pastor to succor and guide her back to the fold, even if I must use force to do so? Therefore, Daughter of Eve, come to the church! Come! Confess to the priest of Our Lord Jesus Christ. Bare your soul fully before him and your heart will immediately reject the squalidness of the flesh. Embrace, as did Mary Magdalene, the feet of God's representative, until God takes pity on you, sinner! Deum colenti stat sua merces!"

And the canon stood for a moment looking toward the ceiling with his arms upraised and his eyes blank.

"Very well, Godfather, very well!" said Ana Rosa, impressed by this speech. And she unceremoniously disarmed the priest from his ecstatic posture: "I'll go to your confession, but stop all this and don't keep on talking like that, for it's bad for my nerves. You know quite well I'm nervous."

It was finally decided that the mass requested by Maria Bárbara would be held on the first Sunday of the following month, and that Ana Rosa would go to confession.

Mônica, always full of zeal and affection for the child she had suckled, was in on Ana Rosa's secrets, and every time she went to the fountain to do the washing, she would drop by Raimundo's house to take word from him to Missy.

One night, Canon Diogo, wrapped in his everyday cassock, sat leaning over an old holywood table, his feet crossed on top of a well-worn wildcat skin from his days in Rosário, and his head inside a silken cap that had been delicately embroidered by his goddaughter. By the light of his lantern he was reading a thick volume with an old-style binding, on whose frontispiece was written: "*Ecclesiastical History*. Volume Eleven. Continuation of the Christian

Centuries or the History of Christianity: Its Foundation and Development from the Year 1700 to the Current Pontificate of the Holy Father Pius VI. Translated from the Spanish. Lisbon. Rolandiana Typographers, 1807. By Permission of the High Court." The dear old man was lost in some tedious descriptions of the Pietist sect, founded during the late seventeenth century by Spener, a pastor from Frankfurt, when three discreet and cautious knocks sounded at his door. He immediately marked his place in the book with the sliver he had been using to pick at his teeth and went to open the door.

It was Dias. He seemed thinner and more bilious than ever, but with his features always masked by that chronic smile of cunning passivity.

"Am I disturbing you, Canon?"

"That's a good one! Come right in."

And, as the visitor lacked the courage to speak, the canon added, after a pause:

"Did you take care of that letter I gave you?"

"Yes, he's already got it. I dropped it myself through the shutters of his window on the eve of his so-called embarkation."

"Have you discovered yet where he's now living?"

"I haven't had any luck yet, no sir, but it seems the rat is nesting over in the Caminho Grande area."

"Keep a sharp eye. The good-for-nothing may pop up suddenly and play a trick on us. Yes, keep a sharp eye. Have you been doing what I asked?"

"Concerning what?"

"Concerning the syping."

"Yes, sir, I have."

"Well, then, what have you found out by now?"

"For the time being, nothing worthwhile. But have faith in me, Canon, I'll not fail. Aside from that search I made on St. John's day, there's not a moment, whenever I can get away from work, that I'm not observing what goes on in that house. But from what I've picked up, the only thing relating to our concerns was a conversation between Dona Anica and the old woman."

"Dona Maria Bárbara?"

"Yes, sir."

"And what was it?"

"Just that after asking her grandmother to feel sorry for her and to try to obtain permission from her father to marry the nigger, she began crying and lamenting like a lunatic. And she said she was very unhappy, that no one in the family held her in high regard, that they all wanted only to thwart her . . . just because she might do this or might do that."

"But what did she say she'd do? What a devil of a way you have of telling these things!"

"It was foolishness, Canon, the prattle of young girls: that she'd kill herself to run away or enter a convent! And the marriage this, the marriage that! In short, she meant that a woman should never be forced to marry. Finally, she threw herself at her grandmother's feet, sobbing and saying that if they didn't allow her to marry Raimundo, she'd not be responsible for what happened!"

"Well, does the old woman know by now that Raimundo stayed on?"

"It seems so. The girl, in any case, said that her grandmother and father would surely suffer much grief if they didn't consent to the marriage!"

"And what did she do?"

"Who, the girl?"

"No, the old woman."

"The old woman got quite riled and threw her out of the room, swearing that she'd rather see her stretched out under the ground than married to a nigger, and that if the boss . . ."

"What boss?"

"Manuel, her father!"

"Oh, of course."

"Yes, sir. But if the boss for some reason were to give in, she'd be the one who would not yield on her granddaughter's marriage, and she'd break off with her son-in-law!"

"Good, good! We're doing well. And the girl?"

"Well, the girl went whimpering off to her room and, unless I'm mistaken, began to pray."

"Praying, eh?" the canon asked with interest.

"Right, she's praying more these days."

"Very good, perfect! We're doing marvelously!"

"And she's all full of odd notions. . . . Just the other day, I noticed she was hanging something inside the well. As soon as I could, I ran to see if I could find out what it might be. Now what does your excellency think it was?"

"A St. Anthony?"

"Correct, a tiny St. Anthony, just like this," confirmed Dias, marking an inch on his index finger.

"Fine," said the canon. "Just continue watching, but . . . be very careful. No one must know, especially my goddaughter, do you understand? If they discover you're sniffing about, all is lost. Pretend you're a fool. Have faith in God! And courage! Whenever you latch onto some news, come here immediately. Don't let up with your spying. Remember, the weapon we'll use to crush the nigger is still in his own hands."

"Well, Canon, I'm already getting worried. I confess to you that. . . ."

"Don't be an idiot, you have no reason at all to lose heart. Keep trying, see if you can discover something, especially something big with which we can get the goods on him, because then your marriage will be that much easier. Remember, pay attention to whoever enters and leaves. If they're no longer corresponding, which I doubt, then their correspondence will resume later. At any rate, the prudent thing is not to resort to their letters for the time being. Just let them write, and I'll tell you when to seize their letters. To be of use, the fruit should be gathered in one swoop!"

"Well, Canon, may I leave?"

"Of course."

"Then I'll be off."

"Sis felix!"

"What?" asked Dias, turning around.

"Don't let down your guard. Off with you."

The clerk made a bow and left. Diogo closed the door and went back to his *Ecclesiastical History* until his housekeeper, Inácia, came to call him to supper. Then, after turning down the lantern, he went out to the veranda and sat down sluggishly before a bowl of broth. At once a huge and fat Maltese cat settled into his lap, meowing affectionately and turning its glowing pupils toward him, pleading for caresses.

One might say that in that modest and tidy nook there reigned the blessed peace of the righteous.

The following Sunday the happy din of the bells of the main cathedral called everyone to mass. It was the one promised by Dona Maria Bárbara.

There was a large throng of people. The most devout women piously climbed the crumbling steps of the atrium and, with heads bent, went to kneel in the main part of the church. One could hear the rustling of ancient and puffed out camelhair cloth skirts, their color restored by black tea, the plopping of heavy new slippers on the sonorous stone flooring of the temple, and the tinkling of babassu palmwood rosary beads being squeezed between the tremulous fingers of the old ladies during the fervent whispering of their prayers. The upper parts of their embroidered blouses, replete with intricate lace, were visible; so, too, were the large white linen shawls hanging from the fleshy shoulders of the mestizo and mulatto women. Their enormous tortoiseshell combs adorned with gold shone brightly, and pretentious beads were coiled round and round their plump shoulder blades and bullish necks. Further up, in the reserved seats near the altar, ladies' hats decorated with feathers and ribbons stood out, and hand fans fluttered restlessly, making a brassy noise as they beat against brooches and breast pins in a jumble of astonishing colors. These were all devout upper-class women and young girls who flaunted flamboyant jewels and strong perfumes and, in gloved hands, held copies of prayer books bound in ivory, velvet, silver, and mother-of-pearl.

The rustic aroma of Brazilian cherry trees and fragrant clover permeated the cathedral. From the vestry door one could discern at a glance several priestlings hurrying through their paces and putting on the surplices for ceremonial days. From the crowd there arose a murmur of impatience like that from the main floor of a theater. The sexton, looking after the various accessories for the mass, moved from side to side, as busy as a call boy when the curtain is about to rise.

Finally, at the nasal cue of a very thin priest who, at the foot of the altar, droned some psalms for the occasion, the orchestra struck up the symphony and the spectacle got under way. The muffled sound of bodies kneeling ran through the church; all eyes converged on the sacristy door; there were whispers of curiosity amid which soft coughing and sneezes stood out. And Canon Diogo appeared, as if entering on stage, radiant, haughty, master of his role, and accompanied by an altar boy frenetically swinging a censer made of white metal.

And the old actor, like some magical god in the midst of a cloud of incense, and covered with the gold graid trimming and spangles of a king, from the height of his full solemnity cast a curious and rapid glance at his public, while across his face spread that victorious smile of those few great actors whom success never abandons.

Indeed, the spectators adored him, though by now he seldom performed. But those few times when he did deign to appear, as on this occasion out of deference to an old lady friend, his triumph was magnificent and assured. People came from afar to see him, to admire the grandeur, the renown, and the graciousness in the man's bearing. Many went out of their way to attend his masses. Sexagenarian ladies from his earlier days would have their old palanquin chairs taken out from under the stairs and dusted off, and would surprise the neighborhood with a jaunt out into the streets. And there, those creaky and wrinkled bodies, which had aged along with Diogo, seemed to revive for a few seconds, like cadavers subjected to an electrical shock, and they would tremulously bite their purple and wrinkled lips, throbbing with recollections.

On the way to the altar the eminent actor gazed from side to side, spoke to his helpers in a low voice, and boldy faced his audience with the circumspect smile of a sovereign. But suddenly his smile expanded into a more accentuated one of pride: among the zealous women he had caught sight of Ana Rosa, kneeling on one of the steps in the nave with head bowed and a penitent air, praying fervently at her grandmother's side.

The censers exuded more incense; spirals of it billowed about, dissipating in the open space. The atmosphere became saturated with sacred and enervating perfumes, and all the women huddled together, eager for mystical ecstasies. The celebrant finally reached the altar, after kneeling rapidly, as if making a hurried bow, before the more important saints who sat haughtily on their artificial brocade thrones. The local dandies, separated from the principal altar by a black wooden grille, were removing musk-scented handkerchiefs from their pockets and kneeling on them in a dapper pose. Young girls hid their mouths in little prayer books, their eyes wandering furtively toward the side where the black tailcoats kneeled. Those who had been on their knees, praying and awaiting the mass for some time, changed positions. The opulent hips of the black women creaked, and the bones of the old men popped. Tiny children let out cries of appreciation for the festivities, and others whined. But, finally, everything took on a false air of tranquility; a hush fell, and, to the sound of the organ, the solemn mass began.

When the bells chimed again, everyone arose with a clamor. The young men straightened out the baggy knees of their trousers, and the girls rearranged their crinolines and bows. The devout old ladies shook out their everlasting skirts, which by now were puffed up from the pressure of kneeling. The orchestra struck up some secular tune, as merry as a farce following a drama. And in the sacristy Canon Diogo removed his picturesque apparrel made of embroidered silk, which the sexton gathered together religiously in his consumptive hand, to store in the vast blackwood drawers.

The people, comforted by religion but dying for lunch, were squeezing impatiently through the large doors of the cathedral. Beggars lined up along the exit, tearfully pleading for alms for the love of God or the divine wounds of Our Lord Jesus Christ; devout women disappeared into the square as rapidly as hunted cockroaches; a few ladies stood in the entrance basking in the sun, waiting for someone to greet them and conversing garrulously about the splendid execution of the mass, the excellence of the voices, the richness of the priest's garb, the altar cloth, and the careful observance of the rites. Everything had been quite satisfactory.

The church was almost empty. Dona Maria Bárbara and her granddaughter were awaiting the hero of the occasion.

"Here's your goddaughter, Canon! Give her communion; see if you can yank the devil out of her!" said the old women upon seeing him.

And, speaking more softly, she asked him with great solicitude to advise Ana Rosa well and to shake the idea of that nigger out of her little head. And finally she went away, tracing a cross in the air in the direction of her granddaughter.

"Go now, God will make you virtuous, for it's not an evil heart you have, my little fool."

And she went out to the hall to await her with Benedito, who had just then appeared, driving a carriage from the coachworks in Porto.

Canon Diogo had reckoned well. The staging of the mass, the enervating perfumes in the church, the still fasting stomach, the venerable mystery of the words in Latin, the religious ceremonial, the splendor of the altars, the eerie yellow light of the immense candles, and the plaintive sounds of the organ had deeply affected his goddaughter's delicate and nervous sensibilities and overwhelmed her tenacious spirit, predisposing her to confession. The poor girl sensed her own guilt; for the first time she understood that what she had done with Raimundo was a sin, and she felt the waning of that steel-like vigor that had inspired her love. And so, at the end of the mass, when her grandmother deposited her in the charge of that religious old fox, she wanted only to weep.

Overcome with emotion, she knelt in a seat next to the confessional and stammered the Confiteor, hardly pausing for breath. But the more she prayed, the more a dense timidity dulled her senses.

"Come," her godfather said, when she had finished her prayer. "Have no fear, my daughter! Confide in me, for I'm your friend. Plus videas tuis oculis quam alienis! Why are you crying? Tell me."

Ana Rosa trembled.

"Come now, stop crying and open your heart to me. Just answer as if you were speaking with God himself, who hears and pardons everything. Make the sign of the cross."

She obeyed.

"Tell me, my goddaughter, haven't you been neglecting religion lately?"

"No, sir," stammered Ana Rosa from behind her handkerchief.

"Have you been praying whenever you go to bed and whenever you get up?"

"Yes, I have, sir."

"And during those prayers, don't you promise to obey your parents?"

"Yes, I do."

"And have you been obeying them?"

"Yes, I have, sir."

"And does your conscience seem tranquil? Do you think you've been faithfully fulfilling everything you promised God, and everything the Holy Mother Church commands?"

Ana Rosa did not answer.

"Well, out with it!" said the priest tenderly. "Don't be afraid. This is nothing more than a conversation you're having with your own conscience, or with God, which is much the same thing. Tell me everything! Open your heart to me. Speak, my goddaughter. Here, I represent your father. If you were married, more than your husband. I am the judge, do you understand? I represent Christ! I represent divine judgment! Come, then tell me everything frankly. Tell me everything, and I will obtain absolution for you. I shall ask our merciful Lord to pardon your sins."

"But what must I tell you?"

And she sobbed.

"Tell me: what is it that has made you so sad of late? Do you feel possessed by some passion that is tormenting you? Speak up!"

"Yes, Godfather," she answered, without raising her eyes.

"For whom?"

"You already know, sir."

"For Raimundo?"

She responded with an affirmative movement of her head.

"And what are your intentions in that regard?"

"To marry him."

"And don't you remember that this offends God in various ways? You offend Him because you're disobeying your parents. You offend Him because you're harboring in your bosom a passion forbidden by your entire society and above all by your family. And you offend Him because through such a union, you'll condemn your future children to an ignoble destiny of shattering misery! Ana Rosa, this Raimundo has a soul as black as his blood! Besides being a mulatto, he's also an evil man, with no religion, with no fear of God! He's a . . . a . . . Freemason! He's an atheist! Wretched be the woman who joins with such a monster! Hell does exist, here is your proof! Hell is filled with unhappy women who, poor things, had no friend to counsel them as I'm counseling you at this very moment! Observe closely and notice, my goddaughter, that the abyss is at your feet. At least consider the precipice that threatens you! As your pastor and your godfather I am obliged to defend you. You shall not fall, because I will not allow it!"

And, as the girl displayed a certain air of doubt, the canon lowered his head, and said mysteriously:

"I have knowledge of horrible acts committed by that sorcerer! It is not only his color that brought down your father's opposition."

Ana Rosa made a gesture of surprise.

"Do you, by chance, know what preceded the birth of that man? Do you know how he came into the world?"

And altering his voice to a more sinister tone:

"Horribile dictu! He is the product of a swarm of crimes and shameful deeds! He is sin itself personified! . . . He is a devil! He is hell in flesh and blood! I would not tell you all this, my daughter, if it were not necessary. But you must realize that, if he wants to marry you, it is because he has a mortal hatred for your father and intends to take revenge on the poor man through the person of his daughter!"

"But why does he want vengeance on Papa?"

"Why? For many, many things that he won't forgive! These are family secrets you're still too young to know of and judge! But one of the reasons, and I'll tell you here in the sacred secrecy of the confessional, is the fact that your father inherited a considerable sum from his brother."

"That isn't possible!" exclaimed Ana Rosa, trying to get up.

"Child!" reprimanded the canon, forcing her to her knees. "Pray immediately, so that God may take pity on such folly! On your knees, sinner! You're much more at fault than I supposed!"

The girl fell to her knees, dizzy under the bombardment of these imprecations, and muttered the Confiteor, striking her breast repeatedly whenever she said "mea culpa" and "mea maxima culpa." And then they both grew quiet for a moment.

"Well?" said the priest finally, returning to his former soft tone. "Do you still feel the same or has some reason finally penetrated that little head? Speak up, my goddaughter!"

"I cannot change my resolve, Godfather."

"You're still thinking of marriage with . . . ?"

"I cannot stop thinking of it. Believe me!"

The old priest rose tragically, furrowed his eyebrows and raised one arm like a prophet.

"Well, then," he recited, "be aware, unhappy girl, that upon you will weigh eternal damnation! You know I have great influence on your father and could make him withdraw his blessing from you! You know that. . . ."

He was interrupted by a gasp from Ana Rosa, who had fallen at his feet in a faint.

"Oh, damn!" he muttered between his teeth.

And he popped out of the confessional to place his goddaughter on one of the long black wooden benches nearby.

Fortunately, it was nothing. The girl let out a deep sigh and rested her head on her godfather's lap, weeping silently, her eyes shut tight.

The priest remained for some time contemplating her in that position, which made her look more beautiful, and, lost in nostalgic reminiscences of his youth, he admired the soft curve of her breast throbbing under the pressure of the silk, the delicate whiteness of her cheeks, and the charming harmony of her features. "O tempora! O mores!" he said to himself and tenderly placed her against the high back of the bench.

"Come now," he continued, whispering almost like a lover eager for peace after a spat. "Come now, don't be obstinate. Don't be bad. Make your peace with God and with me."

"If for that," stammered Ana Rosa, without opening her eyes, "I must renounce the marriage, then I cannot."

"But why can't you, my little fool?" her confessor insisted, gently taking her hands. "Hum? Why can't you?"

"Because I'm pregnant!" she replied, turning scarlet and covering her face with her hands.

"Horresco referens!"

And the canon jumped back with a start and stood there, mouth agape, for quite a while, shaking his head.

"Yes, ma'am, you've really done it this time!"

Ana Rosa continued to cry, hiding her face.

"Yes, ma'am!"

And the old man probed her entire body with his gaze, as if trying to discover in her the physical confirmation of what she had said.

"Yes, ma'am."

And he took a pinch of snuff.

"Now you see," she ventured finally, between tears, "that I've no choice other than. . . ."

"You're entirely mistaken!" interrupted the canon, energetically. "Entirely! What you must do is marry Dias, and at once, before your guilt is evident!"

Ana Rosa made no reply.

"And as for this," added the old fox, disdainfully jutting out his lower lip toward her belly, "I'll take charge of finding you some remedy to. . . ."

Ana Rosa rose in one movement and cast a fierce eye on the canon.

"To kill my child?!" she exclaimed, livid.

And, as if fearing that the priest would yank the child from her womb right then and there, she fled headlong from the church.

She exited on the side facing the public gardens. Maria Barbara was only able to catch up with her in the coach.

"Indeed," she said to Ana Rosa, vexed. "You look like you've come from hell rather than from the house of God!"

"And I have!"

"Why the devil are you behaving like this, Anica?" the old lady admonished. "No one did things like this in my day! Why are you frowning so, my child?"

Ana Rosa, instead of replying, turned her face away. And they exchanged no further word until they reached the house, despite the grandmother's persistent nagging all the way home.

And yet Ana Rosa felt horribly oppressed and in need of unburdening herself to someone. An insane desire was consuming her: to run and find Raimundo, to tell him everything and beg his advice and support, because in him alone, and in no one else, could she confide fully. Her body burned with a carnal need to see him, embrace him, and clasp him to her with the most ardent kisses, and then to drag him far away, to some isolated place, some sanctuary unknown to the others, where the two would surrender exclusively to the joyous self-centeredness of their love.

Ever since she had realized she was preganant she had been unable to bear her girlish little room; her maiden's hammock stirred profound feelings of revulsion in her. And now, after blurting it all out to her godfather, she felt she had the strength for anything. A strange and compelling force surged through her blood; she thought of her child with rapture and pride as if he were gloriously conceived from her intelligence. And, obsessed with that idea, she grew detached from everything else, not even contemplating the falsity of the situation in which she found herself. She eagerly anticipated the pleasures of maternity, as if she were achieving them through licit means, and she trembled all over with dread at the simple idea that her baby might lack the tiniest attention or the most superfluous comfort. She would live exclusively for it, that mysterious little being dwelling in her body. The child was her cherished thought at every moment; she spent her days guessing what it would be like, whether a boy or girl, large or small, robust or delicate, whether it would take after its father. She had forebodings and became more superstitious. But despite all the dangers and difficulties, she felt happy to be a mother and would not have traded her position for the most honorable and secure one if it meant the sacrifice of her child. Her child! That alone made up for everything, that alone was truly important. Everything else was trifling, incomplete, false, or ridiculous when compared to the truth that was mysteriously occurring within her, as if by a miracle. Ana Rosa felt a happiness that from hour to hour and moment to moment was growing in her womb like a living treasure taking shape. In her womb she carried that other being, branching out from her own, and it was a throbbing fragment of her beloved, her Raimundo.

On arriving home, she ran straight to her room, locked herself inside, took up pen and paper and, without stopping for breath, composed a voluminous letter to him. "Come," she told him, "come as soon as possible, my friend, for I need you, so as not to believe that we two are monsters! If you only knew how much I miss you, how your absence pains me, you would have pity on me! Come and fetch me. If you don't come before the end of the month, I'll go to you, I'll do something crazy!"

But Raimundo replied that it was still too soon and asked her to wait patiently for the moment to put their plans into action.

The young man was now quite dejected, very nervous and irritable. In his state of melancholy, he wanted to see no one. At times he would be thoroughly startled when his servant would unexpectedly enter his room. He let his beard grow and paid little attention to his appearance; he read little and wrote even less. His acquaintances, made mostly through his uncle, vanished like sand along the shoreline. He would seldom leave his house for, as Ana Rosa was his sole reason for staying in Maranhão, only she interested him and could entice him to go out.

Ana Rosa, however, was being closely watched, as she had been ever since her cousin's unsuccessful departure. And Manuel's visitors, too, refrained from mentioning Raimundo; the event was treated with a hypocritical indifference, and no one uttered a word about it, but everyone sensed perfectly that the scandal still lingered, muffled but stirring, awaiting the first chance to burst open once more. And the coterie that gathered at Manuel's house waited and waited, seated together in the evening until the inevitable hour for tea and toast, conversing about dozens of subjects, except the one of most interest to them all, for no one had the courage to bring it up.

But the first week went by uneventfully, then the second, the third, and the fourth. Two months passed, and the coterie, disheartened, began to disperse. Little by little Eufrasinha stopped coming; Lindoca, anchored to her obesity, kept Freitas at her side; Campos finally vanished to the country; José Roberto went off also, and lived here and there between sprees. The only one who did not desert the house, who appeared with her usual regularity, was Dona Amância Souzelas, always ready for anything, always speaking ill of others, never ceasing to complain that the good old days were gone and that the niggers wanted to stick their noses into everything.

"But it's the girls who encourage them," she said one night, squinting an oblique peep at Ana Rosa.

Manuel's daughter instinctively folded her arms over her belly.

17

Three months passed. Ana Rosa, contrary to all expectations, seemed calmer. The vigilance exercised over her had diminished considerably. The canon, either by design or through mere fulfillment of his duty, had kept her confessional secret. Manuel's house had at last lapsed back into its listless and profound bourgeois tranquility.

Of all this Raimundo had kept faithfully abreast, and he now decided to play his final card. He wrote to his lover to mark the day of their flight. Ana Rosa fell ill with happiness. It would be on the following Sunday. He would have a coach await her at the corner of the street, and, once together, they would flee to a safe place. Her abductor would not be easily recognized, because his whiskers had totally altered his appearance. "Still," he said in his letter:

> . . . at Sunday night at eight, when your father is usually chatting in Vidal's pharmacy, when the neighbors and clerks are still out for the evening, and your grandmother is being tended to by Mônica, who's on our side, a bearded fellow dressed in black will whistle a familiar tune outside your door. That will be me. When I signal, you'll descend cautiously and with complete security. I'll take care of the rest, the house where we will go and the priest who will marry us—all will be ready. Courage! Until Sunday night at eight.
>
> P.S. Take every precaution!

During the few days remaining before their flight, Ana Rosa did little more than dream of her future happiness. She was frightened and at the same time radiant with satisfaction. She scarcely ate or slept, brimming with an excited impatience which gave her feverish dizzy spells. In the selfishness of her maternal happiness she ill humoredly put up with both the few girl friends who sought her out and Manuel's old companions, who from time to time appeared for supper. But no one seemed, however remotely, to suspect her plans. On the contrary, at home they talked openly about her loyal obedience, her resignation to her father's wishes, and they whispered devoutly about the salutary effect of the confessional. Maria Bárbara was resplendent with triumph and, like the others in the family, intensified her solicitude toward her granddaughter. Ana Rosa was treated like a child convalescing from a deadly illness; they surrounded her with little niceties and loving gestures, avoiding any unpleasantness and excusing her whims and petulance. Despite what he knew, the canon had never acted so paternal and tender. And Dias, unalterable Dias, went dully about, continuing to gain his ascendency over his colleagues, who had already begun to treat him with the respect due the boss, for they sensed his impending marriage to Ana Rosa.

"He's got a foot in the door! He's already there, entering society," Pescada's clerks would snort, after commenting on the new tone with which the girl addressed Luís.

She, indeed, now greeted him with less repugnance, once she even smiled at him. But that smile, so misinterpreted by everyone, was nothing more than her satisfaction at looking back at the precipice near which she had passed, and from which she was now safely removed.

The fact of the matter was that Manuel was now as happy as could be. He was overheard humming while at work and was seen at the neighbors' doors, hatless and at times in shirtsleeves, noisily jesting and choking with laughter; and at night, when the canon arrived at the house, he always clasped him in an embrace.

"You're a real old devil! No one can put a thing past you!"

"Davus sum non Aedipus!"

Members of the coterie privately discussed the great event. "Who will be the guests of honor at the wedding? . . . Who will be invited? . . . What will the trousseau be like? . . . How about the banquet?" And soon, throughout the province, the approaching wedding of Pescada's daughter was discussed. They gossiped about it, predicting good and bad consequences. They all laughed loudly about Raimundo, and in general praised Ana Rosa's behavior: "Yes, sir, she's behaved like a sensible girl." All the family friends began to prepare for the celebration—even before receiving invitations. Sparky was soon going around worrying about the impromptu poem with which he hoped to redeem himself from his fiasco on St. John's day. Freitas outdid himself with discourses in honor of the event, while still feeling sorry for Raimundo, whose articles and poetry he had truly admired. Casusa railed against all Portuguese, furious that such a lovely and darling Brazilian girl was going to fall into the hands of a stinking Portugee. Amância and Etelvina wiled away hours gabbing about the marriage, the widow insisting she would believe it only when she saw it. Everywhere people were wagering that the celebration would be magnificent.

They expressed wide-eyed amazement that ice cream would be served, and even mentioned that Pescada was going to revive the ice machine from Santo Antônio just for that day.

But the fateful Sunday that Raimundo had chosen for the flight finally arrived. It was, by chance, a tedious day for Manuel's family, for the canon did not make his customary appearance for a chat, and no one knew just what Dias was up to. With no visitors, dinner passed uneventfully, but in good spirits. At the table the merchant repeatedly commented on his daughter's future; with a Lisbon wineglass in his hand he seemed happy and cheerful, recalling familiar family anecdotes, jesting about marriage, and teasing his daughter that he would arrange Tinoco or Major Cotia as a fiancé for her. She laughed a great deal; she was flushed, very fidgety, and nervous. She wanted to embrace her father, to hug and kiss him while bidding him farewell. During dessert, she felt an absurd desire to tell him frankly all her plans and, for the last time, to ask for his approval of Raimundo.

At six o'clock Dona Amância arrived and found them still finishing their coffee. Ana Rosa felt a twinge in her heart. "What bad luck!" The old lady declared that she was tired and quite out of breath. She asked them to permit her to rest a while.

"What toil on your part, gracious! To climb up eight hills on the same day!"

"Eight, eh?"

And Ana Rosa bit her lips, smiling but annoyed.

"One by one! Why it's enough to truly exhaust a creature!"

And they conversed at length about the hillsides of Maranhão.

"Well, that one at Vira-Mundo, God bless a soul!"

"It isn't any worse than the one in front of the provincial palace."

"Now just a minute there, how about the one on your street, Manuel? I tell you, it has quite a slope!"

"And the one on the Rua do Giz?"

"It's an inferno," declared the old lady, still gasping, "for a soul to be always going up and down like some cursed thing. Heavens!"

The conversation continued, and Ana Rosa grew frightened. Amância seemed ready to waggle her tongue; she would not be leaving soon. The clerks had already retired, and Ana Rosa trembled with impatience. "Won't that old crow ever leave? Goodness!"

Time hurried by.

Manuel, a short while later, declared that he would not be leaving the house. He went to get his newspapers from Portugal and sat down to read at the dining table on the veranda.

Ana Rosa almost screamed. She ran to her room, seething with rage and sobbing. "Now this! Once again they seem to be conspiring against me!"

The large clock struck. It was seven-thirty. Ana Rosa beat her fist against her head. "The devil!"

Manuel was yawning. Amância seemed resolved not to leave.

Ana Rosa returned to the veranda, her hands ice-cold and her heart jumping out of her chest. She felt an impatience saturated with fear. She wanted to scream out, to cut off that old woman's idiot chatter, to throw her violently out into the street. "Why doesn't she go bother Grandmother?" Such obstacles to her escape seemed to her unjust and inconsiderate. Even the desire to complain to her father crossed her mind, to protest these setbacks that were making her suffer.

A quarter of an hour slipped by. Manuel got up and stretched himself, the newspapers in his hand.

"Well, if you'll excuse me, Dona Amância."

And he went off to his room to sleep.

"Finally!"

Ana Rosa felt restored. She had a desire to embrace her father, to thank him for such a kindness.

"Well, I'll also be moving along," said Amância. And she rose.

"Already?" Ana Rosa muttered, for the sake of courtesy.

The visitor sat down again. Ana Rosa felt an urge to strangle her.

Maria Bárbara came from her room and struck up a conversation with her friend.

Ana Rosa was gasping. "The devil!"

It was already five minutes before eight. Amância at last got up and said good-bye. "At last, thank God!"

Maria Bárbara went to the hall.

"Remember" Amância shouted. "Don't forget, right? Three drops of lemon and a teaspoon of orangeflower water. A saintly remedy, another invention of our deceased Maria do Carmo!"

And she went down the steps.

But once downstairs, she turned back, calling for Maria Bárbara. "Say, Babu!"

Ana Rosa was almost out of her mind. She let herself fall into a chair.

"It's true, you probably haven't heard. Well, I nearly forgot." Eufrasinha is sweet on a student from the Lycée."

"What a harebrain!"

"A fellow fifteen years old, mind you."

And she related the entire story, spicing up and exaggerating the details.

Ana Rosa, seated on the veranda in a rocking chair, tapped her fingernails against her teeth.

"Well now, good-bye, my dear."

And Amância kissed Maria Bárbara on the cheek.

"Finally!"

Ana Rosa immediately dashed to her room. Raimundo had advised her to bring nothing, absolutely nothing, from the house, for he was prepared and would see to all her needs.

The clock rasped out eight steady strokes. Maria Bárbara withdrew deep into the house; Manuel continued to sleep in his room. A few moments later, in the silence of the veranda, Ana Rosa heard Raimundo clearly whistling an Italian tune.

Ana Rosa, whose heart was doing gymnastic exercises in her chest, shakily gathered up her skirts and, with the agility of a bird fleeing its cage, went tiptoeing down the stairway. Once downstairs, she threw herself into the arms of Raimundo, who was awaiting her on the bottom steps.

But on passing through the door to the street, she let out a scream. Raimundo stopped in his tracks and turned pale. Outside, Canon Diogo and Dias, accompanied by four policemen, moved forward to confront them, blocking their passage.

Dias, left to himself, was merely a poor ass, incapable of even the slightest intellectual subtlety, and with little ability to focus his thoughts. Placed under Canon Diogo's command, however, he had become a dangerous weapon, with a wider range and greater aim. Guided by his master, the imbecil had never ceased prying, and had remained constantly suspicious and alert, sounding out everything that seemed odd to him. Many a time he had awakened in the middle of the night to go groping about in the dark, spying and eavesdropping in the hope of uncovering something. The stealthy conversations between Ana Rosa and Mônica, whenever the latter returned from the fountain, did not escape his notice, and Dias thus found out about the correspondence with Raimundo, from the very first letters.

"I should intercept them, isn't that right?" he asked the priest.

"No! Not now! It's still too soon," answered Diogo.

And the canon continued assiduously to frequent Manuel's house, ever solicitous of his goddaughter's health, and inquiring with paternal interest about the tiniest things concerning her. He wanted to know on which days her appetite was better, when she felt happy or sad, when she cried, when she dressed up, when she woke up late, and when she prayed. As an old family friend, he insisted that everything be told to him, and Manual willingly did so, satisfied to see things return to normal and his house restored to its former tranquility. The canon had in no way revealed Ana Rosa's confessional secret, for as Dias's ally, he feared that in such an ugly state of affairs the merchant might forget everything and prefer marrying his daughter to the man who had robbed her of her virtue. As for his protégé, neither was it fitting to tell him the truth, for he was afraid that the clerk, through either scruple or dread of his rival, would give up on the marriage. And if Dias were to back out, Diogo would be in bad straits, for Ana Rosa would immediately marry Raimundo, and he might end up subjected to the revenge of the mulatto, whom he had feared, and with good reason, ever since their little conversation when Raimundo had returned from São Brás. "I know perfectly well," rationalized the old fox, "the good-for-nothing hasn't the least bit of proof against me. But it's in my interest to get him out of Maranhão—whatever the price! Better safe than sorry! What keeps him here is the hope of still obtaining Ana Rosa. But once she's married to that fool Dias, she'll go with her husband on a trip to Europe, and Raimundo will naturally take off as well. But if by chance before leaving he wants to discredit me publicly, they'll all reject whatever he says as pure spite, and he'll end up looking not only ridiculous but also like a slanderer." And satisfied with his scheme, he rubbed his hands together and concluded: "Whoever told him to butt into my territory?"

And so, whenever Dias came and told him of a new letter from Raimundo, the canon, with his practiced eye, would seek to discern its effect on his goddaughter. Seeing the girl's excitement after the most recent, he hurried to tell the clerk:

"The time is now ripe, my friend. Get moving! We need this letter!"

"And why didn't we need any of the others?" Luís asked stupidly.

"Why? Well, I'll tell you—and you asked me at just the right moment. The other letters were the simple, idle chatterings of love. They weren't worth the risk. And besides, if my goddaughter had suspected something, she'd have increased her precautions. And, now, our acquisition of this indispensable one wouldn't be as easy as it surely will be, do you understand?"

But the old trickster did not reveal the real reason. He had not wanted the clerk to read Raimundo's earlier letters for two reasons: first, because he feared Raimundo might make some revelation about the crime at São Brás; and, second, he dreaded that the letters might by chance refer to Ana Rosa's embarrassing condition.

What was certain, however, was that such a plan unquestionably facilitated the surreptitious removal of the letter in which Raimundo set the date of their escape. The clerk, enticing Benedito with a ten milréis note, obtained it right away, copied it quickly, returned it, and ran to Diogo's house.

Now in possession of their enemy's plan, the two allies set about to prevent his flight and went straight to the police, who provided them with four officers.

As could be expected, the commotion attracted a crowd on the Rua da Estrela. Manuel awoke with a start at the shouts of his mother-in-law, Brígida, and Mônica, who, still unaware of Ana Rosa's absence, were frightened by the appearance of the policemen and the din of the mob gathering at the door of the house. Maria Bárbara, stunned out of her wits, scurried screaming to her room, where she embraced the statue of a saint and hid in her hammock—it wasn't her department to deal with uniforms and bayonets. She had right off felt an itching in her legs and her stomach had knotted up. "Good heavens!"

Raimundo, meanwhile, did not lose heart at this turn of events. Without hesitation, he went back up the stairs, leading Ana Rosa, who was half in a swoon. At the top, he came face to face with Manuel and abruptly halted. The two stared at one another with equal firmness, for each was fully aware of what was at stake. The priest and clerk came up immediately, accompanied by the policemen.

With all of them together the situation turned tense: silence hovered heavily about, immobilizing them. Finally, the canon pulled out his ample handkerchief of Indian silk, noisily blew his nose, and stated, after a Latin proverb, that as a friend of Ana Rosa's father and godfather to the girl, he had perceived it to be his duty to forestall the criminal abduction that Dr. Raimundo had attempted to perpetrate against a member of the family.

Ana Rosa gathered her wits on hearing her godfather's words and listened with her head lowered but still resting on Raimundo's shoulder.

"I was going of my own free will," she murmured, without raising her eyes. "I was fleeing with my cousin because it was the only way to marry him."

"And you, how do you explain this?" the canon asked Raimundo in an authoritative tone.

"I'll not defend myself, nor accept you as judge. I'll simply state that this lady bears no responsibility for what has just happened. I alone am to blame. For better or worse, I thought, and still think, that I must marry her, and toward this end I shall employ every means possible!"

Ana Rosa was about to say something, but the canon cut her off: "Let's all go inside."

After dismissing the police, they headed to the sitting room, at the door of which Maria Bárbara, still confused and skittish with fright, stood spying on them.

"Now that we're among the family," Diogo added, shutting the door, "let us, as people of good and sound judgment, resolve this touchy situation as best we can. Hodie mihi cras tibi! Manuel, you first! You have the floor!"

Manuel was pacing back and forth the length of the room. He stopped, faced the sofa where they were all seated, and addressed the group. The poor man had an expression of deep sadness on his face; his bewilderment was apparent in his gaze, commanding the respect and compassion that resigned pain always inspires. It was obvious that he lacked words, and that the unhappy man was struggling to explain his ideas in an honest and clear manner. Finally, he turned toward the canon and stated that he quite valued his presence at his side at that moment. Diogo had always been his helping hand, his companion and best friend, as he had just proved once again. He should remain, then, and listen in, for he was one of the family. Then he asked his mother-in-law to join the group. Her presence and opinion were equally indispensable.

And, finally, he mentioned the clerk. Dias should also remain as he was more than a mere employee in Manuel's store; he was an efficient co-worker and a future partner, who would shortly acquire officially the position that in fact had been his for some time. Consequently, they were among family and he, much to the relief of his conscience, could speak straightforwardly to Dr. Raimundo and tell him everything he thought about what had happened, without pulling his punches.

And, after a brief pause, he declared that ever since he had first pondered the marriage of his daughter, it had always been with her future and happiness in mind. Surely no one imagined he wanted to marry her to some enchanted prince or Greek wiseman? No, indeed! All he wanted was to give her to an honest man, as hardworking as he. But, well, what the devil! Someone who was white and who could assure a decent and secure future for his grandchildren. So, then, he had thought of Dias; something inside told him that Dias would make a good husband for Anica.

One fine day he discovered a certain inclination for her on the part of the clerk—and that suited him just fine. So he immediately promised himself to make Dias a partner in his firm if the marriage took place. Now, everyone could see how, in all that, Manuel had thought only of his daughter's well-being. And they couldn't possibly believe that there were parents so perverted as to want grief to befall their very own offspring. Nothing of the sort! What they often wanted was to prevent such grief as was sure to appear afterward! Now just how could he, who had only his daughter, only his Anica, who had brought her up as best he could, and whose hair had turned white with worry over her happiness, he, who had always given in to all her whims, all her fancies; he, who was capable of the greatest sacrifice out of love for that child; how, then, could he go against her and cause her grief, just because he felt like it? So, did they think this all made sense? . . . He wanted to see her married, by God, that was what he wanted! He hadn't raised her to be a nun! But, for heaven's sake, he wanted to see her married in their own circle. He wanted to see her happy, satisfied, and surrounded by relatives and friends; but, darn it, he wanted her right there in Maranhão, at her father's side! The very idea! Can it be that a man, just because he's old, no longer has a right to his children's affection? Or, who knows, that a daughter, being quite grown up, should forsake her father? Or should say to him: "Oh, go drop dead, you old toad, what do you matter to me?" No! For God never set things up that way, either. Did she want to go off? To leave her poor old father there all by himself, without anyone who cared about him, without anyone to look after his aches and pains? Well, she could go! Let her leave! But let her wait a moment for his eyes to close first, ungrateful child!

And, drying his tears on his coat sleeve, Manuel concluded in a quivering voice:

"I've just told you what I intended to do. But, with the devil's own luck, who should arrive from Rio de Janeiro but my bastard nephew, the son of my deceased brother José and that Negress Domingas who was his slave! As was to be expected, given that I always looked after my brother's affairs, and lately those of my nephew too, I put him up here in my house. Raimundo grew attached to my daughter, and she, by the looks of it, reciprocated. So he comes and asks me for her hand in marriage. What can I do? I refuse him. He wants to know why, and I tell him the reason straightforwardly. Well, then, just look! This man pretended to leave town just to trick me, and, after sneaking about out there and hiding from everyone, he reneges on his word of honor, and. . . ."

"Sir!" shouted Raimundo.

"Sir, no! You gave me your word you would never attempt to marry Anica! Therefore, I say and I repeat: after reneging on your word of honor, you cunningly come to abduct my daughter! Is this right? Don't the legal codes of this country have a punishment for such an outrage?"

"They do," said Raimundo, regaining his composure. "They do, whenever the offender refuses to atone for his offense by marriage. I, however, desire nothing but that!"

"Aaaaack!" blurted Maria Bárbara, jumping forward. "Marry my granddaughter to the son of a Negro? Can't you see what you are?!"

The merchant felt embarrassed.

"I appeal," Manuel pleaded, "to the conscience of each and every one of you. Put yourselves in my place and tell me what you would do? But it does seem to me that what we should do is put an end to all this and avoid an even greater scandal. I understand perfectly that Dr. Raimundo shares no blame for his origin and, as he is a man of common sense and extensive knowledge, he will, I hope, at our request, leave Maranhão as soon as possible."

"Amen!" the canon seconded.

"And I now," ventured Luís, obeying a signal from the canon, "request Dona Anica's hand."

"I refuse!" shouted Ana Rosa. "Even if Raimundo abandons me!"

"You're doing me an injustice," Raimundo remarked to her. "I know perfectly well how to do my duty."

"What do you mean your 'duty'?" challenged Maria Bárbara, grinding her teeth.

"Yes, my lady, my duty."

"So, then, you won't leave. Is that final?!" intervened Manuel.

"I swear that I shall not leave Maranhão without marrying your daughter," answered Raimundo, calm and resolute.

"And I declare," shouted the old woman, "that you shall never marry my granddaughter as long as I live!"

"And I shall withdraw my blessing from my goddaughter if she does not obey her family," reinforced the canon.

Raimundo nailed a stare on him that upset the priest.

And Ana Rosa jumped up, raising her head. Her face, dulled by tears, now shone with the luster of a great and painful decision. Everyone looked at her. She was pale, overcome with emotion, her lips trembling; but finally, overcoming the flushed wave of modesty that was suffocating her, she stammered:

"I absolutely must marry him. . . . I am pregnant!"

It came as a great shock. Even the canon, to whom the girl's condition was not a secret, was flabbergasted at her words. Manuel collapsed into a chair with his eyes wide open, fulminating and gasping. Dias turned the color of a corpse. Raimundo folded his arms, and Maria Bárbara, foaming with rage, jumped to her granddaughter's side, shielding her with her body as if to protect her from her lover.

"Never, never!" she howled like a beast. "Pregnant? So be it! But I'd rather have her dead or a prostitute!"

"Shhhhh . . ." whispered the canon. And, in a mysterious and pleading tone, he said:

"Quiet . . . quiet! Remember, they can hear us from the street, Dona Babita."

"So you're with child?" Manuel finally exclaimed, getting up, his face purple with anger.

And he started toward his daughter, fists clenched.

Raimundo pushed him away without a word.

"You, sir, are wicked!" the poor father inveighed, heading toward a corner, sobbing.

Raimundo went over to him and humbly asked for his pardon and for Ana Rosa as a wife.

The merchant did not answer and began cursing through his tears.

"Calm down! Calm down!" advised the canon, putting his arm on Manuel's shoulder. "Let's just see what we can arrange. It's only death that has no remedy. Mentem hominis spectate, non frontem!"

"Arrange whatever you can, except my granddaughter's marriage to a Negro!"

"Yes ma'am, Dona Maria Bárbara. . . . Minima de malis!"

And, after taking a pinch of snuff, the canon turned politely to Dias:

"You, sir, a while ago asked my friend for my goddaughter's hand, is that not so?"

"Yes, sir."

"Well, your request is still under consideration, and I'll give you the answer tomorrow afternoon. You may leave now."

"But. . . ."

Diogo did not allow him another word. He led him to the door and whispered rapidly to him:

"Wait for me at Prensa corner. Go now."

Dias excused himself and left.

The canon returned to the middle of the room to address Raimundo.

"As for you, Doctor, you say you are willing to make amends for your crime."

"That is correct."

"Yes, sir, that's quite natural . . . even quite gallant. However," he continued, smacking his lips, "on the other hand, Manuel, Dona Maria Bárbara, and I, your humble servant, all say you are not in a position to make restitution. Suspecta malorum beneficia! What you call amends, instead of saving her, would injure and vilify your victim even more!"

"You scum!" shouted Raimundo, completely losing his patience and grabbing the priest by the neck. "I'll smash you right here, you crook!"

And he relaxed his hands, afraid of killing him.

Manuel and Maria Bárbara hurried to help, brimming with indignation at Raimundo, while the canon put his lace collar back in place and straightened his cassock, muttering:

"Wait a moment, my friend. Force will resolve nothing. Hoc avertat Deus! We're quite aware that you are an excellent person, indeed! But . . . you must agree that you've no right to lay claim to my goddaughter's hand. Not even physical force can make me deny that you're a. . . ."

"A nigger!" concluded the old lady with a shout. "You're the son of that black Domingas! Freed at baptism! You're a half-breed, a mulatto!"

"But, what the devil? What are you all driving at?" shouted Raimundo, stomping his foot. "Spill it out!"

"It's just that we," answered the canon in a steady tone, "in order to prevent this scandal from continuing, are once again going to offer you the only expedient to follow. And remember that we can, without further delay, have charges brought against you, if we so desire. But . . . why deny it? We simply do not believe you violated the innocence of this girl. Her declaration a few minutes ago was nothing more than a ploy cooked up by you in the hope of accomplishing your plan. But you were wrong! We know she's as pure as ever! Therefore, what must be done is this: you, Doctor, will leave the province as soon as possible. You will leave immediately, under threat of being legally prosecuted if we see fit!"

Raimundo went to get his hat. The canon blocked his path.

"Well? What have you decided?"

"Go to hell!" Raimundo answered him and went over to Ana Rosa who was sitting against the wall, crying.

"We still have one way out. You're of age. I'll send word tomorrow. I swear I shall be your husband!"

"And I swear I am yours!" she exclaimed, jumping up to accompany him to the door.

"Shut up" ordered Manuel, forcing her to sit down again with a shove.

"Well," muttered the priest as soon as Raimundo had left. "So be it!"

Ana Rosa ran to lock herself in her room.

Manuel dropped into a chair, muffling his sobs in his hands; Maria Bárbara continued to curse, now turning all her despair against her son-in-law; and the canon, walking back and forth, first to one, then to the other, attempted to calm them, promising to take care of everything. "Now, let's get past this quarrel. The situation isn't that bad. It's not worth fretting like this! Have confidence in me, and I'll work everything out quite decently. This business about the pregnancy was a whopping lie, cooked up at the last minute. If there were any truth in it, wouldn't she have confessed it to me?"

And a little later he went down the stairs, the steps creaking under his polished shoes.

"Here I am, Canon. Can we go?" Dias asked him as soon as they met at Prensa corner.

"Just wait! Hold on, my friend. In what direction did our man go?"

"He went down the Prensa alleyway."

"Then we still have things to do around here."

And he walked over to a coachman parked at the corner, spoke to him in a low tone, and the coach trotted off.

"Fine," he said, returning to the clerk. "Now, let's hide here, behind this stack of barrels."

"What for?"

"So the nigger won't see us when he passes by."

And there they remained, conspiring in low voices until Raimundo appeared, coming back out of the alley entrance. He had gone to dismiss the boat awaiting him and Ana Rosa down on the beach. The light from the corner streetlamp hit him fully in the face, for his felt hat was tilted back toward the nape of his neck. He stopped for an instant, hesitant, looking for his coach, and finally resolved, with a gesture of impatience, to walk down one side of the Praça do Comércio.

"Good!" murmured the priest mysteriously to his companion. "Follow him, but from a distance, so you won't be seen. And if he tarries at all on the street, do what I told you. Take it!"

And, without raising his arm, he handed him an object that Dias was reluctant to take.

"Well?" insisted Diogo.

"But. . . ."

"But what? Now don't be an ass. Take it!"

Dias still resisted, so the canon added:

"Don't be a fool. Seize this opportunity God offers you. Do what

I told you—you'll be rich and happy! Audaces fortuna juvat! Give thanks to Providence for the easy path presented to you, and which I now see you don't deserve! The majority of powerful men had to overcome far greater ordeals to reach their ends! Go, and don't be ungrateful to the fortune that watches over you. Besides, that would be the last straw: for one moment of infantile fear, your labor of so many years would vanish! I guarantee he wouldn't have the same hesitation if it were you, which might just happen anyway."

"But, Reverend, do you think that. . . ."

"I don't 'think,' I'm fully certain! 'He who spares his enemy, will die by his hand!' But even if he himself does not kill you, is that reason for you not to destroy him? Tell me frankly here and now: are you or are you not determined to marry my goddaughter?"

"Yes, sir, I am."

"Fine! Then let me just remind you that a colored man, a mulatto born a slave, has dishonored the woman who is going to be your wife—and this, for someone in your position, is a greater insult than adultery! Therefore, you are fully within your rights to avenge this outrage to your honor. Indeed, this right has now become a duty dictated by your conscience and by society!"

"But. . . ."

"Just imagine yourself married to Ana Rosa, and that fellow is out there enjoying his life. And there's the child who we already know will resemble his father. Well, then, one fine day when you, my friend, are out with your family, on the street or in some shop, you meet up with that nigger! Just how will you act, Dias? What will you look like? What won't people say? And let's face it, they'll have just cause! And the child? The child, if he's still living, what won't he think of the idiot who raised him? Be clear about one thing: as long as Raimundo exists, his child will be fated to find out who his real father is. There won't be a shortage of people to tell him!"

"Yes, but. . . ."

"But, despite everything, if both sides were equal, that's one thing. But that's not the way it is. You attained your position in that firm through years of dedication, with ceaseless effort, day by day, hour by hour. You buried your youth there and mortgaged your future. You gave your all, everything you had, so that you might now get back your capital and the accumulated interest. And Raimundo? He is simply an intruder who blocks your way. He's an opportunist, an adventurer who wants to seize what you've earned. What, then, should you do? Get rid of him. We've run out of threats to him, but he persists. So kill him! What right does he have? None! A Negro freed at baptism cannot aspire to the hand of a rich white lady. It's a crime! It's a crime the malefactor wishes at all cost to perpetrate against our society—especially against the family of the man to whom you are dedicated, a family that, one might say, is already yours, because Manuel Pedro has been a real father to you, a true friend, a protector who at the very least deserves the sacrifice you now hesitate to make for him! This is ingratitude, nothing more, nothing less! But, Dias, divine justice never sleeps. God has tried to make you an instrument of His sacred designs, and you refuse. . . . Very well! I'll have nothing more to do with this! And to hell with your conscience! I wash my hands of it! . . . As a priest and as a friend of your benefactor, I've now done and said all I should. The rest is not up to me! Do whatever you wish!"

"Yes . . . but. . . ."

"I'll make only one more observation: even if Raimundo does not manage to marry Ana Rosa, keep in mind that because she's of legal age and Raimundo does have the law on his side, you can be sure that as long as he's alive the mother of his child will never pay the least bit of attention to you. That I guarantee you!"

"But her father can make her marry me. . . ."

"Don't be such a dumb ass! A girl in that state marries only as she herself wishes. But, even if it were that way, and we accepted the absurd hypothesis that her father could force her, then that would be even worse for you! At any time Raimundo need only say to Ana Rosa, 'come here,' and she, your wife, my dear friend, would follow him immediately, like a puppydog! Do you have any idea how a woman feels about the first man to possess her, especially when he gets her pregnant? She's a spoken-for animal! She'll follow him wherever he goes and do just as he wants! She's an automaton, she does not belong to herself! She has no will of her own! Married to someone else? What does it matter! She'll be off after her lover and follow him through all kinds of degradation! She'll laugh at her husband's expense and heap shame upon him! She'll be the first to call him names! And you, you dunce, you'll be there only to spice up their delights, to give them now and then a piquant bite of the forbidden fruit of sin! And consider, for just a moment, the terrible consequences of your cowardice: the black sequence of shame that awaits you won't stop at that! Sooner or later, Raimundo will surely tire of his lover, as we eventually loath all illicit things. Once the initial phase of illusions has passed, the ardor that binds him to Ana Rosa will vanish, and all his dreams will then center on acquiring a magnificent position in society. Well, as soon as Ana Rosa no longer fits into his plans, his political and literary conquests, she'll become an obstacle to his career, a hindrance to his future, an impediment that he will kick away at the first opportunity and replace with a legitimate wife of whom he can take advantage to rise even higher. Ana Rosa will then be passed on to a second hand, then to a third, a fourth, a fifth, until, exhausted and worn out, she'll slide into the mud of the waterfront slums, into sailors' taverns, or, in short, any place where she can sell herself to stave off hunger. And remember: In all this she'll never cease to be your wife, accepted at the altar, in the eyes of God and society! Now tell me, Mr. Dias, does it not seem to you that by avoiding such calamities you will be carrying out the will of our Creator and our fellow beings? Do you still doubt you're accomplishing a good deed by removing the sole agent of so much misfortune? Let's go, my friend, don't be selfish. Save that innocent lamb from the whirlpool of prostitution! In the name of the church, save her! In the name of decency! In the name of goodness!"

And the great actor raised his arms toward heaven, exclaiming in a plaintive voice:

"Quis talia fando temperat a lacrymis?"

Dias listened, frowning. The canon pressed on, changing his tone:

"Let's reverse the coin! Let's see now what will happen if you follow my advice: the girl will cry for a while, but not for long, just a short while, because I'll console her with my words. Then, because she'll need a father for her child, she'll marry you, and there you are, my friend, from one day to the next, rich, happy, your own man! Not to mention the inner joy you'll feel at having delivered your benefactor's daughter from certain perdition. She'll cease to be a lost woman and become a model wife!"

"That's right!"

"Well, get the deed done! Anyone who finds a thief in his house, stealing mere money, has the right to blast his brains out with a bullet. How, then, can anyone stand by with arms folded when he sees his honor, his fortune, his woman and his tranquility threatened? Yes, he can . . . if he's a wretch and a fool!"

"Reverend, I swear that. . . ."

"Then, be off! The only opportunity God grants you is slipping away. Tomorrow will be too late! He'll already have her legally and, even if by chance they don't marry, the scandal will be known! Decide now, or leave the field free once and for all to the strongest and most clever!"

"Good-bye, Canon Diogo."

"May the Most Holy Virgin Mary go with you!"

And Dias, his head lowered, his steps long and muffled, went up the Rua da Estrela. Suddenly, he returned, called the priest and whispered a question in his ear.

"That's better, yes."

The clerk then took the Rua de Santana.

An hour later, after savoring a hot broth and rubbing the shiny back of his Maltese cat, the canon, all washed and sweet smelling, said his usual prayer and tranquilly stretched out in his cotton hammock, ready to pass a restful night.

18

Ana Rosa, meanwhile, was crying in her room; Manuel continued to pace back and forth in the parlor with his hands clasped behind his back, his head bent as if a leaden anxiety were weighing it down; and Maria Bárbara was having supper on the veranda, muttering as she dunked slices of toasted bread into her cup of green tea. The night went by, the hours yielded to one another like mute sentinels, and none of the three sought sleep. Finally, Maria Bárbara compelled her son-in-law to retire and then went to join her granddaughter, preparing to keep her company until dawn. Before long, however, the old lady was snoring, and both father and daughter, through their tears, watched the new day dawn.

As for Raimundo, he had wandered through the streets of the city, his heart flooded by a massive despondency. He was plagued less by the difficulty of the situation than by the brutal obstinacy of that family, which preferred to see their child dishonored rather than have to give her in marriage to a mulatto. "Surely, they are carrying this business of blood to great extremes!" And despite the vigor and firmness with which he had until then faced all setbacks, he now felt depressed and miserable. In the disturbed current of his thoughts, that of suicide appeared like a threatening undertow. Raimundo rebuffed it with disgust, but it lingered stubbornly. For him, suicide was a ridiculous and shameful act, a kind of dereliction of duty. And to restore his courage and regain his self-respect, he recalled to his memory the brave heroes who had struggled far more than he against the prejudices of all times. Then, jumping from one thought to the next, he imagined himself in a perfect domestic bliss, by the side of his loving family, surrounded by children, and happy, full of confidence, working hard and with no ambition other than to be a useful and respected man. But these hopes no longer awakened the same echo of enthusiasm in his spirit. What now bothered him most was his humiliation and his outraged love; he wanted to marry Ana Rosa, he desired this as never before, but now it was as a kind of vengeance against those accursed people who had reviled and debased him. He wanted to bind her to his destiny as if he were tying her to an ignominious pillory. He wanted to scatter his blood about, because wherever it would fall, it would leave a glowing stain. To suffer less, he needed to see someone else suffer; others must weep bitterly, so that he, in his turn, might laugh for a change. Oh, he would have his laugh! Ana Rosa would belong to him by right! And why not? He had the law on his side! Who could impede him from taking her away legally? And besides, with his child in her womb, she'd obey him like a slave!

And brooding over these projects, pretending he was fully in control of himself, but with an overwhelming sense of despair howling within him, Raimundo, his hands in his pockets, roamed the streets, wavering like a drunkard, waiting for dawn. Impatient for the following day, he seemed to lure it to him with his growing anxiety. That long and silent night weighed upon his shoulders like a soldier's knapsack in the midst of a battle. Yes, dawn had to arrive soon! He wanted to defend his own interests, to put an end to that entire irksome business. Twelve hours more, just twelve hours, and it would all be finished. On the following day everything would be prepared, and he could leave for Rio de Janeiro on the first steamer, accompanied by his wife, happy and independent, never again having to remember Maranhão, that province which was like a cruel stepmother toward its offspring!

Reaching the Largo do Carmo, he sat down on a bench. A fresh wind swayed the trees, and rain threatened to fall. The muffled and distant roar of the ocean could be heard, and nearby, at some party, a woman's voice sang "La Traviata" at the piano.

Riamundo wiped his brow and noticed he was in a cold sweat. Two o'clock struck. A policeman approached slowly and asked him for a cigarette and light, then continued on his way with the lassitude of someone fulfilling a useless and boring formality. Raimundo sat listening to the patrolman's vibrating footsteps, which had the monotonous regularity of a pendulum.

The clock struck three. A light rain was falling. Raimundo got up and continued down the Rua Grande. Perhaps now he could sleep a little. He was so weary! As he crossed the Campo de Ourique, he thought he sensed someone following him. He looked to both sides but could not make out a living soul. Surely he was mistaken . . . perhaps it had been the echo of his own steps. He continued walking, until he reached his house.

But from the darkened bay at the edge of the outer wall, a shot rang out at the very instant he was turning the key.

The shot had come from the revolver with which Canon Diogo had provided Dias. Even then, at that crucial moment, the poor devil had lacked the strength to kill a man, but the priest's words surged through his mind, surrounding his obsessive idea. "How could you now, in a mere instant, lose the work of a lifetime, destroy your gilded castle, your one concern, the best thing in your life? To lose the gamble at the best try! To become useless, to reduce yourself to mud, when with just one slight movement of your finger everything would be saved!"

This was what Manuel's clerk mulled over while hiding in the dark behind a pile of stones and timber near a tumbledown shack. But time was passing rapidly, and Raimundo was about to enter his house and vanish beyond an unassailable border, only to reappear the following day, by the light of the sun. He had to hurry! An instant later would be too late: Ana Rosa would pass into the mulatto's hands and the entire city would be aware of the scandal, relishing it and laughing at the loser! And then, all would be finished forever! With no recourse! And he, Dias, covered with scorn and . . . !

At that moment the lock creaked. The door was opening like a burial vault into which the wretched Dias sensed his future and happiness slipping. And yet such a calamity was contingent on so little! The great obstacle of his life was standing there a few steps away, in perfect position for a shot.

Dias closed his eyes and concentrated all his energy on his trigger finger. The bullet flew, and Raimundo, with a groan, collapsed against the wall.

* * *

A dull day had dawned, replete with drizzles and humidity. Few people were on the streets, no sun appeared, and a widespread tedium yawned everywhere. Thick and somber clouds plodded through the sky, heavy with the weight of their moisture; the atmosphere could scarcely hold them up. Thunder, sounding like bullets rolling along the floor, could be heard in the distance.

Manuel's house wore the silent calm of mourning, its windows closed, its residents sad, its veranda and sitting room completely abandoned. In the warehouse down below, the clerks pretended to know nothing. The blacks in the kitchen were whispering, afraid of speaking out loud, but spreading gossip throughout the neighborhood, which was already abuzz with the previous night's scandal.

Manuel put in an appearance only at the lunch hour, which on that day was delayed because the slaves, deprived of Maria Bárbara's watchfulness and busy with their gossip, had neglected their duties. The poor man wore his pain and insomnia stamped on his face; his eyes were dark and swollen. He scarcely touched his plate and, instead, set his silverware down and with his napkin wiped away a tear that Ana Rosa's vacant place had wrung loose. The sadness of that unoccupied chair seemed to be telling him: "Resign yourself, you poor fellow, for a daughter you'll never again have." He refused to go down to the warehouse and instead locked himself upstairs in his office, telling them to send Dias there when he arrived.

The thrush warbled in despair on the veranda. They had forgotten to fill its feeding trough.

Ana Rosa had not yet gotten out of her hammock. She was agitated, ill, quite nervous, with an upset stomach. Her grandmother, out of sorts, had brought in a small pot of herb tea for her fever, and, after counseling her granddaughter to stay in her room and try to sleep, she shut herself up with her saints to pray.

Ana Rosa was unaware of what was taking place outside. Amância was the only visitor to come by, and she spoke at length of the pallor she had noted in Ana Rosa.

"I even found her breath to be bad," she said to Mônica, as soon as she left the sickroom.

"It's from her stomach," the mestizo explained. "The poor thing still hasn't had a bite to eat today, and she hasn't had any sleep since yesterday morning."

The old lady went into the kitchen to look for Brígida, to inquire what the devil had happened in that house for everyone to be going around so gloomy.

Ana Rosa, in fact, was deeply depressed and in a dangerous state of exasperation and weakness. Mônica made her swallow some porridge, but she immediately vomited it up.

"Say, Missy, that's not right," the Negress objected maternally. "There's not a thing left in your tummy."

"Mammy," Ana Rosa then asked, "can I go out as far as the sitting room? There's no breeze; the windows are closed."

"Go on, Missy, but put some cotton in your ears. Wait! Cover up your head!"

And she wrapped Ana Rosa's head in a vermillion silk kerchief.

"Do you want me to help you, Missy?"

"No, Mammy, just stay here. You must be tired."

The Negress sat down next to the hammock, drew in her legs, which she enfolded between her arms, and began to doze, pressing her face against her knees. Ana Rosa got up very weakly and, supporting herself on the furniture, slowly crossed through the disarray of her room and went out to the sitting room.

The sight of her sluggish and sad step, accompanied by those sighs and drooping eyelids, produced an unpleasant impression. She seemed to be convalescing from a long and serious illness; she had a waxy color, with large purple circles under her eyes, and looked exhausted. Her hair, uncombed and dry, was hanging out from under the vermillion kerchief, which gave her head a certain picturesque and graceful appearance. Her entire being exuded a melancholy and sorrowful air. Her long gown, unbuttoned across her stomach, dragged carelessly on the floor. Her arms were limp, her hands weak, her neck slack, her lips half-open and cracking with fever. Her gaze was inert and unhappy, but still permeated with tenderness. Everything about her sounded a tacit lament of profound hidden pain. Her dainty feet dragged two tiny slippers along the floor and through the opening in her gown appeared her wrinkled lace chemise and a gold chain hanging against the whiteness of her bosom, with a small crucifix that swayed between her breasts.

And with the resignation of an ailing person unable to leave the sickroom, she promenaded her isolation about the room, attempting to amuse herself by minutely examining the objects on all the tables as if she had never before seen them. She took the little quartz greyhound in her fingers and stood gazing at it endlessly. Her mind was not present; it wandered about outside, seeking Raimundo, seeking her dearly beloved partner, author of that crime she felt within herself, filling her with happiness and fear. She loved him much more now, as if her love were also growing like the fetus that stirred in her womb. Despite the distressing situation, she found that she was ever happier; she had dreamed of the felicity of becoming a mother and sensed it taking place in her body, in her belly, from moment to moment, with a mysterious, incomprehensible and inevitable impetus. She was a mother! . . . It still seemed to her like a dream!

She was growing impatient to prepare her child's layette, which would be an excellent one with nothing, nothing, missing. Ah, she knew perfectly how all that was done: which was the best flannel for the diapers, the best bonnets and woolen booties. In her dreams she pictured a cradle next to her hammock with the little creature in it among laces and pink ribbons, whimpering in the beginnings of a human voice. And she imagined herself anxiously burning lavender incense to sweeten the child's clothing, preparing sugared water to cure its colics, avoiding taking too much coffee and any food that might affect her milk, because she wanted to be the only one to raise her child and for nothing in the world would she entrust it to even the best of nursemaids. And thinking of these things, which no one had in fact ever attempted to teach her, she forgot entirely about the vexations and problems her difficult position would surely cause. The possibility of not marrying Raimundo did not enter her mind. That was the way it had to be, regardless of whatever happened and whoever might suffer.

In this way her day wore on. She only awoke from her daydreams at two-thirty in the afternoon, when the bell of the main cathedral tolled the death knell. "From whom can it be tolling?" she asked herself, caught up in compassionate curiosity. It seemed preposterous that someone would consider dying just when she thought only of giving life to that other someone who so preoccupied her.

Nevertheless, the tolling continued in the distance, pressing through the air like an expanding sob. And that mournful sound there in the closed room seemed to make the day sadder and the sky more somber and rainy. Ana Rosa felt a slight tremor of ill-defined fear tingle her flesh. She thought of going to pray and even took a few steps toward her room, but the murmur of voices coming from the street held her back.

She went over to the window. The buzz from the crowd was growing. "Some scuffle," she thought, leaning her face against the windowpane to peek at what was happening outside.

The tumult swelled as a large group of men and women, filled with curiosity, approached. Ana Rosa then realized the cause of the gathering: in a hammock, whose bamboo poles they bore on their shoulders, two black men were carrying a body.

"Goodness, what an omen!" she said, troubled.

She started to withdraw from the window but remained out of curiosity. "Some poor sick fellow going to the hospital . . . or perhaps someone has died, poor thing." And she attempted to concentrate on her child, to undo that unpleasant image.

The body, completely covered by a linen sheet, seemed to be that of a man of some stature. A few crimson stains stood out here and there against the whiteness of the cloth.

Ana Rosa now felt a certain terrified interest. She again started to back away from the window, but by now what was taking place in the street below irresistibly attracted her gaze. The funeral procession meanwhile kept approaching, drawing closer to the wall near her side of the house. She was finding it harder to see, but, because of the wind, she did not want to open the window, besides which, it looked like rain, and it was in fact starting to drizzle. She continued staring attentively, her face flattened against the glass.

The hammock advanced slowly, jolted by the unevenness of the street and the discordant motions of the two bearers. This caused the sheet to move up and down, making large momentary billows. Ana Rosa felt anxious and frightened, as if all that had something to do with her. The hammock was about to disappear completely from her view, for as it moved ever closer to the wall, her eyes could scarcely reach it.

Heavens, it seemed to be heading toward Manuel's door!

A gust of northeastern wind whistled on the windowpanes. People's hats blew off like dry leaves, and the windows of the neighboring houses rattled against their casements in a harsh burst of wrath. The wind howled more fiercely and, in a final gust, wrested away the sheet covering the hammock.

Ana Rosa shuddered profoundly, shrieked, turned livid, and raised her hands to her eyes. In that bloody corpse, she imagined she recognized Raimundo. Uncertain and too disheartened to reason clearly, she suddenly threw open the window.

It was, indeed, Raimundo.

The crowd looked up in time to witness a horrifying sight: convulsed and demented, Ana Rosa stood clawing her nails into the wood of the window sill, her eyes rolling ominously, her mouth wide open in a dreadful laugh, her nostrils dilated, her arms and legs rigid.

Suddenly, she let out another howl and fell backward.

Her black mammy came running to help and dragged her inside the room.

Behind her, on the floor, Ana Rosa left a thick trail of blood, which was seeping out from under her skirts, staining her feet. And, at the spot where she had collapsed, an immense red pool covered the floor.

19

The next day, in all the streets of São Luís, in the government offices, the commercial district, the butcher shops, the fruit and vegetable stands, the sitting rooms and bedrooms, there were widespread murmurs about the mysterious death of Dr. Raimundo. It was the event of the day.

The episode was recounted in a thousand ways; legends were invented and romantic love affairs dreamed up. The Santa Casa Hospital had already taken the body away. An examination had been performed, and it was ascertained that the victim had died of a gunshot wound, but the police were unable to apprehend the killer.

That same afternoon Manuel's clerks, dressed in mourning clothes, went from door to door distributing this announcement:

> Manuel Pedro da Silva and Canon Diogo de Melo Freitas Santiago announce that they have received sorrowful word of the demise of their highly esteemed and greatly lamented nephew and friend, Raimundo José da Silva. As he is to be laid to rest today at 4:30 in the afternoon, in the cemetery of the Santa Casa Hospital, they trust that you will accompany the bier from the home of his inconsolable uncle at Rua da Estrela, No. 80. They profess their immediate and eternal gratitude for your act of kindness.

The Santa Casa Hospital ceded a burial plot for sixty milréis. The funeral procession went on foot and was heavily attended. Many merchants accompanied it out of consideration for their colleague; a larger number of persons appeared out of mere curiosity.

The canon anointed the body with holy water and committed it to God.

Maria Bárbara, to fully ease her conscience and so that others would know she did not have a cold heart, promised a special mass for the soul of the mulatto.

Dias appeared at the house only in the afternoon, at the hour of the funeral procession. Everyone noticed that the good fellow had been much shaken by the death and that, as the coffin was being lowered into the grave, he went off by himself, naturally to weep without restraint. It was not known whether anyone, besides Dias and the canon, wept.

Returning from the cemetery, Freitas conversed with Manuel's clerks, as well as with Sebastião Campos and Casusa, and piously lamented the pitiable demise of the unfortunate young man. He said he very much regretted that the police had not discovered the perpetrator of the crime, but that in his humble opinion it had been neither more nor less than a suicide, and Raimundo had reached the door in his death throes.

"A calamity!" he concluded philosophically, using his handkerchief to dust off his highly polished shoes. "I'll just never be able to get used to this darn red dust out here in São Pantaleão! But, believe me, poor Mundico's death has really moved me. He was such a talented young man. And so clever in turning out verse!"

"But so conceited, let's admit it!"

"No, no, the poor fellow! He was quite learned, he truly was! That can't be denied."

"But, after all, he wasn't what he wanted to be!"

"Well, yes, I can't contradict you," Lindoca's father agreed politely, for he generally never contradicted anyone. "A calamity," he repeated, shaking his head.

"And the situation might get even worse," Sebastião observed. "The girl is still in danger."

"That's right! I heard she was."

"Dr. Jaufret ordered her taken out of the city."

"They'll be going to Ponta-d'Areia quite soon."

"No, to Caminho Grande!"

"My, but she sure was crazy about Raimundo."

"What foolishness. . . ."

They then abandoned the subject to listen to Casusa, who merrily told the story of the drunkard who one day stopped in a cemetery to sleep and had been locked in. Afterward, awakening late at night, he had gotten up and gone over to the entrance to get a match from the watchman, who was smoking rather inattentively and leaning against the gate. The poor fellow, feeling the drunkard's cold hand on his neck, took off at a run, shouting for help at the top of his lungs.

They all thought it funny, and Freitas right off the bat told a comparable story about an incident during his adolescence. This tale inspired still others and each man told the stories that he knew. Thus, by the time they turned onto Rua Grande, still covered with the red dust from São Pantaleão, they were having a good laugh, despite the profound sadness of the twilight, which on that day lacked its usual pomp.

As soon as the bad weather lifted, Pescada packed his daughter and mother-in-law off to a farm in Caminho Grande, but there Ana Rosa's condition declined even further. Manuel called in a regular team of doctors.

From that time on Manuel lived a very troubled life. It was said his hair had turned totally white, and that he now worked as never before, with the furor and despair of one who drinks to forget his misfortunes.

In the meanwhile, the new commercial firm, Silva & Dias, came to life, and enjoyed the most complete prosperity.

* * *

Six years later, in the middle of February, there was a gathering at the Family Club. It was sponsored by the Liberals to pay their respects to a political ally from Rio de Janeiro who had recently arrived to assume the presidency of the province of Maranhão.

It was at the peak of the rainy season, and rain had fallen all afternoon. The reddish lights from the gaslamps cast a zigzag pattern on the sidewalk; drops still fell sorrowfully from some of the rooftops, and the sky, entirely black, hung over the city like a lead cover. Nevertheless, many people were arriving for the party. All kinds of old carriages filed through the Rua Formosa, depositing mounds of silk and cambric. Ladies, wrapped elegantly in their puffed-out dresses, ascended the stairs, lifting their trains and going toward the ballrooms on the arms of grave men dressed in tails. Ostentation prevailed. The flights of the stairway had been strewn with defoliated flowers and the leaves of mango trees, and every fourth step was decorated with huge plantless vases of rock powder. Tall mirrors in the corridors reflected from head to foot all the couples who passed. White lace curtains hung in every door.

The president had just arrived, and the Fifth Infantry Band down below struck up the national anthem. Everyone crowded around to catch a glimpse of him. Comments were made in somber voices about the figure he cut, his movements, his walk, coloring, and shirt buttons.

In the Gilded Room the ladies sat bolted into their chairs in a kind of ceremonious resignation, discreetly craning their necks to see "the new president." The young men, their hair parted into two locks hanging over their foreheads, smoked in the halls or sipped at the buffet. Out on the terrace, unending hands of ombre were silently played. The entire building reeked like a French perfume store.

A heavy and dull constraint hung over the club. Few felt inspired to chat, and no one laughed. But the orchestra unexpectedly struck up the first dance, and a wave of men burst noisily through each entrance into the main hall. It was a confused inundation: there were long white gloves, tails without gloves, blue silken handkerchiefs peeping out from the breast pockets of three-button cutaway coats, and enormous starched cambric dress ties with their bows carefully extended over black lapels. Some displayed pretentious tics; others an embarrassed and flushed air. Everyone began to perspire.

The sons of the rich merchants, who had gone to Europe to "study commerce," and the students home for vacation from Rio de Janeiro, Recife, and Bahia, stood out from the others. The dancing loosened up the crowd: ladies were already rising; chairs were dragged around; gaslight bit into bare shoulders and made jewelry flash. The fiddles began to wail.

Quadrilles and waltzes succeeded one another with virtually no interruption. Enthusiasm brightened all spirits.

The atmosphere quivered with the faint sound of whispers about amorous affairs, tiny delicate laughs, the tinkling of bracelets and rustling of skirts, the murmur of hand fans, and the muffled dragging of feet on the carpet.

Held at the waist, the women whirled about the floor in voluptuous abandon, their heads resting on their partners' shoulders. The atmosphere was saturated with the tepid and close smell of hair and flesh, mingled with Lubin extracts. Exhausted couples fell to the settees, weakened by a sensual torpor, their nostrils dilated, chests heaving, and eyelids drooping in a feverish prostration.

Shortly, however, a sudden frenzy electrified the couples: "Galop!" they shouted, and an unfettered mad whirl of people rushed headlong through the rooms, bounding in and out in a blur of silken dress trains and coattails, twisting, colliding, and finally bursting into a frightful and thundering hubbub—like the roar of a wave crashing in full storm.

Dresses were torn, lace ruffles ripped, and coiffures sagged in the midst of delighted squeals.

After a quadrille, one fellow went limping onto the veranda, seeking refuge. Someone had stepped on his worst corn.

"Damn those people!"

And he went off to sit down in a corner, tenderly holding his foot.

"Oh, Sparky, please say something to your old friend," said Freitas, coming up to him and holding out his hand. "I wasn't aware that our part of the country had the pleasure of your presence, Doctor."

Freitas was still the same person, starched and stiff with his usual high collar and highly prized long fingernail. "Well, then, what's happened to you since your last visit? My, it must be going on three years now."

Sparky, a third-year law student in Recife,[1] was on vacation.

Freitas noted how he had blossomed into a handsome young man, quite polished, and so grown up!

Sparky smiled. Indeed, his shoulders had broadened, and his body had filled out. He now had side whiskers and seemed less foolish, but much less sharp. The two railed haughtily against that barbaric new style of dancing. The student described the pain he'd felt when his corn had been stepped on and swore never again to dance with such clumsy people. They then spoke of the new president. Freitas vented his complaints about the Liberal Party: "A mob of childish pranksters!" he said indignantly. "They're just too young to run the country properly! The so-called cabinet formed on January 5th,[2] why, they're a bunch of big babies likely to wipe their hands on the walls! Incompetents! Pure incompetents! They then turned their attention to the past, to recollections of the late Manuel Pescada and the now-deceased Maria Bárbara.

"Old Babu," murmured Freitas, overflowing with memories.

Sparky asked for news of Lindoca.

"Just as fat as ever. She's now over in Paraíba with her husband, Dudu Costa, who's been transferred to the local customs house there. Say, did you know that Eufrasinha ran off with some comedian?"

"Yes, I'd already heard that one."

"She was out of her mind! But that poor Casusa, he's the one who was lost. What folly! Sparky, old man, if you saw the guy, you wouldn't recognize him. He's all haggard, his hair's gone white." Sparky said he had not yet run into him since he'd been back.

"What do you mean, 'run into him'? The fellow's in bed, a cripple! One of his legs—that's what it was."

Freitas then let his belly relax and hang out a little.

"What about Sebastião?" the younger man asked.

"Just can't get away from his ranch . . . . No one sees him any more." And in the same breath he added: "Man, do you know who's about to leave us? Our friend Canon Diogo."

"Yes, I'd heard that already."

"The poor man . . . urine retention. He always did suffer from strictures."

"Such a saintly man."

"He certainly is."

And both nodded their heads, in contemplation of that shared conviction. Sparky thought he might write the canon's obituary in the event the poor man died before his return to Recife. They also spoke a little about Cordeiro, who had set up in business with Manuelzinho. Freitas affirmed that they were doing well, because Cordeiro had finally given up his devilish vice. He then interrupted himself to whisper:

"Do you know that fellow there, going by with a girl on his arm?"

"No."

"Why, it's Gustavo!"

"Gustavo who?"

"De Vila-Rica! He was one of Pescada's clerks."

"Oh, yes, now I remember. But, how he's changed! He used to be such a good-looking boy."

Gustavo had in fact completely lost his lovely European coloring; his face was now mottled with syphilitic scars. He was about to marry the girl at his side, one of old Serra's daughters.

"Well, good for him! . . . Sounds like a good match."

At midnight some of the families put on their wraps and prepared to depart. Freitas immediately took leave of Sparky and hurried off.

"After midnight, nothing happens, absolutely nothing!" he observed, as methodical as ever.

But, on the landing of the stairway, he was obliged to wait for a few seconds while one of the departing couples descended. He guessed they were important people because of the warm-hearted smiles the others were giving them; many stepped back hurriedly to make way for them. The president himself accompanied the couple to that point and, with an energetic English-style handshake, thanked them for their kindness in having appeared at the ball.

This fêted couple was Dias and Ana Rosa, who had been married now for four years. He had let his moustaches grow and learned to stand up straight. He even had a rich man's mien, as well as the satisfied and smug air of someone whose ships are about to come in. Ana Rosa had put on a little too much weight, but was still quite handsome and shapely, with clear skin and well-toned flesh.

She went gliding out, quite worried about keeping the train of her dress from dragging and, naturally, thinking about her three little children asleep at home.

"Grand'chaine, double, serré!" resounded through the rooms.

Dias had received his hat in the hall, and, as they entered the carriage that was awaiting them, Ana Rosa affectionately turned up the collar of his coat.

"Cover your neck well, dearest! Last night you still had such a cough, my darling!"

Translator's Notes

Chapter 1

1. *Luís de Camões* (1524–80)—Portugal's national poet; wrote *Os Lusíadas* (1572).

2. *Marquês de Pombal*—Sebastião José de Carvalho e Melo (1699–1782); dictatorial prime minister of Portugal (1750–77).

3. *Portuguese Cultural Center*—Gabinete Português de Leitura; a network of Portuguese cultural associations, reading rooms, and libraries existing, especially in the nineteenth century, in most Brazilian cities.

4. *Alcântara*—a village on the mainland, across the bay from São Luís.

5. Although the majority of Portuguese are brunette, those from northern Portugal are sometimes blond and blue-eyed.

6. *José Cândido de Morais e Silva, "Farol"*—anti-Portuguese political figure of Maranhão; described in Antônio Henriques Leal, *Pantheon Maranhense* (Lisboa: Imprensa Nacional, 1873), 221–32.

7. *mutiny of August 7, 1831*—although Brazil became independent in 1822, Maranhão remained a pro-Portuguese province; this mutiny was an attempt by native-born Brazilians to diminish the power and influence of the Portuguese in residence in Maranhão.

8. *Paraguayan War* (1864–70)—also War of the Triple Alliance; Brazil, Argentina, and Uruguay allied against an aggressive Paraguay, led by dictator Solano López.

Chapter 3

1. *guaraná*—tropical Amazonian fruit, used in Brazil as a base for a popular soft drink.

2. *Rebellion of 1831, Pará*—anti-Portuguese rebellion that took place in neighboring Pará at the time of Farol's uprising in Maranhão.

Chapter 4

1. *Emperor Dom Pedro II* (1825–91)—grandson of King João VI of Portugal, son of Emperor Dom Pedro I of Brazil, and Emperor of Brazil, 1840–89.

2. *Gavião*—like Alcântara, a village in the environs of São Luís.

3. *provincial president*—during the nineteenth century the chief executives of the Brazilian provinces were known as presidents and were nominated by the emperors and sent out from Rio de Janeiro.

4. *Guararapes War*—(1648–49)—skirmishes between the Dutch and Luso-Bra-

zilian forces near Recife during the Dutch occupation of Northeastern Brazil in the seventeenth century.

5. *Gonçalves Dias*—Antônio Gonçalves Dias (1823–64); a major romantic poet; native of Maranhão.

6. *Cunha, Odorico Mendes, Pindaré, Sotero*—literary figures of nineteenth-century Maranhão.

7. *João Lisboa*—João Francisco Lisboa (1812–63), a native of Maranhão, one of the most respected Brazilian historians during the nineteenth century.

8. *réis*—"réis" and "milréis," Brazilian and Portuguese monetary units. The milréis (one thousand réis) was worth approximately $.55 in 1875.

Chapter 5

1. *nhô*—"nhô" and "nhôzinho," African-influenced variations of "senhor," meaning sir, master, or little master.

2. *Paraíba*—state in Northeastern Brazil.

3. *b's and v's*—the Portuguese language distinguishes phonetically between the consonants *b* and *v;* Spanish does not; therefore, Spanish and Galician immigrants are easily recognized by Brazilians.

4. *law school*—the law school course in nineteenth-century Brazil and Portugal was similar to the liberal arts course of the twentieth century.

Chapter 6

1. *Paissandu* and *Humaitá*—small cities in Paraguay, sites of important battles during the Paraguayan War. General Manuel Luís Osório was commander of the Brazilian forces during the war.

2. *Pernambuco*—state in Northeastern Brazil.

Chapter 7

1. *Caxias*—a then-prosperous agricultural city in the interior of Maranhão.

Chapter 8

1. *"Bumba Meu Boi"*—a Brazilian folklore song and ceremony, especially popular in the Northeast.

2. *Juvenal Galeno* (1836–1931)—a popular poet from Ceará, a northeastern state near Maranhão.

3. *Tomás Ribeiro* (1831–1901)—a popular poet of the last phase of the romantic movement in Portugal.

Chapter 14

1. *Rebouças*—André Rebouças (1838–98), mulatto and public figure of Imperial Brazil.

2. *Galician*—Because of the cultural, ethnic, and linguistic affinities between northwestern Spain (Galicia) and Portugal, especially the northernmost Minho province, many Portuguese immigrants to Brazil are referred to as "Galicians."

3. *republican revolution*—Azevedo, writing this novel ca. 1880, was a republican in spirit and conviction. A revolution on November 15, 1889 deposed the Emperor and ushered in the First Republic.

4. *law of the free womb*—in Portuguese, "Lei do Ventre Livre," passed in September 1871, declared that all slave children born after that date would gain their freedom no later than at age twenty-one.

Chapter 19

1. *Recife Law School*—during the nineteenth century only two law schools existed in Brazil: at Recife and São Paulo.

2. *cabinet of January 5*—on January 5, 1878 the emperor formed a new cabinet, replacing older statesmen with a younger group.